Praise for the #1 bestseller *Looking for Jane*

"Heather Marshall speaks to the power of solidarity and of brave women who dare to take a stand."

ELLEN KEITH, bestselling author of *The Dutch Orphan*

"Shines a spotlight on the unsettling truths and heartbreaking realities faced by women of every generation. A compelling, courageous must-read about motherhood and choice."

GENEVIEVE GRAHAM, *USA Today* and #1 bestselling author of *The Forgotten Home Child* and *The Secret Keeper*

"A searing, important, beautifully written novel about the choices we make and where they lead us."

KRISTIN HARMEL, *New York Times* bestselling author of *The Paris Daughter*

"Marshall vividly brings to life the dangers involved with operating Jane . . . a page-turner."

Publishers Weekly

"Heather Marshall's sensitive fictional take on these real-life events illuminates the power of women and of motherhood."

Canadian Living

"A confident debut that offers a fascinating, often disturbing insight into the state of Canadian women's reproductive rights in our recent history. . . . Timely."

The Globe and Mail

"Masterful . . . A poignant celebration of motherhood, and a devastating reminder of the consequences of denying women the right to choose. Fierce, beautifully written, and unforgettable."

FIONA DAVIS, *New York Times* bestselling author of *The Magnolia Palace*

"A beautifully written meditation on the lengths mothers will go to for their children as well as an eye-opening history of women."

JANET SKESLIEN CHARLES, *New York Times* bestselling author of *The Paris Library* and *Miss Morgan's Book Brigade*

"This timely novel about motherhood and choices is a must for all fiction collections."

Library Journal (starred review)

"A brave, generous, capable exploration of what it means to be a mother, to be a woman, and to stand up for inexorable truths."

MARISSA STAPLEY, *New York Times* bestselling author of Reese's Book Club pick *Lucky*

"A powerful debut . . . an emotional but compelling story, inspired by real events."

HELLO! Canada

"Gripping from the moment is starts . . . *Looking for Jane* has the potential to remain pertinent for generations."

Associated Press

"A deftly braided narrative, Marshall keeps the tension high as she reveals the devastating consequences of denying women autonomy over their bodies. A charged topic handled with sensitivity and compassion."

Kirkus Reviews

ALSO BY HEATHER MARSHALL

Looking for Jane

The SECRET HISTORY *of* AUDREY JAMES

A NOVEL

HEATHER MARSHALL

Published by SIMON & SCHUSTER
New York London Toronto Sydney New Delhi

A Division of Simon & Schuster, LLC
166 King Street East, Suite 300
Toronto, Ontario M5A 1J3

This book is a work of fiction. Any references to historical events, real people, or real places are used fictitiously. Other names, characters, places, and events are products of the author's imagination, and any resemblance to actual events or places or persons, living or dead, is entirely coincidental.

Sheet music for "Ilse's Theme" used with permission of Jim Seale.

This Simon & Schuster Canada edition June 2024

SIMON & SCHUSTER CANADA and colophon are trademarks of
Simon & Schuster, LLC

Simon & Schuster: Celebrating 100 Years of Publishing in 2024

For information about special discounts for bulk purchases, please contact S
imon & Schuster Special Sales at 1-800-268-3216 or
CustomerService@simonandschuster.ca.

Interior design by Erika R. Genova

Manufactured in the United States of America

1 3 5 7 9 10 8 6 4 2

Library and Archives Canada Cataloguing in Publication
Title: The secret history of Audrey James / by Heather Marshall.
Names: Marshall, Heather (Heather J.), author.
Description: Simon & Schuster Canada edition.
Identifiers: Canadiana (print) 20230568246 | Canadiana (ebook) 20230568254 |
ISBN 9781982170257 (softcover) | ISBN 9781982170264 (EPUB)
Subjects: LCGFT: Novels.
Classification: LCC PS8626.A76677 S43 2024 | DDC C813/.6—dc23

ISBN 978-1-9821-7025-7
ISBN 978-1-9821-7026-4 (ebook)

For my family

My dream enablers, my cheer squad, my joy.

Prologue

VLAGTWEDDE, NETHERLANDS | APRIL 1945

The soldiers are sitting outside playing cards when they notice the woman staggering down the street.

The small Dutch border town they recently liberated from the Germans is quiet on this spring afternoon, and the soldiers have settled themselves in a circle using cargo boxes as makeshift chairs and tables in the absence of any real furniture. Canteens rest on the dusty ground at their feet whilst the sun shines on the tips of their ears and the backs of their necks, the same sun that warmed their skin back home.

These five soldiers are part of the North Nova Scotia Highlanders, a proud contingent of the province's best and bravest young lads. Or at least, what's left of the contingent. They've lost many men along the way, the boys they grew up with, went to school with. Their mothers belong to the same quilting circles and church bazaar committees. Their fathers go fishing out on the flashing bays of the Atlantic where they smoke cigars and avoid discussions of the last war, burying the appalling realities that they didn't dare reveal to their own sons. They watched, tight-throated and helpless as their boys shipped out in crisp new uniforms, drunk on the dangerous youthful delusion of invincibility that they themselves once felt.

The young soldiers think of their families now as they run their tongues over their teeth. Each man considers the hand he's been dealt.

One craves his mother's fresh-squeezed lemonade. Another longs for the touch of his girl's warm hand on his arm, and hopes that she'll be waiting when he returns. And each man wants to win this card game so that he can line his threadbare pockets with cigarettes. They welcome the burning, dry heat in their lungs on cold evenings, a reminder that they are still alive and breathing where other, less fortunate men are rotting in a constellation of unmarked graves in France.

When they hear a scratch in the dirt on the deserted road, the soldiers' heads snap up. Their eyes squint into the light for the source of the sound. They're always on high alert, even though they've taken Holland from the Nazis. A soldier can never be too careful.

But it's only a woman on the road. No threat.

As she shuffles closer, they see her dress is torn, her blond hair disheveled. She is missing a shoe.

One of the soldiers drops his cards and jogs toward her, reaching her just as her knees give way. He catches the woman and lowers her to the ground, shouts to his comrades to fetch the medic. Her bare foot is bleeding and badly bruised. Her face is dirty, lips cracked and dry. Her blond hair reminds him of his little sister's, and in that moment, he just wants to go home.

He calls for water and a canteen is thrust into his hand. "Drink," he tells the woman. "If you can."

Her grey-blue eyes grow wide and she grips his hand. "English!" she whispers.

The soldier nods. "Canadian."

She tries to take the canteen, but her fingers tremble violently. The soldier rests it against her lips and tips some water into her parched mouth. She splutters at first, then gulps it down. When she finishes, a drop slips down her chin. The soldier wipes it away, revealing pale skin beneath the layer of grime.

"What's your name, love?" he asks.

The medic arrives and squats down. He shines a bright light into her eyes, and her chest tightens like a rubber band. She fights against the memory of the searchlights. The fire.

The medic takes her wrist and presses his fingers down to locate her weak pulse. "What's your name, miss?"

"Audrey," she says, her raspy voice a little louder this time. "Audrey James."

PART I

In the middle of the journey of our life I found myself within a dark wood where the straight way was lost.

—Dante Alighieri, *Inferno*

Chapter 1

Audrey

BERLIN, GERMANY | OCTOBER 1938

"Your tempo is off today, Fräulein James."

From her seat on the gleaming black bench in front of the conservatory's second-best grand piano, Audrey James bit down on her bottom lip, which was normally painted a deep crimson that set off her grey eyes in the style of the American film starlets. But she had been in a hurry to get to her lesson this morning and left the house without completing all her typical ablutions. Frankly, she was lucky to have smoothed the wrinkles in her dress and unwound the curlers in her hair in time to catch the bus across town to the *konservatorium*. She ran out of time for the lipstick.

"Yes, Herr Fogel, I apologize," she said, straightening her posture and resetting her fingers on the ivory. "I will try again."

The mood in the home of her best friend, Ilse Kaplan, where she lived as a long-term guest, had been strained of late, and the tension was affecting Audrey's typically sanguine disposition. Two weeks prior, Ilse's younger brother Ephraim had been attacked by a gang of Hitler Youth on his way home from school. Audrey had seen them around the city, those miniature versions of the Nazis. They'd beaten him badly; he'd needed stitches in two different places on his face, and his black eye was only now beginning to yellow.

Keeping her back and neck as straight as an oak trunk, Audrey closed her eyes and let her fingers dance across the white and black keys, hearing her way into the correct tempo. She'd been working on Wagner's Sonata in A Major for several weeks in preparation for her graduation recital in December. It was one of the most complicated, furious pieces she'd ever undertaken to learn, but the effort required would render the mastery of it even more delicious. She had wanted to prepare Mendelssohn's Number 2, but Mendelssohn was a Jewish composer. Wagner was the darling of the Reich—and Herr Fogel.

"There we are," Herr Fogel muttered.

Several minutes later, Audrey finished, the last note lingering in her ear long after it dissipated. She always loved that moment. She opened her eyes, blinking into the golden autumn light streaming through the large windows of the airy conservatory space that overlooked the quiet Bernburgerstrasse.

"Better. Better," her professor said, adjusting his wire spectacles. "But watch your progressions in the middle of the second movement. I shall see you on Friday, Fräulein James. Good day to you. Heil Hitler."

"Thank you, Herr Fogel, good day," Audrey said. He eyed her, waiting. It was the same look with which he fixed her at every lesson, in anticipation of her first note. Expectant. Relief when she delivered. "Heil Hitler," she added.

When he left the room, Audrey allowed herself to slouch a fraction, releasing the tension in her spine and shoulders. A person could feel the weight of the Third Reich. Even a non-Jew who was not personally impacted by their stringent policies could feel the pressure of what the Nazi Party was doing to the country. These days, one was expected to salute the Führer. At the grocer, the chemist's. When the postman delivered a parcel. It had become the standard greeting for all Germans, replacing genuine geniality with a thinly veiled trial as they tested one another into declarations of allegiance. Because all it took to bring someone down in this Germany was a question mark.

Audrey carefully tucked her music sheets into her satchel (Herr Fogel did not abide crumpled pages), pulled on her coat and gloves, and made her way down the marble staircase to the first floor. As she passed another classroom, a cello strung a haunting tune. She stopped in the foyer and fished a tube of red lipstick out of her bag, slicking it on with a rebellious flare. Painted faces were not the ideal. Hitler preferred women's faces fresh. No trickery of appearance, no allure or drama. No excitement or individuality at all.

When she opened the door to the street, her father's most recent letter, two weeks before, came back to her. He had all but demanded she return to England immediately.

I know you wish to finish your studies, but Germany is no longer safe, and I fear the borders will close. You must *return to England before Hitler makes it impossible for you to do so.*

She had been living with the Kaplans since she began her three-year program at the conservatory, but Germany had always been her home, as it had been her mother Helene's. She'd met Audrey's father, Victor, an Englishman, in Germany during the Great War. A solicitor by trade, he had flown a reconnaissance plane for the Brits, shuttling back and forth between France, England, and the Eastern Front to gather aerial photography of the enemy's encampments and armaments. In the fall of 1917, his plane malfunctioned and he crash-landed just outside of Brandenburg, near Helene's family home. She and her mother put themselves at risk to shelter and nurse Victor back to health. They fell in love, and Helene became pregnant. Audrey knew her father must have been mad about her mother; only a love like that could have caused him to marry Helene and stay in Germany after the war was over. It would have been a love story for the ages, but Helene died of complications from Audrey's birth.

Victor was devastated by his wife's death, and never remarried, but stayed in Berlin to continue to grow his fledgling legal practice and fulfill his promise to Helene to support her aging mother. With no time or knowledge of how to raise an infant on his own, he hired a wet nurse to care for Audrey in her infancy, followed by a nanny, Sophie. She was a kind woman who clapped and cheered when Audrey put on little theatricals in the attic, asked her about the books she read and what she was learning in school. Sophie was Audrey's best friend until Ilse swept into her life like a warm August wind when she was seven years old.

Audrey had been watching from her window as furniture and crates were stacked on the pavement outside the house across the street, curious as to who was moving in. Then she saw a girl her age with soft eyes and braided brown hair who'd waved, smiling in a way the girls at Audrey's school never did. Without hesitation, Audrey had marched over the street to ask to be her friend whilst Sophie hustled along in her wake, apologizing to the Kaplans for the intrusion.

Audrey was spunky but mostly friendless, and Ilse was a good listener with a heart that spoke to Audrey's in all the ways she needed, showing her that she was, indeed, loveable. Sophie was caring, but she was paid to watch over Audrey, and her father was distant and formal in his interactions. Nothing was ever explicitly said, but Audrey knew he held her responsible for Helene's death, and it didn't help that Audrey so closely resembled her mother. A portrait hung on the wall above the fireplace in the sitting room, and though Audrey was never invited into her father's bedroom, she'd once glimpsed several gilded-framed photographs of her mother on the walls before he closed the door, shutting her out of his sanctuary of grief. He never understood that she was grieving, too, for the loss of the mother she never got to have, and the loss of the father who blamed her for it. But Ilse had let her in, and Audrey found a family in the Kaplans, who welcomed her at any hour of the day.

Each summer, Victor returned to England and brought Audrey with him. He hosted his London friends and his sister Minna at their holiday home in Kensington, and took Audrey to the symphony and shows in the West End. Arts were their shared interest, and the only real connection Audrey felt was when they bonded in these moments. But all the while, Audrey counted down the days until September, when she would be back in Berlin with Ilse.

Then, five years ago, Helene's mother died, and Victor determined it was time for them to sell the Berlin house and live full-time in London. His English roots ran deeper than the earth's core, but England had never felt like home for Audrey. Home was Berlin, and home was with Ilse, the sister she'd never had and the one person she couldn't live without. Heated arguments had ensued, but with his promise to his late wife fulfilled, Audrey thought he'd finally just come to a point where he couldn't live in Berlin with Helene's ghost anymore. He had no reason to stay, and plenty of reasons to run.

When Victor announced their plans, Audrey's nanny had resigned, saying Audrey was well on her way to becoming a fine young woman and no longer needed her. Sophie's sister was also leaving Berlin, and Sophie decided to join her.

"We're getting out whilst we can," Sophie had told Audrey before she left. Her brother-in-law was political and deeply concerned about Adolf Hitler's appointment as chancellor. "Eli has job prospects in Brussels, and I figure I can find a family in need of service, anywhere I go."

Audrey tried to be strong when Sophie left, and she summoned that strength once more on the day she herself departed for London. She and Ilse held each other outside Audrey's house in a clutch of despair.

"I shall be lost without you," Ilse said, her voice thick. "Especially if things get worse. You've always been my shield."

Over her shoulder, Audrey spied the house down the street where an awful boy named Karl once lived. He and one of his mates had cornered Ilse when the girls were about ten years old, hurling insults like jagged rocks. Audrey placed herself between them and Ilse, but it was a trap; a third bully crept up from behind and cut off Ilse's long braid with his mother's kitchen shears. The boys had cackled harshly, throwing the braid at her feet and spitting on it. Ilse fled home sobbing. Audrey screamed at the boy, knocked the shears from his hand, and kicked him as hard as she could in both shins. She made sure he was also reduced to tears before she sprinted away after Ilse.

Tears slipped down Audrey's cheeks now even as she brushed Ilse's away. "No," she said, with a sad smile. "I'm not your shield. I'm just the sword." Ilse laughed despite herself. "I know you'll be fine," Audrey continued. "You're stronger than you think. Besides, your biggest pest is going to be Ephraim, now, anyway."

Ilse chuckled as they pulled away.

"You must promise to write every other week," Audrey said. "And so will I."

"Mama says maybe we can come visit someday," Ilse added, hopeful. Her glossy dark hair shone in the morning sunlight.

"And I'll make my father bring me back soon," Audrey said. "I'll find a way. I'll insist."

"I know you will," Ilse said with a watery laugh.

For the next two years, Audrey distracted herself with studying acting and music alongside her finishing school classes in London, but her heart was in Berlin. So, in secret, she applied to the premiere *konservatorium*. It was a prestigious school, but Audrey had guessed—correctly, as it transpired—that her father's soft spot for her artistic interests might be the ticket back to Berlin, and to Ilse. He agreed to let her return to the continent to attend the conservatory, so long as Ilse's mother Ruth, a woman of profound caution, kept a watchful eye on her.

But now, her father wanted her back safely in England. Audrey knew, on a level, that he had a point. The attack on Ephraim wasn't an isolated incident. It was indicative of the climate, the hatred of Jews and anyone who didn't fit the Nazis' own definition of who was a "good" or "real" German. But she wasn't about to waste three years of her time, dedication, and her father's money by abandoning her program so close to the finish. She'd written back, reminding him that her graduation was only a few weeks away, and she would return then.

She caught her bus at the end of the street. As the vehicle meandered through the city, the prospect of leaving again weighed on her mind. She did miss her father, in a way. Despite his aloofness, he was still her family, and their relationship had improved somewhat as she got older. But she hated the thought of going back to London. Victor had allowed her to pursue an artistic education, but he still believed that a woman's place was in the home, supporting her husband and bearing children. Audrey didn't much fancy the looming battle of trying to convince him that she wanted more than a half-life. She didn't want her own aspirations stifled by the effort of supporting a man. She didn't want to live for someone else, masquerading under his name. She wanted to see her *own* name up in lights on a stage someday because of her own talent and hard work.

At her father's insistence, Audrey had her passage to England booked, but she had buried the ticket beneath a stack of cardigans in her dresser drawer, as though hoping to smother it into nonexistence.

She didn't know what the alternative was, but she couldn't imagine leaving the whole Kaplan family when their lives had shrunk so much over the past while. Ilse was forced to abandon her nursing training, and they all had to carry identity cards stating their Jewish heritage. Before the attack on Ephraim, the most recent blow had been when

Jewish passports were invalidated and stamped with a *J*. Prior to that, Audrey had some vague thoughts that perhaps the whole Kaplan family would come with her to London after her graduation. She knew Ruth wanted to leave, as so many Jews were choosing to do, or at least send their children to England on the *kindertransports*. But Herr Kaplan wouldn't hear of it.

"This is our home," he'd said. "And I have my business, Ruth. We cannot pack up and leave all that." He shook his head. His textile company was one of the few remaining under Jewish ownership.

"Yet with each passing day, it becomes more likely our business will be stripped from us, Ira," Ruth pleaded. "So many already have."

"But ours may not. And if we emigrate, we will lose all our wealth to the Flight Tax," he'd replied. "Germany will regress toward the mean. We must simply wait out the madness. Have faith, Ruth."

But Audrey could see that Ruth's faith was tested. As was Ilse's. Even mischievous, twelve-year-old Ephraim was wary after his ordeal with the Hitler Youth, and Ruth's sense of caution had blossomed into full-scale paranoia. None of them went outside much anymore. Previously mundane excursions to the grocer or bank were anxious, fleeting errands where Ruth or Ira tried to conduct their business as discreetly as possible under the black and red swastikas draped with imposing ceremony over doorways and on buildings. The emblem that signified the constant presence of the Führer in their daily lives.

Audrey let out a heavy sigh. The bus was stuffy. The Kaplans' house was still a twenty-minute walk away, but she got off early. She readjusted her grip on her satchel, welcoming the cool autumn air, a tonic after the cloud of gloom that dogged her. When she reached the house, she scaled the few steps up to the front porch, then glanced back across the treed street at her childhood home, now occupied by a couple in their seventies, the Richters.

Audrey turned the key in the lock and the sound of her footsteps echoed inside the expansive entryway. She removed her shoes and headed into the telephone room, which was kitty-corner to the front door. This room was her favourite in the Kaplans' grand home. It was small, perhaps five feet square, large enough for a utility chair, telephone, and a little desk, which sat right beneath the mail slot on the other side of the porch. The post would slide through and land in a large wicker tray next to a brass banker's lamp and a smart, six-inch-long silver letter opener with an ivory handle. Seeing the latest *Modenschau* fashion magazine on top of the pile of post, Audrey hissed in excitement and hurried upstairs to find Ilse.

She knocked but didn't wait for a response before bursting into Ilse's room. Her friend was lying on her stomach on her butter-yellow bedcovers, knees bent, stocking feet drifting side to side like a metronome.

"It's arrived!" Audrey said, holding up the magazine.

Ilse let out a little squeal. "Ooh! Let me see, let me see!"

Audrey handed it over and flopped down beside her.

"How was rehearsal?" Ilse asked, turning a page.

"Good. Fine."

"Are you feeling ready for the recital?"

"I suppose, yes," Audrey said. "But to be honest, the fact that none of you will be able to be there has sort of taken the shine off. It's not right."

Ilse nodded. "I know. I wish I could. You know that."

"But it's really not a big thing, anyway," Audrey said with a wave of her hand. It was, and she was immensely proud of her accomplishment, but she carried such guilt about it now.

Ilse frowned. "Don't be stupid. Of course it's a big thing. You've worked hard for this, and you're talented. I know what you're doing, and you can stop right now."

Ilse had a way of seeing straight through Audrey that was both endearing and occasionally problematic.

"All right. But you should have graduated already, Ilse. It isn't fair that I got to finish this, and you didn't get your nursing certificate."

Ilse sighed. "There isn't much point wailing about it, though, is there? I can't be a nurse if Jewish doctors can't practice, and Mama's made up her mind about our restrictions. She's half-mad with worry."

Audrey knew Ilse didn't blame Ruth. Not really. But she was clearly growing weary of the limitations foisted on them.

"I'll still be useful in some ways, even without the certificate," Ilse said. She'd been the one to give Ephraim his stitches. It was becoming nearly impossible to find a Jewish doctor who was still willing to work, even under the table. "But that's why you need to let me help you choose a dress! At least I can participate somehow. I'm proud of you. You're going to be a concert pianist one day, I'm sure of it. On some big London stage."

Audrey nudged her friend playfully. "I doubt it, but I love you for saying so. Though I'd far rather be here instead of London."

Ilse's eyes were wistful. "I know." She squeezed Audrey's hand. "If we're to be separated again soon, all the more reason to celebrate now, right?"

It had been just as difficult in the weeks leading up to Audrey's first departure to London, years ago. But she'd been not much more than a child then, just fifteen. This time felt as though it ought to be different, that Audrey should be able to decide whether to stay or leave Berlin. She was twenty now, a woman. She told Ilse as much.

"Except no one considers you a woman until you're married, do they?" Ilse said. "As far as making your own choices. Until then, it's your father's call."

Audrey scoffed. "Right. And then after a woman gets married, her choices are limited to what her husband is willing to allow. We're just always under a man's control. What if I don't want that?"

Ilse rolled her eyes. "I know you've never been interested in marriage, or boys generally."

Audrey cast her eyes to the embroidery on Ilse's bedspread, the subtle pattern of forget-me-nots, dark yellow against the lighter fabric. She recalled the only time a boy tried to court her, when she was thirteen and had hardly adjusted to all the new changes in her body. She hated the development of her breasts, the onset of her menstruation and all it meant. That she was a woman now, Sophie told her. But all she'd ever seen of women's lot was death and heartbreak and discontent. And when the son of the grocer two streets over approached her with a bouquet and a request for a kiss, Ilse had had to defuse her ire as Audrey hit him with the flowers. Muttering apologies to the rejected boy, Ilse had marched Audrey home from the market, offering an understanding ear and a gentle lecture on propriety as rogue daisy petals clung to Audrey's hair from the skirmish.

"You might find you want to get married one day, you know," Ilse said now. "People change. They grow."

"You mean they grow *up*," Audrey said wryly. "They concede to what's expected of them."

Ilse turned back to the magazine, and Audrey knew she was giving up the fight for another day.

"I like this one," Ilse said, pointing at a long gown. "The Empire waist—"

"Doing *girl things*?" a loud voice said from above.

Audrey's eyes whipped up to the ceiling, where Ephraim's head had just emerged from the attic access door. Lately he had taken to using the attic for play, as he had done as a young child, and the location of the access allowed him to torment his sister whenever she least expected it.

"Ephraim!" Ilse cried. "Get *out*! How long have you been up there, you *yutz*?"

Ephraim cackled and threw the rope ladder over, then scampered down. He stuck out his tongue at Ilse, who pitched a pillow at his head, which he narrowly dodged.

"Mind my stitches!" he shouted, deliberately loud enough for Ruth to hear, wherever she was in the house.

"He's so childish sometimes," Ilse said as he darted out the door. "What about this one, then?" She folded the magazine over to better display a page.

"Mm," Audrey said, frowning. "I don't think so. The sleeves are too billowy. They'll get in the way of playing. I like the wrap-front on that one though. But I'd need it tea-length, so it doesn't interfere with the pedals."

It seemed a little ridiculous to focus so much on the dress, considering everything that was going on. But it was, as Ilse had said, a way for her to be involved, and served as a bit of welcome distraction from the stress in the house. Audrey also knew that it mattered. Only two women would be performing at the graduation—the rest were male, and would all wear the same black suit, that equalizer of men. But what a woman wore was always important, no matter how skilled—or inept—she might be. The right outfit had a way of validating a woman. Whether that fact was fair or not was irrelevant. Anyone who denied it was a fool.

Audrey and Ilse whiled away another hour perusing the pages of the magazine before wandering downstairs. It would only be another half hour before supper, and Ira was due home any time now.

They found Ruth and Ephraim in the sitting room. Ephraim had settled from his earlier unruliness and was curled in a large leather armchair by the fireplace, working in his notebook. He was always writing. *What* he was writing, no one really knew. But he was rarely seen without ink stains on his fingers. Wherever Ephraim was, a shadow always followed; the negative space his twin brother, Michael, should have filled. He'd died of a dreadful fever before the boys had even reached their second birthday. Audrey had been nine, but she still remembered little Michael's eyes, because they were serious yet warm, just like Ilse's. Such a contrast to Ephraim's mischievous ones.

Michael's death had wrought a permanent change in Ruth, as though a piece of her very body had died that day, too, only she hadn't ever attempted to amputate it. She'd just allowed it to fester and grow gangrenous, seeping into the rest of her cells because the contamination served as a constant reminder of the child she had lost, ensuring he was unforgotten. Audrey couldn't imagine why anyone would ever have children at all, if in the act of doing so, one had to risk enduring such ruinous pain. She couldn't make sense of it. It was one of the major ways in which she and Ilse differed; Ilse wanted so much to be a mother one day.

Now, Ruth was staring into the fire, clutching a folded newspaper so hard her knuckles were white.

Ilse stopped in the doorway. "Is everything all right, Mama?"

Ruth nodded but didn't make eye contact. She was only forty-two, but her light brown hair was streaked with grey, making her look older than her husband, who was seven years her senior.

Ilse exchanged a glance with Audrey, who shrugged.

"Game of bridge?" Ilse suggested. Audrey was a terrible player and always had been, but played on occasion for Ilse's sake.

"I'm sort of enjoying my book right now," she said. Ilse chuckled, then took her usual place over on the navy velvet divan. Audrey followed, settling at the opposite end of the small sofa and picking up the copy of Dante's *Divine Comedy* that she'd been reading. Ilse had been immersed in Virginia Woolf lately, and had already disappeared behind *A Room of One's Own.* The Kaplans' wealth enabled them to boast a fabulous library that Audrey had worked her way through twice in the three years she had been living there. Ilse's father believed that knowledge and self-education were essential for all, women included.

Ten minutes later, a series of clicks at the front door alerted the family to his arrival. Ruth exhaled. There was always an underlying sense of tension in the air when Ira was out, palpable relief when he came home safe.

"Papa!" Ilse said happily, but her smile slipped from her face when Ira appeared in the doorway, looking drawn and tired.

His eyes went to the newspaper in his wife's hands. "Ruth—"

"You saw it, then?" she demanded, cheeks flushed.

"It is not as bad as all that."

"What isn't as bad as all that?" Ilse asked.

"Let us just sit and talk it over," Ira said, kneeling beside his wife and reaching for her hand.

"What is it, Papa?" Ilse asked again.

He hesitated a fraction too long, and Audrey's gut twinged.

"Hitler has ordered the deportation of all Polish-born Jews from Germany."

The room was silent.

"But we aren't Poles, Papa," Ephraim said. "We are Germans."

Ira cleared his throat. "No, son, we are not Poles. But these people were denied entry by Poland and are now living in ghettos on the border. Stateless. Homeless." He paused. "It would seem that a young man in Paris has parents in one of the ghettos, and has exacted revenge by shooting a Nazi diplomat. The propaganda"—he glanced down at the paper still clutched in Ruth's other hand—"makes it clear that Hitler is using this assassination to fan the flames of outrage. So . . ." He trailed off, massaging his forehead in a weary sort of way.

"So . . . what, Papa?" Ilse pressed. "Are we in danger?"

"We are always in danger," Ruth said.

Herr Kaplan shot his wife a placatory look. "We are not in *imminent* danger," he said. "But there is no denying the escalation. We must continue to exercise caution, whilst maintaining our composure and our faith that more secure times lie ahead. I do not wish for you to live in fear. At least, no more than you already do," he added heavily. "But there is no doubt these recent events are pushing Germany to a boiling point. We must take care not to get burned."

Ruth just nodded. "Dinner should be ready now," she said, ending the discussion. "Supper is a more casual affair this evening," she added as the family gathered in the dining room. Matya, their cook and housekeeper, had to leave early, she explained. "Her mother is ill."

"That's not a problem, my love, this looks wonderful," Ira said, sitting down at the head of the table.

"What shall we pray for tonight, Papa?" Ephraim asked.

Over the course of their childhood, and as their guest over the past few years, Audrey had gotten quite used to feeling out of place during prayer times. Though she had been baptized as a child, her family was not particularly religious. She had only attended church at Christmas or Easter. Audrey had always supposed her father had simply given up on God after the death of his wife, his first and true love, and she couldn't entirely blame him for the departure. Whilst she found some measure of comfort in the familiar hum of the Hebrew words, it seemed to her, given all the dreadful things happening in the world, that it was unlikely anyone was listening.

Audrey watched Ira fix his surviving son with a hard look that didn't entirely eclipse the unease beneath. Ilse was also studying her brother, brow furrowed as she took in his stitches, the bruising. Ira swallowed.

"Deliverance," Ruth said softly, her eyes swimming with tears.

But her husband shook his head slowly back and forth.

"Reason," he said. "We shall pray for reason."

Chapter 2

Kate

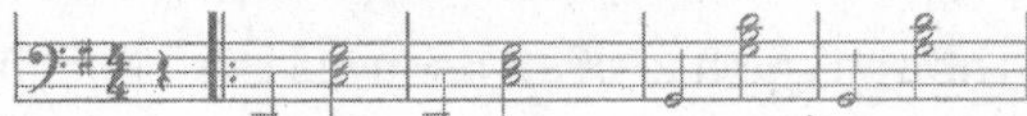

LONDON, ENGLAND | NOVEMBER 2010

Kate Mercer sits cross-legged on her bed, the light of her laptop screen reflecting off her large glasses. Her dog, Ozzie, is curled up beside her. No, not curled up—sprawled. His brown and white mottled legs are spread in a most undignified manner, as though his mission in life is to take up as much space as possible. His head rests on Kate's hip, floppy ears splayed out. The tip of his wet nose nudges the laptop every so often. She scratches his head and the diamond in her engagement ring glints in the soft light of her bedside lamp. She isn't entirely sure why she's still wearing it.

She adjusts her glasses and gently moves Ozzie off her. He keeps sleeping as she walks into the kitchen. She glances out the window that overlooks a quiet side street in Islington, then refills her coffee and heads back into the dim light of the bedroom. Moving boxes line the walls like Tetris pieces, ready for her to move out as soon as she finds her own flat. Meticulously labelled with the full contents, concealing the chaos of Kate's life within.

She rubs her eyes. She hardly slept last night, but that's par for the course these days. And as exhausted as she often feels, it's a double-edged sword anyway. The nightmares are bad enough that sometimes Kate doesn't want to sleep.

She picks up the small 4 x 6 photo album she's been flipping through. It's from her parents' honeymoon, a road trip up to Scotland. When Kate packed up the contents of her closet the night before, she came across the blue binder in a box of her parents' mementos that had been shoved unceremoniously into the back corner. She hasn't looked at this album since they died, nearly a year ago now, when she pawed through their family photos with numb fingers, disbelief gnawing at her insides like a diseased rat as she pulled a selection for the funeral service.

She's been going through the photos all morning, googling the locations, retracing her parents' steps through their road trip, one landmark and restaurant at a time. A handful of them still exist; she's looked at the menus and guest photos online, wondered how much the offerings have changed since her parents patronized them over forty years ago.

She takes a sip of coffee and turns the page. The clear plastic pockets are empty, but there's a couple of loose photos stuffed between them. Kate holds one up. It's a rare picture of both her parents together—her dad was always behind the camera. They're smiling, standing on either side of an embossed wooden sign tacked on to a low grey stone wall with a set of gates.

THE OAKWOOD INN

"Oakwood," Kate mutters, shifting her computer back onto her lap. She types it into the search bar as Ozzie flips over, brushing against her legs.

It's a bed-and-breakfast in Alnwick. Kate's never been that far north, up near the Scottish border. An old picturesque market town, by the looks of it. She navigates back to the website for the guesthouse. It looks like it was designed in 1995 and loads just about as quickly. Kate lets out a little chuckle. Leave it to her parents to stay somewhere so quaint. Her dad was such a history buff, and he loved old things. Used books and antique furniture.

They have character, Kate, he'd said, *secrets and lessons to share, if you take the time to listen.*

He never would have booked a modern hotel with high-pressure showerheads and gleaming tile floors, the kind that Kate's soon-to-be-ex-husband Adam would have preferred. The Oakwood looks exactly like the type of place Kate's dad would have stayed at, especially in a medieval castle town: full of creaky floorboards and tricky locks and maybe even a ghost story, if he got really lucky.

Kate takes a deep breath to loosen the tightness in her chest, then navigates to the About page of the inn and reads about its history. Sure enough, it's been around since the thirties, but the building itself is far older. As Kate scrolls to the bottom, she spots an awkwardly placed text box:

HELP WANTED

She stares at it for a moment, then clicks it.

WANTED: The Oakwood Inn seeks an industrious and patient Assistant Administrator. Role to be filled immediately. Hospitality experience an asset, but not required. Position is live-in. Pets welcome. Ask for Sue.

Kate takes another few sips of coffee. She had to leave her role at the insurance company after the accident to recover from her injuries, and has been living off the modest inheritance from her parents' deaths. But without a job—or any occupation, really—her mind keeps returning to tormenting memories. She's been scrolling job sites since she and Adam decided to formally separate a month ago. She needs something to do.

Getting a job somewhere on the outskirts of the city is one thing, but Alnwick? That far north? She rereads the brief posting. Live-in, pets welcome. It at least sounds better than some corporate admin job in the City that she would loathe for the next three years before moving on out of sheer boredom in a fucked-up game of existential kick-the-can. A contact phone number is listed, but no email address, which Kate finds unsurprising, given the state of the website. She looks at the photo of her parents again. A moment later, she picks up her mobile and dials the number. There will be some benefit to being busy again. Or at least, as busy as one can be in the winter at an inn up near the North Sea . . .

"Er, hi. Could I speak to Sue, please?"

Two hours later, Kate's on the treadmill, watching *The Great British Bake Off* on the television in front of her. She's been going to the gym nearly every day since her physiotherapist cleared her for running. It gets her out of the postage stamp of a flat so she doesn't go mad there.

The gym is a soothing place for her, somewhere people pretty much keep to themselves, and there's no pressure to talk to anyone. Just the welcome distraction of muscle burn and vapid TV. Except today, the woman on the treadmill beside her keeps glancing at the web of scars along Kate's cheek, left arm, and shoulder. She'll be making up her own story about what happened. Kate usually covers the scars with a layer of makeup, but not when she goes to the gym. She wants to hate this woman and her smooth arms, pumping at her sides like an Olympian as she runs faster than Kate ever could. She's thinner too. Doesn't seem to sweat as much. Her eyes don't have dark circles under them like Kate's do.

Twenty minutes later, the other woman's treadmill beeps and she slows her pace to a cool-down. Kate has already hit her calorie burn target, but she keeps running. A minute later the other woman stops, mops her forehead with a small white towel. She flashes Kate a pitying sort of smile, but Kate just increases the pace of her own run, even though she's starting to feel lightheaded. As the woman heads toward the locker room, Kate's mobile starts vibrating where it's resting on the control panel.

OAKWOOD INN flashes up on the caller ID.

She hits the emergency stop button and the treadmill jerks to a halt.

Before she came to the gym, she spoke briefly with Sue, who requested she email her CV for review before hustling her off the phone. Given Kate's recent experience with her job search, her expectations for a follow-up were low. The labour market had been so miserable of late; she'd sent out dozens of applications over the past month and had only been granted one interview, which had gone poorly, probably because she hadn't really wanted the job. But since sending her CV to Sue, she started to picture herself at the Oakwood, the need to connect with her parents' past drawing her to the place. And, she thought, there was certainly some appeal in Alnwick being as far away from London as she could get without leaving the country. A true fresh start.

Breath heaving, she answers the phone. "Kate Mercer."

"Hi, Kate, Sue again from the Oakwood. Oh, can you hold on just a mo'?"

"Yeah," Kate says, pushing her red fringe up off her sweaty forehead, grateful for the moment to try to catch her breath. There's much scuffling on the other end of the line, and Kate hears a door shut.

"Sorry, had to pop in somewhere quiet," Sue says in a Scottish accent thicker than fog. "I had a look at yer CV. Lots of admin experience, I see. No hospitality."

"That's right. But I'm a fast learner. I—"

"Not a problem, just confirming. But you can manage things?

Scheduling and ordering and the like? I see some of that here on your resume."

"Yes, of course," Kate lies, smooth as poured wax. She hadn't done much as a basic phone receptionist at the insurance company, but she's sure she could figure it out. And besides, who doesn't polish up their CV nowadays? Enhance and exaggerate here and there to appear more experienced, more knowledgeable, more educated, more more more of whatever more they think an employer wants to see?

"And you've volunteered at an animal shelter?"

One hundred percent true. "Yes, quite regularly," Kate says. "My dog Ozzie is a rescue and it's a cause close to my heart."

"So he'd be coming with you, then?"

"Yes, if that's all right? I saw in the advert—"

"Yes, pets welcome and encouraged. We've got a wee terrier here. Yours is friendly with other dogs?"

"Absolutely."

"Good."

Kate half-expects Sue to ask to interview Ozzie.

"Now this is a live-in position, you're aware."

"Yes, I saw that."

"Without putting too fine a point on it, it's likely not the best environment for children. Do you—"

"No," Kate says, an edge to her voice that she tries to file down as she continues. "Just me and my dog."

"Jolly good then. Have you ever been up to this part of the country? A bit different here in the North than down in London."

"I haven't, no. But I'm looking to get away from London, actually. Time for a change."

"Can be as good as a rest, can't it?" Sue says. "Well, Kate, I reckon we should give it a go."

Relief courses through Kate like warm water. "Brilliant, thank you!"

She smiles with something that feels like a vestige emotion from a past life. Optimism, maybe.

"We'll start with a probationary period and if all goes well, we'll formalize the role. How soon can you be here?"

Kate thinks of all the boxes lined up against her bedroom wall, as ready as they'll ever be. "I can be there tomorrow," she says.

As her breath steadies, she leans against the treadmill and watches the contestants on the television show craft cakes that are truly a work of art. The judges dig in, excitement glowing on their faces like children at a birthday party as they taste-test the results of the competition. She looks at the layers of icing and reckons it would take at least two hours of running to burn off one piece of that extravagant cake.

It's hard to outrun your bad decisions. But you can certainly try.

Chapter 3

Audrey

BERLIN, GERMANY | NOVEMBER 1938

"That was lovely, Audrey," Ruth said, glancing up from her embroidery. "What was it?"

Audrey turned on the piano stool. "I'm not sure, actually," she said. "Just something I'm playing at."

In addition to her assigned music, Audrey had been chipping away at a little piece of her own for a couple of months. The composition was simple and gentle, yet full of strength. She thought of Ilse when she played it, of her subtle courage and kindness. It at once uplifted and grounded her, like a warm drink. Once she finished it, she planned to give it to Ilse as a parting gift. But something was missing from it still. Audrey glanced over at Ilse, absorbed in her book.

"There's a contradictory feel to it," Ruth was saying with a smile. "I think it's beautiful."

Ruth was the player in the Kaplan family. She'd never had the opportunity to hone her skill like Audrey had, but she used to play all the time before little Michael died. His death had cut through so many layers of Ruth, scarring her very bones. She didn't touch the piano anymore, but enjoyed Audrey's entertainment from a distance, and was pleased to see the instrument used again. It was a rare honey oak baby grand that Ira had commissioned for her.

"Does anyone need anything whilst I'm out today?" Audrey asked, changing the subject.

Lately she tried to run errands for the Kaplans whenever she could, to save Ruth or Ira having to venture out unnecessarily.

"Where are you off to, Audrey?" Ira asked from his seat in one of the large wing chairs. Ephraim was across from him, a chessboard between them.

Ephraim always won, and Audrey never knew whether Ira was in fact terrible at the game or wanted his son to experience a sense of achievement and victory that was—at least at the moment—unattainable to him in any other realm of his life. He was being homeschooled by Ruth now, so he didn't even have his classmates to compete with in studies, or at recess.

"To the shops," Audrey replied, a little embarrassed. "I need a dress for my recital. I don't really have anything smart enough, unfortunately."

With Ilse's help, Audrey had narrowed down the style she wanted, but she was miserable that her friend couldn't join her for the excursion. She felt no small measure of shame at the fact that she could still go about her business without fear of roundups by the Gestapo, or spot checks on her identification papers. She could continue with her studies as though nothing had changed. Audrey had to believe that Ira was right, that this was a terrible season for Jews and Germany. That once Hitler was no longer in power, things would return to normal, and Audrey might come back to Berlin. Surely this climate, these politics, couldn't be what the people truly wanted.

"I need new trousers," Ephraim piped up. "Look! They're inches too short now."

"I cannot believe how fast you're growing," Ruth said from her spot on the couch. "You'll be as tall as your father soon. But I can mail-order trousers for you. Audrey needn't bother with that."

"I really don't mind—"

"We should all go," Ira said, eyes still on the chessboard.

Ilse set her book in her lap. "What?"

Ruth gave Ira a piercing look.

"We can go out?" Ilse pressed. "To the shops?"

Ira nodded. "I think so. It would be good for us all."

"Ira—" Ruth began, but he pressed on.

"We'll go to Hertie's," he said. "It'll be busy enough there. We won't linger, and we'll keep a close eye, as always."

"I'd *love* to go," Ilse said, and grinned at Audrey.

"If we all hide like criminals," Ira directed at Ruth, "what message does that send? We have already altered our very way of life. If we reduce ourselves even further, then they have already won."

Ruth returned her gaze to her embroidery, her lips a fine line. "It isn't a game, Ira," she said.

"No, my love, it is not a game. But it will almost certainly be a war. And one must stand for what is right in war."

After lunch, the Kaplans and Audrey set out for Hertie's on the Liepzigerstrasse. It was one of the two remaining Jewish-owned department stores.

The day was bright, and not too cold, which lifted everyone's spirits a notch as they made their way from the bus stop to the store one block down. Audrey had only been to Hertie's once. It was an enormous five-storey building that took up nearly an entire square city block. She glanced at the triangular red flags emblazoned with the store name as they snapped in the wind atop the roof, and an unpleasant image flashed through her mind of them replaced with the swastikas that had overtaken the rest of the city. A frightening sense of inevitability came over her. In front of her, Ira was staring resolutely ahead, chatting to his wife, who was constantly looking over her shoulders, Ephraim's gloved hand clutched tightly in her own. He was too old to be holding his mother's hand in the street, but he didn't protest, and Audrey wondered whether he felt trepidation at being out in public after his ordeal. She reached for Ilse's hand, who laced her fingers with Audrey's the way she used to when they were little and were forced to pass the nasty boys as they walked down the street to the main road. They called Ilse names Audrey didn't understand at the time and tried to stick chewing gum in the ponytail they would eventually cut off.

At Hertie's, there was a distinct strain about the customers, who were shopping with a harried determination rather than enjoyment. After half an hour of searching in the ladies' formal wear section, Audrey hadn't found anything suitable for her recital. Frowning, she turned to Ilse.

"Do you think we could pop across the street? There's that dress shop not a block down. It might have more selection." She was eager to get this sorted, and wasn't sure if Ilse would be able to come back out with her some other time.

Ilse nodded, wiping her dewy brow. "I'm over-warm in here anyway. We've been so cooped up, I'm not used to any sort of crowd anymore." She breathed an uncomfortable chuckle. "I could do with some air. Let's ask Papa."

They wove their way through racks of men's garments until they located the others. Ephraim was in a dressing room, and Ruth stood nearby with several sets of trousers slung over her arm. Ilse pled their case as Ruth's brow knit tighter and tighter.

"I don't think it wise to separate," she said. "It's already—"

"Ruth, they're only going over the street," Ira said. "We'll be a few more minutes here with Ephraim, and then we'll join them. Perhaps we could all get a cup of hot chocolate from the cart on the corner, as a treat for the way home."

"Yes!" Ephraim called from the dressing room.

Audrey suppressed a laugh. Ruth's face softened.

"I'm sorry," she whispered. "It's difficult to feel at ease right now."

"I know, my dear," Ira said. "Have fun," he added, pulling Ilse's head toward him and planting a kiss on her hair.

He was an affectionate man, generally. He didn't shy away from embracing his children, which had always made Audrey a little jealous. She couldn't recall the last time her father kissed her. A surprising lump formed in her throat, and she was gripped with a homesickness for him that she hadn't felt in the three years since she'd seen him.

Outside, the sky was clouded over and the temperature had dropped. Audrey and Ilse crossed the busy road to the dress shop, the bell above the door jingling when they entered. It was a small store, nice and quiet. There was only one other patron poking through dresses, which were organized in a rainbow of colours on crisscrossed racks throughout the shop. It gave Audrey the feeling of being trapped inside a kaleidoscope.

"*Guten Tag*, ladies," a light voice called from within.

"Hello," Audrey and Ilse said together, searching for the speaker.

A slight woman with light brown hair and a long neck emerged from behind the cash desk. "Heil Hitler. How may I help you?"

She smiled at them both. Her eyes loitered for a moment longer on Ilse, taking in her features from hair to collarbone in an instant, but her expression remained pleasant. Still, it left Audrey with a lingering disquiet, that they had both been analyzed and Ilse had clearly been noted—or suspected—in some way. It shifted something in the interaction.

Audrey forced a smile. "I have a piano recital coming up, my graduation. I was thinking something like this," she said, withdrawing the folded magazine page from her pocketbook. "But I need something with tighter sleeves than that."

The other patron left, and over the next five minutes, the woman pulled a series of gowns from the racks, holding them up for Audrey and Ilse to assess. Ilse sighed wistfully at a navy piece that Audrey didn't care for, but that was more Ilse's style.

"I wish I had somewhere to wear something like this," she said.

The familiar twinge of guilt struck Audrey. "You will. Someday soon," she said, hoping that was the truth.

With a flourish, the saleswoman plucked a floor-length crimson gown from a nearby rack. It had a plunging neckline, but the slim sleeves Audrey was looking for.

"What about this?" she asked, one eyebrow raised. "It is daring, but I see you have the lipstick to match," she added, nodding at Audrey's mouth.

Audrey pictured Herr Fogel's face if she were to turn up in something as flashy as this dress, and nearly laughed. The wrong outfit threatened just as much of an impact as the right one.

"I don't think it's quite what I'm looking for," Audrey said. "I don't want it to detract attention from my playing, you see. I think I'd prefer something more subdued. Pastel. A soft blue, or yellow perhaps?"

A sudden shouting from out on the street made all three women startle. The proprietor brushed past Audrey to the window.

"What is it?" Audrey asked, foreboding flickering inside her.

"The police," the saleswoman said quietly. "Gestapo, I think. Again."

Audrey went to the window, Ilse behind her. They peered out and Audrey's stomach plummeted. Ira was standing on the pavement across the street, facing a uniformed officer.

"Papa!" Ilse gasped. "Good God, what's happening?" Her eyes were wide and round, like prey that knows it's been cornered. Knows what's coming next.

"I don't . . ." Audrey trailed off. She scanned the crowd as the Gestapo officer continued to shout at Ira. There were more policemen. Four or five that Audrey could see.

"Only shopping," she heard Ira say. "Not a crime . . ."

There were Ruth and Ephraim, just behind him, off to the side. As Audrey watched, the crowd of shoppers and pedestrians dispersed, melting into the ether before the soldiers turned hungry eyes on them too. Audrey couldn't process what she was seeing fast enough, and then the officer in front of Ira raised his gun.

The saleswoman screamed as the shot cracked through the cold air and Ira dropped to the ground in a burst of blood.

"Papa!" Ilse cried. "Papa!"

"No!" Audrey shouted.

"Oh God," the saleswoman murmured. She looked at Ilse, then at the street and back again. "Is that—"

Ilse made a dash toward the shop door.

"Ilse, *no*!" Audrey lunged forward and seized her around the shoulders. "You can't! You *must* stay here!"

But Ilse squirmed, trying to shove her off. "No!" she screamed. "No! *Papa!*"

Audrey wrapped her arms around Ilse as tightly as she could and Ilse stopped fighting, collapsing into her. She could feel her friend's heart pounding as sobs racked her body.

This could not be happening. It couldn't.

Audrey glanced out the window again, blinking at the sight of Ira's prone body. Blood was pooling. She pivoted her body to block Ilse's view.

"They're rounding people up," the saleswoman said, her face wan.

Audrey watched over Ilse's shoulder, sickened by the scene unfolding in front of her. A large black van had pulled up. The soldiers were still shouting. Another shot rang out, and a renewed wave of screams crested. Ilse turned around to face the window before Audrey could stop her.

At the sight of her father, she let out a strangled cry.

Audrey's heart was racing. The back doors of the van opened as officers began seizing anyone within reach and shoving them inside. Two more shots, and another body crumpled to the ground. But Audrey's eyes were locked on Ruth, who was kneeling over her husband, tears streaming down her red face as chaos reigned around them. Ephraim approached her from behind, a paper shopping bag still clutched in his hand. A soldier grabbed him by the collar, pulling him back toward the van. Ruth rose, shouting something at the soldier, a plea, and Audrey felt a surge of terror. He waved his gun in Ephraim's direction and Ruth stepped between the pistol and her son. Ilse wailed.

The soldier indicated the van, and then Ira's body. Ruth nodded. As she turned toward the vehicle, her eyes scanned the street, searching, finally landing on the dress shop window and Ilse, who pushed back against Audrey.

The pandemonium seemed to fade into the background in those few seconds when Ruth locked eyes with her daughter. The look in them seared itself on Audrey's memory; the blistering anguish of a woman who knows this may be the last time she will ever set eyes on her child. But there was a softness there too. In what she knew might be her final act as Ilse's mother, Ruth Kaplan's deepest instinct was to comfort.

I love you, she mouthed.

A soldier pushed her toward the van. She took Ephraim's hand, climbed in, and disappeared.

"No!" Ilse cried. "No! Mama! *Mama!* Ephraim!" She made another attempt for the door. "Where are they taking them?!"

"No!" Both Audrey and the saleswoman said together, reaching for Ilse. They held her back as the van doors slammed shut.

"Ilse, you're no good to them if you get taken as well," Audrey pled. Tears were running down her own face now. "Stay here. You *must* stay here, I beg you!"

The saleswoman darted to the windows and pulled the curtains shut with a sharp *swish,* then locked the door.

Ilse moaned like a wounded animal and leaned against Audrey. They heard more vehicle doors slamming in the distance, a few men's voices, then eventual silence.

Audrey twitched her head toward the window. *Is he still there?* she mouthed to the saleswoman, who, to Audrey's surprise, had tear tracks on her face.

The woman pulled the edge of the curtain aside an inch. She peered out, then shook her head. "No one."

After nearly half an hour, Ilse coughed herself into silence, her bloodshot eyes staring down at the dress shop floor as she wrung her hands. Audrey followed her gaze. At some point, the deep crimson dress had fallen and now lay in a puddle. Audrey blinked rapidly to dispel the image of Ira and the blood that had pooled on the ground behind him moments before.

She brushed the hair back off Ilse's wet, swollen face. "Ilse?" she whispered.

But Ilse continued to stare, unresponsive. Suddenly, she began to shake.

"She's in shock," the saleswoman said, and her heels clicked on the wooden floor as she hurried away, returning a moment later with a glass of water and two large woolen shawls, which she tenderly wrapped around Ilse's shoulders.

"You need to get out of here," she said to Audrey once Ilse had finally ceased trembling. "I can let you out the back way, into the alley. But you must go. It isn't safe."

Audrey stood, supporting Ilse. The woman led them to the back of the shop and opened a door into a dim, odorous alleyway.

"Thank you," Audrey offered, but the woman shook her head.

"Get her out of Berlin. Out of Germany, if you can," she said, meeting Audrey's eyes with a hard compassion. "I fear this is only the beginning."

Chapter 4

Kate

ALNWICK, ENGLAND | NOVEMBER 2010

A few hours outside of London, Kate glances at the clock on her car's dashboard.

"Okay, Oz," she says. "Hold on. I'll find us somewhere to stop."

Ten minutes later, she pulls off the A1 into the small town of Knottingly, where she lets Ozzie out for a quick stretch, then picks up a takeaway salad and coffee at a quirky café. Ozzie's face appears in the open window as she approaches the car with her lunch. His tail beats a *thwump-thwump-thwump* against the seat.

In the car, she munches her salad, Ozzie drooling over her shoulder. He loves fruits and vegetables, the oddball.

"Yes, yes, here you go."

She tosses a chunk of cucumber into the back seat, where it's instantly swallowed whole. She takes a sip of coffee, which is remarkably good, and checks their status again on the SatNav.

"A couple more hours, Oz. I'm ready to be off the road as much as you are." She pauses, then fishes in her purse for her mobile, finding it at the very bottom under the detritus of makeup compacts, lip balm, crumpled receipts, and tampons. "All right, let's do this," she mutters, dialing her husband's number. It rings several times before going to voicemail. It's a workday for Adam, but it's also possible he's just avoiding her call. He's been staying at his brother's place for the past few weeks.

"Hey," she says. "It's me . . . I'm out now. And my stuff. Most of it, anyway. The shipping company will be by on Thursday to pick up the last few boxes, and my bookshelf." She's unsure what more to tell him. There hasn't been anything left to say for a long time. "My new contact info is on the kitchen counter, if you need it." She hesitates again, knowing that this is the moment she would normally have signed off with a message of love. She can feel the edges of the hole it leaves, ragged as bite marks. "I'm . . ." Her nose tingles. "I'm sorry, Adam. Okay . . . Bye."

She takes a moment to settle her nerves, then tosses the gear into drive once more.

The view outside the windows becomes wilder and more beautiful as they drive farther north. This landscape is all new for Kate, and she wants the unfamiliar right now. She glances over her shoulder at Ozzie, who's sitting with his nose smeared against the glass. His eyes are wide, as though he knows they're on an adventure in uncharted territory.

Kate skirts past Newcastle Upon Tyne as her thoughts swirl. She stayed up late last night to finish the last of her packing. Before leaving early this morning, she double-checked each room, then stopped to look around the empty kitchen, noted the faded rectangles on the walls from picture frames that once hung there. The residue from happier, more hopeful times. There's nothing keeping her in London, and she feels a thread from her parents' lives tugging her to the Oakwood, so she's letting it. Instinct is as good a guide as any once you've lost your compass.

A while later, she finally spots the signposts for her destination: Alnwick. She turns onto the high road that runs through the centre of the old town. Low stone walls line either side as they cruise through the village, and Kate is pleased when they reach a traffic light so she can take in the streetscape. It's filled with an array of boutique shops, pubs and restaurants, some businesses, and charity shops. After the frantic bustle of London, she already feels more relaxed. Safer, somehow. Her shoulders drop a little. They've been hitched up to her ears for the past few months.

She drives through the heart of the town and past the grand gates of Alnwick Castle. After another minute or two of twists and turns down a narrow county road and over an old stone bridge, they reach the very edge of the village. She slows down, eyeing the building in the field on her left with mounting curiosity. Though it's partially obscured by trees, it looks enormous. Her SatNav announces that they've arrived at their destination as she reaches a break in the low stone wall, beyond which stretches a long gravel drive lined with gold and auburn-leaved oak trees. She spots a sign on the wall next to the gates.

THE OAKWOOD INN, it proclaims in aged copper lettering.

"Well, Ozzie, this is it," she says, turning the wheel.

The gravel crunches as she drives along, the green lawns sweeping out in either direction. A dark wooded area forms a dense wall of evergreens behind the inn and an autumn mist hangs over the trees, lending the landscape a mystical sort of ambience.

Kate pulls up in front of the hotel, and her mouth falls open a fraction as she peers up. It's built in the same beige stone as the buildings back in the town, with three storeys that rise into the overcast sky. The angled roof is all charcoal shingles and Gothic eaves. It looks like a miniature castle, a grand and proud lady who's been sitting on this plot of land since before there were fairies.

"Whoa," she breathes, staring at the dark upper-floor windows and feeling as though she's been transported into the pages of a Brontë novel.

After a moment, Ozzie shifts in his seat, alert to the change in energy now that the car has stopped moving, and Kate is pulled from her reverie. She steers into a spot in the car park—there's only one other vehicle there—turns off the ignition, and gets out. The temperature dropped as the afternoon wore on, and the clouds overhead block out the weak autumn sun. Kate stretches her arms up, extending her compressed spine like an accordion, then retrieves her purse. She clips Ozzie's leash to his collar and he bounds out of the car, shaking himself off as though he's just stepped out of a lake. He pants with excitement at all the new smells.

"Not bad, eh?" Kate says, scratching his ears.

A sign indicates the reception desk is at the front of the house. Kate guides Ozzie to a path up to the navy blue door, where lush ivy creeps across the wall above. She notes the silence; the air is dense out here. There's no noise from the town a short distance away. She doesn't even hear any birds. She breathes in the smell of smoke and leaves and damp, smiles at the absence of petrol fumes.

She presses down on the brass handle and steps over the threshold, tugging Ozzie's leash in tightly. Although Sue said the job and house were dog-friendly, Kate wants him to make a good first impression. He seems to sense this, because he sits down smartly on the entryway rug and cranes his neck to look at her with his large brown eyes. Kate would swear he's smiling.

"Good boy, Oz, good boy."

The foyer is an impressive welcome to the house. A wide, majestic staircase straight ahead leads to a landing and the second floor. The stairs are dark walnut with a thick botanical-patterned runner. Overhead, a large gold chandelier illuminates the entryway and the hall that extends toward the back of the house. Kate glances left into a sitting room filled with overstuffed navy armchairs and a sofa clustered around a floor-to-ceiling brick fireplace, the logs crackling away in welcome.

A small reception desk is pressed against the wall beside the door, piled with neat stacks of tourism brochures. Beyond the reception is what she suspects may be a hall closet, then another door, through which she spots a larger, ornate desk with a lamp casting a dim glow over a mess of papers.

The air smells warm, like coffee and sugar, but she feels an unidentifiable draft. She taps the silver bell on the reception desk to alert Sue to her presence. There's a scuffle on the floorboards down the hall and she straightens, expecting the manager, but a small black terrier emerges from the shadows and trots up to her and Ozzie, whose tail begins to wag as he sniffs the newcomer.

"Well, hello, you," Kate coos, bending to pat the terrier.

"Can I help you?"

Kate's head whips up at the voice. A woman is walking down the same hallway whence came the terrier. She's elderly, and a little stooped. Kate reckons she must be into her nineties. One hand grasps the rounded handle of a cane as the other extends out to the side for balance. Kate remembers her grandmother walking like that, and her heart twinges at the thought.

Kate stands and offers her hand to the woman, noticing as she does so that she has the most remarkable eyes. So light blue they're grey, and spaced just a little too far apart. Her thin white hair is longer than most women her age, and pulled back into a soft bun.

"Hi, I'm Kate Mercer. I think we spoke on the—"

"Who?" the woman asks.

"Kate Mercer," Kate repeats, louder.

The woman scowls. "I'm not deaf. What is your business here? We're closed for the season, I'm afraid."

"I'm sorry, are you Sue?" Kate asks, sure that she isn't. The accent is different. It's English, not Scottish, but there's something off about it. At any rate, there's clearly some confusion.

"No, Sue is my housekeeper."

Kate stares at her. "Oh, okay, er . . . I was hired as the new administrator. Sue told me to come up today."

"You're the *what?*" The woman's face is dark as midnight.

"The er, the new administrator?"

"Is that a question or a statement?"

"I'm sorry," Kate says, "I think there's been a misunder—"

"Like hell there has," the old woman curses. "Sue!" she hollers over her shoulder, louder than Kate would have anticipated, given her age. "*Sue!*"

A door slams somewhere on the main floor and Ozzie shifts against Kate's leg. A moment later, another woman emerges from down the hall. She's somewhere in her fifties, heavyset with a square face and large jaw surrounded by greying hair tied back in a ponytail. She's dressed in leggings and a loose jumper. Sweat beads on her forehead.

"Our new *administrator* has arrived," the older woman says, tossing a hand in Kate's direction.

Sue stands off to the side, eyes darting between them.

"Hi there," she says, accent rolling over the *R*'s like a drum. "I'm Sue. The housekeeper. We spoke on the phone. Now, Audrey," she directs at the old woman, "please just listen for a mo—"

"I told you no!" Audrey barks. "I have everything under control."

"Except you *don't*," Sue insists. Kate stands, frozen, watching the exchange with mounting alarm. "You need someone to help with the day-to-day, and the off-season is the time to get someone trained up. That's why I hired Miss Mercer here."

"Without consulting me."

"Yes, without consulting you."

"Why?"

"Because I knew this is how you would respond, you stubborn old goat."

"Listen, I—" Kate begins, but Sue cuts her off.

"Miss Mercer, why don't you go show yourself around? Choose a room. They're all empty but for Audrey's on the second floor." She flashes Kate a stressed smile, her eyes imploring her not to leave.

If it weren't for the pull Kate feels to retrace her parents' steps, that's exactly what she would be doing. This is a disaster. Sue hiring her without the knowledge or consent of the hotel's owner? It's embarrassing for all three of them.

"Sure," Kate says. She might as well explore this Gothic queen of a house before she's booted right out of it. She tugs Ozzie toward the stairs.

"She's not staying," Audrey snaps at Sue, who retaliates in a low whisper.

They continue to bicker as Kate scales the staircase. Her mind is already skipping on ahead, planning what she'll do if the owner won't let her stay, if this job didn't exist to begin with. She'll have to tell Adam she needs to move back into the flat again until she finds a place of her own. She wishes now she'd waited until tonight to call him.

She rounds the landing to the second floor. The air is still, like the basement of a library, and smells like lemon cleaner. Her footsteps are muffled by a thick, dark blue carpet. The diffuse golden light from the hallway sconces outside each room glints off the polished wood door frames and banister. At the end of the corridor, another set of stairs leads to a third floor.

How many rooms are there? she wonders. The house is even larger than it looks from the outside.

All the bedroom doors are open. They're painted the same navy as the front door with gold words stenciled into them instead of numbers. Kate spots Lily and Lavender. She pokes her head into the latter. The walls are papered in a dusty purple damask print, and she catches a whiff of lavender from the clutch of stems in a pewter vase on the dresser. This room has two single beds, so Kate moves on down the corridor, stepping into each room as she passes: Sage, Wisteria, Lilac, and Fern, all decorated in keeping with their names, and at the very end of the hall: Elder. It's the only door that's closed, so she assumes this must be Audrey's room. She smiles wryly at the fact that the aged proprietor should have the room named *Elder*.

Ozzie has been tight on Kate's heels, and he follows her up the narrower staircase to the third floor; still carpeted, but less grand than the main stairs. She turns right at the landing and pokes her head into Willow (her favourite yet), Marigold (far too yellow), and Oak. The last room is tucked into a little alcove of its own: Rose.

Kate takes a deep breath, thinking of her mother, and pushes the door open wider. With a name like Rose, she expected pink or red, but the walls are papered in white with a striking black floral pattern. White curtains frame both large windows, falling into pools on the floorboards. The white duvet is piled with dark green accent pillows, and a matching throw blanket covers the foot of the bed. A couch, armchair, and glass coffee table are clustered in the corner of the room in front of an old television. Kate catches a glimpse of the woods out the window, a border of green speckled with gold and red. A realization dawns on her. "Wait a minute . . ."

Ozzie raises his head as she reaches into her purse for the small photo album from her parents' honeymoon. She locates the photo she's looking for in the pile of loose pictures stuffed into the back.

The wallpaper is different in the photo, but the dresser is identical. The sofa is the same size and shape too. It's just been reupholstered in a more modern fabric. In the photo, her mother is perched on the edge of it, a stream of sunlight from the window behind her creating a halo around her auburn head. Her mouth is open in a wide smile, eyes glittering with good-natured annoyance; the expression she always wore when Kate's dad took the piss out of her about something. He had a sarcastic streak that was often funny but could sometimes wound, if he was in a depressed mood, or drank too much that day. Even now, she can hear their voices, her dad's low cackle. Her eyes blur with tears and she holds the picture to her chest.

"They were here," she says to Ozzie. "They stayed in *this* room."

Kate sits down in the same spot as her mother and closes her eyes, trying to leech some long-forgotten ray of her mum's quiet, reserved energy out of the cushion. She'd like to believe it's possible. Some people do. But Kate doesn't really know exactly what she believes anymore. Loss has a way of challenging everything we thought was true and right in the world. The lucky ones are drawn closer to whatever it is they believe about the universe, comforted by the idea of a god with some master plan for everyone. Other people just drown in the unnerving knowledge that life is random. It's fair, in a way, that we're all beholden to the outcome determined by the same set of dice, but fairness can be cruel sometimes. It stole her parents from her. It was the nail in the coffin of her failing marriage. It stole something else deep inside Kate, too, something she's not sure she can ever get back.

A knock on the door jolts her. Audrey is standing in the doorway, Sue behind her.

"Go on," Sue says.

Audrey steps into the room. Ozzie tugs toward her but Kate holds his leash firm, wiping an errant tear.

"Gracious," Audrey sighs. "There's no need for tears."

"No," Kate says, embarrassed. "It's, er . . . It's the room. My mother's name was Rose. I lost her recently, that's all." She pushes the memories away like crumbs falling to the floor. She'll clean them up later. "It's a beautiful room."

Audrey's knotted fingers flex on the handle of her cane. In the hallway, Sue clears her throat.

"I've agreed to let you stay on a probationary basis," Audrey says. "Sue has made some convincing, however *pigheaded*"—she shoots Sue a withering look over her shoulder—"arguments about the amount of work required for the continued administration of the Oakwood. It may be time for a bit of help. We'll give it a go until Christmas, perhaps. Are you agreeable?"

A strong sense of relief floods Kate's veins. Now that she's in the Rose Room, she desperately wants to stay.

"Yes," she says, with forced composure. "That would be lovely."

Audrey eyes her a little longer, her mouth pinched. She shifts the leg supported by her cane. "I've lost a lot of people over the years, including my mother. She died when I was born. I lost both my parents young. I am sorry for your loss. It's never easy."

Without waiting for Kate's response, Audrey turns back down the hall, leaving Sue alone in the doorway.

"She's all bark, you know," Sue mutters. "Apologies for the deception, but she needs help and is too damn stubborn to admit it. But here we are. Have you had a chance to poke around the town a bit?"

Kate shakes her head. "Not yet, no. I came straight here from London this morning."

"I think you'll like it. Certainly not the same pace as London, mind." Her grin reaches her eyes. "It does get a wee bit slow between now and springtime, but the shops and pubs are still open. Folks come up here for the castle and the gardens during the high season, and we get swamped."

"I noticed the house seemed rather quiet."

"Aye, everybody's cleared off for the season."

There's a beat of silence whilst Kate absorbs this. "So . . . there are no guests at all during the winter?"

Sue shakes her head. "Nah. Audrey likes it quiet for a spell, 'specially as she gets on, and there's not many tourists in the winter lookin' for lodgings anyhow."

"So it will just be the three of us here all winter?"

"Two; I live in town, and come in to clean. I'll come by every couple o' weeks. Like to take the time to be with me grandkids in the winter, anyway. Works out nice for me."

Kate gets the sense Sue wants her to ask about the grandchildren, but she's still processing what Sue said.

"Now then, yer room," Sue continues, brushing past Kate, who finally releases Ozzie. He rushes around sniffing furniture legs. "We have the full cable package. Audrey does love that new baking competition show." Kate smiles. At least they have one thing in common. "The Wi-Fi password is Sophie. There's a DVD player there for you too; the DVD collection is down in the sitting room. Just help yourself and be sure to return them when you're finished."

Kate wonders silently if either Audrey or Sue has ever heard of Netflix.

They move into the toilet and Sue demonstrates how to coax the faucet to life as Ozzie scoots around their legs, continuing his olfactory tour of the premises.

"And that's about it," Sue says when they emerge back into the main room. "Oh, here's yer keys. That one's for yer room, this one here's for the front door. Welcome to the Oakwood, Miss Mercer."

"Thank you," Kate says, taking the keys.

Sue heads for the door, then rests her hand on the frame, one conspiratorial eyebrow raised. "If I speak truth, Audrey needs the comp'ny as much as the help. Health's not what it once was, I'm afraid. She's done all the admin herself for years, since she took it over from her auntie. But it's too much now, and with me gone most of the winter . . . she needed someone. She's a big ol' box o' secrets, that one, but if you can find the right key, there's a heart o' gold inside it." Sue winks before turning down the hallway.

Kate watches her go, wondering about the losses Audrey mentioned. As she steps back into the room, her eyes fall on the name stenciled to the door: *Rose.* She closes it, glances down at her arm as the knob clicks. Her arms are identical to her mother's—from shoulder to fingertips. She's jarred by the memory of feeling those arms around her as she sat in Rose's lap as a child, relaxing against her chest as her hair tickled Kate's cheek.

Later that night, Kate brushes her teeth and pops her bite plate in. Some mornings she wakes up unsure whether she's going to be able to pry her own jaw open. She undresses, then turns off the lights and crawls into the unfamiliar bed, gently shoving Ozzie over to make space. She stares at the ceiling until she finally drifts off into a fitful sleep filled with uneasy dreams of black roses beading with water from the rain. Of dark and deserted roads that stretch out indefinitely, leading nowhere. Silent and cold.

Chapter 5

Audrey

BERLIN, GERMANY | NOVEMBER 1938

Ouch!" Audrey swore under her breath. She quickly withdrew her hand from the stream of hot water pouring from the bathtub faucet. She turned the cold tap to temper it and then fumbled with the jar of salts on the tub ledge.

Behind her, Ilse leaned against the doorway with a vacant expression.

"Come here," Audrey said gently.

Ilse startled as though surprised to see her there, then moved into the bathroom.

She had cried herself sick at the dress shop, and in the hour it had taken for them to get back to the house, her spirit seemed to have left her body. A sort of mental paralysis had overtaken her, which, in a way, allowed Audrey to guide her easily onto the bus. The vehicle had been full of commuters with shopping bags, children, small dogs. People laughing and chatting to their travel companions, carrying on with cheerful nonchalance. When they'd finally arrived back home and Audrey slid the lock into place behind them, Ilse had looked around, disoriented.

"Let's get you into the bath," Audrey had said. It was the first thing she thought of, to help fight the lingering shakes and thaw the numbness that had settled over her friend.

Now Audrey reached for Ilse and helped her with the buttons on her dress. Something flipped in her gut at the sight of Ilse's breasts, and she averted her eyes as Ilse stepped into the tub. They'd been so close for so long, had seen each other dress, but something about Ilse's nakedness was particularly vulnerable in this moment. Audrey half-expected to see her shattered heart through the layers of skin, as red and raw as her eyes.

Audrey had always responded well to stressful situations and pressure—she was never nervous onstage—though she hadn't experienced anything like this before. So far, her adrenaline was helping her manage Ilse, but beneath it simmered the shock and grief, the encroaching sense of panic at the questions that swirled in her mind.

"Thank you," Ilse muttered, staring straight ahead at the porcelain tub.

"You're welcome. When you're ready, come down, and we'll . . ." *What happens now*? "I'll make some tea," Audrey finished, then left the bathroom, shutting the door behind her.

Downstairs, the lamps were off, but a dim afternoon light cast a grey aura over the sitting room. Audrey could still smell the lingering aroma of potato soup from lunch. She glanced behind her into the dining room. Ira, Ruth, and Ephraim had all sat around that table together only hours ago, discussing their shopping needs. But the house was silent now. They were all gone, taken, in one way or another, in a matter of minutes. It was unfathomable. Audrey expected them to appear suddenly, around the corner from the foyer or through the doors to the dining room.

Matya hadn't worked today, given her mother's illness. Audrey wondered vaguely how they would continue to pay her, and then the questions all began to flow at once. Her mind flicked through the realities of their situation like pages in a book, marking the ones that would require solutions in the short term, wondering what the answers could possibly be in the long run.

How would they pay for anything at all, with Ira dead, and Ruth gone? Would Ilse be able to access their bank account? What did it mean if Ruth was missing, or in custody, but not dead? And—Audrey felt bile rise in her throat at the idea—what if she was? And Ephraim, too? Where did people go once they were rounded up? Audrey had heard Ira speak of holding sites, but had no idea what they entailed or where they were located. How could they find out where Ruth and Ephraim had been taken? And what had they done with Ira's body?

I fear this is only the beginning, the saleswoman had said. The beginning of what? Things were already horrible.

As she waited for the kettle to boil, Audrey leaned against the counter, struggling to fend off mental images of the afternoon's events. Her world was spinning, and her instinct was to clutch the mundane, grasping at trivialities that were familiar and stable. To convince herself that some things hadn't changed, no matter how inconsequential. So she made the tea, and set a small tray with some biscuits and Ilse's favourite blackberry jam to try to tempt her to eat. A while later she heard the tub drain above, and braced herself for the conversation she knew they must have.

Upstairs, Audrey found Ilse in her bedroom, sitting on the edge of her bed, staring dreamlike into the cold fireplace. Her dark hair fell into little damp tentacles over her broad shoulders, and her face was flushed from the hot water.

Audrey set the tray on the bedside table and went to Ilse. She wrapped her arm around her, pulling her close. The spell Ilse had been under finally broke, and she began to sob once more, pouring out her grief into Audrey's shoulder as the tea grew cold and the room dark.

"Mama was right," Ilse said finally, taking a shaky breath. "We never should have gone."

"No, we shouldn't have," Audrey whispered. "And it's all my fault. I'm so sorry."

"It was my—" Ilse coughed, clearing the phlegm in her throat. "My father's decision, Audrey. Not yours. You went to buy a dress. You didn't ask us to join you. We all came willingly. I just wanted to feel normal for an afternoon. That's no fault of yours. But why did they shoot him?"

"I don't know. We didn't see what happened beforehand. I heard him say something about shopping not being a crime. It could have been nothing at all. They can do whatever they want, can't they? Maybe they just wanted a fight."

Ilse sat up straighter. "But why are we *in* this fight? What will become of us?"

Audrey wasn't sure if by *us* Ilse meant the pair of them, or Germany's Jews. Maybe both. But Audrey had no answer for any of it.

She stood and turned on a few of the lights. They both blinked as their eyes adjusted. The bright light felt incongruous with what was sure to be the darkest day of their lives. But it relieved Audrey in a way, and she hoped that perhaps the light might help them see things a little clearer.

"What do we do now?" Ilse asked, voicing Audrey's thoughts as she sat down again next to her. She hadn't wanted to be the one to bring up the urgency of their circumstances when Ilse's grief was so fresh, and was grateful for the segue.

"In the short term, we're going to need money," she said. "For electricity, coal, groceries. Do you have access to your father's account?"

"I—I don't think so. Mama did, but . . ." Ilse trailed off. "And you don't have your own money either, do you?"

"No." Ira had held funds from Audrey's father in trust, paying her tuition at the *konservatorium* and doling out an allowance. "You'll need to come back to London with me. It's the only—"

"I can't. We aren't allowed to travel, remember? Not legally, anyway. Hitler's made it impossible for us to go anywhere except by his own orders." She choked on the last word.

Ruth's and Ephraim's names lingered, unspoken, in the beat of silence that stretched between them. Ilse's grief was deep, as was

Audrey's, for the loss of Ira, but his death also posed a massive problem for their survival.

"I'll write to my father," Audrey said. "For a start. He might know someone who can help. In the meantime, maybe there's another way for him to send money."

"He's going to tell you to come home. He might even try to come fetch you."

Audrey gripped Ilse's hands. "I know. But I won't leave you. Not now. Not like this."

Ilse said nothing.

"I think you should try to eat something. I brought toast and—" Audrey stopped, her ears pricking at a noise in the distance. "Did you hear that?"

"What?"

"I thought I heard something. A shout."

"I don't know," Ilse said, sounding drained.

Audrey strained her ears again, but all she could hear was the ticking of the clock. She shook her head, then went to the tray on the bedside table. The pile of magazines was still stacked there. Only days before, they had sat here perusing them, irritated by Ephraim's interruption. What Audrey wouldn't give to see him climb down from the attic now, mischief sparkling in his eyes. In the span of an afternoon, their lives were set on an entirely different course.

"So," said Ilse dully, taking Audrey's proffered plate of toast. Her hair was beginning to dry, curling up at the ends. "What do we do for money right now, before we hear back from your father?"

Audrey had been thinking about this as she made the tea. Any job she might be qualified for—a salesgirl, probably—would barely put food on the table for the pair of them. She understood now, more than ever, that women's financial dependence on men was a prison. It wasn't just unfair. It could be catastrophic. She steeled herself. "Well . . . I was wondering if we could sell some things. I don't have any jewellery or anything, but—"

"My mother does."

"Yes." Audrey felt anguished at the thought. "Or your father's books—"

"No." Ilse's tone was firm. "Not the books. Not . . ." Her breath hitched. "Not yet."

She was quiet for a while. Audrey thought about Ira, wondered where his body had been taken, and fought back her own tears. He was such a good man. A second father to her.

"But what happens when Mama and Ephraim return?" Ilse said finally. "She'll be devastated, won't she?"

Audrey lowered the bite of bread that was halfway to her mouth. "I suppose she will find it to have been . . . resourceful," she said. "Will she not just be overjoyed to be reunited? I can't see her being angry at you for doing what you must to survive."

The family had never discussed this possibility. Ira had been too optimistic. It seemed foolish now that they hadn't talked about what to do in the event any of them were arrested, let alone killed. But Ira had been steadfast in the hope that things would get better. It was a harsh lesson.

The abduction had been so violent and chaotic, right in the aftermath of Ira's murder. But perhaps Ruth's and Ephraim's detention would be over in short order. An intimidation attempt to incite fear and acquiescence. It was possible. But a dark voice inside Audrey reminded her that that type of optimism had already burned them. They should prepare for the worst, she thought, though she couldn't bring herself to say that to Ilse.

"Where are they, do you think?" Ilse asked.

Audrey inhaled deeply. "I assume at one of those holding centres your father was talking about. Or these ghettos that have sprung up, like that one near the border with Poland."

"But how do we find out?" Ilse set her plate aside, then rubbed her temples. "I can't even think straight."

By the time they finished eating, it was mid-evening. Audrey took the tray downstairs and did the washing up whilst Ilse went across the hall to her parents' room to peruse Ruth's jewellery. When Audrey returned, Ilse was standing in front of her own dresser, fingering a simple silver pendant necklace that was now slung around her neck. In front of her lay several sets of sapphire and ruby earrings, a diamond bracelet and necklace set, two spectacular emerald broaches, three gold rings, and some reichsmarks.

"I've collected everything except the pearl necklace and her wedding ring. She was wearing those today." Ilse's voice was weak. "And this"—she touched the pendant—"was the first piece of jewellery Papa gave her. It's not as valuable as the others. They were younger, not as well established as now." She forced a smile, which Audrey attempted to return.

"She'll be glad you saved that, I think."

"I don't know—" Ilse began, but what she didn't know, Audrey never found out.

A thunderous banging sounded from downstairs, followed by male voices shouting.

Audrey's heart pounded against her tonsils. "What was that?"

One spectacular *bang* and the sound of splintering wood confirmed that someone had broken through the front door.

"Good God, someone's in the house!" Ilse hissed.

Audrey's mind flew to images of the roundup, of guns and blood and Ruth mouthing *I love you*. She could not let them take Ilse. Her eyes flashed around the room, the lock on the door, the window. And then they landed on the ceiling.

"The attic!" she said. "*Go!*"

Ilse struggled on the rope ladder, feet slipping in her haste to climb, but she made it to the top. Audrey scrambled up next and hoisted the rope, tossing it into a pile beside her. There were two different male voices on the stairs now, taunting, somehow simultaneously jovial and angry. Audrey rushed to lower the door back into place and her eyes fell to the glittering array of Ruth's jewels on the dresser below.

"No," she breathed, a new horror overlaying her acute fear.

"What?" Ilse whispered.

"The jewellery."

Ilse's hand flew to her mouth.

In the briefest wild moment, Audrey debated retrieving them, but the men were in the hallway. They could either risk immediate death at the hands of violent intruders or gamble their future survival by losing their most valuable assets.

Audrey pressed her lips together to stop them from trembling. Closing her eyes against what might prove to be a calamitous loss, she shut the attic door.

"They're here for me, aren't they?" Ilse whispered, fear keen in her eyes. "The Gestapo?"

They both jumped as the bedroom door sprang open below and instinctively retreated a few paces from the attic hatch.

"Ha!" one of the men called. "Lars! Right here!"

The other man let out a satisfied sigh. "Christ, it's like they just left it there for us." A nasty chuckle. "Grab it all, and we'll head downstairs for the silver."

"Best score of the night so far though," the first one said.

Audrey's eyes found Ilse's and she was sure that she, too, was picturing this fiend stuffing Ruth's jewels into some dirty sack.

"How many houses left on the list?" the second man asked.

"Not sure. Three or four?"

More thuds and grunts told them that the rest of Ilse's room was being ransacked. A minute later they retreated, their voices on the stairs, and Audrey's breathing slowed a little. She held on to Ilse, whose limbs were curled in on themselves. She felt so frail. Just when it seemed no more could be taken from her, here were two bandits to strip her family home of its heirlooms and valuables. Audrey worried this latest assault would break her.

"He said something about a list," Ilse said, pulling away. "Papa had to register our property back in the spring. Do you think they're going to all the Jewish houses? Or was this just because they think we aren't here? After what—what happened today?"

Audrey thought of the shouting she'd heard earlier. "No, I think this is all some sort of plan."

"A plan for what?" Ilse asked.

Audrey swallowed. Her arms wanted to hold Ilse again, to touch something solid and familiar, because everything was terribly, terribly wrong.

Half an hour later, after the noise had ceased and they could be sure the men had vacated, they emerged from the attic. Audrey's jaw dropped at the sight, astonished at how much damage had been wrought in a few minutes' time. Ilse's drawers were all open, the bedclothes torn off and tossed to the floor. The large brass lamp on the dresser was overturned. They found a similar sight in the other bedrooms.

Downstairs, Audrey went to the front door and listened, picking up the sounds of banging and shouting in the distance. She peered outside, but their side street was deserted, quiet, and there was no sign of broken doors or windows in any of the neighbouring houses. It confirmed her suspicions that the attack on the Kaplans was targeted: they were the only Jewish family on the street. The realization trickled down her spine like cold water. She withdrew into the house, shutting the door against the terror outside, but the lock was broken. Together she and Ilse dragged the heavy coat tree over and shoved it against the door. It would have to do for now.

In the dining room, the curio cabinet had been emptied of its silverware and some of the crystal. The silver candelabras were gone from the sideboard and shards of china plates encrusted the floor. In the sitting room, the large front window that overlooked the street was shattered. It wasn't even for entry. It was purely for sport. Mercifully, Ira's book collection appeared intact. The thieves, it seemed, did not understand the library's value.

Ilse stared at it all with blank eyes, still wrapped in her robe. Her mother's necklace glittered at her collarbone. "We aren't even safe in our homes anymore," she said.

Audrey had no response.

Ilse gestured at the mess. "We have to clean this up. But I can't do it tonight." She said it dully, as though she were simply too tired, or had other commitments. As though it didn't matter either way. And that made Audrey fear for her mental state. There was only so much a person could absorb in one day. Audrey nodded. Better they try to get some sleep and approach these tremendous hurdles with rested minds tomorrow.

They trudged back upstairs. After a brief discussion, they agreed that the house was not secure enough for them to sleep unprotected in their bedrooms. It was cold, but the attic felt safer. Seizing some blankets and pillows, they dressed themselves in their heaviest clothing, then scaled the ladder with a pair of candles. The room felt much smaller than it had when Audrey and Ilse played here as children, but the low, sloped ceilings, yellow warmth of candlelight, and piles of quilts exuded a much-welcome sense of security.

They'd nearly drifted off when another loud noise in the distance jostled them.

"What now?" Audrey muttered. Wrapping a quilt around her shoulders, she walked, ducking against the slope of the ceiling, to one of the two small windows. In the moonlight, she could see into the neighbouring street, and beyond that, the peaked roofs of buildings and churches and—her stomach plummeted—the unmistakable orange glow of fires burning. She creaked open the window. The sounds of screams, crashes, booming echoes and harsh laughter rose up in the night air. It sounded like a riot, like animals tearing each other apart.

I fear this is only the beginning.

Audrey felt Ilse at her elbow. "That's the synagogue," Ilse said, her voice brittle. "They're burning the synagogue."

Chapter 6

Kate

ALNWICK, ENGLAND | NOVEMBER 2010

It's dark. They're on the motorway again, rain beating down on the windshield. In the headlights of the car, the road shimmers like glitter in a pool. Kate can hear the soft whir of water spraying into the wheel wells. There's hardly anyone else on the road. She glances at her dad, his stubbled chin in shadow. The odour of whiskey wafts from him.

But her rage at Adam fills her chest, and she's about to answer her husband when a sound louder than anything she's heard in her life fills her ears with the force and volume of cannon fire. It's inside her, reverberating in her cells. And then there's silence, and confusion, and the red and blue lights of the ambulances through the shattered windows.

Kate jolts awake with a gasp. It takes several seconds for her to realize that she's at the Oakwood, that she's safe. She runs a hand over her damp forehead. Ozzie, who always sleeps at the end of her bed, is resting his snout on the pillow next to her, looking at her with worried eyes.

"Oh, Oz." Kate reaches to soothe him.

Rain lashes against her bedroom windows as thunder rumbles loudly overhead. The noise from the storm must have woven its way into her dream. She glances at the small analog clock on the bedside table: 6:24.

She leans her head into Ozzie's, closing her eyes, but the lights from the ambulance are still imprinted on the back of her eyelids like some chaotic film projection, and she tries to blink them away.

The nightmares started not long after she left the hospital. At first, they were debilitating, but now Kate's learned to focus her attention on grounded things when she wakes from them: the feel of her dog's fur beneath her fingers, the weight of her body on this impossibly soft mattress. Sometimes she picks up her journal and writes things out.

She takes several deep breaths, then swings her legs out of bed, planting them firmly on the woven rug beneath her feet. She goes to her suitcase. She'd only unpacked a little last night. After a frozen lasagna dinner with Sue and Audrey—in uncomfortable silence punctuated by forced small talk from Sue—she'd gone to sleep straightaway. Now, she selects a turtleneck and heavy knit sweater to keep out the damp chill. She wonders if she'll have to do some shopping; she isn't sure the clothes that suited London winters will suffice this far north.

Her mobile vibrates in her purse. It's a text from Adam.

Got yr voicemail. Sorting things out with the solicitor - be in touch when the docs are ready for signature.

She isn't sure what, exactly, she expected. He's never been particularly sensitive in text messages, and there's really nothing left to say, anyway. They've said it all. Cried and shouted it all. But something about the brevity of it, the way he spoke so flippantly of drawing up their divorce papers, makes her wonder if he even gives a shit. If he feels as unmoored as she does, as fucked-up and broken. She turns off the mobile entirely, tosses it back into her purse, then reaches into her suitcase for her silver jewellery box, the size of a deck of cards. A gift from her grandmother on her sixteenth birthday.

She looks at her left hand, the diamond ring Adam gave her sitting atop her wedding band. Whatever power or magic or promises the rings once held have blown away like rotted leaves in the aftermath of everything that happened.

She's left London, left Adam. The Oakwood is her fresh start. It's time to let go.

Swallowing hard, Kate wiggles off the rings. The bands have left a divot in her finger, the lingering outline of a previous identity, like new skin cells knitting into a scar. She wonders if it will be visible forever. She glances at the small mirror on the dresser, turns her face to view her scars. One is thicker than the others but masked a bit by her jawline. The others snake out in different directions, one down her neck, the other farther up her cheek, but they aren't as noticeable from the front. The physical scarring could have been a lot worse. The emotional ones are as bad as they could be. But she hopes they all might fade a little in time.

Pulling her gaze away from the mirror, she sets the rings inside the jewellery box. Her eyes catch on the small silver locket her parents gave her on her twentieth birthday: oval, with an intricate letter *K* engraved in the centre.

"Your dad picked it out," her mum had said, as he watched silently from the end of the table. "He figured you're old enough for real jewellery now."

"Thanks, Dad." Kate smiled. He'd nodded in that gruff way men of his age tend to when confronted with emotion, and got up to refill his wine.

She used to wear it every day, but hasn't since the accident. She turns it in her fingers to access the clasp and look inside, then frowns at something dark crusted in the groove of the locket. Silver doesn't rust. And then it hits her. It isn't rust.

It's dried blood.

Ice floods her veins. She sets it back in the jewellery box and snaps the lid shut.

Half an hour later, Kate creeps down the stairs, Ozzie at her heels. They pass the Elder Room on the second floor. The door is open a crack, but it's dark inside, and Kate assumes Audrey must still be asleep.

She'd taken a shower to warm herself after the sight of her necklace, and she wishes she'd dried her hair instead of just braiding it damp over her shoulder. The house is drafty, and the continuing rain beats a soft rhythm against the roof and windows.

When they reach the foyer, Ozzie darts for the front door and Kate lets him out.

"Don't faff about, Oz, it's raining."

She watches as he trots in little circles, tail in the air, until he finds the perfect spot. The grounds are just as beautiful in the rain. The grass is dark green, and all she can hear is the soft patter of raindrops on the oaks lining the driveway. Ozzie gallops back inside and they head to the kitchen. Kate hauled his food in from the car the night before, but the bag is half-empty. She makes a mental note to look up the pet supply shop in town. Her move across the country had been impulsive, though necessary, but she hadn't exactly made a list of all the new roots she would need to establish elsewhere once she'd ripped up the existing ones. The thought of finding a new doctor, dentist, and groomer makes her tired and anxious, so she pushes it to the back of her mind for now and sets about making a pot of coffee.

Once it's on, she wanders back to the sitting room, and Ozzie curls up on the dog bed in the corner as though he's lived here his whole life.

"Make yourself at home, buddy," she mutters with a chuckle, then, noticing a doorway beyond the sitting room, walks over. Before her is the most intriguing room she's seen so far: part conservatory, part library. Tall bookshelves line the walls with various greenery perched on top. Tendrils of ivy and spider plants cascade down, partially obscuring the spines of the books on the highest shelves. A single large window framed with hunter-green curtains looks out over the extensive lawn on the side of the inn. There's a cushioned seat with a couple of pillows, a perfect little reading nook.

But in the centre of the room is a large, gleaming baby grand piano, its spindly legs resting on a worn, patterned rug. Kate runs her fingers over it, curious about its colour: a warm oak instead of the classic glossy black. She's never seen a grand piano like this. Her dad used to play. Pretty well, too, for an amateur. With a lurch, she wonders whether he might have sat down at this same stool and given it a go. She can hear him playing inside her head, see his head bowed at the old maple upright they had in her childhood home.

The thought makes her pick at her cuticles, so she turns from the piano to inspect the bookshelves. She always likes to explore other people's book collections; it says so much about a person, the books they choose to read, and—perhaps even more revealing—the books they choose to *keep*. The ones they continuously hold on to, even after spring cleanings, moving houses, downsizing, divorce, and decluttering. The books they curated from their life's collection.

Kate walks her fingers over the spines. There's a classic set of encyclopaedias titled with thin gold lettering, loads of aged books on history, botany, and music theory, their titles nearly worn away by the hands of time and readers. Anthologies of poetry, philosophy, and an array of novels both classic and modern. There are dozens of titles in German, too, which piques Kate's interest. She thinks about Audrey's elusive accent.

She's a big ol' box of secrets, that one, Sue had said.

Kate moves down the bookcase. There's a gap in one of the shelves at her elbow where a book is splayed, a pen resting in the fold. A guest book. Kate looks at the entries—exclusively positive reviews and well-wishes from happy visitors over the past several months. They've come from as far away as Singapore, Australia, and Brazil, or as close to home as Edinburgh, just down for a weekend mini-break. Her eyes slide to the books lined up beside this one; the spines each have dates. With a little skip in her heart, she inspects the long row.

And there it is: *1968*. The year of her parents' honeymoon.

Kate plucks it from the shelf and flips through. She locates the guest entries from April through June, and there they are:

> Audrey — thanks so much for everything. Can't express what it was like to be here. —Joseph & Rose Barber, Shropshire

Outside, the rain continues to splatter the library window, but Kate is rooted to the floor as she stares at her dad's note, referencing their visit in his own tall, tight handwriting. She didn't keep much of it, or her mum's either. Maybe a birthday card here or there. You never think to do those things, and then suddenly it's too late. But Audrey clearly made them feel welcome—which is a small surprise to Kate, given her own less-than-warm reception, and she wonders what fond memories they created here.

She caresses the cover of the book, then slides it back into place on the shelf. A creak breaks the silence and she startles, turns to find Audrey standing in the doorway.

"Sorry," Kate says. "I didn't think anyone else would be up yet."

She notices Audrey isn't employing her cane today. The thud of the stick on the floorboards might have announced her presence.

"I normally rise early. I've never been a particularly deep sleeper." Audrey taps her forehead. "Busy mind. And 'Anyone else' is only me, Miss Mercer. It's just the pair of us. And these two."

Ozzie and the black terrier she met yesterday scramble past Audrey and over to Kate.

"Hello again, little one," Kate says.

The terrier's stumpy tail wags back and forth, causing her entire body—including her whiskers—to shake. Kate scoops her up and is rewarded with a lick on the cheek, then she kneels, holding her out to Ozzie, who touches his nose to hers and the tail wagging begins again.

"This is Sophie." Audrey nods at her dog, now squirming out of Kate's arms.

"This is Ozzie."

"Yes." Audrey peers down at him. "We shall have to get the measure of you, hm?"

Kate finds this to be a rather haughty remark toward a dog, but she lets the comment slide in the spirit of unfamiliarity. A moment later she wonders whether it was meant for her.

"Well, come along then," Audrey says with a brusque clearing of her throat. "Time for breakfast."

She leads Kate back through the sitting room and down the hall to the kitchen. She's clearly moving better than she was yesterday, but still very slow, a little too careful.

She stops inside the doors. "I smell coffee."

"Yeah," Kate says. "I was up early, so I put it on."

"I'm glad you like it," Audrey says with a grave expression. "I've been running on the bloody stuff for decades."

Kate's mouth twitches. Between that and the baking show, perhaps they'll get along after all.

"I usually just have an egg and toast when we're vacant." Audrey moves toward the refrigerator. "Nothing fancy. And no fry-ups. I can't stand potatoes."

"That's fine," Kate says, though she wonders what sort of person hates potatoes. "What can I do?"

Audrey heaves a sigh. "If you must, go ahead and get the Marmite and whatever you like for your toast, and some mugs, and bring them through. The coffee, too, I suppose."

"I like Marmite on my egg and toast, too," Kate says, opening a cupboard at random in search of it.

"Some prefer jam or marmalade, but I think a salty punch wakens the morning nerves better than sugar." Audrey fishes the eggs out of the fridge. "Top cupboard beside the stove."

Kate retrieves it, along with some mugs and the coffeepot.

Audrey gestures to the swinging door. "Head into the dining room. I'll come through with the breakfast." She drops an egg onto the tile floor and curses.

Kate moves forward. "Do you need a—"

"I only need you to go sit down, Miss Mercer."

Kate purses her lips on a retort and pushes open the door to the dining room with her hip. She sits at the table where they ate dinner yesterday, stomach tightening on a small knot. She wishes Audrey wanted her here. It's uncomfortable, but she thinks of her dad's message in the guest book. She doesn't want to leave just yet.

She swallows that realization as she surveys her surroundings in the morning light. The dining room is brighter than the other rooms. One entire wall is floor-to-ceiling glass overlooking the dark woods at the back of the inn. Outside, a muted, pale light diffuses through the clouds. It looks like the rain has stopped now. Kate takes in other details she was too distracted to notice last night—the framed prints of various plants sketched in black and white on the walls, the long buffet table, and the smaller dining tables positioned around the room for when the Oakwood is full of guests—and an eerie feeling of isolation comes over her, as though she's the sole occupant of a restaurant after hours.

She's musing on the last time she and Adam went out to eat when Audrey appears in the kitchen doorway with a tray. Kate's instinct is to leap up and help, but she already knows better.

Audrey settles herself down. "Thank you," Kate says, then pours the coffee, slides a cup to her. It's a good sign that Audrey wants to eat with her.

As Audrey reaches for the cup, Kate gets a closer look at her hands. They're speckled with age, as one would expect of a nonagenarian, but the knuckles resemble the knots of a tree, and two of the fingers on her right hand are bent to the side, as though they were crushed at one point. Whatever it is, it's more than just age. Kate tries not to focus on them; she knows how it feels when other people stare at her scars.

Audrey picks up the jar of Marmite, struggles to open it. "Bloody lid."

Kate waits. After a momentary battle, Audrey glances at her, then nods curtly.

"It might need a younger hand."

With a forced wrench, Kate releases the yellow lid and hands the little jar back to her. She watches Audrey for a moment.

"Eat, Miss Mercer," Audrey says, fixing her with a pointed glare. "You're thin as a rail and paler than cheese."

Kate swallows, indignant, but pulls the plate toward her. She *is* hungry. "You can call me Kate," she says.

They sit for a couple of drawn-out minutes, eating their eggs, before Audrey speaks again. Her tone is businesslike.

"So, then. My housekeeper has gone and hired a woman I know nothing about to live in my house." One thinning white eyebrow arches. "Tell me a bit about yourself, so I have some vague idea who I'm cozying up with."

It's a fair question, but Audrey's inquiry isn't as straightforward as she thinks it is. How do you tell someone you just met that your life is in the middle of a massive renovation? That you wake up every morning and go to bed each night not entirely sure who you really are, what you want, or where you're going? Kate sips her coffee, buying time as she rakes together a few scattered details. Just enough to form a pile resembling a whole person.

"Well, I'm thirty-three. I was born in Shropshire, but I moved to London for uni, and I've lived there ever since."

"Do you have any siblings?"

"No."

"And you were married?" Audrey nods at Kate's hand. "The groove in your finger there."

Kate opens, then shuts her mouth. Audrey's well over ninety and wears glasses, for Christ's sake. How did she even notice?

"You know—" Kate begins, but Audrey dismisses her with a wave.

"You don't need to justify it to me," she says. "I'm sure I'll learn the whole sorry tale in due course."

Kate leans back, offended. "How do you know it's a sorry tale?"

Audrey lifts her coffee. "Have you ever heard a cheery story of divorce and heartbreak? It's always a sorry tale. I was going to ask you what a young woman like you is doing abandoning the hustle and bustle of London to come up here to work at a sleepy old guesthouse, but I think the divorce is responsible for the career change, too, isn't it?"

The weight of Audrey's assumptions quashes Kate's appetite. She came here to escape the past, but Audrey is intent on bringing it up. Is this her way of driving Kate away? She doesn't need to put up with this, despite her longing to learn more about her parents.

"Listen, you clearly don't want me here, so I'll just go."

She stacks her fork and knife onto her plate with a clatter, pushes her chair back, and leaves the dining room without another word. In the sitting room, Ozzie is cozied up with the tiny Sophie, his body curled around hers like a chocolate doughnut. He opens one bleary eye at Kate's approach.

"Well, at least one of them is friendly, yeah?"

There's a smattering at the large bay window and she glances up to see that the rain has started up again. She breathes a curse. She doesn't drive in the rain—not anymore. She'll have to wait it out. In the meantime, she stomps up the stairs to repack.

What a disaster, she thinks, heaving her suitcase onto the bed. *Just like everything I do, apparently.*

Except, to be fair, she isn't the problem this time. It's Audrey, who can't even manage a civilized conversation over breakfast. Tears prick at Kate's eyes, and she growls at them.

"Why are you crying?" she whispers aloud as she wrenches open the dresser drawers. "She's just a bitter old crank. It's nothing to do with you."

She pauses for a moment with a stack of trousers in her hands and takes a deep breath at the sight of the sofa across from her, recalling the image of her mum sitting there. Audrey must have been very different then, for her parents to have had such a pleasant experience here. Something must have happened in the interim to make her so aggressive and hurtful. But that's not Kate's problem. She would have liked to stay longer, linger a little with her parents' memories, maybe learn something of them from Audrey, a snapshot of their lives before she was born. But that's clearly not possible.

She shakes her head. She'd started to want this. She'd felt something akin to hope, an unfamiliar sensation warming her cold, pessimistic mind. But she'll have to write this off as a failure, tell Adam she needs to move back into their place. She wipes at the tears, stuffs the trousers into the suitcase. She'll need to ring the shipping company straightaway and tell them not to collect those remaining boxes.

She's in the bathroom retrieving her toiletry bag when there's a smart rap on her door.

"Yes?" she calls, a curt clip.

Audrey pushes the door open. "May I come in?"

"I'm busy. I'm packing."

"I shouldn't have said what I did about your life being a sorry tale," Audrey says in her gravelly voice. "I saw your ring finger and . . ." She seems incapable of completing the half apology. Kate comes to the bathroom door. Audrey's jaw is set, with determination or embarrassment or both, Kate can't tell. "The truth is, as much as it *severely* irks me to admit it, Sue is correct. I do need some assistance. If the time has come where I can't open my own Marmite jars, it would be foolish to pretend otherwise."

"Yeah. *Your* fingers have a sorry tale, too, don't they?" Kate snaps.

Audrey lifts her chin and the air between them thickens like curdled milk.

"I'm sorry," Kate mutters. "I didn't—"

"If you are fortunate enough to live to my age, Miss Mercer, you will understand how loss of independence can weigh on a person. The only thing worse than aging is the alternative." Audrey takes a few steps into the room. "You must forgive me for my pointed questions. But I am uncomfortable with secretive roommates." Her eyes flicker over to Kate's suitcase. "You know, I ended up here when I had nowhere else to go. No place to call home."

Kate's throat tightens a little.

"May I ask why you chose the Oakwood?" Audrey asks.

Kate chews the inside of her cheek. "My parents stayed here once. Years ago now."

"You came here because your parents stayed here once?"

"I told you my mum was dead, but my dad is too. They died in February. And I'm trying to . . . retrace their steps. To feel like I'm there with them." She explains how she stumbled across the job advert after googling the Oakwood.

"And your marriage has ended, so you needed somewhere to run. And you ran here?"

Kate doesn't fancy her trauma being summed up so indifferently, like a statement on the weather or the score of a football game. But she nods, because it's still the truth.

Audrey's cold grey eyes melt a degree. "This place was, and continues to be, one of solace and purpose for me. Perhaps it could be for you too. You're fiery, like I was."

Kate has never in her life been described as *fiery*, and she warms a little to the praise.

Audrey straightens and fixes Kate with another pointed look. "Well, then. Now that we've each lain down our swords, let's go have another cup of coffee and try again, shall we?"

Chapter 7

Audrey

BERLIN, GERMANY | NOVEMBER 1938

His gold pen is gone," Ilse said. "The engraved one Mama gave him for their twentieth anniversary."

Audrey looked up from her seat on the couch in the lounge off Ira's study. Through the open glass double doors between the two rooms, she could see Ilse standing behind her father's desk, the surface of which was strewn with papers stuck together from an overturned inkwell. She was wearing her heaviest dress and a thick wool cardigan. They'd both chosen grey and black clothing today without speaking of it, Audrey realized.

"I'm sorry," she said.

Ilse rubbed her red eyes. "There may have been some money, too, I don't know. This drawer was forced open. It must have been locked for a reason."

They'd spent the morning cleaning up after the looting. It had given them a task to focus on to stem the tide of grief that threatened to overwhelm them. The bedrooms had been ransacked quickly, drawers pulled out in search of valuables. But the thieves must have known there couldn't be much left after the pile of jewellery they'd swiped from Ilse's dresser. The sitting room and dining room had been the worst destroyed. When the women finished sweeping up the shards of china in the dining room, Ilse had moved on to the final room—Ira's study—whilst Audrey sat down to write to her father.

She explained all that had happened yesterday, with Ira's murder, then Ruth and Ephraim's abduction, and the riots.

I have never in my life encountered such violence, Father. Surely it must make the London papers—you may read of it before this even reaches you, and I am sorry for that. I hope you will not be left worrying for long. I see now that you were right, I should have come home. But who was to know this madness would escalate so quickly?

We are safe in the house, though. For now. But we need your help. I have no access to the trust you set up with Herr Kaplan. Ilse's passport is invalid, and I have no knowledge of foreign relations or immigration, where to even begin the process of trying to get her out of Germany. But I need you to understand—since I know you will suggest it straightaway—that I have absolutely no intention of leaving here without her.

Please write back as soon as you receive this.

With affection,
Audrey

Audrey finished the letter and stared at her own handwriting, as though hoping an answer would appear between the lines. She had never craved her father's support and intervention more than she did now. She blinked hard, trying to rouse her tired eyes. They had managed to get a little sleep, but their dreams were of gunshots, and Audrey had woken sometime in the night to rioting in the distance, someone's life being dismantled.

The sound of shuffling papers and soft thuds continued, punctuated with sniffles as Ilse carried on tidying the study. A shiver ran through Audrey. She glanced across the hall at the broken front window. They had hung a thick blanket over it, but it did little to help as the autumn wind blew in from the west.

“It’s freezing,” she said. “I’m going to go feed the furnace.”

“Good idea.” Ilse brushed her hands together. “And I suppose I’ll need to telephone Matya next.”

In the damp cellar, Audrey opened the furnace door, welcoming the blast of hot air on her face. As she shoveled coal, she thought how she’d never done a task like this in her life; this work had always been within the purview of servants. Change could be so sudden sometimes, so drastic. As she climbed the narrow stairs back to the main floor, she wondered how much more change was yet to come.

Ilse was still in Ira’s study, which always smelled of furniture polish and ink. Her face was buried in her hands, and Audrey went to her.

“We should be preparing for his funeral today,” Ilse said, anger echoing off the walls of her hollow voice. “It’s not enough that we lose him, but we also don’t get to bury him properly? To grieve him the way we’re meant to?”

“I know,” Audrey said, embracing her.

When Michael had died, the family sat shiva. Audrey had come over with her father and Sophie to pay their respects, passing the pitcher of water on the doorstep and the shrouded hallway mirror. The ritual made perfect sense to her. The aftermath of a death was a time to sink into oneself, to hold tight to the memories of the person who was lost. To nurture the wound that it was without distraction. Yet here was Ilse, sorting through her dead father’s ransacked office with hardly a moment to spare for her grief. It was cruel.

Audrey pressed her eyes shut, fighting her own tears. As they cried, Audrey squeezed Ilse tightly, hoping her arms might be enough to hold her friend together.

“Where did they take his body, Audrey? It isn’t right.”

"I don't know," she replied, trying not to think about where it might be. "I don't know."

After a few minutes, the wave of grief passed. There would be others, Audrey knew, and she would be here to help Ilse through them, she thought, handing her friend the handkerchief from her pocket.

Ilse composed herself, then returned her attention to the desk she'd mostly managed to reorganize. "Before you came in, I found something I wanted to talk to you about. Look." She lifted a sheaf of paper. "It's Papa's bank statement."

Audrey scanned it, swallowed her surprise at the numbers. Though the family lived well, Ira's textile business was even more lucrative than Audrey had ever presumed. No wonder he had dug in so ferociously to hold on to his company.

"Oh, my. Ilse, this is . . ."

"I know. It's more than I suspected. I didn't even know what bank he used. He never talked about work with me, really. But this money can't possibly sit in the bank now that he's—" She stopped, unable to say the word. "We need to access it."

Audrey reviewed the document again. The name and address of a credit cooperative in Berlin's financial district was listed at the top. "They won't give it to you, surely?" she asked.

"No, not to his daughter. And I can't leave the house." Ilse locked eyes with Audrey. "But they might hand it over to his accounting secretary with a handwritten letter from him authorizing the withdrawal."

Audrey's brow furrowed. "Do you know his accounting secretary? I thought—"

"It's *you*, Audrey."

Audrey took a step back. "Ilse . . ."

But Ilse was adamant. "Go get changed into your smartest skirt and jacket. I'll forge the letter using Papa's handwriting. It doesn't have to be perfect. Just the signature. I can do it."

Audrey's brain whirred, trying to grasp some other possibility.

"You can do it," Ilse said. "I know you can."

There was a firmness in her tone that Audrey rarely heard. She was determined to claim something from the ashes of all she had already lost.

"Okay," Audrey said. "I'll do it."

The cool morning breeze was bracing on Audrey's nerves as she made her way from the post office, where she mailed the letter to her father, on to the bus that would take her to Potsdamerplatz in the financial district. The bank statement was tucked in her pocketbook, which she clutched in her gloved hand. The ruse was simple: she would walk into the bank, confident and nonchalant, introduce herself as Ira Kaplan's accounting secretary, and tell them he had sent her to access the funds. It all felt a bit outrageous, but these were unprecedented, dire circumstances, so she prepared herself for the required performance, hoping she would be convincing.

As the bus wound through the streets of Berlin, Audrey looked out the window, swaying gently with the motion, appalled by what she saw: Another synagogue had been utterly ruined by vandals. The stone edges of the windows and doors were blackened with soot from fire damage and the inside was dark, giving the building the ominous appearance of an empty skull. Most of the shingles were burned, rafters exposed and sagging. Along the route, there were more burned-out buildings and broken windows, glass shimmering on the pavement beneath, families huddled together outside. One shop had been painted with something, but the bus turned a corner before Audrey could make out the details.

What in the name of God had happened? Two days before, she'd been wallowing in her melancholy about having to return to London, but the truth was that her reluctance had nothing to do with leaving Berlin itself anymore, and far more to do with abandoning Ilse to whatever fate this new Germany had in store for her. It was clear now that the Nazi flags weren't coming down. Audrey didn't recognize her own city. Reason was not prevailing, as Ira had hoped it would. She *must* find a way to get them both back to London. But whatever method she found for escape, they would need money.

Her sense of foreboding increasing by the minute, Audrey disembarked and walked the final block. But as the credit cooperative came into view, she stopped in her tracks. A man ploughed into her elbow from behind, muttering his irritation. She hardly even noticed him glance back as she stared at the scene before her.

The bank was ravaged.

Like the Kaplans' home, its front windows were all smashed. A CLOSED sign still hung, absurdly, in the open wall where the window should have been. A six-pointed black Star of David had been crudely painted on the door, and the word *JUD* stood out in large block letters on the wall above it. Crumpled pieces of paper lined the pavement outside the bank, like snow. The words *im Urlaub in Buchenwald* were scrawled on the wall.

On holiday in Buchenwald.

She knew that name. Buchenwald. It was some sort of work camp for arrested Jews. She had overheard Ira and Ruth talking about it, seen the newspaper headline when she went to toss coffee grounds into the bin.

Dread trickled through her veins. In the dizzying aftermath of Ira's murder, she hadn't really considered *where* Ruth and Ephraim might have been taken. That wherever it was, it was a *place*. Something real and horrible. That it might be somewhere like Buchenwald. Everything that had happened yesterday wasn't random. The night of terror was clearly the beginning of something systematic. The violence had crested in a great, orchestrated wave, and Audrey was afraid of how many more people would be taken down in the undertow.

She headed back to the Kaplans' in a distracted haze, eyes on her feet. The bank was inaccessible, and so, too, she presumed, was the money. With the country in this state, she wasn't sure how long it would take her letter to reach her father, or for him to take any kind of action—she had no idea what—to secure Ilse's safe passage to England. All she could do was put one foot in front of the other.

But sometimes, a person could become so fixated on avoiding the obstacles right in front of her that she didn't see the ones creeping in from the sides.

On the Kaplans' doorstep, Audrey unsnapped her pocketbook for her key, but it fell from her hands, which she realized were shaking. Her hands never shook. It was a point of pride for a skilled pianist, to have fingers so controlled that they gave the illusion of movement independent from the player. She stooped to retrieve the key, not noticing the two men approaching from behind.

"Excuse me, Fräulein."

Audrey spun around and felt her stomach drop somewhere into the region of her knees. Two uniformed officers stood at the bottom of the steps. She vaguely registered a black car parked a few feet away from them. The men were about the same height, and dressed almost identically, with black trousers, boots, and long grey overcoats with the eagle and swastika emblazoned on the arm. They peered up at her from beneath the rims of their matching caps. Confusion and fear raced one another around her mind. Why were they here? Had they come for Ilse?

"Yes?" Audrey said. It was a moment too long before she forced a smile. "*Guten Tag, meine herren.*"

She'd gotten used to officers winking at her, making comments on her appearance when she was out in the streets. She usually offered a tight smile to satisfy the underlying demand for acknowledgement, and carried on her way.

"*Guten Tag*," one of them said. The other just watched her. "Is this your house, Fräulein?" the first one asked, and Audrey's stomach gave a jolt as he began to scale the steps toward her.

The other man spoke now. "You have a key," he said, gesturing to her hand.

"Yes," she said, unable to deny it, then answered with the first story that came to mind. "I'm the accounting secretary for the man who lives here. For his business. But he has not been at the office, so I thought I would try his home."

The first officer reached into his overcoat and withdrew a piece of paper. He ran a finger down the page, glanced at her. "You are employed by Ira Kaplan?" he asked, frowning.

He took in her appearance, from her curled hair to her buckled black boots and up again, lingering on her face, her red lips. She was a performer, used to people staring at her, but this man's gaze raked her in a way that made her skin feel as though it had been exposed to the elements. He had rather striking green eyes that were darkened by his narrowed brow. His boxy face stood in direct opposition to his long nose, and his moustache was mostly red whilst his hair shone blond. He looked as though he had borrowed his features from several different men.

"Yes," she said, keeping her expression impassive.

"What is your name, Fräulein?"

Audrey hesitated. Her identification papers showed her name as Audrey Gertrud James. Audrey after her father's mother, Gertrud after her mother's grandmother. Despite growing up in Berlin with an English name, she had never felt uncomfortable with it. But she thought it might raise a flag for these officers, whose tones were already thick with suspicion.

"Audrey James," she said.

The blond man watched her intently as the other one joined them on the steps. "I am Obersturmbannführer Müller," the second officer said. "This is Brigadeführer Vogt. I think perhaps you should come inside with us, Fräulein James."

Audrey felt the blood drain from her face, but she nodded, hoping her rouge and lipstick would suffice to mask her ashen complexion. As she turned the key in the lock, she sent up a silent prayer that Ilse was not downstairs waiting for her. She fiddled with the key as long as she dared, rattling it.

"It sticks sometimes, I do apologize," she said loudly. With a surge of fear she pushed the door open, then glanced around as the two officers swept in behind her. She startled when the one called Vogt pounded on the door with a fist, forcing it shut. It hadn't closed properly since the looters broke the lock.

"What happened to it?" he asked her.

Audrey shrugged. "I'm not sure," she said, allowing her voice to carry.

They stepped past her and into the spacious foyer, taking in the large, open rooms, gleaming hardwood floors, crystal chandeliers, and richly papered walls. She hung back now, unsure how to proceed or what, exactly, was happening. She strained her ears but could hear no sign of Ilse. Hopefully she had fled to the attic or had been there already. Audrey couldn't contemplate the alternative.

She flashed a smile at the officers as she moved toward the stairs to confirm Ilse's whereabouts. "I'm just going to go—"

"Sit there, Fräulein." Herr Müller indicated the divan in the sitting room.

Audrey perched on the edge of the sofa, pocketbook in her lap, trying not to appear too much at home, as Müller and Vogt left the room, each in a different direction. What were they looking for? When Müller went upstairs, she held her breath, tucking one foot behind the other to stop her legs from jiggling. As Müller's footsteps creaked on the floorboards above, Vogt returned from the dining room. The hairs on the back of her neck prickled as he stood in the doorway, watching her. There was something off about this man; she hated looking at him, but she forced an expression of innocence.

A moment later, Müller came back downstairs, and Audrey's

breathing returned almost to normal. He had evidently not discovered Ilse.

He took a seat across from her. He was younger than Vogt by several years and a different sort of person altogether—plain-looking with a brown moustache that at least matched his short-clipped hair, and brown eyes that studied her with a penetrating, though not malicious, stare.

"What do you know of Ira Kaplan?" he asked her.

Audrey sat up a little straighter. "He's my employer. I—"

"Not anymore," Vogt piped up. He was still standing off to the side.

Audrey feigned confusion as her heart stung. "Why not?"

"Because he is dead, Fräulein James."

She raised her eyebrows in surprise. "Oh dear. How did he die?"

"He took it upon himself to talk back to the SS," Vogt said with a harsh bite.

Grief and anxiety coursed through Audrey's body, but she needed answers that these men might be able to provide. "And what of his family? Have they been taken to Buchenwald with the others?"

Vogt once again withdrew the paper from inside his jacket and consulted it. "Kaplan wife and son detained. Not sure where."

"You are well-informed for a secretary, Fräulein," Müller said.

"I have seen the city, Herr Müller," Audrey said. "And the papers. I take it yesterday's events are part of a strategy to eradicate the Jews from Berlin? Is that not the Party's intent?"

Müller's dark eyes sharpened on her. "From Germany, at the very least."

"One daughter unaccounted for," Vogt continued. "Per the register. Ilse Kaplan. Do you know of her whereabouts?"

Audrey seized the opportunity. "No, she is dead," she said dispassionately. "Of a fever, I believe. Last winter."

Vogt checked his papers again. "Are you certain?"

"Yes. Quite."

"Well, less work for us then," Vogt said. "If only more of them died of fevers."

"May I see your papers, please, Fräulein James?" Müller asked.

Audrey had to unstick her throat after Vogt's comment. "Of course."

She fished them out of her pocketbook. Müller examined them, then passed them back.

"English father and German mother," he said.

"Yes."

"And how did you come to be employed in the office of a Jewish textile maker?"

"My parents are both dead," she lied. "I needed a job. I'm good with figures, and it was available."

They waited.

"I'm no friend of Jews," she said, feeling her tongue twist around the words. "I'm not proud of it. I had few options for income."

Out of the corner of her eye, she saw Vogt's gaze linger on her again. "Indeed," he muttered.

"May I ask why exactly you are here today?" Audrey said, desperate to move these strange proceedings along and get the officers out of the house.

"We are here to inspect the home," Müller said as Vogt wandered over to the sideboard and helped himself to a drink. "The place has been looted," Müller continued, scanning the walls. "No silverware, jewellery. Many items are missing from the property register the previous inhabitants submitted in May. And odd things too. Bedclothes," he added, brow pinched in confusion. "I have recently moved to Berlin from the south. Vogt from Hamburg. We require new accommodations, and I believe this will serve nicely."

Audrey's mind was fixed on his comment about the missing bedclothes. It took her a moment to catch up. "I'm sorry?" she asked. "You are . . . you're moving into this house?"

He glanced over at Vogt, who nodded his assent.

"Yes," Müller said. "As some of the finer houses have been vacated by migrating or deported Jews, the Party has reclaimed them as housing for senior officers. It is part of the Führer's broader plan for the Aryanization of Jewish property and industry."

Audrey clenched her jaw. Ruth had feared Ira's business would be taken over, but their *home*?

"We have inspected a few vacant properties, and this is the grandest thus far. Plenty of space. It will do. We will require your key, Fräulein, and that will be all."

If these officers were confiscating the Kaplans' home, she and Ilse would be forced to leave—God only knew how soon, perhaps that very night—and go . . . *where*?

"What about my job?" she asked, buying time as her mind flailed, trying to avert this new catastrophe.

"What of it?" Müller said.

"If my employer is dead, what am I to do?"

He shrugged. "I cannot see how that is of any concern to us."

Vogt finished his drink and set the dirty glass down on the table. Audrey's mind flashed with an idea.

"Surely you will need a housekeeper," she said with a demure smile. "And I need a job. With my parents dead, I *must* work. A pair of busy officers like yourselves certainly don't have time to manage your own meals and laundry. Do the washing up," she added, gesturing to Vogt's glass. "I assume you must have planned on hiring help."

Müller frowned. "I don't think—"

"Hold on a moment, Müller," Vogt said. "Do you know the house well enough, Fräulein?"

Audrey steadied her balance on the fine line she must tread. "I have been here a few times. To collect papers from Herr Kaplan, if he was working from his home. But I'm a fast learner."

"We *will* need a housekeeper, Müller," Vogt said. "She is unemployed and already has some familiarity with the place. A good fit, I think."

She forced herself not to flinch under his unsettling gaze. It was like staring into a tiger's maw.

Müller glared at Vogt. "I do not think that will be necessary."

"I do," he argued.

"I would agree," Audrey added, mustering her courage. With these men in the house, for better or worse, all the household expenses would fall to them. The window would be fixed, coal and groceries would be purchased. In the short term, her and Ilse's immediate needs would be met. The arrangement would enable their survival until Audrey could find a way to get Ilse to England. She felt a strange surge of emotion; relief and panic and disgust all braided together into a noose that scratched at her throat.

"It makes perfect sense to me," Vogt said.

"Then I accept."

"Excuse me—" Müller began, but Vogt cut him off.

"Excellent."

Audrey beamed, her lips dry. "It would be an honour to serve you both, and by extension, the Reich. Perhaps it could be a live-in position? This is a far nicer home than the place I'm currently in, you see." She paused. "There's such competition with Jews and immigrants to let a decent flat. And it would be more convenient to not have to travel to work."

"I think that would be our preference," Vogt said.

"Vogt," Müller said sharply. "A word."

The two men disappeared across the hall, Vogt trailing in Müller's wake as they headed toward the lounge. Audrey took a long, shaky breath. Already her mind was turning to the details, the logistics. She would suggest Ilse's room for herself. Fortunately, Ilse's and the guest bedroom Audrey occupied were the smallest, and surely Vogt and Müller would take the largest rooms for themselves. And then it hit her: Ilse would have to *live* in the attic, hiding, for some indeterminate period of time. She would be a prisoner in her own home, yet, unless something went horribly wrong, her jailers wouldn't even know she existed. Audrey's stomach knotted with guilt, but she couldn't see another way out of this. There was no way she could overpower their decision to confiscate the home, and arguing with them on it would only draw suspicion—or worse.

The men returned a moment later, and Audrey stood up. Müller's face was blotchy whilst Vogt strolled into the room smiling.

"Very well, Fräulein," he said. "We will employ you. You will receive ten reichsmarks a week in addition to room and board."

Audrey nodded. If room and board were covered, they could at least use that income for their eventual escape plans.

"Excellent," Vogt said.

Müller stood with his hands on his hips, overcoat open to reveal the gleaming insignia on his jacket. Judging by the numerous decorations, he was high-ranking. "We will need you to conduct an inventory of the house, first thing," he directed at her. "To determine the entire property's value and compare that against what was catalogued when the Jews registered it. Anything of significant value had to be reported. All Jewish-owned businesses have also been seized, effective today," he added.

Audrey refrained from any reaction.

Vogt handed her the papers he'd been consulting earlier. "Work into the evening, if you must, and have it ready by morning. We will collect our things from our hotels and move in tomorrow."

Tomorrow.

"Yes, sir."

"Be here early in the morning for our arrival," Müller said.

The men made their way to the front door.

"Thank you for the opportunity," Audrey said. "I shall see you both tomorrow."

"Indeed, Fräulein," Vogt said. "Heil Hitler."

"Heil Hitler," Audrey parroted.

When they had driven away, she wrestled the door shut, then leaned back against it and let her breath out, closing her eyes. Her pulse was still racing, and she only now noticed the prickling sensation on her back, perspiration from the stress. She took a moment to collect herself as best she could, dreading what she knew she must do next.

Upstairs, she opened the door into Ilse's room.

Staring up at the attic access, an overwhelming sense of shame at the blow she was about to deliver to Ilse settled on her like a cloak. She wanted to suspend this moment, to go on with their evening, watch Ilse read a book as she played the piano, hide out just a little longer from reality. But they couldn't. What was happening beyond these walls had found its way in, and it was infusing everything, like poisonous gas.

"Come on down, Ilse," she called. "Or let me up. It's safe."

No, it isn't.

The door opened and Ilse's head appeared in the void, eyes wide and bright.

"Audrey! *Baruch hashem*," she hissed. She lowered the ladder and scrambled down. "What happened? Who were those men?"

Her shoulders slumped inward, and she was clutching her hands together in front of a wrinkled skirt. It made Audrey want to weep.

"Their names are Müller and Vogt," she replied. "SS officers. High-ranking, I think."

Ilse gasped. "What did they want? Was it about Mama? Ephraim?"

"No." There was no point in holding back. "Ilse, they've confiscated the house."

Ilse's hands stilled. "What?"

As Audrey explained that the credit cooperative was gone—along with their money—and that the officers had confirmed the attacks and riots were part of a process to transform Germany into an entirely Aryan state, that there was no place for Jews here anymore, Ilse sank onto the bed, hugging her knees to her chest. Audrey hated herself for having to relay everything to her, and she hated the Nazis for stripping Ilse of the only remaining freedoms she had.

"But how—" Ilse choked on a sob. "What are we going to do? Where will I go?"

"You will stay here. I'll keep you safe until we can flee. We'll wait for my father's response to my letter."

"And I'll be trapped in the attic. It's going to be winter soon. I'll freeze up there."

The thought had already occurred to Audrey. "I hope we'll be long gone before winter sets in."

Ilse stared into the middle distance. "How did we get here?" she asked, and her eyes were glazed over, staring back in time at things she couldn't change. "How did this happen? Why was it *allowed* to? How do they wield such power?"

"I don't know," Audrey said, with an ache deep in her heart. "I don't know what we've become. It all happened so fast."

"Except it didn't, did it? And now . . . I'm going to die. Aren't I? We all are."

"I won't let that happen," Audrey said, reaching for Ilse's hand. It was cold. "I'm not going anywhere without you." There was no way she would, even if her father arrived on the doorstep and threw a net around her.

Ilse's eyes shone. "Except I think you have to. How can it possibly be safe for you to work so close to those men? They'll find us out, you know they will. They'll learn you're not what you say you are. Somehow, they know everything about everyone. They're too powerful, Audrey. You have to go back to London."

"I won't. Not until we find a way to bring you with me."

"I don't think I can."

"We'll see what my father says, we'll find a way—"

"That's not what I mean," Ilse said, fixing Audrey with a look. It was the face she made whenever she was about to say something Audrey would disagree with. "I've thought about almost nothing else, and I can't leave without knowing what's happened to Mama and Ephraim. I have to believe they're still alive—until I know for sure that they aren't. We don't know how long they'll be detained, or where."

On holiday in Buchenwald. The words flashed in Audrey's mind.

"We don't know what's going to happen next," Ilse was saying. "But I can't leave without them. What if they come back, and find me gone?"

"Ilse—"

"This is our home. I have to stay here until they come back." She took a deep breath. "But you don't."

"Yes, I do. Ilse. How can you *possibly* survive in the attic without me here and with them living downstairs? How will you eat, drink, go to the toilet?" Her mind was already maneuvering around the minefield of problems in the distance, black as trees in a dark and unfamiliar forest.

"Audrey, be sensible—"

"No, *you* be sensible," Audrey said. "I can't leave you. I love you more than anything." As she spoke the words, she found that she meant them more than ever. A strange sort of feeling trickled through her; at once heat and nervous chill, profound understanding and disorientation. She wanted to embrace Ilse, as they had so many hundreds of times before, but it felt different now. There was something electric in it, something that drew her in and terrified her in equal measure. She fought to shake the sensation. "I'll keep you safe. I promise."

Ilse's eyes stayed on Audrey's. "That's what my father said too."

Chapter 8

Kate

ALNWICK, ENGLAND | NOVEMBER 2010

Kate wakes suddenly, a long, shrill wail still hanging in the air in front of her.

"Kate," a soft voice says. "It's all right. You're safe."

She scrambles upright, panting. It's dark. The only light comes from the moon streaming between a crack in the curtains. In the haze of confusion, she squints at the figure at the foot of her bed.

"Audrey? What—?"

Audrey comes closer, tentatively sits on the edge of the bed. "It's all right. You were having a nightmare."

Kate hesitates, then collapses onto her shoulder with a sob. Audrey stiffens a little, but holds her with one arm, a little awkwardly, as Kate cries out the leftover fear and shock. She hates the sensations that flood her body after her nightmares—first the fear, then the grief, then the twitch of nerves as the adrenaline dissipates. She hates what it means, what it dredges up for her again.

Every damn time.

Ozzie approaches the side of the bed, ears back, and Audrey gently extricates herself from Kate.

"I tried to reassure him," she says, "but dogs are such empathetic creatures, aren't they? We really don't deserve them."

"Oh, Oz. I'm sorry. Come here, buddy."

He leaps up onto the bed, gently nuzzles Kate's arm. She strokes his fur. Outside, it's still raining; she can hear it drumming against the roof above them.

"Here, watch your eyes." Audrey tugs the chain on the bedside lamp. "Things are always far more frightening in the dark."

"This is so embarrassing. Did I wake you?" Kate asks. Her eyes feel puffy.

"Yes," Audrey says. "You were quite loud, but I go to bed so late these days, anyway."

Kate presses a hand against her clammy forehead. "I'm sorry, again. Please, go back to bed. I'm fine."

Audrey studies her. "You don't look fine."

The scene is still flickering behind Kate's eyes. She's having difficulty shaking it.

"I was . . . I was in a really terrible car crash," she says, her lower lip trembling. "And it's stuck with me. Obviously." She waves a hand at her disheveled face, the scars.

Audrey nods with a knowing expression. "I used to have nightmares too. For a long time. After the war. My poor aunt Minna didn't know what to do for the best. I terrified the guests out of their wits during one particularly dreadful episode, back in my thirties sometime. At any rate," she continues, "*I* wasn't fine. I was reliving some horrible moments. I'd wake up sure it was still happening, and then be devastated that it had already occurred in the past. That I couldn't change it. I'd scream and thrash like you were. It was dreadful."

Kate searches Audrey's eyes, looking for validation that she isn't mad, or pathetic. "What were you remembering? During yours? Did you . . . did you lose people? In the war?" She wonders now whether Audrey had ever been married or had children.

Audrey hesitates, but Kate sees the memories, whatever they are, pass across her face, a flitting shadow. "It's not something I talk about," she replies. Her white brows knit together. "It was a bad crash, you said?"

Kate presses her tongue against the inside of her teeth. "Yeah. Both my parents were killed."

There's genuine concern in the stubborn look that usually pinches the old woman's thin lips into a tight pucker. "I'm very sorry. And what did that do to you?"

Kate sits, speechless. Any time anyone asked her about the crash, one of her old friends, the doctors, the police . . . everyone always asked "what happened?" They always wanted to know the *how.* The factual step-by-step of tragedy.

This happened, then that, and then I was an orphan.

No one ever asked what being the sole survivor had done to her. Not even Adam. Kate had often wondered whether people just couldn't bear to hear the reality of it, to imagine themselves adrift in that kind of fucked-up, impossible grief. So they didn't ask.

Now Kate struggles to pin down the answer to Audrey's question. The words wriggle out of her grasp and a sense of inadequacy settles over her shoulders, the same weight as shame.

"I'm not sure I know the full extent of it yet."

She realizes, as she speaks, that this is the most honest thing she's admitted in a long time. To Audrey James, of all people.

Audrey is quiet for a moment. "I know a thing or two about being the survivor, Kate. Some days I doubt whether it really does beat the alternative. But if it's the hand we're dealt by chance, then it's what we must accept."

Kate's throat tightens. "Haunts a person though, doesn't it?"

Audrey doesn't answer. She has her secrets.

"What do you do with the grief, then?" Kate asks. "Where do you put it, if you don't talk about it?"

"I don't entirely understand the question."

Kate shrugs. "How do you process it?"

Audrey sighs irritably. "No offence intended, my dear, but your generation seems particularly fixated on individual emotion. On *processing* everything, like you're an assembly line for feelings. A person could spend their life obsessing over the past. Seems rather exhausting and dramatic to me. In my day, we just got on with it. Kept on keeping on, as they say."

"But you still had nightmares," Kate presses. "Do you think you were really *getting on with it*?" She points to the black notebook on her bedside table. "I write in my journal. It helps to get it out. Have you ever tried that?"

Audrey pushes herself up from the bed with a grunt. "I really don't see the point of that. The past is the past. There's no changing it. And it's a fool's errand to pretend we can. Now get some sleep."

She stumbles a little on the rug but steadies herself, makes her way toward the door.

"Can you leave it open?" Kate asks, feeling childish the moment she says it.

Audrey glances over her shoulder, nods. "Of course. I don't much like closed doors either."

When Kate rises later that morning, the rain has stopped and the landscape outside her window is green and fresh. Maybe she'll go for a run, figure out a route around the inn and the town, but first she needs a hot shower to wake her up. She didn't sleep much after her conversation with Audrey, her curiosity piqued by the woman's vague answers. What were her nightmares about? What has she survived? Rubbing her tired eyes, Kate staggers to the bathroom.

Once she's clean and dressed, she calls for Ozzie, who is still dozing at the end of the bed. But as they round the corner toward the stairs, she stops in her tracks.

"Oh shit."

Water drips in a steady rhythm from the ceiling, and the runner beneath it is drenched. Kate darts back into her room for the bin under the sink, then places it beneath the leak and hurries downstairs, Ozzie at her heels, keen for his breakfast.

She finds Audrey in the dining room, poring over that morning's newspaper with a steaming coffee and a large seven-day pill case. She pours a small pile of multicoloured tablets into her hand before knocking them back with a wince.

"We've got a problem," Kate tells her, taking in the pill case. Her grandmother used to use one of those. She'd been on about eight different medications in her last years. "The ceiling is leaking in the corridor upstairs."

Audrey sets the paper down on the table with a crackle of newsprint and an aggrieved sigh. "Where?"

"Right outside the Oak Room. I used a bin to catch it for now, but the rug is soaked. Shall I call a handyman for you?"

"No, no, I'll deal with it. You have your breakfast." Audrey heaves herself up from the table. She's using her cane today.

"Are you sure?"

Kate feels torn—shouldn't this be something she should handle? Isn't that why she's here? She watches Audrey's gnarled hand grip her cane and thinks back to what she said about having lost so many people. Maybe *keeping on* really is the only way she knows to cope.

"Yes, eat," Audrey says. "One should never starve when there's perfectly good food to be had. Save your restraint for times of scarcity, I say. I'll ring Ian."

"Who's Ian?" Kate asks, but Audrey is already walking away.

An hour later, Kate is back up on the third floor. Audrey had forgotten a doctor's appointment scheduled for nine o'clock. She called Sue for a ride into town, and left Kate to sort out the leak with Ian the handyman.

"When did it start?" he asks her from his perch on the stepladder.

He isn't what Kate expected. He's probably a couple of years older than her, with slightly untidy brown hair and black-framed glasses. He arrived in khakis and a cable cardigan, altogether looking far more like an analyst or librarian than a labourer.

"Not sure exactly," Kate says. "Ozzie, come here." Her dog has been repeatedly scooting over to the base of the stepladder to sniff at Ian. "I came out this morning around half seven and found the drip. The rug was already soaked, so I reckon maybe sometime in the early hours?"

"Yeah, we got a real clobbering with that rain last night," Ian says. "I'm not surprised. This old place is full of holes I keep patching."

Kate seizes the prompt to address her curiosity. "So, do you have your own business, or . . . ?"

He chuckles, a soft bark of a laugh. "No, I work at the bookshop in town."

Kate isn't sure if this information makes her more or less confused. He steps down off the ladder, and before Kate can grab Ozzie, he darts over for a scratch, which Ian enthusiastically delivers.

"Then what are you doing here?" she asks. "Doing this?"

"Well, my granddad dated, courted—I don't know what they called it then—Audrey in the fifties, after they both came back from the war. For whatever reason, they didn't marry, but they stayed friends. After my gran died, Audrey was really there for my granddad until he passed himself, a couple years ago, now. Anyway . . ." he says, waving a hand through the air as though dispelling the details like a cloud of gnats. "Point is, Audrey never had kids of her own, and she sort of took a shine to me. I'm good with my hands so I help out here when things need doing around the hotel . . ."

Kate nods as he continues speaking, but she's only half-listening, fixating on his mention of the war. "Did you say your granddad and Audrey met when they *both* got back from the war?"

"Yeah."

"Was she one of those women who built aeroplanes or something? She hasn't really said. I'd kind of assumed she was on the home front."

"No. I think she was over there. Not sure what she did though. I've only ever heard her mention it once, maybe twice. I don't think Granddad ever knew much either." Ian gives Ozzie another scratch, then points at the ceiling. "I need to get up on the roof and have a look. I'll be outside for a bit if you need me." He picks up his tool case and steps past Kate with a gentlemanly nod reminiscent of a bygone era.

"Are you going to be okay up there? It's freezing outside."

"I don't mind it. You get well accustomed to this sort of weather here in the north. Bit different from London, I expect."

Kate's never understood people who like the cold. She prefers running on a treadmill indoors instead of out, and she'd happily hibernate under a pile of blankets with a hot drink all winter if it weren't so socially and financially problematic.

"It is," she says, "but that's not a bad thing."

"Good," Ian says, flashing her a warm smile. "I've always loved it here. Small-town lad at heart."

She nods. "Do you know if there's a decent fitness centre in town?"

"Yeah, a couple. I can give you the names before I leave."

"Thanks."

Half an hour later, Kate is in the sitting room when she hears the front door open. After struggling with the fireplace for a while, she finally got it burning, but the log is smoking more than it should be. She cranes her head around the side of the wing chair to find Ian brushing his boots on the doormat. His cheeks are ruddy and the rush of fresh air he brings in smells like mud and something green.

"I've mostly got it," he says. "I patched some new shingles over the hole, but I think we might still have to replace part of the ceiling. We'll see how well it dries out. Don't want to get any rot though, 'cause then we'll have an even bigger problem. This place is an old pig of a thing, honestly. I've told Audrey for about two years now that the roof *really* needs replacing, but she's stubborn." His tone is affectionate, fondness permeating his frustration, and Kate smothers a laugh.

"Yeah, I gathered that." She rises from her chair. "Anyway, thanks for doing this. What's the process for settling up? Do I pay you now, or do you invoice us, or . . . ?"

Ian shakes his head. "Don't worry about it. Audrey and I have it all sorted."

Kate lifts an eyebrow but doesn't say anything. She'll follow up with Audrey once she's back from the doctor.

"Well, the least I can do is offer you a coffee. I've just made a pot. Audrey should be home in a little while. From what you've said, I'm sure she'd be happy to see you."

"Sure. That'd be great."

"How do you take it?"

"Milk, no sugar."

Kate disappears into the kitchen to fetch the drinks, and returns to find Ian kneeling beside the fire, which is no longer smoking.

"How'd you do that?" Kate asks.

Ian's expression is that of a kid caught out in something. "Oh, did you build the fire? You had the logs all piled up, is all." He points to the triangular arrangement that's now crackling in the grate. "You need to give the flames some space to breathe. Don't worry, it's a common mistake."

"Can you tell I wasn't a Girl Guide?" she asks wryly, passing him the mug.

He nods his thanks, and they each take a sip.

"I doubt Audrey will be much longer," Kate says after a moment of silence.

"I don't mind waiting," Ian says pleasantly, then strolls over to the library, settles himself onto the piano bench. The grey autumn light from the window is weak, and Ian reaches up to switch on the small lamp on top of the piano.

"Do you play?" he asks.

"No, but my dad did."

Kate remembers the sound of it drifting upstairs to her room on weekend mornings. She'd hated it as a teenager, when she wanted to enjoy a lie-in, and now would give almost anything to hear him play again. Life is so full of extremes. How often that happens, that you end up yearning in ironic desperation for the very thing that once irritated, exhausted, or overwhelmed you.

"One of the ways Audrey repays me is by letting me tinker on this little beauty whenever I'm here."

"I've never seen one this colour," Kate says, blinking away the memory of her dad. "Is it rare?"

Ian pushes his glasses up the bridge of his nose. "Yeah. It's one of Audrey's most prized possessions." He pauses, then starts to play a few bars.

Kate leans against the archway between the rooms, the aroma of the coffee in her hand mixing with the woodsmoke in the fireplace. The melody is bright and simple, yet sentimental. It stirs something in her, something melancholy.

The front door opens, jarring her back to the present. Sue and Audrey have returned. Ian stops playing and heads toward the foyer.

"That was lovely," Kate says, following him.

"Thanks, but it's not mine."

She's about to ask what it's called when they reach the lobby.

"Bloody freezing," Audrey mutters as Sue shuts the door against the damp wind. She spots Kate's coffee. "Is there a pot on?"

"Yeah. Still hot."

"Brilliant. Thank you for the ride, Sue," Audrey says, setting her cane in the umbrella stand near the door.

"Of course, deary," Sue says, but her face is drawn. "Take care o' yerself, naow. Let me know what you need." She pulls Audrey into a hug, whispers something Kate can't hear. "Ian, nice to see you. Kate." She nods, her lips in a thin line, then leaves.

Kate exchanges a look with Ian, who appears curious but unconcerned. "Is everything okay?" Ian ventures.

Audrey straightens. "Nothing a good strong cup of coffee can't fix."

"Why don't you come and warm yourself by the fire Kate's got going?" Ian says, offering his arm, which Audrey takes. A bittersweet longing tugs in Kate's chest as she watches Audrey lean into Ian, like a tree bowing to stop itself breaking in the wind.

Kate fetches Audrey's coffee and returns to find the two of them in conversation by the fire. Ian is telling some sort of amusing story about a customer at the bookshop. Kate sets Audrey's mug down on the table and steps back to leave them to their chat. There's washing-up to be done in the kitchen, anyway.

"Hold it, there, dear." Audrey stays her hand. "I understand you and Ian have sorted the roof?"

"Yeah, we did," she says, looking at Ian, who smiles and takes a pointed gulp of his coffee. "Oh, but it might need replacing full-on, very soon."

Audrey shoots Ian a good-natured glare. "Got her campaigning for you now, have you?"

Ian raises a hand in mock defense. "The more people convincing you, the better. It's a disaster up there. You won't make it through another year without massive leaks, Audrey."

She scoffs. "God help me now if the pair of you are in cahoots."

There's a beat of silence before Ian glances at the clock. "I should be off," he says. "It's been a pleasure to meet you, Kate. Audrey," he adds, "I'll see you soon, yeah?"

Audrey grasps Ian's outstretched hand, a broad smile on her face that, until now, Kate didn't think she was capable of. It's the first true warmth she's seen from the woman, and it fills her with more questions about Ian. "I heard you playing when I came in. Do me a favour and tickle the ivories once more before you leave?"

"Of course."

Kate returns to the kitchen and Ian strikes up another tune, different than the last piece. Debussy or Ravel, maybe. As the notes drift through the house, Kate fills the sink with hot water and soap, begins to clean the dishes from breakfast.

Orange-scented steam warms her face as her thoughts wander back to Audrey. So, she was on the continent during the war, according to Ian, but doing what? Her mind assembles the details she's observed about the woman, trying to fit the pieces together. There's that collection of German books in the library. Was Audrey in Germany, of all places? Had she lived there? Her aunt owned the Oakwood before her, so Kate had just assumed Audrey was English. But it could explain the strange lilt in her accent.

Her thoughts shift to Ian. He clearly brightens Audrey like no one else does, and the tenderness between them reminds Kate a bit of her own parents' relationship, or the way it was with her and Adam in the beginning.

She scrubs aggressively at some caked-on grease as she pokes around her feelings. She thinks of the Marmite jar, the dropped egg, Audrey's cane and medication. Audrey does need help, that much is clear. And maybe Ian needs Audrey too—he seems genuinely pleased to be here. Everyone wants to be needed in some way, including Kate, she admits. She's felt adrift in her own life. Perhaps Audrey and the Oakwood could be her anchor, some direction, as unexpected as that may be.

She scans the kitchen for more dishes, then returns to the sitting room to collect the coffee mugs. The piano has stopped, and Ian is gone, but Audrey is staring into the fire, her eyes glassy.

"Are you done there, Audrey?" Kate asks gently, feeling certain she's interrupted some deep thought.

Audrey blinks up at her. "Oh, yes, thank you."

Kate scoops up Audrey's mug and looks for Ian's, spotting it on top of the piano. She retrieves it, then does a double take at the sight of a water ring on the surface.

"Oh, goddamnit," she mutters, using the sleeve of her cardigan to try to wipe away the white mark. It doesn't budge.

"What's that?" Audrey asks from the next room.

Old as she may be, her hearing is clearly still perfect.

"It's just, er . . ." Kate continues to scrub ineffectually.

"What?"

"There's a water ring on the piano." No matter how she says this, it's going to come out like an accusation. "Where Ian set his mug. I'm sorry. I can look up how to shift it, I'll see what I can do. Or maybe Sue—"

"That wasn't Ian's cup," Audrey interrupts her. "Don't worry. It's been there for decades."

"I really think it was though, Audrey. I'm sorry. It's right where—"

"I said don't fret about it. Ian didn't leave that water ring." She turns in her chair, fixing her eyes on Kate's. "A Nazi bastard did."

Kate freezes at Audrey's pronouncement. "Pardon?"

Audrey gestures to the armchair across from her. "Come and sit."

"Ian said you were in the war," Kate says, sitting down. "Is that where your nightmares come from? Things you saw?" She wonders for a moment if she's being too bold, too intrusive. But Audrey nods.

"Yes."

"And the mark on the piano was left by a Nazi?"

"It was. In Berlin."

Audrey's hand grips the arm of her chair, the misshapen knuckles protruding. A log pops in the fireplace.

"I'd love to hear it," Kate says, "if you're willing."

"I haven't been willing. Not really. But now . . ." She trails off, staring into the depths of the fire as though trying to retrieve something long lost to the ashes of time.

Nearly a full minute passes, and Kate starts to wonder whether she's going to say anything more at all. Finally, Audrey shakes her head.

"Truth be told, I'm unsure where to start. Or what good it will do, really."

Kate considers her response. "I felt a lot better after I talked to you last night," she says. "What you said about being the survivor. What that does to you." She clears her throat to dislodge the stuck memories. "If you've never really talked about it, how do you know it won't do any good?"

Audrey pierces her with a look that's both vulnerable and resentful. "No one other than you has ever asked me to talk about it."

Kate frowns. "What about Ian's grandfather? Or Ian?"

"Ian told you about that?"

"Yes."

"I think . . ." Audrey turns to the fire again. "When everyone came back from the war—when the survivors came back, I mean—no one wanted to talk about it. And no one wanted to ask. There was this gaping chasm between the people who had seen the war and those who hadn't. The horrors aren't articulable, Kate. They've made films and things, of course, depicting it. But being there is—*was*—something very different. Ian's grandfather didn't want to talk about it, and neither did I. We made a go of it, tried to find comfort in one another's company. But it was a very"—she casts around for the words—"isolating experience. It was enough to drive a person mad. And it did for many. I think my auntie thought me mad at times. And I couldn't tell her any of it. I wanted to move on, have a fresh start here."

Kate picks at a ragged cuticle. "Like me."

Audrey nods. "I assure you I'm as surprised as you will be to hear this, but I hadn't really recognized myself in anyone until now. Until you."

She glances over at the library, the piano, and a sad smile pulls at her lips. "It all started with Ilse," she says. "She was everything to me. Absolutely everything."

Chapter 9

Audrey

BERLIN, GERMANY | DECEMBER 1938

Audrey was elbow-deep in suds from the washing-up when Vogt entered the kitchen. She glanced over her shoulder, swallowed, then turned back to the dishes. She hated having her back to him, or being alone with him. She always felt like cornered prey.

"*Guten Abend*, Audrey."

He opened the icebox and helped himself to some of the leftover chicken that Audrey was hoping to give Ilse for breakfast tomorrow. She cursed him inwardly.

"*Guten Abend*, Herr Vogt. I could have brought that out to you."

He ripped a piece of the chicken with his teeth. "I am aware," he said, licking the grease on his lips.

It was the men's weekly poker night. She had learned in the first few days that Müller and Vogt would be hosting these gatherings every Friday. When Vogt informed her that she would be expected to cook beforehand and clean up after, she had been ironing his shirts. She smiled graciously but her gut swirled with apprehension that there would now be several more Nazis hanging about the house.

"But I'm sure you're up to the task, Audrey," Vogt had said, taking in her appearance from her feet all the way up to her chest. "You look like the sort of woman who knows how to take care of men."

Audrey hated herself for blushing. She had never been spoken to like that by a man. She felt naked in front of him. She tried to believe that his hand had only accidentally grazed her bottom when he'd left, but, a month later, she knew better. Even now, he passed by her unnecessarily close on his way out.

Once he'd left, her shoulders relaxed, and she set the last of the dishes in the wooden drying rack beside the sink. There would be many more glasses to clean when the evening was over. All she wanted was to take a bath and crawl into bed. But she had work to do. She began to prepare a small plate of biscuits to go with the men's after-dinner cocktails.

She wished they could have kept Matya on to help with the food preparation, which was not in Audrey's bailiwick. Her first couple of meals weren't outstanding successes, but she did her best with the box of kosher recipes Matya had kept on the kitchen counter, added some pork every so often and hoped it was good enough. She and Ilse felt awful about letting her go. Matya was valued by the family and relied on her income to support both herself and her aging parents. Audrey wondered from time to time what would become of them. They weren't targeted on the night of the pogrom, but she wouldn't be surprised if they were trying to flee somehow.

Audrey felt that the key to survival was making herself useful, keeping the men as happy and well fed as possible, and ingratiating herself so that she could pick up on any information Müller and Vogt might have. It required all her skills as a performer, but she was up to the task. Now, plate in hand, she pasted a smile on her face and swept through the door to the dining room.

A cloud of cigarette and cigar smoke hung over the brightly lit room. The men were seated around the Kaplans' lace-covered dinner table,

Müller and Vogt at either end, heads at a table they had no business eating at. She couldn't stand seeing them sit where Ira and Ruth should have been, and was grateful that Ilse would never witness it.

There were three other men in the poker club, to whom Audrey had been cursorily introduced at their first visit: Claus Von Holten, a stocky fellow in his midtwenties who was shaped rather like a gorilla. Based on snippets of conversation she'd overheard, she surmised he worked in weaponry of some kind. There was also Ludwig Thurman, upper-middle-aged, the oldest of the group by about a decade. He seemed to hate sitting still, and did so reluctantly for each hand of poker. Whenever there was a break in the game, he would stand and pace the room, an overflowing rocks glass and a cigar clutched in the same hand, the other stuffed deep into his trouser pocket. The other men often dressed in more civilian wear for the festivities, but Ludwig wore his uniform as though it were a second skin. Aldous Stoltz was the third guest, a weedy young man with small glasses who didn't seem to fit with the rest of the group. He walked with a slight limp and used a cane on occasion. She'd never seen him in uniform, though she figured he must be a Party member.

"Ah, Fräulein James," Müller greeted her now as she offered each man the biscuits in turn. "Thank you for these, but you needn't fuss over us any longer. We can manage by ourselves for the rest of the evening, and if you bring round any more delights, we may burst. Good night."

She bobbed a curtsey. "Yes, Herr Müller."

Despite Müller's gruffness when they first met, and his hesitancy to hire Audrey, he was reasonable enough to work for. He attempted to make conversation with her, inquiring about her family and experience. She'd embroidered her own history and developed a character to play, which helped her to separate her true self from the persona of a loyal German that she despised, but that was necessary to portray if she wanted Ilse to remain undetected.

In the kitchen, Audrey pressed her ear up against the door to listen in on the conversation. In the days after the pogrom, she'd learned that Jewish children had been banned from attending school, and that the Nazis had fined the Jewish community to pay for the damage done to the city during the riots. That had made international news. Sometimes their boisterous voices dropped to whispers, and Audrey often wondered why. Even now, there was silence beyond the door. Then she heard one of them—Claus, maybe—mutter.

"Nosy one, isn't she? What are we going to do about that, Fred?"

Audrey blanched.

"I don't—"

Another voice, Ludwig's. "We can't talk about any kind of plan or news with her poking her head in every ten minutes."

"I know how to keep her busy," Vogt offered.

"*Enough*, Vogt," Müller snapped.

"We could gather at my place instead," Claus said. "It would be safer without any other ears around."

Audrey's breath caught on a hook of fear. Did they suspect her of spying?

"Do your wife and children not have ears, Claus?" Aldous asked.

"Just dismiss her," Ludwig said.

A creak, as someone shifted in a chair. "I don't think she's of any concern," Müller said. "But I can tell her not to wait on us, if you prefer. She can go upstairs when you're here."

"Well, where's the fun in that?" Vogt asked. "Besides, I've got an idea that will please us all. Fräulein!" he shouted. "Audrey, get back in here."

"*Vogt—*"

"Audrey!"

Audrey paused a moment, then pushed the door open, adopting a mask of innocence. "Yes, Herr Vogt?"

"You've been to finishing school, haven't you? Learned your pianoforte like all good girls do?"

She paused, nodded.

"Play for us," he ordered, gesturing at the piano with his thumb. Müller's mouth was tight. Ludwig rolled his eyes up to the ceiling and took another drink. "Something cheery," Vogt added.

"Yes, sir," Audrey said, swallowing the resentment. How dare he warp her talent and joy into some sort of hackneyed diversion, as though she were a circus animal. She wanted to say as much, but dutifully took her place at the bench.

Since the arrival of Vogt and Müller, she'd rarely had a chance to play. The housekeeping and cooking kept her busy, leaving little time for rehearsal, but she was also simply distracted by the stress of their predicament, the uncertainty of their future. But every so often, when the men were away, she would take a reprieve from her chores and sit down to play. She did it for Ilse as much as for herself, to provide some mere delight to her friend, who could still just hear the music upstairs.

It was in those moments that she missed her lessons the most. She'd telephoned Herr Fogel in the first week after Müller and Vogt moved in, fed him a story of familial strife until she could sort out whether it was possible to continue with her program. He'd been disappointed, but hadn't pressed. She had been *so* close. The recital was only two weeks away, but Audrey wouldn't be there. The imminency of that achievement had been thrust into the background of her life by all that had transpired over the past few weeks. She had no emotional energy to spare for the loss of her studies, which paled in comparison to all that Ilse had lost and continued to lose every day she sat trapped inside her own attic with cobwebs and piercing grief for company. Perhaps one day, when the world had turned the right way up again, Audrey could complete the program.

At the piano now, she spared a glance sideways at the dining room. All the men had their heads together, speaking in low tones, except for Vogt, who had risen from the table and wandered over. Audrey clenched her jaw and considered her choice of music. With a rush of brazen defiance, she began to play Mendelssohn's Piano Sonata Number 2, the piece she'd wanted for her recital but couldn't use because Mendelssohn was a Jew. Vogt was too vulgar to recognize such a cultured piece, she thought, satisfied at her own trickery.

Leaning against the side of the piano, Vogt set his drink down on the gleaming wood, and Audrey watched as the condensation dripped off the glass. He really was such a brute. She could only imagine what Ruth would have said.

With a pinch in her throat, Audrey cut the piece short and stood up. The other men ceased their conversation and looked over at her and Vogt.

"You didn't tell us you could play like that," Vogt said, his voice slick with chagrin.

"You didn't ask."

"Mendelssohn," he said.

She felt her cheeks warm, but said nothing. She'd underestimated him.

"Go." He flicked his head in the direction of the stairs.

She didn't need to be told twice.

"And Fräulein," he called after her. "Next time, you will play Wagner. And you will play to the end."

Ten minutes later, Audrey locked Ilse's bedroom door, then tapped gently on the wall beside the attic access, the all-clear message for Ilse. The hatch opened with a soft creak and the rope ladder fell, the ends swishing on the floorboards as Ilse climbed down.

"Oh, God, I have to go," she whispered.

Audrey opened the door a crack to check that the hall was still deserted, then slipped out to give Ilse some privacy to relieve herself in the basin Audrey kept in the room. Audrey had been bringing water to her bedroom in a large ceramic jug every night. Müller had noticed it once, and she'd told him she found it so terribly dry in the house now that the weather was getting colder, but really it was so Ilse could attempt to bathe herself.

Crouching beside the door in the dark hallway, Audrey wondered, as she did almost every hour of the day, how it had come to this. A few minutes later, she snuck back into the room. Ilse was sitting on the edge of her bed, staring at the floor with a vacant expression.

Quickly, Audrey disposed of the fetid contents of the basin in the toilet, then returned to the bedroom, locking the door behind her.

Ilse hadn't moved. Audrey hated to see her so diminished. Ilse never complained, but she was coiling into herself. Her dignity had been stripped away. She was alive, yes, but what sort of existence was this? They were fugitives in hiding; the moments they had together were few, confined to whispered exchanges in the middle of the night.

"Come here." Audrey opened her arms for Ilse, who fitted herself into them, resting her weight against Audrey's chest as her body shook with suppressed sobs. She exhaled in staccato pieces, broken and detached. Audrey stroked her soft hair. "I don't know how much longer you can go on like this, Ilse. It's only been a month, and it's seemed an eternity."

It never felt like long enough when she held Ilse, who always moved away first, as she did now.

"I'm fine. I'm just having a weak moment. I can manage this. I *can*," she emphasized, in response to Audrey's look.

Both women jumped as a burst of laughter sounded from the floor below, which set Audrey's heart racing.

"This is getting more and more precarious. Vogt—"

"What? What did he do? Did he say something?"

"No, but we're not safe with them here. Their friends. God, there are eyes *everywhere*. We can't sustain this much longer without being caught out." She didn't know, exactly, what the penalty would be for harbouring a Jew. But it didn't really matter. If Ilse were caught, Audrey's life would be forfeit anyway. She knew she loved Ilse more than she should; their current situation had thrust that truth to the forefront of her mind. Though she was still trying to understand what her feelings meant, the thought of anything terrible happening to Ilse was intolerable.

"We can," Ilse said. "We have so far. I know it's not safe, but we just have to wait a little longer."

Audrey still hadn't heard back from her father. His replies typically arrived within a few weeks, but who knew how the postal service might be impacted by all these new rules and systems the Nazis had implemented. She'd been checking the post daily, not just because she was anxious for news, but because she had told Vogt and Müller that her parents were dead. Also, his letter was sure to contain some reference to Ilse and the Kaplans. If the officers discovered it, the girls were finished. To be safe, she had burned all of her letters from her father and taken responsibility for checking and delivering the post to Müller and Vogt, setting their correspondence—which was occasional—beside their plates on the breakfast table.

She had mixed feelings about what her father would say. Ilse insisted on remaining in the house in case Ephraim and Ruth came back, and Audrey knew, if her father managed to sort out some way to get Ilse to London, that it was going to be a fight. Ilse was so desperately clinging to the prospect of her family's safe return that she couldn't see the rope was rapidly fraying beneath their fingers. Audrey had to get her out. If her father didn't reply soon, she would write again.

"Ilse, if your mother and Ephraim do come back, what then? These men aren't going to vacate the house just because—"

"Then we'll all leave, go somewhere, anywhere we can. We'll find something. Maybe your father will have a solution? Perhaps they could come with us to London."

Audrey took a deep breath, recognizing the discussion was at an end for now. "Yes, perhaps," she said.

They listened to the low tones of the men, who seemed to have moved to the sitting room. Glasses clinked.

"I heard you playing," Ilse said after a pause.

"Yes. Vogt made me."

"Ah. Well . . . I'm sorry. But I can't say I mind. You know I love hearing you. What's that other piece you've been playing lately?"

Audrey's stomach jerked. "Just something of my own I'm picking away at."

"What's it called?"

Claus raised his voice downstairs, and Müller hushed him.

"I, er, I don't have a name for it yet."

"I love it."

Audrey smiled in the darkness. "I'm glad."

"Do you remember when Papa took us to see *Peter Pan* when it opened?"

Audrey did remember. That performance, along with another at the Staatsoper Opera House in Hanover around the same time, had sparked her love of music and the piano. "Yes," she said. "What was that . . . eleven years ago?"

"Yes. A few months after Michael died. Papa took us to distract us, cheer us up. Mama was in a terrible state." Audrey reached for her hand, squeezed it. "You couldn't stop staring at the pianist. I'm not sure you took in a word of the play."

Audrey chuckled softly. "No, I suppose not."

"It was always one of my favourite books, you know. *Peter Pan*."

Audrey lay back on the bed. "I know."

"I always thought Peter was foolish," Ilse said, reclining beside her. "For not wanting to grow up. Though I think he might have been right. It's not been what I expected."

"No," Audrey murmured. She could feel her eyelids growing heavy. "It isn't."

"But then I think of little Michael. I suppose the only thing worse than growing up is the alternative. Isn't it?"

Audrey woke with a start, Ilse still asleep next to her. She berated herself for dozing off. What if one of the men had knocked on the door, wanting something? She thought of Vogt and his many demands.

She sat up, blinking in the dark room. Ilse was breathing deeply, the curves of her frame curled into a ball, as though protecting herself even in her dreams. Audrey wanted to stay like this all night, to bask in a fantasy that things had gone back to normal, that the family was still alive and whole, the house full of love instead of the scent of Nazi boot polish and malice. Without thinking, she bent to kiss Ilse on the head, something she'd never done before.

Ilse stirred.

"You should get to the attic," Audrey whispered.

Though half-asleep, Ilse scooted up the ladder and shut the attic door.

Through a crack in the curtains, Audrey checked her watch in the light of the streetlamp. Two thirty. She wanted to undress and crawl back into bed, but she'd missed checking the evening post after suppertime, so preoccupied she'd been with the poker night.

She crept downstairs into the dim foyer, lit only by a single lamp casting an orange glow from the sitting room. On poker nights, Müller usually went to bed around eleven thirty, Vogt around midnight. He was most often alone, but sometimes with a woman, a different one each time. Audrey was sure they were prostitutes, and loathed changing Vogt's sheets, which stank of sweat and perfume and transactional lust.

Audrey opened the door to the telephone room, glanced at the post basket, but it was empty. Tomorrow evening, she would write again to her father.

As she turned back to the hall, she was met with a puzzled-looking Müller in his red velvet dressing gown. She jumped, held a hand to her mouth.

"I'm sorry I frightened you," he said. "What on earth are you doing at this hour?"

"I couldn't sleep," she said, recovering quickly. "I came down for some warm milk. And then I realized I hadn't collected the post this evening."

"How meticulous of you."

Audrey attempted a smile. "I try to be thorough, Herr Müller."

He stared at her for a moment with a quizzical eye. She wasn't in her nightdress, which was suspicious.

"Well, good night, sir," she said, sliding past him toward the staircase.

"Your milk," he said.

She stopped. "I'm sorry?"

"You said you came down for a glass of warm milk."

"Oh, yes. Thank you."

She hurried to the kitchen to prepare the drink she didn't want. As she opened the icebox, she heard Müller's soft footsteps behind her.

Just leave me alone, she thought.

"I couldn't sleep, either," he said. "I will take some too. Please."

"I could get you a drink, if you prefer."

"No, thank you. Milk will be fine."

Audrey lit a match to start the stove element, and Müller took a seat at the small scrubbed wooden prep table in the kitchen. He crossed one leg over the other, the tassel on his slipper waving gently with the movement.

"How have you been enjoying your position so far, Fräulein?" he asked as Audrey emptied a bottle of milk into a small pot.

"Oh, very well, sir," she said. "I was pleased to have found new employment so soon after . . ." She trailed off.

"Were you close with Ira Kaplan?" His tone was conversational, but Audrey knew better.

"Not particularly, sir. I only worked for him for a little under a year. I was already looking for another position when all this transpired."

He nodded slowly. "I see. And you collected papers from his home so often that you were granted a key? I would have thought a man of his wealth could employ a maid to receive them at the door."

Audrey swallowed. "I'm not sure, sir," she said, tossing a modest smile at him. "I just did as I was told."

He watched her for a while until the milk was hot. Audrey poured it into two porcelain cups and handed one to Müller. "Here you are. If that's all, I'll be heading back upstairs—"

"Sit with me, Fräulein," he said.

"I'm just the housekeeper, sir," she replied. "I don't think it's proper for—"

"I insist."

Audrey obeyed, and took a seat across from him, feeling flushed.

"Are you quite all right?"

"Oh yes. Just a bit warm standing over the stove." She waved a hand over her steaming cup. She needed to redirect the conversation, and fast. "So what exactly do you do at the—"

"I must admit that I discovered certain discrepancies during my initial inspection of the house that first day," he said, cutting across her. "For instance, all the bedrooms were missing blankets from the beds, save for the room you are currently occupying."

Audrey shrugged. "I cannot speak to that, sir. You said the place was looted. Perhaps—"

"And I have wondered for some time who put the blanket up in front of the broken window." He twitched his head back in the direction of the sitting room.

Her pulse quickened, but she attempted nonchalance, tracing the rim of her mug with her finger. "Perhaps someone was, what . . . squatting, is it called?" she suggested. "If the house appeared vacant?"

Herr Müller's face was impassive, but his eyes scrutinized her. "Perhaps. It is possible. Although if an intruder had been doing so, they arrived and left in the time between the Jews' exit and our arrival two days later. That seems an odd ploy."

"Speaking of the Jews' exit," she said, seizing an opening, "if the remaining Kaplan family was detained, what happens when they return? I assume their detention is somehow temporary?"

Müller's eyes were hard. "They will have been sent to one of the camps. Buchenwald. Dachau. Sachsenhausen. They are intended as permanent institutions for the prisoners. All part of the Führer's scheme for the purification of Germany, Fräulein."

"Permanent? Surely you—"

"You know, I am not convinced that you are as flighty as you pretend to be. I do not believe a dull mind could ever develop the skill you have as a pianist." He set his cup down on the table with a thud. "That was most surprising. And you say you were an accounting secretary, so your maths must be above average, particularly for a woman. May I ask why the ruse?"

Audrey took another sip of her milk, willing her cheeks to cool. "Sometimes it is easier, or more advantageous, for a woman to pretend to be less intelligent than she truly is, Herr Müller."

"Advantageous, how?"

She hesitated, then decided to offer a kernel of truth. "For example," she said, delivering an expression of mild concern that she hoped would elicit sympathy, "I feign ignorance of Herr Vogt's advances on me, because it serves me to avoid its manifestation."

Müller shifted in his seat. "Your concern is not without foundation," he said quietly.

A twinge of foreboding plucked at Audrey's insides. It was one thing for her to feel it herself. Quite another to hear Müller confirm it so readily.

"I am not blind, as I'm sure you have by now surmised." He stood. "I will speak to him, Fräulein James. I regret he has made you uncomfortable."

Audrey nodded. "Thank you."

"But I cannot be in the house at all times. It would perhaps be prudent for you to take precautions."

Audrey cleared her throat. "Yes, sir."

"Good night," Müller said.

"Good night."

Audrey waited until she heard him on the stairs, then took a deep, steadying breath. When she'd finished cleaning the mugs and pot, she went back to the telephone room. Trying to keep her mind from diving too deeply into what she was doing, she retrieved the long silver letter opener, then headed upstairs, her steps heavy with the weight of the conversation. In the hall, a yellow slit of light shone in the crack beneath Vogt's door. Heart thudding in her ears, Audrey hurried to her room and shut the door.

The house was silent, everything still as night stars. If he was awake, she hoped Vogt wouldn't hear the sharp metallic click as the lock slid into place.

Chapter 10

Audrey

BERLIN, GERMANY | DECEMBER 1938

It was a frigid Tuesday morning, and Audrey was struggling with the Christmas tree.

Though it was only days before Christmas Eve, Vogt had insisted upon having one. He'd ordered a junior officer to drag it home behind him the previous night after work, leaving Audrey to sweep up the needles they trailed through the house.

She was now affixing two dozen small candles to the branches, thinking of Ira and Ruth. She had discovered a box of Hanukkah decorations in the cellar one evening when she was fetching wine for the men. She'd nearly wept at the sight, knowing where each object belonged: the grand silver menorah in pride of place on the sitting room windowsill, where it grew cold to the touch from the chilly draft. The blue spun glass bowls filled with multicoloured boiled sweets adorning the mantel. She ached to bring one of the smaller menorahs to Ilse, but knew she couldn't risk being discovered with it, and Ilse couldn't use candles in the attic in case their captors smelled the smoke.

Audrey had written her father again, but there was still no word from him. All she could do was wait, keep Ilse alive and hidden, and hope for some way out of Berlin. Since Müller's gentle interrogation a few weeks before, Audrey was even more careful to maintain her character, lest his veiled accusations of her deepen. He hadn't mentioned the irregularities he'd observed again, and she hoped she'd sufficiently deflected his attention onto Vogt's behaviour.

Audrey brushed an errant spray of pine needles off the honey-coloured wood of the piano and thought of the recital and graduation she'd missed on the fifteenth. At this point, she was meant to be on a train to London to spend Christmas with her father, which would have likely involved a heated discussion about his goals for her—marriage—and her dreams—an artistic career. For months, she'd dreaded the prospect of leaving Ilse. Now she would give almost anything to be in London, so long as Ilse was with her.

All she could do now was keep on keeping on, and so she wrestled the finicky candles onto the tree, though it seemed strange to be celebrating anything at all right now. Christmas was a time of family, friends. Warmth and hope in dark times. But their current circumstances were painfully lacking in that regard. It felt as though her world itself were on fire, and here she was, acting the fool, lighting candles to augment an already scorching blaze.

The propaganda splashed over the covers of the cold newspapers she collected from the porch every morning made it clear Hitler was preparing for war. And from what she'd overheard during the poker nights, he planned to invade Bohemia and Moravia in the coming months, expanding Germany's reach into Czechoslovakia.

The metallic *clink* of the mail slot interrupted her thoughts. The morning post. With one last look at the tree, she rose and wandered to the telephone room, flicked on the small desk lamp. There were two pieces of mail. One was for Müller, evidently from some relative named Gisela.

The other was from her own aunt Minna.

After weeks of waiting for her father to respond to either of her letters, why was there a letter from Minna?

She tore it open.

1 December, '38

Dear Audrey,

It is with a heavy heart that I must relay news of your father's passing.

Audrey gasped, and tears sprang to her eyes.

He died suddenly on 26 November of a stroke. The Dr (or coroner? I do not know) told me he could not have suffered long, if at all. That has brought me some measure of comfort, and I hope it will for you too. We buried him today in the family plot in Brompton.

I know it was his wish that you return home after your graduation, and you must now sort out your inheritance, the sale of the home, etc. His solicitor is Wm. Bailey in Lombard St—you must contact him to make the necessary arrangements. Your dowry remains available for your marriage, and you would honour your father by coming home and securing a strong match. I am headed back to Alnwick tomorrow—your letters can find me there.

I expect I shall see you soon, and that we might share our grief together. It pains me to lose him so soon after my own dear Alfred. I am sorry, dear.

Affectionately,
Aunt M.

Audrey read the letter over and over, willing her aunt's words to change, but the terrible truth was there in black and white. She needed Ilse. Letter in hand, she fled upstairs.

When Ilse saw Audrey's tear-stricken face appear in the access, she scampered down the ladder. "What is it?"

Audrey couldn't speak. She just held out the letter.

"From your father?" Ilse said.

"No," Audrey managed.

Brow furrowed, Ilse took the paper, then her face crumpled. "Oh, no. Audrey." She held out her arms and Audrey curled into them, sobbing. They sank to the floor, but Ilse didn't let her go. She just held her as Audrey cried out her grief as quietly as possible. Even though the men were out and they had locked Ilse's bedroom door, she still felt the need to muffle her cries, as though the very walls might hear and betray them.

She was fighting an internal battle now, grappling with the questions in the dark arena of her mind, that place a bereaved soul descends to in the aftermath of tragedy. What if she had been there with him when the stroke hit? Would he have stood a chance, if she'd been able to send for a doctor straightaway? Had he known what was happening? Had he died alone?

"I'm so sorry," Ilse murmured, stroking Audrey's hair. "I never thought the loss of our fathers would be a tragedy we shared so soon."

Audrey closed her eyes against Ilse's soothing touch.

She thought about how her father had been happier after they returned to London. The distance from Berlin had helped him leave some of his heartbreak behind, and he made a little space for Audrey in his life.

Growing up, Audrey had never had a birthday celebration because it was also the anniversary of her mother's death. It was as though the two events somehow cancelled one another out in the great cosmic scoreboard. The James family let every August third pass by in silence whilst they stared at it, like some beast that might attack at the smallest sound.

But on her sixteenth birthday, her father had come home from work and found her at the bench of their black baby grand, playing Debussy's *Reverie.* She heard the creak of the door, the *thunk* of the lock, but kept playing. Victor had walked silently into the room and sat behind her in his favourite green club chair with the brass studs, and listened. When she finished, she'd turned to face him with a small smile and was shocked to see that he was struggling to hold back tears.

"She would have been very proud of you," he said.

It was the only time in her life that Audrey's father had ever made any reference to her mother's existence. She wished she could go back to that moment, wrap her arms around him, and tell him she was sorry for the pain in his soul.

"What are you going to do now?" Ilse asked gently, pulling Audrey from the past.

"What do you mean?"

"Well . . ." Ilse wavered. "You'll need to leave, won't you? Go home to settle things, like your aunt said?"

Audrey sat up. "Don't even speak of me leaving, Ilse. Of course I'm going to stay."

She had hoped that if her father came up with a way to get them to England, she still might have been able to convince Ilse to come with her, despite the unknown fates of her mother and brother. But that door was closed to them now. Minna didn't have the connections her father did, or the resourcefulness.

Come what may, they were entirely trapped in Berlin. Trapped with Müller and Vogt.

The sliver of light in the dark—the thread Audrey clung to in her grief—was Ilse.

"I can't go back to London. This is my home," she said. "Here. With you. It always has been."

Chapter 11

Kate

ALNWICK, ENGLAND | NOVEMBER 2010

Kate sits back in her armchair, brow furrowed in sympathy. Since Ian left two hours ago, she's been listening as Audrey relayed her experience of her time in Berlin before the war broke out. Her childhood, all the way up to the Night of Broken Glass in the fall of 1938, Ira Kaplan's murder, Ruth and Ephraim's abduction. Working for the Nazi officers when they confiscated the house. Her father's sudden death.

Sue was right: *box o' secrets,* indeed.

There's a queue of questions in Kate's mind, and she stares at the fire, wondering where to begin. She added a log a while ago; it's low and glowing now.

"Did you know, after the fact, the extent of the pogrom during Kristallnacht?" she asks.

Audrey presses her wrinkled lips together. "Yes, we heard stories of that night. Hitler's ultimate objectives became clear very quickly after that. I overheard more detail from Müller and Vogt than what was in the papers. And later, at work, I learned things."

Kate waits for her to elaborate, but Audrey shakes her head.

"It doesn't bear repeating, my dear. There are some things we can't ever unsee. Unhear. Even if we want to. I won't be the one to put those images in your head."

"I understand." Kate's dad was Jewish. She's well educated in the Holocaust. She can imagine what Audrey's referring to. "How did you manage it?" she asks instead. "Living in the house with those monsters? Keeping Ilse hidden from them?"

"Immense caution. A great deal of sacrifice. And pure determination, I think. It was incredibly difficult."

She's already provided some glimmers of the answer, but Kate ponders how to frame her next inquiry. It wouldn't be a loaded question for a woman of Kate's generation, but Audrey's time was very different.

"So . . ." she starts. "You said that you stepped out with Ian's grandfather when you came back from the war."

"In the fifties sometime, yes, for several years. We were very fond of each other; he was a good man. Soft and transparent and kind. Just like Ian. Refreshing, particularly for a man of his generation. But I broke his heart. It is one of my greatest regrets. And I assure you," she says with a knowing look, "that is a competitive category. I thought I could stiff-upper-lip my way into a new life, you see. Everyone was carrying on, after the war. Trying to forget the impact the whole thing had on the world. On their friends, families. Everything they had lost and would never know or see again. The entire axis of the world shifted, but we were meant to just keep on because there was no other option. You've run up here for a new life, Kate, because your old one caved in beneath you like some great sinkhole. I came up here, met Martin, and ran headlong into a courtship that was doomed from the start because I was desperate for companionship and stability and a *fix* for all that had gone wrong. For requited love. But I failed. I failed in moving on, and I failed in loving Martin as he deserved to be loved because I hated myself," she says. "And a person can't love through a shield of self-loathing. It simply doesn't work."

They meet eyes, and there's a vulnerability in Audrey's that pushes Kate forward.

"You were in love with Ilse, weren't you?"

"Oh, yes, very much so," Audrey replies, her eyes bright. "It was the most consuming love I've ever experienced. I don't know whether you've known that kind of love, Kate, but my God. It changes you on a cellular level."

Audrey's frankness surprises Kate: the guilelessness with which she speaks about her feelings for Ilse brings a lump to her throat. She picks at the cuticle on her thumb, uncomfortably aware that she doesn't, in fact, know the kind of love Audrey is talking about.

"What happened to her? To Ilse?"

Audrey drops her gaze, taps the edge of her mug. "I don't believe I'm ready to talk about that yet, dear. In fact, I think that's all I can manage for now."

They sit in silence together for a few minutes as Kate's mind fills up with more questions. Audrey seems to see them floating to the surface before Kate has even opened her mouth.

"That's enough for today."

Kate nods, trying to figure out how to move on from such a weighty conversation. "What would you like for dinner?" she asks finally. "I'll go—"

"Don't worry about it, dear."

"But I could just knock up something simple. Beans and toast?"

"For yourself, if you like. But I must confess this exchange has rather sapped my appetite. I'm tired." She pushes herself out of the chair with a grunt and stumbles a little, shifts her weight from one foot to the other, working out the stiffness.

"If you're sure," Kate says, watching her with concern. Though she isn't very hungry herself either.

"I am. I'm going up. Good night."

As she passes by, Audrey squeezes Kate's shoulder in an affectionate sort of way—hesitant, but tender—and it catches Kate off guard. She rests her hand on top of Audrey's papery skin just as the older woman is pulling away.

As Audrey disappears up the stairs, Sophie trotting along in her wake, Kate's mind turns to her own family. When she was seventeen, not long before her maternal grandmother passed, her dad had taken a photo of her hand on top of her mother's and grandmother's, three layers of generations together, the skin progressively thinner, more mottled. Kate had always liked the photo, but wasn't old enough to fully appreciate that her time with her grandmother—and her parents—was limited. That the opportunities to ask about their lives, hear their wisdom, were withering by the day. There's a lot she wished she had asked that was now unknowable.

Her parents' hands never even got a chance to grow old.

Later that night, Kate takes a long, hot bath, still ruminating over the conversation with Audrey. She pulls on flannel pyjamas and makes herself comfortable on the bed with Ozzie. She picks up the novel she's been chipping away at over the past couple of weeks, a contemporary anti-rom-com about single life that she'd hoped would raise her spirits. Her eyes slide over two pages until she realizes she isn't taking in a word of it. She keeps thinking about what happened to Ilse. Unable to stand it much longer, she tosses the book aside, seizes her laptop, and opens a fresh search tab.

She's about to google "Ilse Kaplan" when a prick of guilt pokes at her. Audrey is sharing her story for the first time ever. She's put an enormous amount of trust in Kate, and it would be disingenuous to listen to her experiences whilst secretly knowing the details. Besides, given the survival rates of Jewish people in Nazi Germany, she can pretty much assume what happened to Ilse, and Ruth and Ephraim too. It's understandable that Audrey doesn't want to talk about it. At least not yet. But Kate feels a need to know *something*. The name Ilse Kaplan wouldn't necessarily retrieve anything concrete in a search . . . but the names of the Nazis might. She picks at a nail bed. Surely it wouldn't be a breach of confidence for her to know who, exactly, the men were. Whether they ever received their comeuppance for their participation in the holocaust.

Kate adjusts her glasses. She can't remember the surnames of a couple of the poker night men, but Friedrich Müller she knows. Audrey hadn't mentioned Vogt's first name. And there was a Ludwig. Ludwig Thurman.

She starts with Müller, and finds his name and Thurman's on a list of men in the Nazi High Command who were tried at Nuremberg in 1948. As Ozzie snoozes beside her, she reads that Müller was sentenced to life imprisonment. There is no mention of his death on this page. Thurman got sixteen years. She can't locate a Vogt that fits Audrey's description in any kind of definitive way, and wonders what happened to him. Plenty of Nazi perpetrators evaded justice, fleeing to Argentina, Chile, and elsewhere. Maybe Vogt slipped out. He wasn't as high-ranking as Müller, though. Perhaps that had something to do with it. Maybe he was tried in some lower court, or at a later date.

She stares a little longer at the web page, at the names of the men who systematically destroyed the lives of so many millions. Overwhelmed, she shuts her laptop, runs her fingers over the scratches on its once-pristine surface, lost in thought.

After she turns off the bedside lamp, she lies awake for a long while. At least Kate can grieve the loss of her family in safety and comfort. She closes her eyes and imagines Ilse up in that drafty attic, with its bare floors and spiderwebs and Ephraim's toys and games. The remnants of his interrupted life. She can almost feel the chill of that old Berlin house, and pulls the duvet farther up her shoulder. It's well after midnight before she drifts into a fitful sleep, her unsettling dreams painted red and black and haunted by the faces of the dead.

"Dark roast, ground. Two pounds."

Kate repeats the order to herself as she drives into town to pick up coffee. Audrey likes a particular blend sold at Barter's, the local bookshop café, and apparently no other brew will do. Kate doesn't mind though. Other than a run through the woods around the inn a couple of days ago, she hasn't left the Oakwood since she arrived and she could do with a reminder that other humans exist. The inn has a dreamlike quality to it, set on the edge of town with the crows and old creaking trees. Kate could spend a decade there, wandering the dark halls or lounging by the fire with Audrey as the snow piled up around the foggy windows, to find that only a few days had passed. Living at the inn was like falling into Narnia, or some sort of slipstream in time.

Head bowed against the misty autumn drizzle, Kate ducks into the shop and is greeted by several rows of fiction, the scent of coffee and dust, and a couple of patrons browsing the shelves. There's a small brick fireplace to her left with several cushy red chairs clustered around the flickering flames. She wanders farther into the shop, which opens up into a larger, brighter space with even more shelves. At a ticking sound, she glances up; above her head is a children's electric train, the tracks suspended from the ceiling, circling their way around the shelves beneath a peaked glass ceiling. Her jaw falls open a bit.

"It's quite something, eh?"

Kate turns to find Ian, smiling politely a few feet away.

"Oh, hi," Kate says. "How are you?"

He pushes his glasses up. "I'm well. How's the roof doing in this rain?"

"It does seem to be holding. Thank you."

He sidesteps to allow a pair of exuberantly chatty women to pass. "You just in to browse?"

"I was actually looking for the café. Audrey sent me here for beans. Some kind of magic beans, I take it." She raises her eyebrows. "She lives on the stuff, eh?"

Ian laughs heartily. "I've wondered more than once whether coffee is the elixir of life. It would seem to be for Audrey, anyway."

"How old *is* she?" Kate drops her voice conspiratorially, as though she's uttered something indecent.

"In her nineties, for sure. At any rate, if you're getting beans for Audrey, why don't you get a cup now too? My shift just ended. I'll join you."

Kate hesitates for a moment. She *did* want to get out and about a bit today before tackling Audrey's filing system in the front office this afternoon. It's ancient and can certainly be digitized.

Ian's smile is so genuine. She's interested in finding out more about him—and Audrey. She can stay for a cup and still have time to get a bit of work done before supper.

"Yeah. That sounds great. Where is the café, anyway?" She glances around at the rows of books and bustling shoppers. The place is busy for a weekday. It must be a popular spot.

"Have you not been here yet?" Ian asks, a little incredulous.

"No."

"It's a bit of a tourist trap in the high season, like most of the town, with the castle and everything," he explains. "But it's good for business. And the café has the best chips around. Back here."

He leads her farther inside. The store appears endless, and is already decorated for Christmas. Fairy lights drape over and between the towering rows of books. Large red armchairs call out to patrons to settle in for the afternoon, and Kate can't tear her eyes away from the interior brick walls and the thousands of books in her view.

"It's an old train station," Ian says, slowing down to match Kate's pace. "The trains stopped running here sometime in the sixties, but they didn't tear it down. Later they renovated it into this." They enter a small room off the main shop with several two-person tables. "This was the waiting room."

"You've given this tour before, haven't you?" she asks, smirking.

"Once or twice, yeah." He winks, then approaches the counter. "What would you like?"

"No, no," Kate says, a little flustered at the offer. It'll feel too much like a date if he buys. "Thanks, but I'd really like to get these. I'll order."

Ian shrugs good-naturedly. "If you insist. Hey, Craig." He nods at the barista. "Flat white, please. And a plate of chips."

"Chips?" Kate queries. "With coffee?"

"Chips are an anytime food. Didn't you know? I'll go find a table."

Kate gets a coffee for herself and when the order's ready, she joins Ian at a table near the fireplace. She sets down the drinks and plate of greasy chips, slinging her jacket over the back of the chair.

"You don't mind hanging about after your shift? Don't you want to get home?"

"Nah," Ian says. "I love it in here. And you can't have a proper coffee shop without lines of spines. No point going anywhere else."

Kate smiles. "I can appreciate that. What's with the mugs?" She gestures to their white cups, which are emblazoned with the familiar KEEP CALM AND CARRY ON phrase printed in dark red.

"Ah, this?" Ian lifts his. "You know this was an old wartime morale poster, right?"

Kate nods.

"So funny enough, these are the best known, but they never actually got posted anywhere. Almost all the copies were destroyed after the war, but the owners of this shop found one in a box of books they bought at auction a decade ago." He can't talk without his hands. If you asked him to sit on them and tell a story, Kate's sure his elbows would just start dancing instead. "We've got the original up behind the cash desk. You can see it on the way out. The shop's famous for it."

"Huh," Kate says, inspecting the words on her own mug.

Ian reaches for a chip. "Help yourself." But Kate shakes her head, clocking the calories. "So how'd you end up at the Oakwood, anyway?" he asks. "Audrey didn't say."

"That's because she didn't know I was coming," Kate replies. She explains about the advert Sue posted, and her arrival.

Ian chuckles. "Audrey can be . . . brusque. But why the Oakwood?"

It's a simple question, a polite inquiry, but the answer is so complicated. She sees all the factors and moments and bad fucking luck that got her to this point line up in her mind before the first domino begins the cascade, one falling into the next until Kate packed up her car and arrived at the inn.

"A new start, I guess," she says, a grossly inadequate summary, but the closest thing she can say that sounds like a normal reason.

"Oh yeah?"

She meets his eyes but doesn't say any more. Soft instrumental Christmas music floats around them like snow. Kate doesn't spot any obvious speakers; it's as though the music is issuing from the walls themselves, reminding her that the holidays will be everywhere soon, and she can't dodge it, no matter how much she might want to this year.

Ian takes the hint and another chip. "You're up from London, then? Your accent."

"Yeah. Never been this far north before. It's beautiful. Have you lived here your whole life?"

"Mhm. Everyone always wants to leave for the bigger cities, but I love it here. My dad died when I was a teenager, but my mum's still here."

Something familiar plucks at Kate's insides. "I'm sorry."

"Thanks. He had a degenerative disease called Huntington's. Affects the brain. He didn't last more than a couple of years after he was diagnosed."

Kate's brow knits. "That's awful."

Ian clears his throat. "Yeah, it was. Particularly hard on my mum. But we mustn't let these sorts of things define us, right? I had fifteen years with my dad, and thirteen good ones. I'm grateful for the memories I do have." He sits back a little. "Are your parents still in London, then?"

"No." She's hesitant to share, but Ian's transparency has put her more at ease. "They're dead," she says, the words gritty on her tongue.

"God, sorry," Ian says. "What happened?"

Kate looks down at her coffee, swallows her fear.

What happened, Kate?

"There was an accident," she says. "Last winter."

Ian looks pained, but she doesn't take it as the same brand of pity she received from well-meaning friends who couldn't relate. Ian's been in these particular trenches. He knows that you never quite get the mud out from beneath your fingernails when you're trying to climb back up to the surface.

Her stomach jolts, but she tells him. "A car crash. They died. I didn't."

He doesn't press for details, though his eyes scan the scar on her cheek.

Kate blusters on. "And I guess . . . well . . . I picked the Oakwood because they stayed here on their honeymoon. I just kind of wanted to see it."

"I get that. So is this your first Christmas since they've been gone?" he asks gently.

"Yeah. Hanukkah too. It's going to be hard. And—"

Her mind wanders to Adam, wonders for a moment whether this holiday would have been any easier if they were still together. But she knows the answer to that.

"It's shit, honestly," Ian says.

Kate lets out a weak laugh. "Got any advice for me?"

Ian heaves a breath. "You can't expect it to feel normal, but you also don't have to enjoy it. Not for a while, at least. Took me a few years."

Kate feels certain it will, at least, be marginally easier to manage the holidays if she spends them in an unfamiliar place. No heirloom tree decorations, no missed rituals. No tripping hazards.

"But," Ian continues, "in the end, the only way out is through. Though I'm sure I'm not telling you anything you didn't already know."

They're both quiet. Even though they're just getting to know one another, it's a comfortable silence; their loss has forged a quick bridge. This is what happens when people share parts of themselves, Kate thinks. Maybe that's why Audrey connected with Ian. He's an open book that welcomes you to sit down and read.

Kate attempts to lighten the conversation. "Do you have any siblings?" She immediately regrets the question, fights a cringe. It feels like first-date banter.

"Yeah, a brother. Doug. Bit older than me."

"Does he still live here too?"

"Nah. Manchester. We don't really get on." He doesn't elaborate and Kate senses something silent pass by. "How about you? Any brothers or sisters?"

"No. Just me."

She takes a big sip of her drink, scrambling for another question to ask. Her eyes flick over the slogan on her mug. KEEP CALM AND CARRY ON. A bit of a condescending mantra for anxious introverts and the trauma-plagued. But it reminds her of the war.

"I've been talking with Audrey about her time in Germany," she says.

"Really?"

"Yeah. Well, so far it's the time before the war, but she was in Berlin." Kate stops, unsure she should be divulging this to Ian, who, however fond Audrey may be of him, clearly hasn't heard it from her. "I'm hoping to hear more."

Ian's eyebrows pop up, impressed. "How'd you get her to talk?"

She thinks about the water ring and her immediate suspicion that Ian had been the culprit. "We sort of stumbled onto it."

He's expectant, but Kate sips her coffee. Her cup is nearly empty, but she finds herself debating on a refill. It's rather cozy here in the café.

"I've been thinking more and more that she should write it all down," she says. "Her story."

"She doesn't want to?"

"I get the sense she just wants to talk about it."

Ian pushes up his glasses again, runs his thumb over the handle of his own mug. His brow knits below his sweep of fringe.

"Well . . . what if you wrote it down *for* her?"

The next day, Kate is cleaning the kitchen after supper whilst Audrey finishes some business paperwork in the office. She's been private about the financials, and Kate wonders how she's going to successfully take on her new role as the administrator when her employer appears hell-bent on refusing to relinquish any modicum of control. Perhaps this job will turn out to be a failed experiment, but at least she'll have gotten to spend some time here, tracing her parents' footsteps and getting to know Audrey, who mentioned during supper that she wanted to have another of their "chats" tonight, a euphemism for opening up again about her story.

Kate sets the final dish on the rack beside the sink, puts the coffee on, and heads to the sitting room. Audrey is already settled into her usual chair, Sophie on her lap.

"Coffee'll be ready soon," Kate says.

She gives Ozzie a thorough belly rub over on the dog bed before taking the seat across from Audrey. The curtains have been drawn since dusk—four o'clock this far north, at this time of year—against the snow that began late this morning. A fire crackles on the hearth.

"Did you enjoy your trip to Barter's yesterday?" Audrey asks her, stroking a deliciously relaxed Sophie, who closes her eyes against her mistress's hand. If she were a cat, she'd be purring.

"Yeah, it's a great place. Ian showed me around."

"You ran into Ian?"

"Yeah. We had a drink when I got your beans."

"How is he doing? I haven't talked to him since he was last here," Audrey says.

Kate doesn't feel qualified to answer, really. "He seemed fine. Good. We had a chat."

"Oh yes? What did you talk about?"

Kate's getting used to Audrey's directness, though sometimes she feels a little like she's being interrogated. "This and that. He told me a bit about his family. His dad. Sad story there."

Audrey nods slowly. "It was a dreadful thing, that. Tore the family apart."

Her words chafe at Kate like rough wool. "He said it was particularly hard on his mum."

"Oh, God, yes. I don't think Janet's moved past it, all these years later. And for what the whole Huntington's business did to the boys . . ."

"What do you mean?" Kate asks.

Audrey shoots her a sidelong look. "How much did he tell you?"

"Er, well, I don't know. He said his dad died of a brain disease when he was fifteen. And that he and his brother don't get on, but his mum is still here in Alnwick."

Audrey shifts in her seat. "Huntington's is hereditary. Ian's father didn't know he had it until after they'd had the boys. There's a blood test to determine it. I don't think Janet wanted them to take it, but both boys did, several years ago. Doug has the gene. Ian doesn't. And it ripped them apart."

Kate gapes in dismay.

Audrey sighs. "Doug hasn't spoken to Ian in years. I suppose that's one of the reasons why poor Janet was against the testing. Perhaps she foresaw the impact on the family, of knowing another of them was doomed to the same terrible fate. Or perhaps she didn't want to know herself."

Kate considers it for a moment. "I can understand wanting to know, though. I think *I'd* want to know, if it were me."

Audrey watches her. "Why's that?"

"I like knowing what to expect," Kate says, swallowing hard. "I'd want to . . . I don't know. I'd want to be able to plan. Decide what I'm doing with the time I have."

"Isn't that what we all do, every day?"

"Yeah, but you know what I mean. It's different."

"Mm. I'm not so sure," Audrey says. "I wouldn't be too hasty for knowledge you can't unlearn. Particularly with something so profoundly impactful. Too much information can paralyze a person."

Kate feels a twinge of judgment. It's different for someone like Audrey, who has lived for so many years. Maybe it seems more comfortable at her stage of life to not know when the curtain call will be.

"I couldn't have managed half the things I did in my life if I'd known what was coming," Audrey says. Her face is grave, but a spectre of something else shadows her features. Amusement? Satisfaction? "In Germany there were plenty of times I thought I was about to die at any moment. Had I known I was going to make it out alive, I wouldn't have had the sense of imperativeness that I did. There's a lot to be said for the power of raw nerve, of adrenaline, in pushing a person to the verge of her ability."

"Like when?"

Audrey doesn't answer.

"Audrey," Kate says, meeting the old woman's eyes squarely, "I know you've wanted to keep these conversations casual. But from what you've already told me, your story is important. I think it warrants a record of some kind, beyond my own recollections of our chats." She hesitates a beat, thinking of her parents, of the unknown stories and secrets that must have died with them. "How would you feel about me writing your story down?"

Audrey is quiet for several long moments as Kate waits. She takes a shaky breath. "Yes," she says finally. "Given what's to come . . . I think perhaps you should."

PART II

But the stars that marked our starting fall away.
We must go deeper into greater pain, for it is not
permitted that we stay.

—Dante Alighieri, *Inferno*

Chapter 12

Audrey

BERLIN, GERMANY | DECEMBER 1938

Audrey glanced at the large mantel clock from her seat on the piano stool—it was half past four, and dusk was descending fast as snow swirled outside. It was two days before the New Year, that strange, weak echo of Christmas littered with empty liquor glasses and emptier promises. Audrey had hoped Müller and Vogt might beg off to visit their families—for she assumed they must have them, parents or siblings, at least—so that Ilse might be afforded more freedom for a day or two. But she'd been disappointed. They'd both remained in the house over Christmas, which was passed with little more than a large dinner and Müller's lukewarm greeting of "*Frohe Weihnachten*" tossed in her direction.

Müller had told her he would be home late today, and not to worry about his supper, so after she was done with her housework, she squeezed in a piano practice. She still had some time to take a bath and eat with Ilse in the attic before Vogt returned wanting a meal. Audrey's stress always increased as soon as the men arrived back and she had to set the stage for her nightly performance. After checking in with Ilse, she crossed the hall to the bathroom, sinking her tired muscles into the warm water. Her sigh of relief was followed by the usual pang of guilt that Ilse couldn't do the same.

She was just rinsing when the sound of the front door closing echoed up the stairs. One of the men was home early. She strained her ears, and by the rhythm of the footfalls could tell it was Vogt, not Müller. There was a rattling downstairs, a clinking of glass on glass. Audrey growled with frustration and quickly rose from the tub, water splashing onto the floor in her haste to reach the ivory towel on the small chair next to the sink.

"Audrey!" she heard Vogt call from down the hall. She glanced around for her dressing gown and nightdress, and cursed. She'd left them in the bedroom. Wrapping the towel around herself, she pulled the plug on the tub as a creak sounded outside the door. The knob rattled. The door was locked, but she gripped the towel tightly around her chest.

"Yes?" she called, trying to keep her voice steady. She hated the idea of him knowing he made her uncomfortable, but she didn't want him to see her like this.

"Are you indisposed?"

For the first time ever, she wished Müller was home, for his presence and authority seemed to keep Vogt at bay. "Is there something you need, Herr Vogt?"

"I am ready for dinner," he said. "But the stove is cold."

"I will be out in a moment."

His footsteps retreated. Ensuring everything of importance was covered, she went to the bathroom door and listened. Silence.

She turned the handle and stepped out into the hallway, nearly jumping at the sight of Vogt a few feet away in the shadows.

"Good evening," he said, staring at her as if he could see straight through the towel.

Audrey fought a shiver, her damp shoulders chilled in the cool air.

"Herr Vogt, I am sorry. I didn't think you'd be home so soon. I'll be right down to prepare your dinner."

She walked away from him, feeling his gaze bore into her half-naked back. She slipped into Ilse's dark bedroom, but as she went to shut the door, his foot shot out, blocking her.

Audrey yelped and lurched back as Vogt shoved his way in.

"What are you doing?" she gasped.

But she knew. And so did he.

A sickening dread gripped her insides. Her thoughts went to Ilse above her. She couldn't cry for help.

"Please, don't do this," she said quietly. It took everything in her not to scream. "Please, leave."

"Be a good girl, now," he snarled, reeking of alcohol. He stepped toward her.

Audrey clutched at the towel with one hand and lashed out at Vogt with the other. He batted her arm away, then seized her shoulders, pushing her toward the bed. Despair surged up her throat like black bile. Her towel fell as she fought Vogt with both hands now, panting with the effort and her own horror. The cold air hit her body. As Vogt took in her nakedness, she landed a punch to his throat. Anger shone in his eyes. She tried to race around him, but he stopped her with his other hand and threw her onto the bedspread with a grunt, pinning her down with his muscly body. A scream escaped her lips.

He covered her mouth with one hand. "Shut up," he hissed, fumbling with his belt as he pressed her head down into the mattress.

In a flash, she remembered the silver letter opener in the drawer of her bedside table. Audrey bit down on Vogt's fingers and he swore, recoiling. She flung an arm out, clawing at the drawer pull, but Vogt wrenched it back down. She thrust her elbow up into his face, tried to twist her body out from under him. She had to reach the blade.

But Vogt's body was heavy on hers, his breath hot on her face. She cried out again as she fought to free her arm. Then, over his shoulder, she saw a shadow.

Ilse.

Audrey recognized the outline of the brass lamp clutched in her hand. Vogt's fist was pressing painfully into her thigh, searching. Ilse approached the bed, holding the lamp like a cricket bat. And then she swung.

Blood splattered Audrey's face as Vogt was thrown off her. He rolled off the narrow bed and landed with a tremulous crash on the floor, out of sight. Audrey scrambled off the other side of the bed, her breath coming in shallow gasps. She seized the blood-splattered bedspread, covering herself. Ilse stood in her slippers and dressing gown, towering over Vogt, the lamp still poised for attack. But he didn't stir.

"Ilse, oh my God!" Audrey breathed. "Thank you. Thank you."

She flung her arms around her friend.

When Ilse didn't respond, Audrey pulled away. In the blue light of the moon, there was a shimmer of something she had never seen in Ilse's eyes before. Rage. Audrey's gaze followed Ilse's to the floor. "Is he . . ."

"I don't know. We'll have to check him."

Audrey's heart felt as though it were trying to jump out of her chest. She padded around the bed to the other side.

Vogt had landed face down, his limbs at odd angles. "Be ready," Audrey said, then nudged his leg with her bare foot. He didn't move. She gave it a kick, but he didn't flinch. And then she saw the pool of blood on the floorboards beneath his head, shining sinisterly maroon in the dim light.

"Oh, God."

"What?" Ilse asked. She looked a little more like herself now. The trance had worn off.

"I think he's dead."

Audrey rolled Vogt over with an effort, hating that she had to touch him at all. His eyes were half-open, mouth agape, and a large break in the skin on his temple was oozing blood.

"Let me see," Ilse said. She placed her fingers at the base of his stubbly neck, and waited. Then she stepped away, panic in her eyes. "He's dead. He's dead." She tossed the lamp on the bed. "I only meant to get him off you. I didn't think!"

"I know. I know," Audrey said, turning away from Vogt's staring eyes. "Of course you didn't. But he wouldn't have—" Her breath shuddered. She felt separated from her body. She wobbled, and Ilse reached out at the same moment. They gripped each other's cold fingers tightly.

"I've killed a man," Ilse said, aghast.

"I'm so sorry you had to do this. I'm so sorry." Audrey pulled Ilse into a hug. "But you saved me. Thank you. Thank you."

"I just couldn't let him do that to you," Ilse whispered as they clung to one another in the darkness. "If anything had happened to you . . ." She trailed off, and Audrey held her tighter.

"I know. I would have done the same for you."

Audrey wished desperately that they could go back to the way things were when they were children playing clapping games on Ilse's front stoop, when the biggest mess they had to clean up was the pile of jacks strewn across the attic floor. The keenest fear was whether the monsters under the bed were going to get them whilst they slept. But Audrey didn't know then that the monsters were real. That they weren't hiding under the bed.

"What do we do?" Ilse murmured when they broke apart.

"We have to get rid of the body."

"But where? How?"

Audrey pushed her damp hair off her face, then grimaced. Her hand was sticky with blood. Suddenly she had to be clean, free of Vogt's mark. She wiped the blood off her hand as best she could on the bedcover, then went to her dresser for a nightgown, her mind spinning as she considered their options.

They were few.

They couldn't very well keep him in the house. The thought alone made her stomach turn. And they couldn't bury him; it would be obvious the ground had been disturbed, and it was frozen now, anyway. No one would believe this was an accident or a suicide. And Vogt was important enough that the authorities would go looking for him.

Audrey pulled the nightgown over her head with relief, letting the soiled covers fall to the floor, and tucked her feet into her slippers.

Ilse was sitting down on the edge of the bed, head in her hands. They simmered in tormenting silence for a few minutes until Audrey finally spoke.

"I think we need to get him outside," she said. "It's dark out now. He was pretty much a drunk . . ." She tried to construct a plausible story with a mind that felt foggy and stuttered. "Maybe if we leave his body somewhere outside, it would look like he got in a brawl, and was killed on his way home."

But there was Müller to consider. Would he believe that Vogt got into a drunken brawl? Audrey glanced down at the body again, wishing his eyes would close. She was immensely grateful to Ilse. She had risked everything to rescue Audrey. But where did they go from here? Müller was an inconveniently sharp, inquisitive man. Could Audrey fool him? She would have to. It was imperative.

There was nothing like trying to get away with murder to test the depth of one's own resourcefulness.

"Come on, Ilse," she said, summoning her fortitude. "Let's take him downstairs."

"I can't go outside. I can't." Ilse was wild-eyed now, wringing her hands. Anxiety had usurped her previous rage. "I'm too afraid."

"I know. And you won't have to go outside." Audrey nodded, encouraging. "Just help me take him as far as the front door, then come back upstairs. I'll do the rest."

“Okay,” she agreed.

Audrey picked her way over Vogt’s sprawled limbs to his head. She tucked her arms under his shoulders, gagging on the stench of alcohol, hair oil, and the tangy, iron scent of blood. “Take his feet,” she told Ilse, who grimaced but complied, and the two women shuffled to the bedroom door, Audrey walking backward as they stepped into the hall. They panted under the weight of the lifeless body. Audrey kept expecting Vogt to suddenly wake. She couldn’t believe what they were doing.

They turned the corner toward the stairs and Ilse gasped. Audrey’s head whipped around, and her heart stopped.

There, standing at the end of the corridor, was Müller.

“Fräulein James?” he said. He scanned the scene: her damp hair and nightgown, Ilse, and finally the body they were carrying between them. “What the hell is this? Good God, is that *Vogt*?” he shouted. “And who is that?” He pointed at Ilse, who dropped Vogt’s legs in panic.

Audrey nearly collapsed to the floor under the weight of the body. She lowered Vogt’s shoulders. They must have been so distracted with the gruesomeness and effort of the task that neither of them had heard the front door open.

Müller found the light switch. It flicked on, and both women recoiled, the evidence of their crime illuminated in gory detail for him.

“Herr Müller, I can explain,” Audrey began, casting around for what that explanation could possibly be.

But Müller drew his gun from its holster and aimed it directly at them. “Don’t move.”

Chapter 13

Audrey

BERLIN, GERMANY | DECEMBER 1938

"Herr Müller," Audrey said again, stepping in front of Ilse and raising her hands. She stared down the dark barrel of the pistol and felt as though she might vomit. All she could do now was tell him the truth. Or a version of it. "Sir, you need to understand—"

"What's happened to Vogt?" he demanded. "Is he dead?"

"He—he tried to violate me," Audrey said. "He came home when I was in the bath. He forced his way into my room. He was about to . . ." Müller's gun was still raised, but he was frowning now. "You must believe me, sir. He would have succeeded, but—"

Ilse spoke from behind her. "I killed him, sir."

"Ilse!" Audrey hissed.

"It was me. I'm sorry. I hit him with a lamp. I didn't mean to kill him though. I only meant to get him off her. I didn't think beyond that. He had her pinned, you see. On the bed."

Tears ran down Ilse's stricken face. She was trembling.

"He tried to violate you, Fräulein?" Müller asked.

"Yes." Audrey looked directly into his eyes, hoping that their conversation about Vogt in the kitchen might count for something, might be a notch in this disaster that she could convince him to hang his belief on.

After a breathless moment, Müller lowered his gun. "You called her Ilse," he said.

Audrey's mind raced to create an excuse for Ilse's presence. "Yes. She's a friend of mine. I know I should have asked you first, but she's just staying the night. She—"

"Ilse *Kaplan*," Müller said.

Audrey sputtered. "How do you know—"

"Because your name was on the registry for this household," Müller said sharply to Ilse. "*You*"—he glared at Audrey—"told us she was dead."

In one wild moment, Audrey eyed the gun at Müller's side, wondered if she could wrest it from him. But no. This was it. They were done for. "Please." She clenched her fists so hard the nails dug into her skin. "Please just let—"

"I assume you've been where . . . in the attic?" he asked Ilse, who nodded. Müller shook his head. "I don't care that she's here," he said, after a pause.

The women stared, speechless.

"But I do need to understand who the hell *you* are, Audrey James."

Blood was thudding so hard in Audrey's ears she could hardly hear him. She was nobody. And he didn't care about Ilse. He didn't seem upset that his comrade was dead. What was going on?

"First, we need to deal with *this*." Müller twitched his head at Vogt's lifeless form. "What were you planning to do with him? Where were you going?"

Audrey shifted. "We were going to put his body out on the sidewalk. Make it look like he was attacked on his way home. A brawl, you know. He stinks of liquor."

Müller cocked an eyebrow. "That's not a bad idea."

"What?"

"We have to get rid of him," Müller said, an impatient snap to his voice. "Unless you want to leave him here in the hallway to rot."

Audrey cringed. "No."

"Right, then grab his feet."

Audrey thought she must wake up from this bizarre dream at any moment, but did as Müller instructed.

"You there." He gestured to Ilse. "Why don't you go pour us each something strong?"

Ilse's dark eyes darted from Müller to Audrey.

"I'll be right back," Audrey said.

They shared a meaningful look. Was this Müller's way of separating them? But he was armed, and they were not. There was no need to divide them. He could shoot them where they stood, if he was so inclined, and receive congratulations for it the next morning. But he hadn't, and she was desperate to understand why.

Müller led the way down the stairs, Vogt's torso heaved onto his back and shoulders. Audrey staggered awkwardly behind, holding Vogt's feet. Ilse followed in their wake, a grotesque processional of pallbearers. By the time they reached the front door, Audrey was in a cold sweat.

Müller poked his head outside, paused, then proceeded onto the dark stoop. Audrey assumed the coast must be clear. It was late, and the side street was normally quiet. Snow was still falling as they dumped Vogt's body on the pavement several feet away from the flagstone path up to the house. They looked around once more to check whether they had been noticed, then scurried back inside. Audrey bolted the door behind them, wondering whether she was locking the threat inside or out.

Müller strode into the sitting room and flopped into one of the wing chairs. Ilse was standing awkwardly by the sideboard, a drink in each hand. Audrey went to her, and they waited for Müller to speak.

"Come on," he said, gesturing to the divan. "I'm not going to hurt you. Have I not proved that? All is not as it seems in this house. You have some explaining to do. As do I."

Audrey and Ilse exchanged a glance, then Ilse handed Müller a glass, from which he drank immediately, and the other to Audrey, who merely held it in her hand. It smelled like Schwartzhog liqueur. Ilse didn't drink alcohol. They both took a seat on the divan, where they had so often sat before, and waited. Müller spoke first.

"Tell me again how he was killed," he said.

Audrey met his eyes across the coffee table. "He was attacking me. I tried to fight him off, but I couldn't. I even took the letter opener from the telephone room up to my bedroom. You know. Just in case. After what you said. But I couldn't get to it. Ilse came down from the attic and hit him with the brass lamp from the dresser."

"I didn't mean to kill him," Ilse said again.

She was having difficulty making eye contact with Müller, and Audrey could hardly blame her. This was the first time she had seen him. He was still in his uniform from the office, the swastika and eagle badge encircling his arm like a pack of wolves. His shoes shone, reflecting the gold flames from the fire. He was a Nazi. Living in her home, sitting next to a Christmas tree. Yet he did not care that Ilse was a Jew.

"I regret that I was not here," Müller said. "I have tried to arrive home before him, or with him, to ensure . . ." He took another swig of his drink. He drank fast, as though eager to be rid of it. "I am sorry, Fräulein."

Audrey didn't know what to say.

He leaned forward, resting his elbows on his thighs. "How long have you both been hiding here?"

Ilse squeezed Audrey's knee, signalling to her to speak for them. Audrey explained what had happened at Hertie's. "Then you arrived the next day."

"And who are you, Fräulein James? What are you doing here?" he asked.

Audrey told him how she grew up in the house across the street, about her studies at the *konservatorium.* "I was planning on returning to England after my graduation."

"But you aren't?" Müller asked.

"Well, no," Audrey said. "I need to stay with Ilse now. Her passport is invalid." She caught the anger creeping into her voice, tamped it. "She can't come with me. So I'm staying here."

"And I need to wait for my mother and brother to return," Ilse said.

Müller glanced at her but said nothing.

Audrey was a flutter of nerves. "We still don't understand. Why do you not care about Vogt? About Ilse being here?"

Müller rose suddenly and refilled his glass at the sideboard before returning to his chair. He surveyed them both, then pulled off his hat and raked a hand through his hair. "I am part of a resistance cell in Berlin. So was Vogt. We are working against Hitler from inside the secret service and military ranks."

The silence that descended on the room was so dense, Audrey felt as though her ears had been filled with cotton padding. Ilse clutched her elbow, and Audrey was reminded of the time she'd stood up to the bullies down the street, when the third had approached from behind. Somehow, this too felt like a trick. A Nazi resister?

"You do not believe me," Müller said.

Audrey's mind was reeling. "So . . . these poker games you've been having here—"

"Strategy meetings, yes. Very astute, Fräulein," Müller said with half a smile.

"All those men are in it?"

"Ludwig, Vogt, and Claus all work for the military or SS in some capacity. I've known Aldous for years, since our school days, and he is particularly useful to us as a forger and middleman. He has some contacts in the other cells." Müller tilted his head at Audrey. "I thought you suspected us, you know. I thought you were spying. You had Claus and Ludwig quite concerned for a while there. That's why I didn't want to hire you in the first place. The last thing we needed was an unknown pair of eyes on us."

Audrey scoffed. "I thought you lot suspected *me* of not being . . . exactly what I told you."

"And you aren't, are you?"

"But why didn't you tell me?" she pressed. "That night in the kitchen?"

"What night in the kitchen?" Ilse asked.

Müller relayed the conversation that had transpired when he caught Audrey creeping down to check the post. Oddly, he seemed to be rather enjoying this exchange.

Audrey was still trying to absorb it all. She leaned forward on the couch, still thigh to thigh with Ilse. "But how did you come to be part of a resistance in the very heart of the Nazi regime? I hardly believe you."

Müller nodded. "There aren't many of us. But there are enough to try to effect some kind of change. There are a few other cells that we know of, aside from ours. I work in the Abwehr division of the SS. The counterintelligence office. My job is to locate and eliminate resistance cells just like ours."

Audrey and Ilse studied him with a mixture of disbelief and intrigue.

"Most of the officers who resist simply feel Hitler has gone too far," Müller continued, "become megalomaniacal in his rule. Many believe in the superiority of the German people and state, but that diplomacy is a far more reasonable method for asserting our rights in Europe. On the current path, Hitler will pull Europe into another war, and we cannot let that happen."

Audrey thought of the millions of soldiers and civilians slaughtered, and felt her skin crawl. Everyone had said it would never happen again. *The war to end war*, they had called it.

Müller went on. "Others, like Vogt, just like a good fight."

"You're not sorry he's dead, are you?" Audrey asked.

"No. He had the right passion for the resistance, but he was reckless, and as a man he was a piece of shit. Obviously."

"And you? Why did you get involved?"

"Well . . . I agree that if we do not avert the Reich's trajectory, if we try to annex any more land, invade another state, we will be at war again. That is a certainty." Müller ran a hand over his cheeks, his eyes on Ilse now. His long fingers twitched his moustache before he answered. "Also, my mother is a Jew," he said.

Of all the reasons Müller might have given for resisting, Audrey hadn't expected that.

"She went to England before the outbreak of the Great War. I was just a child. My father never married her," he said. "But he cared for her. There was a load of anti-Jewish sentiment before the war, and he could see things heating up. So he sent her to live with his brother until she could get herself established on her own. My uncle is a professor of German literature at Oxford. His family has lived there for years. Longer than I have been alive, I believe. I have never met him." He exhaled. "And he kept me here to be raised by my stepmother. I was his son and heir. My stepmother was only ever able to have one other child, my sister."

Ilse shifted beside Audrey. "You don't really look Jewish," she ventured.

Müller's face glowed in the light of the fire. "I know. I take after my father."

"Don't they know you're Jewish?" Ilse asked. "The Party, I mean? Your papers—"

Müller shook his head. "My stepmother is listed on my birth certificate. My father fixed it. So there is no suspicion. And besides, who would expect a Jew to show up looking for a job in the German secret service? Much the same idea as hiding in one's own attic whilst Nazi officers move in downstairs," he added, inclining his head at Ilse. "Sometimes the best place to hide is the last place anyone would look."

They were all quiet for a while, each sorting through their own thoughts.

Müller cleared his throat. "I find this a relief, truth be told, to have everything out in the open. Far less skulking around in the shadows for everyone. And now you, Fräulein Kaplan, can come down out of the attic. That can't have been pleasant or comfortable."

Ilse's eyes were glassy, but she had finally found her voice. "This is my *home*," she said. "I've been a silent prisoner in my *own home.* You took it over, threw parties. Put up a Christmas tree." She gesticulated at the candlelit fir. "I've been grieving my family in a dark attic whilst you slept in my parents' bed and ate at their table."

Müller was solemn. "I am sorry," he said. "Truly. You must believe me. I had no idea you were here. I—"

"Will you leave?" Ilse asked.

"Excuse me?"

"Will you leave, now that you know who we are? This is *my* home."

Müller's gaze flicked from Ilse to Audrey and back again. "Forgive me, but what recourse do you have for income if I leave? Who will pay to heat your home, put food on your table?" His tone was stern, but not unkind.

"Could you not access my father's funds for us? Are they—"

"All Jewish businesses have been seized by the government," Müller said. "Your father's wealth is now the property of the Third Reich."

"What about when my mother and brother return?" Ilse demanded. "What then?"

Müller swallowed, his Adam's apple bobbing up and down beneath his clean-shaven throat. "I do not think it fair or compassionate to lead you into a thicket of false hope." He paused. "I think it is unlikely they will return. If they do, it will certainly not be anytime soon."

Ilse fixed him with a hard stare. "Unlikely."

"Yes."

"But possible?"

Müller shifted one of his glossy shoes. "Possible, yes. I suppose."

Ilse straightened. "Fine. Then I will hold on to my hope, no matter how deluded you may find it. This is my family. And if they return, I will expect you to leave."

Audrey marveled at her friend's uncharacteristic assertiveness, then glanced at Müller for his reaction. But he said nothing.

Ilse rose from her seat. "I'm going to have a proper bath. It's been weeks."

As she made her way toward the stairs, Audrey found herself locked in an internal battle. Her loyalty told her to go with Ilse, but she was desperate to know more from Müller. Everything had changed. Audrey stayed where she was.

"Is there any way for you to find out where they've been taken?" she asked quietly. "Ilse's family?"

"I can try," Müller said. "But I make no promises. To be frank, the father might be the lucky one. A bullet to the head is far more humane than what may await the rest of the family at the camps."

Despite the heat from the fire, a shiver snuck up Audrey's spine. "What are the camps like? You only told me they were meant to be permanent."

Müller shot back his last dose of liquor. "That isn't a conversation for tonight, Fräulein," he said, and the hollowness in his eyes frightened her nearly as much as the gun in his hand had.

"I think the hope of them returning has been all that's kept Ilse going," she said.

"Then we shall let her keep going." He seemed to consider something. "You clearly care deeply for your friend."

Audrey's heart swelled. "Yes. She's my family."

Müller pulled a hand through his hair again. There was conflict in his eyes, which made sense now that she knew more about her mysterious housemate. "I think now that we have come clean with one another, we need to consider what happens next," he said.

"I agree." Audrey was happy to move on from the topic of her feelings for Ilse.

"In the morning, you will need to call the regular police to report Vogt's death. You'll need to do it before I've finished breakfasting and left the house."

"Why me?"

"Because you are the least likely suspect. You're a small woman, a dutiful housekeeper. You're attractive and young enough to garner sympathy. Just be sure to act shocked and put on some hysterics if you can." Müller studied her. "You fooled me for a time, Fräulein. You are well suited to the dramatics. Tell them you went out to fetch the milk and found his body on the pavement, nothing more. The fewer details, the better. Liars always say too much."

Audrey nodded. She was still trying to grasp all that had transpired, reaching for the details like marbles scattered in all directions. She remembered the blood on the floor upstairs. It would need to be cleaned before Ilse took her room back. But they could share the bed in Audrey's old guest room for tonight. In the morning, she'd call the police. And then what? She looked down at her glass, decided to drink it after all. She knocked it back, tasting the bitter orange, vanilla, and spice.

"You said there are other resistance groups?" she asked.

"A few. We have a distant relationship with one other group. It isn't centralized though. Its members hail from all over Germany and Holland, whereas ours is Berlin based," he said. "I would imagine it has its advantages, though, to be spread out. Less chance of discovery. But much more difficult to communicate without being exposed. There isn't any kind of organization," he continued. "It's all very fractured, different groups advocating for different things. But the SS refers to all the cells collectively as the Red Orchestra."

"Why the Red Orchestra?"

"The people in my office, the counterintelligence officers, suspect some of the resisters have ties to the Soviets. And they may be right. But they have no idea how deep this runs within their own ranks. It is my job to divert and distract them, to prevent them from learning the true extent and identity of the resisters here."

Audrey felt a tingle of something at the thought of these clusters of resistance. "What's your objective then?"

Müller met her eyes. "To kill Adolf Hitler."

Chapter 14

Audrey

BERLIN, GERMANY | DECEMBER 1938

Audrey woke suddenly the following morning, as though a loud noise had roused her. She opened her eyes into the darkness of the winter dawn, blinking several times until she made sense of where she was.

It was her old room, the Kaplans' guest room, and all was quiet. Ilse was still asleep beside her, her form rising and falling softly beneath the quilt. For one short-lived moment, Audrey forgot why they were in the guest room together, but then the events of the previous night crashed over her like an icy wave.

Vogt's breath on her face.

Ilse raising the lamp.

Müller's revelation and the Red Orchestra . . .

It was all too much. Curling her body in closer to Ilse's, she pulled the blanket up around her neck and took a steadying breath.

"*Kill him?*" she'd asked Müller last night, incredulous.

"Yes," he'd replied. "He's a madman. He's going to destroy Germany, and who knows how many other countries along with it. He's driving us into another great war within Europe, make no mistake."

"But how do you kill someone like that?" she'd asked him. "It seems impossible."

The whole regime of the Third Reich was so grand in scale, they breathed Hitler like an intoxicant. He was larger than life.

Müller had smirked, eyes hard. "He is not a god, Fräulein. He is only a man. Flesh and bone and blood, just like you or me. Any man can be destroyed. All you need is the right weapon."

But where did that leave Audrey and Ilse? Audrey looked at her friend. They hadn't lain awake whispering the way they would have years ago. There was much more to talk about now than there ever had been before, but it was all so complicated, so violent, that it was difficult to find the words.

At least Ilse would be free to move about the house now. She had been clear she wouldn't leave Germany without knowing Ruth and Ephraim's fate, but they couldn't live in the house with Müller indefinitely; they couldn't wait around for the end of Hitler's rule.

Action. That's what was needed. A plan.

Audrey could provide emotional support to Ilse in the best way she knew how, but her role in their relationship had always veered toward what she could *do.* That was the sphere in which she was most comfortable, where she knew herself best. But what to do now? Audrey felt as though she had only just secured her footing from the tectonic shift of that fateful day at the department store, and now here they were again, scrambling to steady themselves on a ship that kept pitching in stormy seas.

The Kaplan fortune had been stolen by the Reich, but Audrey would have access to her father's money in England. If they could only get to London, they could live in the Kensington house together until—Audrey's throat tightened at the thought—Ilse eventually married. Her mind turned over possibilities, then she remembered something Müller had said the night before.

Tucking the quilt around Ilse, she slid out of bed and dressed quietly. In the hall, she caught the aroma of coffee. It was early, but Müller was already up.

She found him sitting in the kitchen, steam curling from his cup, but before she could say good morning, he spoke.

"You should call the police straightaway. Before the post or the milk arrives. It's still dark, but once it's light, someone else will find him."

"Oh." Audrey's stomach turned, remembering Vogt's body outside. She hoped she would never see anything that grisly again. "Yes. Of course."

"Don't forget the theatrics," he said with a wry smile.

Audrey went to the telephone room and dialed the number for the police. As the line rang, she tapped into the mindset of a woman who had just found her employer dead on the pavement outside the house. With false alarm in her voice, she reported Vogt's body, then hung up and returned to the kitchen.

"It's done," she told Müller. "They're on their way over though. We haven't long."

"They will interview you, ask questions," Müller said. "Stick to the story. You know almost nothing. You retired before Vogt returned home last night, and you came out to get the milk this morning and found him outside the house. Leave it at that."

"All right," Audrey said.

"I will take care of the rest."

He'd made toast in her absence, something she'd never seen him do. He pushed a plate and pot of jam toward her. Gingerly, she took a seat across from him, another first, and tucked into her breakfast. He and Vogt had always sat at the dining table to eat, she in the kitchen or—unbeknownst to them—upstairs with Ilse. Their relationship had altered overnight, the entire dynamic of the house tilted onto an unfamiliar angle.

She took a sip of her coffee. It was good and strong. "You make it better than I do," she admitted with a reluctant smile.

"You're not much of a cook, really, Fräulein, I am sorry to say."

Audrey barked a laugh, then pinched her lips shut. Everything felt too serious for amusement right now. "I'm not, no, Herr Müller. Difficult to bluff that one, I'm afraid. But I did my best."

"I think you can call me Friedrich now," he said, finishing his coffee. "I would be far more comfortable if we dispensed with the formalities at this juncture."

"All right." She nibbled her toast. "I know we haven't much time, but I wonder if I could ask you something."

He watched her, but said nothing, which she took as an invitation.

"Last night, did you say Aldous is a forger?"

Müller nodded. "His father owns a print shop, so he has easy access to the required materials."

"Do you think he could forge a passport for Ilse? So I could get her back to London?"

Müller sat back in his chair. "I could approach him about it."

"Even for a Jew? He'd have to know, wouldn't he?"

"Yes. I do not think he would care, but I will need to consider this. However, it seemed clear to me last night that Fräulein Kaplan will not leave until she knows for certain what has become of her family."

Audrey sighed. "But you said you would try to find them."

"And I will. You have my word. Though it may take some time, and I told you both, I suspect the outcome will not be what she hopes for."

"Thank you." In the meantime, she would continue to chip away at Ilse's resolve to stay, even if her efforts proved futile. Audrey paused, surveyed Müller. His hair was speckled grey at the temples, one ear slightly higher than the other. "What's it like for you?" she ventured. "Doing what you do. Your double life?"

He chewed his cheek, his moustache twisting to the side. "It's . . ."

He shook his head. "It is impossible. I betray myself every day. Do you know what that's like?"

Audrey held his gaze and thought of Ilse. She knew that her feelings were more than friendship. Every day she tamped them down, fought them. Sometimes it felt as though she were wearing someone else's skin.

"In a way, yes," she said.

They sat for a while, and the kitchen was silent but for the tick of the clock near the door until a loud knock sounded from the foyer.

After the police left, Audrey went back upstairs to check on Ilse. She'd slept late, and Audrey was glad of it. Ilse hadn't had anything resembling a decent night's sleep in weeks, up in the chilly attic with no proper mattress.

"Ilse?" she murmured, opening the curtains with a swish. Weak winter sunlight filled the cool room.

Ilse rolled over. "Hi."

Despite the chaos of last night, she looked more rested than she had in a long time. She was such a beautiful person, though she never thought so herself.

When Audrey perched on the end of the bed, Ilse sat up, adjusted the neck of her ivory nightgown. "What is it?" she asked.

Audrey told her about the police interview, which was short and to the point. As Müller had instructed, she'd kept it straightforward, and after they'd taken her statement, the police spoke with him for several more minutes, cutting Audrey out of the conversation entirely. She was only the help, after all.

"Müller thinks they bought it," she said. "Vogt had a reputation, and a bar fight gone sour is entirely in line with his normal behaviour."

Audrey's thoughts were full of Vogt, and she wondered how long it would take to shake the unpleasant images that flashed in her mind every time she closed her eyes. "Hopefully that's it. I'm so sorry, again, that you had to do that. And thank you. It never should have happened."

"No," Ilse agreed. "But it did get us here, didn't it? I don't have to hide anymore. When Mama and Ephraim come back, Müller will move out, and . . ." Her lip began to tremble. "And that wouldn't have been possible if the situation hadn't pushed Müller to reveal himself. I'm grateful for that, at least."

"Ilse . . ." Audrey met Ilse's eyes, imploring. "Müller says one of the men in the resistance cell—Aldous—is a forger. He can falsify *passports*."

"No. Audrey, I told you, I can't. I need to know they're okay. I need to stay. And now it's more feasible for me to do so. I needn't freeze and hide."

Audrey took a deep breath. It was the answer she expected. She was restless to know what had become of Ruth and Ephraim, too, but her primary concern was Ilse's safety, and remaining in Berlin under Hitler's rule when there was a chance to get her to England felt like a gamble against a house that was holding all the cards.

"Müller says he's going to try to find out where they were taken," she said. "He gave me his word."

Ilse brightened. "Really?"

"Yes."

"And then maybe they can come home? He could have them released?"

Audrey thought of Müller's warnings as she looked down at the bedcovers—an old quilt sewn by Ruth's mother. It was a mercy, perhaps, that she had died a few years ago. She never had to witness the destruction of her family tree. "I don't know, Ilse. You could ask him."

"I will," she said. "So, what do we do today, then? Or tomorrow, or the next day." Ilse choked out a sarcastic laugh. "I could take over some of the domestic tasks, if you like. I know you hate all of it, and it would give me something to do."

Audrey was glad to see any vestige of humour in her. "I won't say no to that. You're a better cook than I am, anyway."

"I let Matya teach me. You never listened when Sophie tried."

Audrey smiled, but the thought of Sophie clenched at her heart. "I miss her. I wonder often how her family is faring. I hope they'll be safe from this madness in Belgium."

Ilse nodded sadly. "And you? You could finish your studies at the *konservatorium*," she said.

Audrey looked up, surprised. "Maybe someday, but not now. It doesn't feel right, after everything that's happened."

"Well . . . Audrey, *you* can still return to England. I'm safe here now, to some degree, with Müller. You can go, if you need to. I told you before, when your father passed—"

"Do you *want* me to go? Why do you keep—"

"You know I don't. You know I want you with me. I'd be terrified without you, truly. But I also feel like I can't ask you to stay now that things have changed so much."

Audrey fought the urge to lean forward and kiss her. "Ilse, I've told you, I *cannot* leave you. For the same reason you can't leave until you know what's happened to your mama and Ephraim. I will *not* leave you here. I—" Audrey stood and began to pace the creaking floorboards, fists clenched, the nails digging into her palms. "I love you, Ilse."

"I love you too. But what's—?"

"No." Audrey stopped, her breathing shallow. The words erupted from her in a burst. "I *love* you."

Ilse's brow furrowed, and then understanding spread slowly across her features, like wine seeping into a tablecloth. Her shoulders dropped, and she exhaled slowly.

"Oh."

The heat of the moment was overwhelming, and Audrey needed to douse it. They could not talk about this. They couldn't. She needed to control it, pretend that nothing had just passed between them.

"Audrey—" Ilse began, her voice soft, but Audrey cut across her.

"I need to do something useful, if you're going to do the housekeeping," she said, pacing the room once more as she tried to steer the conversation away from the eye of the storm. "I can't play the goddamn piano all day, waiting for this to end."

"What—what do you mean?" Ilse shook her head slowly, as though working to follow Audrey's train of thought.

"I don't know. But I need some sort of occupation."

Ilse looked at Audrey as though she were made of glass. "Could you help Müller in some way? Does their group need any kind of . . . I don't know . . . assistance?"

Audrey seized the suggestion, grateful that Ilse was following her lead. "Such as?"

Ilse shrugged. "Reconnaissance? Maybe you could help with that, with your skills. You were prepared to do it at the bank, right? Pretend to be someone else? You could put your theatrical training to use here. If you're staying," she added with a shadow of hesitation.

Audrey cleared her gummy throat, nodded. "I'll—I'll talk to him today. See if I can be of help." She needed to leave, to be alone with her spinning thoughts. "I'll see you downstairs later."

"Audrey, we should talk—"

"No," Audrey said, forcing a smile through her lips to stop them trembling. "Because there's nothing to talk about, is there?"

Ilse dropped her gaze, her voice hollow. "No. I suppose there isn't."

Chapter 15

Audrey

BERLIN, GERMANY | JANUARY 1939

"Are you nervous, Fräulein?" Friedrich asked, finishing his drink.

Across from him on the divan, Audrey realized her foot was jiggling, and stilled it. "I suppose so, yes."

"You've met them all before, though."

"I know, but this is different. You're asking them to trust me now. Not only trust me, but let me take part. I lied about who I was for months."

"And *that* right there will be the sell. Your ability to take on the character. As you said, you managed to dupe Vogt and me for a long time. You might have continued to, if not for . . ."

"Vogt."

"Yes."

Tonight wasn't all that different from the night of Vogt's death, when Audrey and Friedrich sat across from each other, revealing themselves. She'd had difficulty believing what he was saying that night; that there was any kind of resistance against Hitler at all, let alone within the SS ranks. And now she was waiting for a group of them to arrive and decide whether she was a worthy foot soldier in a fight that felt both imperative and utterly futile.

After Ilse's suggestion, she'd sat at the piano and let her fingers play automatically whilst her mind ruminated on how to broach it with Friedrich, and what she might be useful for, trying desperately to block out thoughts of what had just come to light with Ilse. She thought of administrative tasks, but surely the cell wouldn't keep records of anything. Then her thoughts went to her father and his reconnaissance flights, how he had worked to gather information for the Allies from the air, details that would help the infantry on the ground to push back against the country he would come to call home after meeting the love of his life. With a stab of regret, she thought how he might have even been proud to know his daughter was taking action.

When Friedrich returned from work, she cornered him in the sitting room to ask whether she might help the resistance effort, perhaps do some reconnaissance herself. "I think your outfit could benefit from a woman," she'd said.

Friedrich sat back in Ephraim's chair by the fire, crossed one leg over the other. "Why would a woman be helpful?" he'd asked. His brown eyes lingered on her face, but his gaze didn't burn like Vogt's had. It was a brusque assessment, not predatory.

Audrey had tapped her finger on the edge of her cup, searching for the words. "Women are far less suspect. We form the background of men's lives," she'd said, thinking of maids and servants, whose worth was defined by how inconspicuous and small they could make themselves. She thought of how the police had turned to Friedrich for explanation of Vogt's discovery, ignoring her entirely once a man was present. "Women exist *around* you, behind you. We're rarely the subject of the painting itself."

Friedrich had scoffed, though not unkindly. "Underestimated, you mean."

"Precisely," Audrey said, one eyebrow cocked, a little surprised that he had arrived at the conclusion so quickly. "I've never embraced that invisibility. If you need confirmation, ask Ilse. I want to be on a stage one day, performing. It's what I love. Let me help. Whatever you need."

Friedrich had agreed. He'd told the group that Audrey had sussed them out but was sympathetic to their cause and might be of use. He was honest with them about her dual residency and English father, but had omitted anything about Ilse. As far as they were concerned, the cover story still stood: she had been Ira Kaplan's accountancy assistant and upon his death, accepted the housekeeping job to make ends meet.

Now, Audrey shifted her shoulders. "And what have you told them about Vogt's death? Don't they have questions?"

"They had no difficulty believing the story we fed the police. Vogt was such an ass, no one has particularly missed him inside the administration. Meanwhile, the police are out halfheartedly chasing the phantom assailants we conjured. Leave them to me. I do not believe it will be a problem."

She had no choice but to trust him. This was either the best idea she'd had or the worst. Either way, it kept her mind from lingering on Ilse's baffled face when Audrey had confessed her feelings. They'd tiptoed around each other since then, neither of them mentioning it, and their conversations had been surface-level. It made Audrey feel as though she were falling away from herself.

But she didn't have time to dwell on it further as the other members of the resistance cell arrived. Claus, Ludwig, and Aldous each eyed Audrey with interest as they entered the room, but said nothing.

Once they were all settled with drinks, Friedrich stood, cleared his throat. "As you all know, this is Audrey James, my housekeeper. And she has approached me with a proposal to join our outfit."

She studied them with a new curiosity, eager to know more about this group of men who were risking their careers and their very lives to resist the Führer.

"Hello," she said, smiling.

"Nice to meet you more, uh, officially? Truthfully?" Claus said, cocking his head to one side on his thick neck.

"Audrey, Claus Von Holten," Friedrich said. "He works in weaponry in the military training office. You know Ludwig Thurman," he continued. "He's from the military operations office of the SS."

Ludwig directed a curt nod at Audrey from over near the sideboard, though he said nothing. He took a large gulp from his rocks glass.

"And Aldous Stoltz." Friedrich nodded to the weedy man on the opposite end of the divan. Audrey had rarely heard him speak at their poker nights. "He's, well . . . what would you say you are, Al?"

The man shrugged. "The kinder term is 'conscientious objector,' I think. We're deemed cowards for not entering military service. But I'm lame from a bout of polio when I was a child, so they wouldn't have me anyway. People like me are a threat to 'national health,' according to Goebbels. I figure I'll be next once they've ejected all the Jews and homosexuals."

Audrey's jaw clenched at the word. How did the government even know who was a homosexual?

"So I thought it necessary to do what I could," Aldous was saying. "My motivation isn't entirely altruistic, Fräulein. You'll have to forgive me."

"And then there was Vogt, of course, whom you knew," Ludwig said in a booming voice. "He would have been able to keep providing us intelligence from within Hitler's own office, if the moron hadn't gotten himself beaten to death." He took another swig of his drink. "Probably fucked the wrong man's wife this time."

"Lud, language around the lady, yeah?" Friedrich said.

Audrey winced at Ludwig, hoping it would pass for a sympathetic frown.

Claus sat forward, broad shoulders rolling in. "So, Fred tells us you can contribute some particular skills to our little organization here."

Audrey nodded. "I do hope so."

"And what exactly is it that you can bring to the table?"

Four sets of acute male eyes bored into her own.

She straightened. "For one thing, I'm fluent in both English and German, and I'm a performer. A trained one. A good one," she added with confidence. "And I'm a woman, which means I go unnoticed." She summarized the arguments she had made to Friedrich.

"How much did you learn whilst serving up bread and beer, Fräulein?" Claus asked.

She could tell by the set of his face that he was genuinely curious. "Enough to know what you were doing and ask Friedrich if I could join. In addition to listening in, I can flirt my way into places where I'm not supposed to be," she said, glancing around at them all. "Can any of you say the same?"

Claus chuckled.

"My concern, Fräulein James," Ludwig began in his deep voice, shifting his massive weight from one foot to the other, "is what your set of skills adds up to."

"What do you mean?"

"In my line of work, I would have serious concerns about someone who can speak multiple languages, who acts and lies to get himself into or out of sticky situations, and who possesses a proclivity for passing unnoticed. You are describing a spy."

She felt pinned under his sharp gaze. "I'm not—"

"You are speaking to a group of exceptionally observant men. You may have underestimated us."

"Ludwig, we have been over this," Friedrich said sharply. "I told you, she—"

"Are you a fool?" Ludwig shot back. His eyes flashed with anger and something else, something sinister. "Did you bed her? Is that how she convinced you of her innocence?"

Audrey's cheeks burned at the insinuation. She glanced at Friedrich, then back to Ludwig.

"You're right," she said, doing her best to match the intensity of his distrustful glare. "I am not precisely who he says I am." She could feel Friedrich's eyes on her, but ploughed on. "I was not Ira Kaplan's accountancy secretary." The men stared back at her with confused faces, and she realized they didn't recognize his name. "He is the dead man whose furniture you now sit on," she snapped. "Whose crystal you drink from. He was murdered in the street." She needed to offer Ludwig a clearer truth to dispel his doubt, but she would not tell them about Ilse. A half-truth would have to suffice. "I was in this house when Friedrich and Vogt arrived because I am a friend of the family. I was living here when Kaplan was killed and his family taken. I grieve the loss of my friends, and I do not want others to suffer the same fate. That is why I want to join you."

The room was silent for a moment. Audrey swallowed the lick of fear that flicked in her throat.

"And when did you learn this?" Ludwig asked Friedrich, ignoring Audrey.

"Not long after Vogt died, I suppose it was," he said, offhand.

"Did he know the truth of her as well?"

"No."

"How did you find out?"

"She told me," Friedrich said, defiant. "Ludwig, we—"

"Why?" Ludwig demanded.

Audrey could tell that interrogation was a part of Ludwig's job. She wondered how many times he had played interrogator, how persuasive he had been, what other tools he had in his arsenal for extracting the truths he sought.

"We got to talking," Friedrich said. Audrey could tell he was agitated, casting about for a story to tell in place of the truth about Vogt and Ilse. "It became clear that we were very much on the same side. You don't need to know the details."

"Do we not?" Claus this time.

"No," Friedrich said loudly. "Suffice it to say that she is on our side. And she is valuable. Have we interrogated one another about how we came to resist this regime?" he asked his comrades. "No, we haven't. It is enough that each man is here."

"All right," Claus said after a while, still watching Audrey. "I'm convinced."

"As am I," Aldous added.

"Good," said Friedrich, exhaling his frustration.

Ludwig would not look at her.

A moment passed in which everyone refreshed their drinks, clearly an attempt to regroup after the tension of the argument. There appeared to be consent that she could participate, but Audrey knew Ludwig would be on the lookout for the smallest misstep on her part, any reason to prove Friedrich wrong for having divulged their secrets and let her join. Why was it that women always had to work harder than men to prove themselves?

"So what did you have in mind, Fred?" Claus asked, sitting down beside Audrey now. Aldous retreated to a wing chair. "For the fräulein here."

Friedrich took a swig of his drink. "Nothing yet. We needed to propose her involvement to you first."

"You said she did an inventory of the house for you," Claus said, massaging his goatee with a meaty hand.

"You thinking Weber?" Ludwig grunted at him.

"Yes," Claus said.

But Friedrich was frowning. "We're not throwing her to that swine," he said firmly. "We'll find somewhere else."

"But that's *exactly* why this might be the best way we can use her," Claus said.

They argued for another full minute. Audrey was beginning to feel like a child, shunted to the side of an adult conversation. She watched the men talk around her again before her irritation bubbled over.

"Who is Weber?" she demanded.

They all turned to face her, as though surprised to find her still in the room.

"He manages the Department of Property Reclamation in the Ministry of Economics," Friedrich said.

"What's that?" she asked.

"The government branch responsible for assessing Jewish valuables and real estate and dispersing them."

Audrey flexed her fingers. "So that's how you got this house. They sent you here?"

He nodded, his expression apologetic.

"And you did an inventory of the property, Fräulein. Correct?" Claus asked.

"Yes," she replied.

"We aren't sending her to Weber," Friedrich said again.

"Why not?" Claus pressed. "Look at her." He extended a hand, palm up, like a ringmaster. "She's perfect for it."

"Why?" Audrey asked.

Claus leaned toward her. "Weber's an easy mark for intel. He's got loose lips and even looser morals. And he has connections to Hitler. Back in the summer and autumn, Weber was at a couple of parties and dinners put on by Hitler's confidants—his driver, his secretaries. Vogt had good connections in Hitler's office, but we've lost that conduit now. And since that previous attempt on Hitler's life last year, his inner office has kept his schedule locked down tight. They only release the details, what, a day in advance?" He looked to Ludwig, who nodded.

"Someone tried to kill Hitler?" Audrey asked, shocked.

"A couple of times now," Friedrich said. "But they've been slapdash attempts with little forethought. To plan something effective, we need enough time. We need to know where he'll be and when, at least a few days ahead."

"Weber must hear things," Claus said. "With the right type of persuasion, he could be valuable."

"But why me specifically?"

"Weber is known for his . . . preference for young women," Friedrich said.

It took a beat before the penny dropped. "You want me to seduce him?" She thought of Vogt's prostitutes, the transactions, the fact that she'd never been with a man. The encounter with Vogt was still too fresh; it coloured her nightmares red. This wasn't what she'd thought she was signing up for. Spying was one thing, listening in, but—

"Not as such," Claus said. "But a little flirtation, some suggestion, could go a long way. You could endear yourself to him, see what you can find out. Just get him to talk."

She thought about what a little "suggestion" might lead to. "You mean bait him," she said.

"Yes."

The prospect put Audrey on edge. But her contempt for the Reich and need for action galvanized her. If this was something only she could do, then do it she would.

Ludwig spoke up. "How do we know she's capable?" He was leaning against the wall now. He raised his glass in Audrey's direction and the amber liquid swirled around. "She's just a girl; she could blow the whole operation. What happens if—"

"I can do it," Audrey interrupted, defiance shining in her eyes. She hadn't liked him from the first poker night, and knowing he was resisting Hitler's regime had not softened her distaste for him as it had the others.

"Excellent," Claus said, clapping. He grinned at Audrey. "This is good. This is good."

She returned the smile, but her eyes still sought Friedrich, whose face was dark, lips pressed together beneath his trimmed moustache. She knew him well enough now to see that he only wanted to spare her from another encounter like the fateful one with Vogt.

"But if you are to work with us, you must have a more German name," Claus said. "They'll never hire a buttery English girl to work at headquarters. They'll definitely think you're a spy."

Audrey raised an arched eyebrow.

"An *English* spy."

"But I'm half German," she protested. "Mostly German, really. I was born here. This is my home."

"Ira Kaplan was German, too," Friedrich said. "A person's name matters now. It has, in fact, come to mean everything. A man's name can determine whether he lives or dies."

The image of Ira's body flashed behind her eyes. Perhaps this was the next, natural step in truly becoming the character she had invented for Friedrich and Vogt. She would assume a new name when she was outside these four walls, slip into the skin of a lioness.

"I can sort that, no problem," Aldous piped up from the wing chair.

"How soon can you have them ready, Al?" Friedrich asked.

"A day. Maybe two." He addressed Audrey next. "You're sure about this?"

Audrey looked to Friedrich.

"Weber could prove highly useful," he said. "This could be the best opportunity we'll get to knock a wedge into his office."

"And anything I might learn could help you?" Audrey asked.

"Yes."

"To get rid of Hitler? To stop all of this?"

Claus sighed. "That's the goal."

Audrey smoothed her wool skirt, the fabric rough beneath her fingers. She thought of Ira, of the need for someone to avenge his pointless death. Of Ruth and Ephraim and who knew how many other Jews, imprisoned at these work camps. The reign of gunshots and swastikas and unbridled violence. The looming war that was certain to destroy the country she loved. Of Ilse. Her face—free and happy—shone brightest in Audrey's mind.

"Then yes," she said, unflinching now at the four sets of male eyes analyzing her, weighing her value and wondering if she would be worth the price. "I'm sure."

Chapter 16

Audrey

BERLIN, GERMANY | JANUARY 1939

Fräulein Jakob?"

Audrey turned at the sound of her newly minted name. She was Ada Jakob now, with a fresh set of identification papers in her pocketbook, carefully worn and handled by Aldous to appear several years old.

"Yes, Herr Weber?" Audrey asked.

Her new boss, Rolf Weber, was leaning against the door frame of his office. A tall yet distinctly porcine man, Weber was responsible for the Department of Property Reclamation, the government office in which Audrey was now employed as a Junior Inventory Specialist.

Once the cell had decided that Audrey should secure a position within the department to try to gather intelligence, Friedrich had told Weber all about Audrey's inventory of the Kaplan household before he and Vogt moved in, embroidering the details to amplify her skill set. Not that it would have mattered to Weber. He had taken one look at her and hired her on the spot.

"I need you and Schulze to go through the files from '38. Confirm, then collate the year-end figures," Weber was saying now. "Broken up by category. I need it by day's end. Then this afternoon you'll be going out with Ebner for on-site orientation."

"Yes, sir," Audrey replied. She'd been in training for several days, but this would be her first on-site assessment.

Johanna Ebner stood at her desk. "Might I have a private word, Herr Weber?" she asked.

"Yes, of course." He beckoned her into his office, and she followed, shutting the door behind her.

Alone, Audrey allowed herself to relax. Johanna was the Senior Inventory Specialist who had been overseeing Audrey's training. She was rather aloof but had been patient with Audrey, who couldn't help but note the resemblance between them. Audrey guessed the young women Weber employed were all slim and blond.

A *tsk* from reception piqued Audrey's ears and she walked through the doorway to find Frau Schulze, Herr Weber's secretary, at her desk shaking her head. Audrey guessed she was in her fifties. She had iron-grey hair, was built like an icebox, and gossiped worse than a fishwife, which Audrey hoped would come in handy. If Frau Schulze could supply useful information for the resistance, Audrey could keep her distance from Weber.

"Did you catch that?" Audrey asked. "About the numbers?"

"Yes. He's got some big meeting on the books for tomorrow. Guess they want a progress report. Come here, we'll see to it."

She crossed the room to a large beige filing cabinet and began withdrawing various folios. As Frau Schulze handed them to Audrey, she tried hard not to think about how many ruined Jewish lives the pile represented.

"He calls her in there a lot, doesn't he?" Audrey said quietly.

"Yes, it's rather obvious, isn't it?" Frau Schultze whispered. "I've walked in more than once to find him with his arm slipped around her waist. With all the advances he makes on her, it's a wonder he ever gets any work done. Though Johanna, she doesn't seem to mind."

"You don't say," Audrey mused. "But isn't Herr Weber married?"

"Oh yes, he is. Doesn't seem to make a jot of difference to him though. The one before Johanna—Ursula, her name was—finally had enough and left. To be frank with you, I'm glad I'm old enough to not be of any interest to him." She tutted again. "My advice? Make sure he keeps his hands where you can see them when you're in there alone, Ada, if you know what's good for you. Pretty thing like you, with eyes like that. Well, none of the girls he hires are ugly ducklings, now are they?"

Audrey turned her attention to the files in front of them, picking up one with the name COHEN. "So what's the big meeting tomorrow?" she asked, offhand. "That we're preparing all this for?"

Frau Schulze didn't glance up from her work. "There's to be a new decree in February. For the surrender of precious metals and stones in Jewish ownership. They're to turn them in."

Audrey thought of the stolen pile of Ruth's jewels and felt the familiar stab of rage, but she focused on her mission.

"Who's attending the meeting?" she asked, hoping Frau Schulze might know who Weber's associates were.

"Oh, the usual," she said with a wave. "So that'll be a whole other kettle of fish now," she continued. "You and Johanna will have to record the metals and stones specially. There'll be a new process for the reclamation because we'll need to compare your inventory to the property registry from last year. We can be sure a fair number of them lied. So more goddamn paperwork."

Audrey watched her, this unremarkable office worker in her blue blouse and grey skirt. She thought of how many small cogs like Frau Schulze there must be in government departments and the SS, all turning in unison to propel the limbs of this monstrous machine.

Frau Schulze caught herself and flashed Audrey a smile. "Don't mistake me, I'm not complaining. It's an honour to serve. Heil Hitler."

Audrey nodded, her head bobbing up and down like the puppet Ada Jakob was, wooden and hard and painted the colour of obedience.

"Heil Hitler," she said.

After lunch, Audrey plastered a smile on her face and went with Johanna to conduct an assessment of a Jewish home. As they walked along the snowy streets toward the upscale Mitte neighbourhood, their heels clicking fast on the pavement, Audrey tried her best to engage Johanna in conversation, but her colleague answered in single, passionless words. It occurred to Audrey that Johanna might not be as detached from the impact of what they were doing as she pretended to be, that the job might cost her something.

"Here we are," Johanna said finally, consulting the clipboard in her hand to confirm the address affixed to the large, stone row house before them. She withdrew a small envelope from a file on her clipboard and shook a key out of it. "And here you go."

Audrey fingered the bevelled brass key in her hand and considered who it belonged to. A father who pulled it out of his pocket as he ascended these same steps at the end of a long day of work? A wife whose thoughts were already focused on what to make for dinner when she turned it in the lock after returning from the market or synagogue? The key felt unfamiliar in Audrey's hand, as though she were wearing someone else's ring, and she wondered whether the owner would ever hold it in their hand again.

Once inside, she took in the surroundings.

Johanna brushed a stray blond hair off her forehead, then handed the clipboard to Audrey. "All right, Ada. It's pretty straightforward, though it requires an eye for detail. They want to know *everything*, so you'll list the contents of the home by room, just because that's easiest in the moment, then back at the office we'll recategorize them. I'll shadow you to make sure you don't miss anything. And you know we need to record the gold and jewels separately now."

The brusqueness with which Johanna spoke dispelled Audrey's earlier suspicion—or hope—that she was bothered by this.

"You'll need to learn this quickly." Johanna paused. "I'm resigning tomorrow. So, it'll just be you. Until he finds someone else."

"What? Why?" Audrey asked, surprised.

"It's time for me to move on," she said firmly.

A string of questions formed in Audrey's mind, but Johanna's expression was set. There would be no further inquiry. Audrey turned back to the room, wondering if Johanna's news had anything to do with Weber, and began to snip off the dangling threads of this family's life. She moved through the main floor and noted the tableau before her eyes: an unfinished meal in the dining room, forks and knives haphazardly strewn across the freshly starched lace tablecloth. The food hadn't yet begun to smell. The family must have been interrupted by the police in the middle of their dinner just last night. She could see, through the veil of the present, the family seated, talking about or perhaps ignoring the question of what would become of them. She could hear the pounding on the door as their fate demanded entry, see the wide, fearful eyes that snapped toward the hallway, knowing there was no possibility of escape.

The candles in the centre of the table were nothing but messy pools of hardened wax, burnt down to their nubs. Audrey imagined the unfinished plates of food lit in the glow from those candles as they burned into the night, lighting the table for no one, finally extinguishing and sending grey curls of smoke up to the ceiling in the early hours of the morning. She stared at the yellow wax and wondered where the family was at the moment the last candle went out. In a holding cell somewhere in the basement of the Gestapo headquarters on the Prinz-Albrecht-Strasse, a place people at work had talked around, but never about? On a train careening toward Dachau?

Aware that Johanna was watching her closely, Audrey forced herself to breathe. She was Ada now. She could not show emotion. She focused on the assessment, opening hutch drawers, inspecting the inventory of silverware, counting the crystal glasses, and noting the number of chairs at the table. With a steady hand, she filled out the survey.

Then she made her way upstairs. The upper floors were in less disarray than the dining room and sitting room. The bedrooms were much the same as those in the Kaplans' home, but young children lived here, four by the looks of it. Two rooms boasted two beds, each with toy chests at the feet. Audrey picked up a bear that was perched on one of the pillows. She ran her hand over it, let her own humanity seep through Ada's harsh exterior before placing it back down, hoping the child would return one day, cuddle it to sleep once more.

In the doorway, Johanna let out an odd noise, like a cough or cry.

"I'll meet you downstairs," she said to Audrey as she fled the room.

"Are you all right?" Audrey called.

She made a sound that Audrey took as an affirmative. With a sigh, Audrey completed her inventory of the second floor, then scanned her notes. An index of these people's lives, reduced to an itemized list.

Seating for 10 at dining table – cherry

Dinner service, silverware, crystal for 10

4 bedrooms

1 bathroom

3 crystal vases

2 crystal chandeliers

Pianoforte

4 pc bedroom set – oak

9 rugs

1 emerald ring – gold

1 set diamond earrings – gold
1 set cuff links – silver

These may have just been things, but they told a story, didn't they? Around that dining table that sat ten people, there were conversations, birthday celebrations, family arguments, and Passover dinners. In the bedrooms, childbirths and lovemaking. There were special occasions that called for pearl necklaces and cuff links. Music coaxed out of the pianoforte. Diamond earrings given from a husband to his wife on a special anniversary, never dreaming they would one day adorn the ears of anyone but his love.

Audrey knew the valuables would be assessed and distributed or left in place for an incoming officer, depending on Weber's instructions. The items would take on new identities then, generate new stories for imposter families as the rightful owners' memories turned to dust and eventually blew away.

Could she really do this? Could she go into these homes over and over, cataloguing the remnants of people's lives? If it meant finding some piece of information that would end this nightmare, she had to. She took a steadying breath, then went back downstairs to find Johanna. She was standing over the kitchen sink, and Audrey caught a whiff of vomit. Johanna looked up and began to cry.

"What's wrong?" Audrey asked. "Are you ill?"

"I only put up with it because I need the work. I don't even fancy him. But he offered me a pay rise, and my father's gone, and it's just me and my mum. She cleans houses, but it's not—and I don't—" She broke off in a fit of sobs, leaving Audrey scrambling to understand.

"What is it?" she asked. "What's he done?"

"It's *his* child. Rolf's. Herr Weber's."

Audrey glanced at her flat stomach. "You're—you're pregnant?" She knew very little about pregnancy beyond how it came to be. She didn't know it could make a woman sick.

Johanna nodded.

The hair rose on the back of Audrey's neck. Was this a trap? Had Johanna been told to concoct this story, fake her emotions to test Audrey's allegiance? She *had* disappeared into Weber's office for some mysterious conversation right after he'd mentioned the assessment. And wasn't Audrey doing the same? Fabricating lies to extract the truth. Still, her gut told her this might be real. And so she stepped out onto this high wire behind Johanna, balancing with enough care that she could still hop back to safety should the rope prove unstable.

"He didn't force you, did he?" she asked gently.

"No," Johanna gasped. "Not as such, anyway. But . . ." She pressed her lips together. "Men like that, these men in the higher ranks . . . they don't give you much choice. Not truly."

Vogt's face flickered.

Be a good girl, now.

Ludwig and Claus were right; this was Weber's routine. She wondered how many Johannas there were within the Party and the government administration, how many derailed lives and illegitimate babies, all because these men in power simply took whatever they wanted. Weber had made a career of appropriation in more ways than one.

Johanna fished a glass out of the cupboard, filled it with water, swished, and spat. She dabbed her face with a hand towel embroidered with someone else's initials.

"It's not just me," she said, sniffling. "There was Ursula, before me. I knew why she left, knew I was next. And I still let it happen."

"Oh?" Audrey prompted.

"It happened in bits and stages, before I really realized what he was doing. He picks us for what we look like, to impress those friends of his in the Führer's office. He's a bad man, and I'm a fool. It's your first week, Ada." Her little nose was swollen, eyes raw as a winter night. "If I were you, I would leave. Find a job elsewhere, any job that's not near him."

Audrey's mind spun far beyond the walls of the kitchen.

She'd been tasked with becoming the bait to Weber. That's what she'd agreed to do. Johanna's presence had allowed Audrey to remain at arm's length from him, and her departure meant Audrey's buffer from Weber's advances was gone—but it also opened the door to get closer to him, walk the razor's edge of seducing him *just* enough for him to let slip something that might be useful to the resistance. She would be next, just as Johanna had been after Ursula. An unnerving awareness engulfed her—who would be her own replacement? And why?

Johanna reached for Audrey's arm and held fast. "You seem like a nice girl. He *will* take advantage. Be careful."

Audrey's heart beat fast. The weight of her mission settled on her shoulders, pressing down like a hot iron, branding her.

"I will," she lied.

Chapter 17

Kate

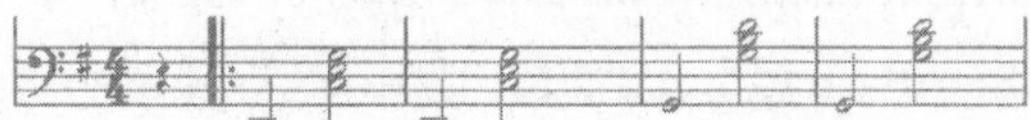

ALNWICK, ENGLAND | LATE NOVEMBER 2010

Kate can't stop thinking about Audrey's story as she scans old records in the Oakwood office. She's spent most of this cold, snowy morning digitizing the inn's files, finally getting somewhere with modernizing the administration after purchasing a brand-new scanner and shredder—neither of which Audrey had. She's begrudgingly allowed some progress—albeit with ample doses of grunts and frowns—but she's also seemed more preoccupied since she and Kate began their chats.

When Kate referred to her recorded experience as an interview last week, Audrey had scoffed. "Interviews are for employees and celebrities." Kate had tried "memoir," but Audrey flapped her hands and insisted on the term "chat," clearly preferring to keep her recollections to Kate firmly—though ostensibly—casual.

As she scans then shreds the yellowed, typewritten invoices, working her way backward through the 1980s, '70s, and now into the '60s, Kate considers the monochromatic monotony of her previous work at the insurance company—the grey carpets, Lego block furniture, and inane corporate culture—things that feel laughably inconsequential in comparison to Audrey's dive into the dark waters of the Third Reich. Kate's gut would swirl over pissing off her bland, inept manager, and here Audrey was, spying on the German government with a false set of papers as she conspired about the downfall of the system.

Kate had been astounded at Audrey's description of the Red Orchestra. "But why have I never heard of any of this?" she'd asked.

Audrey had shrugged, scratched her scalp. "I don't write the history books, dear. And I've never met anyone who does. Have you? Makes you wonder where they get it all from."

As Kate feeds the paper through the shredder—a task that's immensely satisfying—she glances at the mess of pens, letters, and scrap paper across Audrey's desk. She can't quite believe how sloppy this office is. It's evident that Sue never comes in here to clean. Either because it's too untidy or because Audrey refuses, Kate isn't quite sure, but she suspects the latter. Kate has always had a tidy and meticulous nature. *A place for everything, and everything in its place*, as her mum used to say. No anxious last-minute searching, no questions. Nothing missed or lost. It was one of the things that made her and Adam a good match at the time.

She pulls the manila folder for 1968 out of the old metal filing cabinet against the back wall, and her stomach lurches with excitement. The year of her parents' honeymoon. Shoving some stationery detritus aside, she splays the file out and shuffles through, searching for the invoice from her parents' stay. She's sure it's nothing special, not a handwritten note like her dad's entry in the guest book, but it's another piece of the picture, another thread of connection to the Oakwood, this place that's starting to feel like home. She sifts through the file, but doesn't see their names.

"Hm."

Brow crinkled, Kate double-checks, but still, nothing. She pauses on the last invoice in the file, notices it's been misfiled. This one is from January 1969. She sighs, unsurprised that Audrey's record keeping hasn't exactly been scrupulous. Maybe she'll find her parents in the 1967 folder. Or maybe, she thinks with a prickle of irritation, she already shredded it with the 1969 batch. She hadn't really paid attention to the details of the invoices, but she's sure their names would have jumped out at her.

"Ah, here you are." Audrey's face appears in the doorway.

At the sight of the shredder, she gives an affected shudder, as though Kate were disposing of animal entrails and not decades-old paper. Kate only barely refrains from rolling her eyes.

"The toilet in the hall is on the blink. I rang Ian to come take a look at it," Audrey says.

"What's wrong with it? It was working fine earlier."

Audrey pinches her lips the way she does when she doesn't like a question. "No idea. That's why Ian's coming round."

He arrives within an hour, brushes a dusting of snow off his wool coat, then hangs it in the hall closet. The battered toolbox in his hand is starkly at odds with his crisp khakis and tweed blazer. He moves about the Oakwood with a comfortable familiarity that somehow doesn't overstep or presume.

He greets Kate with a genuine smile. "Nice to see you again so soon." His glasses fog up a little in the warmth of the foyer.

"You, too," Kate says. She realizes she means it, and it takes her a beat to recognize the feeling in her gut.

"So, it's the toilet, this time, yeah?"

Kate clears her throat. "Yes."

She follows him down the hall, then leans against the door frame and watches as he removes the tank's lid and peers inside. His brow wrinkles in concentration for a minute or two.

"Hm. Interesting."

Kate waits for the diagnosis. "What is?"

"It looks like the chain has just been pulled out. I have no idea how that would happen unless someone was mucking about with it. But you haven't had any guests, have you?"

"No. Just us."

"And you haven't touched this?"

"I don't make a habit of fiddling with toilet tanks, generally," Kate says.

"Well, I can't see how it happened. But at any rate, it needs a new chain. I can pop by with one later."

As they return to the front hall, Audrey comes out of the office. She braces her weight with one hand on the wall, her stature stooping slightly.

"Ian!" she says, flashing him a tight smile, almost pained. "My dear boy, how are you?"

He sets the toolbox down and she pulls him into a hug, kisses his cheek as though she were indeed his own gran.

"Do you have a moment?" she asks him in an undertone.

He glances at Kate, then steps into the office. The door shuts with a soft thud and Kate moves into the sitting room, where Ozzie and Sophie are cuddled together.

Twenty minutes later, Audrey calls, "Lunch, Kate?"

Kate smiles. Anything Audrey asks her to do falls into that awkward ditch between a request and a direction.

"Ian is joining us," Audrey says.

"Audrey," Kate hears Ian protest, "I don't—"

"Don't be ridiculous, dear, you're staying."

In the dining room, Audrey appears as stoic as ever, but Ian looks distinctly rattled and his nose is pink. He remains quiet as they munch on a quick meal of tomato soup and cheese sandwiches, despite Kate's attempts to catch his eye. She wonders what sort of exchange occurred to elicit this reaction from him. Audrey peppers Kate with suspicious questions about the new electronic filing system, then announces her need for a nap and heads upstairs, patting Ian's arm on the way by. Sophie follows at her heels.

Ozzie looks rather lonesome and lost without his constant companion, and Ian is still acting odd.

"I thought I might take Oz out for a good walk around the grounds," Kate says, taking their dishes over to the sink. "Want to join? Or are you heading out?"

Ian nods tightly. "Yeah, that'd be great actually. I need some air."

Ozzie's tail pounds against the hallway rug as they pull their coats on. Outside, the snow has stopped, leaving a thick dusting of fluffy white over the sweeping grounds. The smell of smoke from the chimney emits the scent of pine and nostalgia.

They forge a new path in the crisp surface of the snow. Some crows call out in the distance, protesting Ozzie's presence as the three of them loop around the edge of the woods.

"So," Ian says, stepping into conversation. "How are your talks going with Audrey?"

Kate turns her coat collar up against the cold. "It's been good. I took your suggestion, and she agreed to tell me. I'm recording her so I can transcribe the whole thing later, and taking some notes too. We've developed a good rhythm." She describes how they sit down after lunch or dinner nearly every day, how open Audrey's been. "Every time she tells me she's done for the day, I'm always left with more questions."

Kate has done her best not to push, but there's no denying that these talks have fundamentally shifted their relationship. The stories that fall from Audrey's aging lips seem to linger in the air of the Oakwood from day to day, like the scent of strong spices wafting from a kitchen. Enticing, and certainly not unwelcome, but undeniably distracting for them both.

"She seemed a bit mysterious with you today, though," Kate says. "Mind if I ask what that was about?"

Ian exhales, fogging the air. "She told me she's been talking to you about Berlin, and the war. She didn't say much about the details, though."

Ozzie barks at a sparrow that's landed on a nearby tree.

"Yeah, I sense a hesitation," Kate says. "Like she's scared to talk about it, but needs to."

"We need to do the shit that scares us though," Ian says. "Especially, well . . ." He shrugs. "I guess she won't be around forever, right?"

Kate acknowledges the hard truth. "At least I feel like I'm really getting to know her now, and the people from her past too." She thinks of Ilse, of the massive sacrifices and risks Audrey took to keep her safe. "She had a great love before she came back to England. Before your granddad."

"Yeah?"

"Yeah. And she was brave. My God, she was so brave." Kate stuffs her cold hands deep into her coat pockets. "I'll be honest, it's made me consider the narrow parameters of my own life."

"How so?"

"She was audacious, daring. Especially for her time. She defied so many conventions placed on women back then. And I've just . . ."

University. Unstimulating office jobs. Marriage. A plan for children that never materialized. Kate was never one for the spotlight—she hated it even at her own wedding—whilst Audrey leapt enthusiastically into the glare, ready to put on a show when duty called for it. Audrey led such a big life. When you live a small life, then lose some of the people at the centre of that limited circle, it has a way of isolating you in short order. Bigger lives with greater reach have more tethers binding them to the ground. If one of them gets cut, you don't need to feel quite so vulnerable. There's still plenty to hold on to. Kate lost so many people, so quickly. Her parents, her husband, her few friends and coworkers. Everyone disappeared, in some way, in the aftermath of the accident, consumed by the dark vacuum that follows tragedy. Her friends were good people who just didn't know what to say. Didn't know how to handle something so broken.

"Audrey's remarkable, that's all," she says.

"She is," Ian agrees, watching her.

Kate remembers his own losses, wonders if he's ever felt this unnerving sort of weightlessness too. "She's like family to you, eh?"

He nods.

"I'm sorry about your brother. The Huntington's gene. Audrey told me."

Ian stares down at the snow. "She's a closed book with a big mouth, that one. Full of contradictions," he adds. "Doug's not sick yet. But he will be. It's a time bomb. No one knows when it'll hit. He decided he didn't want to have kids. Didn't want to risk passing on the disease. But his wife wanted children. She left him last year. He acts like he's dead already, really. It's like he's just waiting for the beginning of the end."

Kate feels a stab of guilt. She didn't intend for them to veer into such dark topics, but Ian has proved he isn't one for small talk.

"My mum didn't want us taking the test, but we both felt we had to know," he continues. "I just wish we'd both had the same result, regardless of what it was."

"I'm so sorry, Ian. That must feel terrible."

His Adam's apple slides up and down as he swallows the pain. A strong wind blows from the north. The snow has started up again.

"It feels like . . ." He faces her. "Like I've cheated death somehow." He gives an uncomfortable half chuckle. "Dodged some bullet that missed me by a hair, but hit my brother instead. Not many people can understand what I mean, but—"

"I can," Kate says, shifting her cold feet.

"I know."

Ozzie tugs on the leash and they resume their walk. They're nearly at the front door of the inn now.

"How do you cope with the guilt?" Kate asks, watching Ian out of the corner of her eye.

He stands a little straighter. "I reckon it's a bit different for me. I've had years more experience with it. But the way I see it, there's just no point dwelling on it. There's no trying to understand it. It isn't my fault I didn't get the gene. It isn't your fault you survived the crash when your parents didn't."

She blinks back tears as they mount the stairs to the covered porch.

"Life deals out shit to some people and roses to others," Ian says. "There's no cheating it, no making sense of it. Maybe it's easy for me to say, not being in my brother's shoes, but I decided to live like the whole rest of my life was a gift. All of this," he says, pulling his hands from his pockets and opening his arms wide, as though embracing everything around him, "is a bonus I could have easily been denied. So, I squeeze everything I can out of it. I try not to live with regrets. I try to just *live*."

Ozzie tugs Kate toward the front door, eager to get inside.

"At any rate," Ian says, clearing his throat, "I hope I haven't scared you off."

Kate shakes her head. "No. You haven't. I don't know anyone else who can relate. It's been . . ." She tries to identify the feeling.

"Lonely?"

"Yes."

Their eyes linger on one another, understanding passing between them.

"Well," Ian says finally, "I told Audrey she doesn't need to sabotage the house anymore to get me to come out here. I like spending time with her. And you," he adds.

"What?" Kate asks.

"She ripped the chain off the toilet for an excuse to see me." He rolls his eyes. "I told her she needn't bother. I'll come round more now."

Her stomach flutters, and she recognizes why. It thrills and unnerves her. "Why's that?"

"A couple of reasons," he says. "Would you like to have dinner with me sometime, Kate?"

Her memory reaches deep into the past, recalling how she'd met Adam all those years ago. Her girlfriends from uni had dragged her out to celebrate a mutual friend's engagement, and the guest of honour had chosen an overpriced basement cocktail bar in Soho with deafening house music and lighting dim enough to disguise the fact that both the establishment and its patrons were aging faster than they would care to admit.

Adam found her on the street outside the bar around midnight. He'd been eyeing her all night. He was a friend of a friend, one of those tertiary people in her circle whom she knew by name and face. They'd started walking, flirting as they enjoyed the evening breeze, and lost track of time. Adam ended up escorting her sixteen blocks across the West End to her flat's door, inside, up the stairs, and into her bedroom. Things moved quickly after that. She'd said "I do" a couple of years later and figured she'd had her last first date, her last first kiss.

Best-laid plans and all that.

But this feels different. Ian is different. As he waits for her answer, she sees a vulnerability flicker in his eyes.

"Yeah," she says. "Yeah, I would."

Chapter 18

Audrey

BERLIN, GERMANY | FEBRUARY 1939

Abrams.

That was the name of the family who had lived—until the previous evening—in the large grey house in front of Audrey. A bitter wind gusted around her legs, lifted her hair.

"Two adults, four children, per the register," Herr Weber had told her that morning when he handed her the file. He had been sitting at his desk, smoking a cigarette and squinting as though trying to see through her. "Big house, and we want it ready for Commander Haas by the end of the week, so work fast on this one, Jakob. I know you will," he added with a wink.

Audrey had immediately pictured the family in her mind's eye, a father and mother who looked like Ira and Ruth, and four children lined up beside them. Outwardly, she had beamed at him. "Of course, Herr Weber." She grazed his hand as she took the file.

She had diligently completed all her administrative work in the morning, leaving the assessment for later in the day so that she could go straight home afterward. The evenings came so early in the winter, and she didn't like the shadows that followed her around street corners. Her role in the Department of Property Reclamation and her false papers should have afforded her some ostensible sense of security. Yet she felt more exposed than ever under the gaze of the swarms of severe-faced men in starched uniforms who wove in and out of her office. She felt eyes everywhere. Berlin had been emptied of half of its residents, and those who remained were all supporters of, or feared, the Reich. People continued to disappear; neighbours turned against neighbours. Children were encouraged to report on their parents if they harboured any kind of anti-Hitler sentiment. Everyone was watching one another's movements, their language. The city was a prison whose walls kept inching closer together.

Outside the grey house, she fingered the key inside her pocket, a morbid habit now. She had tried to harden herself, tell herself that she wasn't really Ada Jakob and that she would never become her, would never lose herself in this persona she wore like a freshly skinned fur, carefully perfumed to mask the scent of the animal it had belonged to. But sometimes she wondered.

When she told herself it would be easier to do her job and help the Red Orchestra bring down the Reich if she simply turned off the human part of her, she wondered. When she ignored the family portraits on the walls, the engraved initials on the jewellery and watch backs, she wondered. She wondered sometimes what she might become if she survived all of this for too long.

There was just one person who knew who she really was—Ilse—but their relationship had altered. Audrey was out of the house most days now and the cell conducted strategy meetings on Friday evenings, which had once been enjoyable, quiet nights with the Kaplans as they observed the Shabbat. But now she sat with Claus, Ludwig, Aldous, and Friedrich in the chairs formerly occupied by Ira, Ruth, and Ephraim, whilst Ilse hid in the attic. Audrey chose to believe this was the reason her interactions with Ilse had changed, as opposed to Audrey's disastrous admission. She continued to wrestle with her feelings—the love she felt for Ilse was deeper and more dangerous than any kind of love she'd known. It was worse late at night when there was no work to be done and the silence of the house provided no steadying point of reference for her spinning mind.

She rolled her shoulders back, shoving the thoughts aside. She had a job to do here, and there was no point loitering outside in the freezing cold. Scaling the steps, she pulled out the key. But there was no need; the door had been forced. It was splintered and stood a few inches ajar.

Audrey entered the home as she did all the others—quietly. The Nazis liked to break down doors when they came to call. Scream. Shatter breakable possessions and people. This felt like the last respectful act she could honour the family with, even though they were already gone.

She inventoried the sitting room and hall, and was entering the dining room when her eye caught a sudden movement. Yelping, she clutched her clipboard to her chest as a small brown mouse scurried onto the table and helped itself to the uneaten dinner. This creature had wasted no time moving in and stealing whatever it liked, she thought, then she realized—no matter how much she hated herself for it—she was doing the exact same thing.

With a sigh, she left the mouse and went about her task. She had it down to a mechanical method now, and quickly worked her way through the main floor before scaling the stairs to the second- and third-floor bedrooms. She had just popped her head into a bedroom when she heard a weak mewling sound. The hairs on the back of her neck stood up.

When she heard it again, her heart fell. This wasn't the first time she had encountered a beloved family pet left behind in the raid. She'd discovered a cat a few weeks ago. It had lapped up the milk she poured for it, but stared at her as if it knew she had no rightful business there.

After nearly an hour of wretched internal debate, she'd set it free outside even though its chances of survival in the freezing winter were slim. It was a kinder fate than what the cat would face at the hands of the Nazis, who treated its human owners like street rats.

Audrey followed the sound down the hallway to a bedroom, already preparing to set this pet free too. But when she opened the door, she gasped. The mewling sound wasn't coming from a cat.

It was coming from a baby.

The child was lying on its side in the crib, its face pale, brown eyes half-open under swollen lids. Looking at the child, Audrey's first reaction made her loathe herself perhaps more than anything she had yet done.

This baby would change everything.

"Oh no. God no," she moaned.

She knew that she would have to take it, and hiding a child would put them all at even greater risk. A baby had constant needs. A baby could not control the volume of its own voice. A baby was too young to understand the concepts of death and evil, the lethal precariousness of existing as a Jew in Germany. Taking it meant gambling the exposure of Ilse and their little resistance cell, all they were trying to accomplish.

But wasn't the whole point of their resistance to save lives just like this one?

Standing in this empty house in a city at once spotlit and cast into darkness, with this baby before her, Audrey understood that they could try to kill Hitler, yes. But what was truly going to matter by the end of all this madness was the actions of individuals.

Today, she could try to save this child.

She rushed to the crib and reached in. She didn't know if the baby was a boy or a girl, but she guessed it wasn't quite a year old. A stench told her it was badly soiled, but what was more pressing was how limp it was in her arms. The infant wasn't crying, just whimpering into her shoulder. Her mind raced. The poor thing would have been alone since the arrest the previous evening, nearly twenty-four hours ago now. It must be hungry, and dangerously dehydrated. Panic crawled up her spine. Was it already too late? What might happen if she ended up with a dead child on her hands?

Audrey snatched a blanket from the crib to wrap around the baby, then fled down the hall to the stairs and out the front door. It was dark now. She hurried along the pavement, past the glowing yellow squares of the other houses' windows to the Kaplans' street a few blocks over, scanning her surroundings as she went.

She didn't have a free hand to fiddle for the key in her coat, so she pounded on the door. No one answered. She hammered harder, her mind whirling. At this hour, Ilse would be making herself scarce upstairs, and Friedrich might not yet be home from work.

A door creaked behind her. She glanced over her shoulder and saw Frau Richter, their neighbour who lived in Audrey's childhood home, illuminated in the streetlamp. The woman stepped onto her stoop. Audrey silently swore, turning away. She shifted the baby as best she could onto one hip, fear cresting at how still the little one felt in her arm.

She wrestled with her pockets until she fished out her key. She rammed it into the lock, then slammed the door shut behind her.

"Ilse!" she screamed. "Friedrich! I need help!"

She heard a muffled scraping from above as she hurried into the sitting room and set the child down on the rug near the hearth.

"Ilse!" she yelled again.

The baby whimpered, staring up at her, and she knew she would never forget those eyes, that look, this moment, for the rest of her life. Everything she had tried to do but couldn't, everything she feared, all the ways the world had failed its children were reflected in those two glassy orbs.

Soft footsteps sounded on the stairs.

"Ilse!" Audrey gasped. "Thank God."

Ilse glanced left and right as though waiting for an attack. "What is it? What's wrong? What's—oh!" Her eyes landed on the baby and she darted over.

"It's your neighbours' baby. The Abramses," Audrey said in a rush. "It was still in the house. It's been alone since last night, I found it in its crib."

"This must be Daniel." She began checking him over. "He's breathing. But he needs fluids. Milk. Water it down and bring it in some kind of a bottle. Use the milk bottle itself if you have to."

Audrey sprinted into the kitchen. When she returned, she found Ilse had wiped the child down as best she could, then wrapped him in a blanket from the divan. Ilse reached out a shaky hand for the proffered bottle.

"It should be heated, but we'll try it and—and see," she said as she put the bottle up to the baby's mouth and dribbled a few drops between its greying lips.

Audrey held her breath.

The baby spluttered, but the milk went down. Ilse tried again. The baby swallowed, then opened his mouth for more. Ilse continued feeding as he slowly sipped. Audrey sighed with relief. Her heart began to slow as the adrenaline that had been coursing through her veins since finding the child ebbed away.

Ilse's eyes shone with tears as Audrey's mind ran through all that had just happened. "The register said there were four children," she said.

Ilse shook her head. "Four children and one baby. He was born just in the summer. It was . . ." She sniffled. "Happy news. For a change."

Daniel's eyes were now locked on Ilse. Audrey watched the two of them stare at one another in the glow of the firelight. In other circumstances, it would have been a tender sight.

"Then he must have been born after the register was taken. Or maybe they found a way to hide his existence?" Audrey said. "But he was in his crib upstairs. How could they have missed him? Why would they leave him? They take all the other babies, or . . ." She'd heard what the SS sometimes did to babies, because it made transport of the family more difficult.

"It's a miracle they didn't," Ilse said. "A miracle you found him."

A lump came to Audrey's throat at the image of the Abramses being shunted from the house at gunpoint, not knowing where they were being taken but knowing their baby was asleep upstairs. Knowing that if they didn't die, he most certainly would. Slowly, and alone. The hideousness of the whole thing hit her, and finally, Audrey broke down.

Ilse reached out for her hand as she sobbed, the dam in her heart bursting at everything they had lost. The Kaplans, her father. Their city and their future, now so clouded and intangible. Even her dreams of a career in music, of a life beyond the confines of expectation. All snatched away. The blows had come in such quick succession, and nothing would ever be the same again. It was as though a permanent night had fallen, cloaking a path that was no longer visible.

She gripped Ilse's fingers, grasping at the only constant in her world, the person she was forging on ahead for, and with, as they fought their way through with nothing but a flicker of hope to light the way.

Chapter 19

Audrey

BERLIN, GERMANY | MARCH 1939

"Here's more," Frau Schulze told Audrey, handing her a stack of CVs to add to the pile she was sorting through.

"Thank you," Audrey said, not making eye contact with her.

They were hiring for a new office girl. Inge, who looked like she could be Audrey's cousin, had been brought on to fill Audrey's role when Johanna's departure precipitated her sudden promotion. Audrey had been training Inge on the assessments just as Johanna had trained her, and was looking forward to handing over the responsibility to Inge entirely once they hired an extra body. Since discovering Daniel Abrams, Audrey was terrified of what might happen if she ever came across another child on an assessment.

In the intervening weeks, Audrey had worked to get closer to Weber, an effort that had not gone unnoticed by Frau Schulze.

"On your head be it," she'd muttered. "Foolish girl."

She flirted with Weber, probing for useful information, and Weber was clearly interested, which was a good thing. But Audrey was unnerved by his indifference to Johanna's flight, and hoped his behaviour was a sign he didn't know of the pregnancy. She didn't want to consider how callous a man would have to be to outright ignore such a thing, move on to his next conquest in the same breath.

Weber opened his office door now. She looked up.

"A word, Jakob," he said gruffly, with half a glance toward Frau Schulze's retreating back.

She smoothed her skirt and followed Weber, straightening as she walked.

Audrey was invited into his office at least once or twice a day now. He, like Vogt, found reasons for his hands to wander. Every time he slipped an arm around her lower hips or made some insinuation, she thought of Ilse and all the Kaplans, of Daniel's family and the countless other ghosts whose homes she had helped confiscate, and she knew there was only one way to end it. Her worth as Ada Jakob lay in whether she could leverage her skills into something valuable. In a game that seemed to have no rules, the winner would be determined by who was willing to risk more for the victory. And so she responded to his flirtations with enthusiasm. He blew a little hot and cold, but Audrey had learned that the volatility was all part of the seduction.

"Yes, Herr Weber?" she asked as he took a seat behind his desk.

"Do we have a decent pool to draw from? For the new girl?"

"Yes, sir," she replied. A pause stretched between them. "Is there anything else I can help with, Herr Weber?"

He drummed his fingers softly on his leather desk pad, studying her. "You've been working very hard, Jakob. I should think you are due for a pay rise soon."

She inclined her head. "Thank you, Herr Weber. That's very generous."

"Would you join me for a drink after work, Ada?" It was the first time he had used her first name when addressing her, as he had with Johanna. It was a signal. An invitation. "A few of us were going to head over to The Adlon at six. The Roths. The Jagers. Otto Basner and his secretary."

Audrey didn't know these names, but it was clear he thought they should impress her, which meant they could be rather important. He dropped each of them with intention and let them land at her feet, waiting for them to resonate. The cell had a meeting tonight, but there was still plenty of time for a drink before eight. A rush rose inside her, a surge of determination that cauterized any lingering fear.

"Oh," she said demurely, flicking her eyes down so that her eyelashes swept her cheeks. "I'm not sure, sir, it's been a long week."

She looked up to find a grin playing around his mouth. He liked her denial, her innocent pushback, and Audrey understood now what Johanna had meant about his slyness, that she hadn't realized what was happening until it was too late.

"All the more reason to have a drink with me." His tone was stained silk.

She nodded. "Then I would be delighted."

Are men really this easy? she wondered as she walked back to her desk, ignoring the inquisitive glances from Inge. Could she, in the end, get what she needed from Weber with little more than a playful game of cat and mouse?

Perhaps.

But the cats are the ones with claws. And even the most patient among them will eventually tire of the chase.

Audrey exited the smoky haze of the cocktail lounge at The Adlon Hotel that evening in a state of excitement. The Roths, it transpired, were Gerta and Ernst Roth—and Ernst was Adolf Hitler's personal driver. Her introduction to him had been brief, but she was clearly being initiated into Weber's social circle. Hopefully, eventually, it might all lead to something the resistance cell could use.

She could still feel the weight of Weber's heavy arm slung around her shoulders, pressing on the back of her neck. His dangling fingers had caressed her as he ordered drinks she didn't want and tried not to finish. She had tried to edge toward the other women, but they were overbearing and chatty and didn't ask Audrey many questions about herself. Had they befriended Johanna? Did they wonder at all where she had gone, and Ursula before her, or were Weber's escorts interchangeable? Had they ever met Weber's wife?

Audrey's heart rate quickened as she approached the looming Brandenburg Gate. Five enormous bright red Nazi flags draped between the columns, illuminated by the great spotlights that shone up from below. She hurried along, feeling as though she were walking under the gleaming blades of a guillotine that might fall at any moment. But her gaze was pulled sideways as she passed one of the columns. A leaflet was stuck to the wall, one corner flickering in the breeze.

WIDERSTEHE

RESIST

Audrey's breath hitched. She glanced in all directions. A few evening commuters milled around, and what appeared to be a pair of tourists, necks cricked as they gazed and pointed up at the gate. But there was no one near her. Adrenaline tore through her like a scythe and she snatched the leaflet from the column, stuffing it into her coat pocket. Then she picked up her pace, low heels clicking on the pavement as she headed south down the Ebertstrasse.

Turning onto the Kaplans' dark street, she tried not to break into a run. She was nearly at the steps when a voice spoke from the shadows to her right.

"There you are, Fräulein James."

Audrey's heart shot into her throat. Frau Richter was standing on the front porch of her childhood home, pipe smoke curling above her head. Audrey's breathing calmed a little. Since returning to Berlin three years ago, Audrey had spoken to Frau Richter a handful of times, but never her husband. He wasn't well, Ruth had said, and Audrey had only ever encountered his wife, bespectacled and smoking, on the porch of their home, watering the herb planters or putting the cat out.

"*Guten Abend*, Frau Richter," Audrey said now with a nod of her tense neck. "I hope you're well."

Frau Richter descended the steps with more agility than Audrey would have guessed, and walked over to her. Audrey cursed her inwardly. All she wanted right now was to get home and show the leaflet to Friedrich before it burned a hole through her pocket or got her thrown in prison.

"I know about you, Fräulein," the old woman said.

"Frau Richter," Audrey said with a forced smile, "I really do need to get—"

Her face was a foot from Audrey, who took an instinctive step back.

"I know about you," she said again, and her smoke-scented breath puffed in Audrey's face. "You're a traitor."

Audrey froze, nerves frayed. Her gloved hand clenched the leaflet in her pocket. "I don't—"

"You're a sympathizer," Frau Richter hissed. She tossed her head in the direction of the Kaplans' house across the street, but kept her eyes on Audrey's. "After all they did for you. They were good people. *Good* people. And you go and work for these . . ." She pinched her mouth in disgust. "I saw you with a baby. Last month. That one of theirs? You a nanny to some jackboot now?" She spat. "In Ruth and Ira's house? You should be ashamed of yourself. Ashamed."

Turning on her heel, Frau Richter retreated inside and slammed her door, the sound echoing in the silence of the little side street.

Audrey was speechless. Frau Richter was loyal to the Kaplans, not the German government. The realization made Audrey want to go after her, defend herself, tell her it wasn't what it seemed. But it wasn't worth the risk. She could trust no one but Friedrich and Ilse. Hopefully, in time, Frau Richter would learn the truth.

She unlocked the Kaplans' door and once inside, withdrew the crumpled paper from her pocket, smoothed it out against the textured burgundy wallpaper of the front hall.

Aufruf an alle Deutsche! Audrey read, scanning the page. *Appeal to all Germans!*

It was heavy with text and appeared to be some sort of student manifesto from the University of Munich. The White Rose, they called themselves.

Isn't it true that every honest German is ashamed of his government these days? Who among us has any conception of the dimensions of shame that will befall us and our children when one day the veil has fallen from our eyes and the most horrible of crimes—crimes that infinitely outdistance every human measure—reach the light of day?

Friedrich needed to see this. Audrey stopped at the foot of the stairs, listening to his and Ilse's voices drift down. She found them sitting on the floor of Ilse's room, Ilse feeding Daniel a bottle, a pile of multi-coloured wooden blocks on the rug between them. She had retrieved a box of Ephraim's old toys from the attic, and it had been bittersweet to see them bringing joy to another child.

Audrey hung back, just outside the door.

"May I feed him?" Friedrich held out his hands.

"Of course," Ilse said.

Friedrich maneuvered him into a suitable position on his lap. Daniel stared up at him, chin pulsing in and out as he sucked happily at the bottle clutched in his chubby palms.

To Audrey's surprise, Friedrich had welcomed Daniel, and in the past weeks, Ilse's resentment at Friedrich's presence in her home had lost its serrated edge. Audrey had told herself that this change in demeanour toward Friedrich was because of Daniel, that becoming a mother had transformed everything for Ilse as it redefined her purpose. But seeing the two of them together like this—a little family that Audrey observed from the outside—reminded her of the growing distance between them. It was as though she and Ilse had been a pair of magnets, and one had now turned the other way. They could get close, but some unseen force kept them apart.

Audrey had to admit, though, that Ilse was in her element now. The isolation had taken a toll on her, and it was only in seeing her come alive again with passion and purpose that Audrey fully understood how close Ilse had come to disappearing. She had nursed Daniel back to health, pouring her love into him as though she were feeding some deep hunger within herself too. The past months had aged her, in a beautiful but stark way. Now she seemed a different person than the one Audrey had always known, an entirely new version of herself.

Audrey continued to watch from the doorway, unnoticed.

Ilse smiled now. "I know it's more risk, but you really don't mind having him here, do you?" she asked Friedrich.

"No, I don't mind. I'd like a family of my own one day. But . . ."

Ilse waited. "But what?"

"We'll see how things turn out, after all this," he said. "It helps me to not look too far ahead into the future just now."

He gave a shrug, as though the thought of his own potential demise was inconsequential, but Audrey understood. They had to simultaneously believe that a good future was possible whilst knowing that death could snatch it away in the process of trying to preserve it. The same things that were worth living for were the same things that were—ultimately—worth dying for.

Friedrich's eyes moved from Daniel to Ilse again, dancing to a song Audrey recognized. Friedrich and Ilse lit each other up, and a knot twisted in Audrey's throat.

She cleared it, and all three of their faces turned to her in surprise.

She forced a smile. "Hi."

"You're home late," Ilse said. "How was work?"

"I finally got asked to join Weber for drinks today. At The Adlon."

"Well, he didn't exactly take you to a dive, did he?" Friedrich said.

"Gerta and Ernst Roth were there, Friedrich."

"Hitler's driver." His eyebrows raised. "That's fantastic. Did you learn anything—"

"Not yet, no. But it sounds like they go out together regularly. It might lead somewhere. But look what I found on my way home," she said, holding out the White Rose leaflet.

Friedrich passed Daniel to Ilse and took the crumpled page. "Where did you find this?" he asked, brow furrowed.

"Posted on the Brandenburg Gate."

"Did anyone see—"

"No," she said, a little irritated. "I was careful."

His eyes were still on the leaflet.

"What is it?" Ilse asked.

"A leaflet from some student group at the University of Munich," Audrey told her.

"The White Rose," Friedrich said. "I have never heard of them. But if they aren't careful, they're going to get themselves killed. I will give this to Aldous." He tapped the pamphlet against his palm. "See if he has any insights on what print shop it might have come from. Maybe we can trace them from there."

"They'll all be here in a while, Friedrich," Audrey said. She felt a need to break up this little domestic scene.

"You're right. This is just . . ." He grinned at Ilse and Daniel. "Far more joyous and hopeful than anything else we're doing."

"I'll get him to bed soon," Ilse said.

Friedrich nodded, brushed past Audrey on his way out of the room. Ilse kept her eyes on Daniel, who was reaching out to grasp his own toes, and Audrey lowered herself to the floor where Friedrich had sat.

During the past Red Orchestra meetings, Daniel had been asleep upstairs, watched over by Ilse, but Friedrich had already floated to Audrey that he was considering how they might suggest a change of location to one of the other members' houses without drawing suspicion, as it was going to become increasingly difficult to conceal a child.

"You don't like him spending time alone with me, do you?" Ilse asked, flicking her eyes over Audrey's shoulder.

Audrey made a face. "What do you mean?"

"You know what I mean."

"I don't know. I suppose I miss you, that's all. Daniel takes up all of your attention now. Work takes up mine. We've hardly had any time to speak, just the two of us, since Daniel came. And I guess . . ." She was unsure how to express why Friedrich enjoying time alone with Ilse irritated her.

"You're jealous of Daniel?" Ilse asked.

"I didn't say that." Audrey exhaled an exasperated sigh. She was still on edge from the excursion with Weber and his friends, and the unpleasant encounter with Frau Richter, which she'd wanted to relay to Ilse. Her nerves were frayed, her patience at a premium.

Ilse shook her head. "You have your work. You get to leave the house every day and go try to accomplish something of value. Until Daniel came, I had nothing. Nothing to do but sit and remember when my father was shot and killed before my eyes, wonder what the hell might be happening to my mother and brother whilst I'm reasonably safe right here, and whether they're ever going to come back. But Daniel has given me a *purpose*. A person to wake up for each morning and go to bed thinking about each night. Can you not understand that?"

At their raised voices, Daniel began to fuss in Ilse's lap.

Audrey and Ilse rarely argued. She couldn't even recall a time Ilse had spoken to her like this. She felt dizzy, as though the very foundation of her life was spinning. Tears pricked at her eyes.

"It's not about Daniel! It's that you seem to make time for Friedrich, but not for me."

Ilse bounced Daniel on her knee. "I enjoy his company, Audrey, and he's affectionate with Daniel. I'm allowed to be friends with him, you know. We—"

"I know. I know you are. All right?" She regretted saying anything at all. Regretted her own feelings. "It's fine," she said, her voice breaking. "Just leave it, Ilse." Audrey stood, swiping at her cheeks.

"Audrey," Ilse called after her. "Audrey, wait. Please."

But Audrey was already racing down the staircase, pursued by the spectre she couldn't seem to fight off, no matter how hard she tried.

Chapter 20

Audrey

BERLIN, GERMANY | MARCH 1939

Three weeks later, the cell arrived just after eight o'clock, bottles in hand, as usual. Audrey waited in the sitting room in her spot on the divan, inhaling the bitter richness of her after-dinner coffee whilst Friedrich answered the door.

Things had been tense with Ilse for a day or so after their argument, but had now, more or less, returned to normal. Ilse claimed she'd been tired from waking each night with Daniel, and Audrey wrote it off as a symptom of the absurd situation they all found themselves in. On a level, she agreed with Ilse that it was a good thing they each had a purpose beyond each other. Motherhood was what Ilse had always craved, but the way she and Friedrich were now interacting with one another was undeniably painful.

She chose to throw herself into her mission with Weber. They went out at least twice a week for dinner, dancing, or drinks. Sometimes she asked for the Roths to join them again, told Weber she'd gotten on so well with Gerta. It was an exaggeration, as Gerta spent most of her time on the dance floor, but she seemed to collect friends like other women collected handbags, and Audrey had a mind to leverage Gerta's sociability to get closer to her. At the office, Frau Schulze hardly had a word for her anymore, and had bonded with Inge just as swiftly as she had with Audrey in the beginning. But Audrey didn't care; all that mattered was Weber's view toward her, and she did all she could to make herself sparkle in his eyes.

The conversation with the cell began swiftly, as it always did, the volume and intensity increasing with each emptied glass. Their meetings had been more sporadic lately. Both Ludwig and Claus had been out of the city on military business, and Aldous had been ill. There was a lot to catch up on.

"Have you been able to learn any more about the White Rose group?" Audrey asked Aldous, who perched on the edge of the sofa next to her, his cane resting between his knees.

"I've been trying to narrow down the print shop that produced the leaflet, but obviously there's no identifier on the paper itself, like there normally would be. I've poked around a little with a couple of friends I trust at the University of Munich, trying to get a contact name. No luck yet, but these things are delicate. It takes time to find people who know when to talk, and when to shut up." He sighed, shifted his thin legs. "These kids are brazen though. They'll have to be careful unless they truly don't care about getting caught."

Ludwig was in his usual spot, standing near the doorway between the sitting room and front hall. Despite his vehemence that they all risk everything for this cause, he always seemed to have one foot out the door, as though readying for a quick exit. He was an enigma, Ludwig. He was an adamant resister of Hitler, but not entirely to all the regimens of the Third Reich. He believed strongly in the importance of rank, and rarely violated societal mores or etiquette. He was in full flow about the recent invasion of Bohemia and the fall of Prague to the Nazis when a child's scream floated down from the floor above.

Audrey froze, coffee cup halfway to her lips.

All the men stared at the ceiling.

"What was that?" Ludwig demanded, turning to Friedrich, dark brows narrowed over his black eyes.

Daniel let fly another shriek that was quickly muffled.

"Who's upstairs?" Claus asked.

Audrey's mind whirred, searching for a plausible explanation.

"Audrey's friend, with her child," Friedrich said calmly. "She's just staying for the weekend, on her way to visit her grandmother in Hamburg."

"Audrey's friend?" Ludwig barked.

Another shriek from above. Blood pounded in Audrey's ears. "Yes," she said.

Ludwig's face was a storm. "You fucking fool, Müller. You let her have a friend come to stay? On a meeting night when we are here discussing, among other things"—he dropped his voice—"how to *destroy Adolf Hitler*?"

Disbelief painted Claus's normally amused features. "What the hell are you doing, Fred?"

"You can't have *visitors*," Aldous added. "They could expose what we're doing—"

"She won't," Audrey snapped.

"How can you possibly know that?" Claus asked.

Audrey bit her tongue.

"She won't," Friedrich echoed. He looked pointedly at Audrey, imploring her for help.

"Don't look at her, look at me," Ludwig snarled. "I've about had it with your exceptions and excuses, Müller. You are gambling our lives with your recklessness!"

"We were—"

"In case you have forgotten," Ludwig said, "we agreed at the outset that it would only ever be we five. Us and Vogt. And then you moved in here and hired *her.*" He practically spat in Audrey's direction. "Because you and Vogt wanted to get your cocks wet—"

"Steady on, Ludwig," Aldous began, glancing apologetically at Audrey.

Friedrich took a step toward Ludwig, chest heaving with anger.

"And what's happened since you brought her into the house?" Ludwig continued. "Vogt died in what you said was a bar brawl—"

"It *was*!"

"—and now you've gone and let her have friends come to stay, like this is some fucking holiday home. Friends who might very well turn round and—"

"She will *not* turn on us!" Audrey shouted.

Ludwig swatted the air as though wishing he could actually hit her. "You cannot know that!"

"Yes she can," Friedrich snapped.

"Why?"

"Because the woman is a *Jew*!"

His words reverberated off the papered walls of the Kaplans' sitting room in the profound silence that followed. Audrey's breath was coming in shallow spurts, heart hammering against her collarbone.

"Friedrich," she breathed, but he didn't look at her this time.

"What the hell are you doing, Fred?" Aldous asked, watching his friend's face. He wasn't angry, but concerned, as though he feared Friedrich had taken leave of his senses. They had known each other a long time, after all. "Ah," he said after a beat. "She isn't just staying for the weekend, is she?"

"No," Friedrich said, holding his chin up. He was pacing back and forth, as agitated as a wet lion. "She's living here. For now, at least. For safety. But no one knows, and she will not—"

Audrey cut across him as anger came to her aid. "How can any of you object to this? Are we not trying to save Jews? Isn't that why we're risking everything—"

"We are not trying to save Jews, girl," Ludwig shot at her. "We are trying to save *Germany*, our Fatherland, from the retribution of England and the other states that will flay us alive for what we are doing, just like they did after the war!"

"Fred, surely you must see that we can't spend the very limited risk credit we have trying to harbour individual Jews," Claus said, scoffing. "This is far, far bigger than that now. Don't be stupid, man."

"And for the love of God, stop listening to *her*," Ludwig fired at Friedrich, indicating Audrey. "She has turned your head. We never should have allowed a woman—"

"Give it a rest, Ludwig," Aldous said quietly.

"You need to find somewhere else for her to go," Claus said, his gaze flicking back and forth between Audrey and Friedrich. "You must. You *must*."

Friedrich was staring at the wall behind Claus, avoiding his eyes.

After a moment, Ludwig threw his crystal glass into the fireplace, making Audrey jump. "She is to be gone within forty-eight hours, or so help me, Müller, you will get into a *bar brawl* of your own!"

He seized his coat from the front hall and exited, slamming the door behind him. Then, one by one, the others turned to go, but Audrey didn't stay to watch. She raced upstairs to Ilse.

Daniel was on the floor, hammering one wooden block as he chomped on another, drool pooling around his mouth.

"I heard shouting. They heard him, didn't they?" Ilse asked, panicked.

Audrey watched her with a sort of disconnected grief. "Yes."

"It's his teeth," Ilse said. "They're cutting on the top and bottom, and it's driving him mad. I couldn't stop him from shrieking. I tried everything I could think of. I'm so sorry." She stopped. "What did they say?"

"It wasn't . . . good," Audrey began. She explained how they'd tried to cover up who Ilse was, but the truth had come out. "They're insisting you and Daniel be moved elsewhere."

Ilse's face fell. "No."

"Ludwig could report us for harbouring Jews if he wanted to. And he threatened Friedrich. It isn't safe for you here anymore."

Ilse's voice rose. "I thought they were working against Hitler. Why would they . . . ?" She trailed off at the sight of Friedrich in the doorway, looking flushed.

"Audrey's right," Friedrich said. "It's not safe for you here." He said a few choice words about Ludwig. "It isn't your fault, Ilse. We were foolish to think we could continue this arrangement. As Daniel grows, concealing him will become more and more difficult." He took a deep breath, but he still seemed deflated, as though all the fight had gone out of him. "The fact is that we are no longer able to protect you here. I know you do not wish to leave your family home, but we must find an alternative. For all our sakes, but primarily yours and Daniel's."

As Friedrich spoke, Ilse looked down at Daniel, tears in her eyes.

"But how?" Audrey said.

Friedrich turned from Ilse. "Aldous."

"Aldous?"

"He stayed after Claus and Ludwig left." Friedrich paused. He seemed to be struggling with what he was about to say.

"He has a connection with another cell in the Red Orchestra through one of his university friends. One of their members, Wendelein Von Albrecht, has a country home outside of Enschede, in the Netherlands, not far from the border. Her family is wealthy. She and her Dutch husband have been using it to smuggle Jews to safety for the past year, I'm told, with great success. They might have a room for you and Daniel. He's going to try to reach them tonight."

Daniel offered Ilse a red block. "Ma ma ma," he said. Ilse took it, blinking rapidly.

"Aldous can make you false papers and if you keep them with you, there is no reason anyone should ever suspect you. You can remain there safely until we have reclaimed Germany from Hitler's grasp." Friedrich twitched his moustache thoughtfully. "He told me these would not be the first papers he has made for Jews trying to flee. I didn't know he'd been doing that."

Audrey's esteem for Aldous rose immediately. "I wonder what Ludwig would make of this information," she muttered. Friedrich didn't answer.

Ilse was quiet a moment. "How long would we be gone for?" she asked.

Audrey exhaled. She must be considering it.

"A year, or longer," Friedrich said. "Truly we cannot know. A war is coming, that much is clear. No one will allow Germany to keep invading its neighbours without consequence. But I cannot tell you how long it might go on."

"And what happens if my mother and brother return whilst I'm away?"

Pity rippled across Friedrich's features before he answered. "If that happens, I will bring them to you at the Von Albrechts." He took Ilse's hand and looked deep into her eyes in a way that made Audrey pink with jealousy. "I promise you, Ilse. You have my word."

Audrey struggled to find her voice. "So you'll do it?" she asked, her nails digging into her palms.

Ilse wiped her tears. "Yes, I'll go. For Daniel."

Friedrich's face cleared. "I'll call Aldous."

When he was gone, Audrey sat down on the edge of Ilse's bed, fingering the familiar embroidered yellow flowers. "You're doing the right thing," she said.

But Ilse shook her head. "There's no control anymore, is there? No true choices. For any of us. It's always just life or death, and nothing in between." She looked down at Daniel. "I do love him so. Though he's someone else's. Is that fair? Is that right?"

"I don't think it could ever be wrong to love a child. He's yours. For now, at least."

"What if his parents return?" Ilse asked.

A shiver crept over Audrey at the memory of Daniel's home. She knew Ilse had to believe that their return was possible, because if it wasn't, that might mean Ruth and Ephraim were doomed as well.

"We will cross that bridge if ever we come to it. In the meantime, the best thing we can do for him—and the parents who love him—is to keep him safe, and love him as they would have done."

Ilse gazed upon his little form. "I would do anything for him," she said. "This love of mine."

Audrey swallowed, the thorns of her own feelings cutting at her throat. "I understand."

An hour later, there was a soft knock on Audrey's door, and Ilse came in. She was in her nightgown and slippers now, wrapped in a robe to ward off the late winter chill. She sat at the bottom of Audrey's bed and they simply stared at one another.

"You're going to stay here, aren't you?" Ilse said finally.

Audrey nodded. She'd spent the past hour coming to the same conclusion. "I think it would be best." For Ilse. For her.

Ilse traced a seam on Audrey's quilt.

"All I've ever cared about is that you're safe," Audrey said. "And you'll be safe in the Netherlands."

Ilse's dark eyes filled with tears and her nose swelled. "I hope so. I wouldn't be going if not for Daniel."

"I know. I know how difficult this is for you."

Audrey sat up a little straighter at the head of her bed. "So much has changed since all this began. The resistance. Daniel. Friedrich, and . . ." She thought of the way he had looked at Ilse, felt a fresh wave of despair.

"I'm sorry, Audrey," Ilse said. "That I don't . . . that I can't . . ." She shrugged, unable to give voice to Audrey's greatest, impossible wish. "It's not who I am. You're the sister I never had. It's different for me, I suppose."

"You were always the sister I never had, too," Audrey said, as her chin quivered. "And then . . . I don't know. I don't know what happened." She didn't want to feel this for Ilse anymore. She wanted to go back to the way it was before, the simplicity and comfort of it. This was too confusing, too complicated and painful. Illegal. She couldn't explain, even to herself, why her feelings had deepened in the way they had.

But they had.

"I can't ever give you what you want," Ilse whispered.

The truth of it ripped through Audrey's chest, fraying the edges of her heart like torn linen. "Because of Friedrich?" she asked.

Ilse hesitated. "It's not *only* because of him. I thought maybe . . . it doesn't matter now, anyway. I'll be gone. We might never even see each other again. He has a job to do here."

"And so do I. There's a new purpose for me here," Audrey said. "We can try to stop it, stop him—Hitler. I've been making progress with Weber. I'd like to see it through. And in a way . . ." She exhaled. "It might be easier for me, knowing you're safe at a distance. I won't need to worry about what could happen to you if we're found out."

The silver pendant resting on Ilse's bare collarbone glittered in the moonlight. She hadn't taken Ruth's necklace off once, not even to bathe, not even when Daniel's curious fingers snatched at it.

Audrey thought of Ruth and Ephraim, what their fates likely were, of the hope Ilse still harboured for their return.

"And if your mother and Ephraim come back, I'll be here to greet them, to explain. They would have no reason to trust Friedrich's word alone, would they?"

Ilse nodded, mopping her jaw. "And you could always come join me, right?"

"Sure I could." But she knew that, for one reason or another, she probably wouldn't.

Ilse crawled to the head of the bed and they held each other for a long while, both sniffling. Audrey closed her eyes and breathed Ilse in, committing the moment to memory.

When they broke apart, Ilse padded to the door. "Will you come with us though, to drop off me and Daniel?"

Audrey forced a smile, willing Ilse to leave so that she could submit to the emotional storm she'd been fending off since Ludwig threw his glass into the fire.

"I would do anything for you, Ilse."

Chapter 21

Kate

ALNWICK, ENGLAND | EARLY DECEMBER 2010

I can't believe they eliminated the lemon cupcakes," Audrey says. They've just witnessed the finale of *The Great British Bake Off*.

"Neither can I," Ian says, throwing his hands in the air next to Kate on the couch. "A travesty."

Audrey chuckles, holds her coffee mug aloft. "Which one of you would like to go get me a refill?" Kate leans forward but Ian pushes himself off the couch first to oblige. "Thank you, dear," Audrey says, and he disappears down the hall. "So the two of you are headed to the Christmas market tomorrow, then?" she says with a small smile. "Sounds lovely."

"Yeah," Kate says. She's a little unsure of the trip, but truth be told she could use a breather from Audrey's weighty recollections, and she's trying to lean into Ian's suggestion that the only real way to face this holiday is to push straight on through it. She's felt better lately, despite the occasional nightmare. But she's having fewer of them than she did back in London, so she takes that as a sign of progress. "I've never been. Have you?"

"Once or twice, years ago now. I love Edinburgh though, used to go there often when I was younger and my legs didn't creak like rotting branches. It's a bit too hilly for me nowadays. The train ride was sometimes my favourite part. You get quite close to the sea along the way." She shakes her head. "It's funny. I've lived landlocked my whole life, despite how much I like being by the water."

"It's not too late, you know," Kate says gently.

"Yes, it is," Audrey replies, her expression soft. "But thank you."

Ian returns with her refill. "I gave it a little jolt of whiskey. Your baking horse lost. This is for the sorrow."

"Cheers." Audrey winks at him. When she takes the mug, a little sloshes over the side, and Ian guides it down to the cork coaster on the side table for her.

"You okay?" he mutters.

"Yes, thank you, dear."

"I'll get a cloth."

Ian's solicitousness sparks a warmth in Kate, but she watches Audrey with concern. She's been unsteady on her feet recently. Kate can tell she's truly struggling because she's accepting—or grudgingly asking for—Kate's help with basic tasks, and getting up and down the stairs. Audrey is unlikely to accept anyone's help unless the need is dire. Her past is evidence enough.

Her story has been playing over and over in Kate's mind like a film for the past several days. Vogt's attack and Müller's shocking duplicity. Her feelings for Ilse. Joining the resistance and rescuing the baby. As much as age may have diminished Audrey on the outside, the core of this woman is made of seriously tough shit. No wonder she reacted so negatively to Kate's arrival—after holding it together for so long, she wasn't prepared to admit she wasn't coping on her own anymore. Kate's respect for her has grown by the day.

"You're sure you don't mind me going out for the whole day tomorrow?" Kate asks her now as Ian disappears again to fetch the cloth.

Audrey waves her hand. "I shall be fine. If I need anything, I'll call Sue. But I suspect being rid of the pair of you for twelve hours will do wonders for my health and sanity."

The three of them pass another pleasant half hour in conversation before Audrey announces she's heading to bed. Ian gives Audrey a peck, then moves toward Kate and loops his arm around her as he kisses her cheek. "I'll be back at eight to pick you up," he says.

She almost pulls him back, but lets him go, her face warm, the feel of his lips still lingering on her skin.

After Ian leaves, she turns to Audrey, who is watching her, a little grin playing around her mouth. "Do you want your peppermint tea?" Kate asks. Audrey has a cup every night for her digestion, and Kate has taken to preparing it for her.

"Yes, thank you. But I think I'll take it upstairs tonight. I'm quite tired."

When Kate returns with the tea a few minutes later, Audrey hasn't moved from her chair, clearly waiting for help with the stairs.

"Thank you, Kate," she says, standing slowly and reaching for the cup.

"No, I'll carry it."

"Oh, just give me the damn tea," Audrey snaps. "I can manage perfectly well on my own."

They exchange glares.

"It's hot water, and you need to hold the handrail," Kate says firmly. "I don't want you scalded on my watch."

"On your watch? I'm not your charge, you know. You're not here to babysit."

"No, but I *am* your roommate and I'm about sixty years younger than you, so I'll carry the tea."

Audrey scowls and heads up the stairs, gripping the railing tightly. "I don't know what came over me, bringing a nag into my home. I didn't marry all these years to retain my independence, and now I'll be spending my final days under the dictatorial thumb of a bossy ginger know-it-all."

Kate stops in her tracks. "Final days? What are you talking about?"

Audrey halts briefly, then flaps the comment away. "I don't mean that literally. But I am ninety-one years old, and, you know . . . it's a figure of speech. The point is, you're an insufferable nag."

Kate smirks. "Fine then, I'll leave. Bye."

"Oh, shut it."

The train journey from Alnwick to Edinburgh wasn't quite as idyllic as Audrey had described. Kate and Ian spent most of the trip squashed into a corner near the toilet. The train had oversold the tickets and the cars were stuffed with noisy families. Kate hadn't even caught a glimpse of the North Sea as it sped past the window.

"I promise it'll be worth it," Ian had muttered as they were shunted aside by a large tourist carting three even larger hot pink suitcases and complaining loudly about the British rail system. "But still, I think we'll just drive next time, yeah?"

They finally disembark onto the busy platform around eleven o'clock. A brilliantly lit Ferris wheel soars above them amid a sea of Christmas lights. Ian squeezes her hand, and they make their way through the throng to street level. Beyond the bridge and the rail lines, the market stretches on for ages, a dazzling holiday exhibition that winds up and down park paths lined with red carpets.

They weave through the horde on Princes Street, past the dozens of stalls offering everything from cuckoo clocks and mulled wine to giant pretzels and tree ornaments. Ian gives her a cursory tour of the New Town, never letting go of her hand. An hour later, they end up at an Indian place for lunch, ravenous. They didn't eat much breakfast before their journey.

"This might be the best sag aloo I've ever had," Kate says. It's loaded with oil and countless calories, but she finds she doesn't care as much as she would have before. The need to control her diet seems to have waned.

Ian nods fervently, mouth full of food.

Kate spears a chunk of potato, and a question comes to mind. "Do you know why Audrey doesn't eat potatoes?"

"No. I hadn't noticed."

"She hates them, apparently. I don't think I've ever met anyone who hates potatoes. There's just so much to love," Kate says, chuckling. "I should ask her."

"She's gotten more particular as she's gotten older though," Ian says, taking a long draught of his beer. "I guess a lot of people do. Why put up with anything you don't like? I doubt I'll eat broccoli for about the last decade of my life."

"I could never get my ex to eat *any* vegetables aside from potatoes," she says. "He was like a toddler that way." The words are out before she has a chance to consider them. She chews her food, racking her brain for a change of subject.

He looks up. "Your ex?"

She hadn't wanted to talk about Adam yet. There was no greater buzzkill for budding romance than to conjure the ghosts of relationships past.

"Yeah," she says. "A while ago now."

The last she'd heard from Adam, he was sorting out the divorce with a solicitor and would be in touch when it was ready to be finalized. Kate doesn't want to have to explain what happened with Adam to Ian—she wishes she could tell him she's already divorced—until she knows where this is headed. She likes the comfortable familiarity of Ian, hopes their connection will progress, but her guard is still up. He doesn't need to know the ugly details yet.

Ian studies her face but doesn't press for more. "I had the opposite problem. My ex was a vegetarian and was always trying to convert me."

"What happened to her?"

Ian takes another drink. "I asked her to marry me, and she up and left for Manchester with another bloke."

Kate sets down her water. "Wow. Shit."

"Thanks. That's about the same face I made when I found out she'd been cheating on me," he says, with a half smile that lightens the moment. "But hey, it's led to this, right? I get to be here with you."

He keeps talking, moving on from his ex, but Kate watches him, takes in the laugh lines around his mouth. Despite the hardships of his life, he's still nearly always smiling. He's somehow managed to maintain his positivity. She wishes she could be more like him, wonders if she has it in her. She fingers the condensation on her water glass, notices that the ice has split. Most of it is floating, but two pieces are joined together and stuck to the bottom. Variations in ice density determine whether a piece sinks or floats. The ones at the bottom are under more pressure. But give the glass a little swirl, a gentle agitation of encouragement, and the chunks at the bottom will eventually rise to the surface.

Revived and full, they explore the neighbourhood a little. After wandering the narrow, pedestrian-only Rose Street, they come to a busy thoroughfare blocked off with a wall of police barricades.

"Sniper?" Kate asks at the same moment Ian says, "Parade?"

They glance at each other. Ian's face splits into a grin and Kate begins to laugh. It feels good, as though one of the weights on her shoulders has tumbled off. Ian has that effect on her. He's looking at her now, still smiling, but there's a tenderness in his eyes.

He leans down and kisses her, right there on the crowded sidewalk. Kate responds with enthusiasm, her body warm and tingling despite the cold.

"Should have seen that coming, I guess," she says when they break apart.

His nose brushes her cheek. “You can’t predict everything in life.”

They circle back to the Christmas Market in the midafternoon, hand in hand. The air smells like baked goods, beer, and hickory. Kate used to love these sorts of artisan markets, buying whimsical gifts for her girlfriends and parents. There was a time she would have left this one with bags full of scarves, ornaments, and kitschy mugs, but as she sets a scented candle back down on the vendor’s table, it hits her—she has no one to buy for this year besides Audrey and Ian. She thinks of her few girlfriends back in London, all married with children now. In the wake of her trauma, Kate had curled into herself, then written off their lack of attention with valid excuses: they were simply too busy, too tired out by their own young families, too emotionally taxed to spare much energy for her. But now she wonders whether she should have asked more of them—that they stick by her, check in with her, even on the days where her bed felt like the only answer to the impossible riddle she’d been tasked with solving.

“See anything worthwhile?” Ian asks, jostling Kate’s wandering mind back to the present.

“Nothing I’ve really decided on.”

“How about a drink?”

“Sure.”

Ian leads her down the red carpeted path to a stall offering mulled wine, hot toddies, and apple cider. They carry their drinks out of the crowd and find a place to sit on the edge of a low stone wall. Kate sips her cider, letting the spicy scent waft over her face as the unpleasant memories float away on the chilly wind.

Ian inhales the steam from his toddy and looks sideways at her paper cup. “You don’t drink much, eh?”

“No. Not for a while now.”

“Mind if I ask why?”

She blows on the surface of the cider, watches a woman hold up a red knitted baby cardigan at the stall across from them, and turns away, huddling into Ian.

"My dad drank too much sometimes," she says. "And it kind of turned me off it."

"Ah," Ian says, resting his free hand on her thigh. "I think people sort of go one of two ways with that, don't they?" he says gently.

"What do you mean?"

"When I was at uni here, I used to tend bar on weekends at a pub just off the Royal Mile." He gestures across the rail lines to the Old Town. "There was this old bloke, Archie, with no front teeth and this yellowing moustache who used to spend hours at the bar every Friday and Saturday night. He was always one of the last to leave. After all the students and the band had cleared off, he'd stagger the two blocks to his flat. We all knew where he lived. Sometimes we had to walk him to his door; he could hardly stand." A ripple of pity passes over Ian's features. "This one night he was more shattered than I'd ever seen him. Even after we cut him off, he just stayed there at the bar. I don't think he wanted to leave. Not sure he had anyone, you know? I ended up walking him home that night, and he stopped at the door to his flat and said it was the anniversary of the day his old man beat his dog to death in a drunken rage. When Archie tried to stop him, the bastard kicked his teeth in." Kate gasps. "He said he drank more than his dad ever did, pickled himself so hard that he couldn't have thrown a fist at anyone if he'd wanted to." Ian pauses. "Do you know why your dad drank?" Tinny music from the nearby Ferris wheel sings out in the background, just audible over the constant murmur of the crowd.

Kate shakes her head. "He had depression, I know that much. Not always. It came and went. And I've wondered how much the drinking contributed to it. He was open about a lot of things, but very private about others. I'm still trying to figure him out, to be honest. My mum was a lot more transparent. But she was too tolerant of his drinking. Or, I don't know . . . maybe she'd just given up trying." She clears her throat with a sip of cider. "Do we ever really know our parents? Like, really? Did you feel like you knew your dad?"

Ian opens his mouth to answer but is interrupted by shouting over near the main road. They twist around, looking for the source of the commotion, and see a cluster of people bent over a middle-aged man with greying hair lying prone on the pavement.

"He just dropped!" they hear a woman wail.

"Whoa," Ian mutters.

An ambulance blares down the street, lights flashing. They're so close that the sirens shred the air. Kate sets her drink down on the stone beside her and covers her ears, eyes still on the ambulance as a pair of paramedics exit with a slamming of doors.

"He collapsed," the woman cries out again. "He was talking one moment, and the next—"

"Okay, ma'am, step aside, please."

Kate trips down into her own memory, falling through the rain. The paramedic is pointing something at her face as her eyes flutter open.

Miss? Miss? Can you see this light? What's your name?

And later, the glaring overhead halogens of the hospital room.

What happened, Kate?

She squeezes her eyes shut, but all she sees is the dark, wet road. Her parents' faces. The blood. The flashing lights are there no matter how much she blinks.

"Kate?" Ian's voice is at her ear. "Are you okay? Kate?"

Her eyes flash open, but she can't breathe. She turns away from the emergency lights and Ian's concerned face, pushes through the crushing, chattering crowd.

"Kate!" Ian calls.

She breaks into a run, trying to get as far away from the scene as possible.

Ian catches up to her at the gates to the Princes Street Gardens. She hurries down the stone steps, panting as she comes to a stop near a border hedge. It's darker, quieter here. The castle is lit now, glowing orange on the rocky cliff behind her.

Ian grasps her shoulders, breathing hard too. He ducks down to look at her properly. "What's going on? What is it?"

He lifts her chin and in his eyes, she sees the lights of the castle that has stood on that overlook for a thousand years, stalwart and secure and reliable. A constant amid the tumult.

She clutches Ian's wrists, feeling her legs giving way. "I killed them," she whispers. "I killed them. It was all my fault."

Ian steadies her. "Who?"

"My parents."

"How is the accident your fault?"

Kate shakes her head in despair. "Because I was the one driving," she says weakly. "It was me. It was raining, and . . . and . . ." She takes a breath, tries to tell him the whole truth, but the words won't come.

Ian pulls her in to his chest, where she buries her head in his scarf as the wind chills the tear tracks on her face. "It's still not your fault, Kate," he mutters. "Any one of you could have been driving, and the same thing would have happened. The roads still would have been wet. You can't blame yourself for this."

Oh, but she can.

"Do you think your parents would, if they were alive to hear you say this? Jesus. Would they not just be grateful you survived? Come on, Kate. You have to forgive yourself. You have to."

Kate tilts her chin up. He kisses her gently and pulls her in for another hug. Over his shoulder, the Ferris wheel is fully illuminated now. Each car is a different colour, and she watches as the red one drops down behind some trees, out of her view. It slows down a little with time, disappears for a while as the other cars take their turn at the fore. You would think the red car was gone. But then it rises back up, almost camouflaged in all the sparkling, twinkling lights, but not quite. It's always there, whether you want to see it or not.

PART III

At grief so deep the tongue must wag in vain;
the language of our sense and memory lacks the
vocabulary of such pain.

—Dante Alighieri, ***Inferno***

Chapter 22

Audrey

BERLIN, GERMANY | MARCH 1939

They left Berlin after dusk. The sky turned from purple to indigo as the late winter sun sank below the horizon, a great fish dipping beneath the surface of the dark water. Audrey, Friedrich, and Ilse, holding Daniel, stepped outside and scanned the street. The Richters' house was dark.

This was the first time Ilse had left the house since that terrible day, nearly five months ago now. As they pulled away from the curb, she glanced out the window at her family home.

"It will be all right," Friedrich said.

"I appreciate the sentiment, but you cannot know that," she replied.

Friedrich turned his attention to the streets. The drive to the Netherlands would take most of the night, six hours or so, he'd said.

As they drove, Ilse took in her once-familiar surroundings. All the Jewish landmarks and businesses were shuttered, destroyed. Audrey had hardened herself to these sights, but now saw them anew through Ilse's eyes. A tear slipped down her cheek as they passed the remains of her synagogue. After the fire, it had been left to steep in its own destruction, like some half-eaten animal carcass at the side of the road. Gaping and hollow. Stripped of its dignity, even in death.

They traveled in silence until they reached the edge of the city and traffic slowed to a stop.

"What's happening?" Audrey asked, craning her neck from the back seat, but all she could see was the car in front. "Why are we stopping?"

"Probably just a checkpoint," said Friedrich.

"A what?"

"A security checkpoint. They want to know who is coming into and leaving Berlin."

"What?" Ilse gasped.

"This was entirely expected," Friedrich murmured, looking over at Daniel, who was dozing in Ilse's lap. "We have our papers. Everyone just remain calm. Remember our cover story."

Audrey steeled her nerve as they neared the front of the queue. Eventually a police officer tapped on Friedrich's window.

Friedrich cranked it down. "*Guten Abend*," he said, leaning his elbow on the window ledge.

The policeman's eyes flicked to the decorations on Friedrich's shoulder. "*Guten Abend*, er . . ."

"Obersturmbannführer Müller."

The officer visibly straightened before saluting Friedrich. "Heil Hitler."

"Heil Hitler."

Ilse stared ahead, but a nerve jumped in her clenched jaw. She hadn't seen Müller's performative Nazi behaviour like Audrey had.

"I'm afraid I must ask for your papers, Obersturmbannführer," the policeman said. "For yourself and these ladies, please. Forgive me, it is policy."

Friedrich nodded and gave no argument. "I applaud your diligence, officer . . . ?"

"Hermann."

Friedrich withdrew his and Audrey's real German documents and

Ilse's false one from his inner vest pocket. Aldous had made a variety of fake identification papers including a second set for all three of them, as Dutch citizens. "Here you are, Officer Hermann. This is my wife and son, and our nanny in the back."

The officer skimmed the papers before returning them. He didn't even look at Audrey or Ilse. "Where are you travelling to this evening?" he asked.

"My business is my own," Friedrich said, curt but without heat.

"Very good, Obersturmbannführer Müller. Have a pleasant journey."

The officer saluted again as Friedrich pulled away from the checkpoint.

"Was that it?" Audrey muttered. "Will that be the only one?"

"I don't know," Friedrich said. "I would anticipate another at the Dutch border, at the very least, but perhaps we will get lucky."

As they left Berlin behind and drove through the dark countryside, Audrey felt some of the tension in her shoulders loosen, like a slackened line that had been pulled too tight to begin with. She grew sleepy, lulled by the car's movements, and nodded off.

A couple of hours later, she awoke to Daniel crying. It made Audrey's ears ring, such loud shrieking in a small space, but Ilse calmly retrieved a bottle from the bag she'd packed, and soon Daniel quieted. She never appeared flustered or perturbed by him. Her patience with Daniel was admirable, and far exceeded Audrey's own.

"Where are we now?" Audrey asked, moving her head to release the stiffness in her neck.

"About halfway there," Friedrich said. "We got past Hanover without a checkpoint."

As they drove through Lower Saxony, the sky began to lighten. Audrey had never been this far west. The pastoral sight of the rolling hills untouched by traces of the Third Reich was somehow simultaneously disquieting and reassuring. Just two hundred miles away, Berlin was infected by the malignancy of Nazism. Its tentacles had grasped Bohemia and Austria. But here, it was as though life were carrying on mostly as normal. As they sped past the fields, she could almost imagine it was all nothing but a bad dream.

Almost.

They passed through small town after small town. Just outside the town limits of Osnabruck, Friedrich pulled over beneath a large oak tree. Without a word, he retrieved a bundle from the trunk strapped to the back of the car, then disappeared behind the tree. Audrey glimpsed a bare arm and shoulder and turned away. He was changing into his civilian clothes, she realized.

She leaned forward. Daniel was asleep again in Ilse's lap, head resting against her chest. "How are you doing?" Audrey asked.

"I'm all right. A bit nervous to be alone there, actually. I'll manage though. I hope it will give Daniel some stability at least. He's had such upheaval for a child so young. It's dreadful. But maybe Friedrich will be right. With our false papers, and outside of Germany, this madness might not touch us. We can go outside. Live our lives a little more fully. Perhaps, well . . . maybe it's a blessing in disguise."

"That's exactly what you deserve, Ilse," Audrey said. She imagined Ilse at liberty, playing and laughing with Daniel in the Von Albrechts' garden a few months from now, a warm summer breeze lifting her dark hair.

"But you'll still be right in the middle of that madness, Audrey. Please be careful. Promise me you will." Her voice broke.

Audrey nodded, but in her heart, she knew she couldn't keep that oath.

Friedrich emerged from behind the tree wearing slacks and a plain brown jacket, a newsie cap on his head.

"He's a good man, Audrey," Ilse said softly.

"He is," Audrey admitted.

"Please take care of each other."

"I will," Audrey said, but she couldn't suppress her relief that Ilse would be parting ways with Friedrich. Good as he was, selfishly she'd preferred it when Ilse was disdainful of him.

Friedrich opened the door.

"What about your uniform?" Audrey asked, noticing his empty hands.

"I left it behind the tree. My real papers too. Can't risk anyone finding it if they search the trunk. We will stop off here again on our way back. It will be fine."

He had a habit of saying that, Audrey noticed, and she wondered how much he believed it, and how much was solely for her and Ilse's benefit.

Twenty minutes later they slowed down, approaching the border.

"Here's the checkpoint," Friedrich said.

As if on cue, Daniel stirred. Ilse bounced him and took a deep breath.

"Remember your roles," Friedrich said. "Say nothing unless called upon. They will expect me to do the talking anyway."

The sun had risen fully, and Audrey watched as the border check came into view. There wasn't much to denote it aside from a couple of lean-to booths and a rather sad-looking fence running in both directions. The night before, she had asked Friedrich whether they could make an attempt on foot and avoid this road into the Netherlands entirely.

"Aldous's work is impeccable. Flawless," he'd assured her. "If we cross with those papers, no one will challenge us. If they see us creeping through the woods in darkness, there is a very good chance they will simply shoot before requesting our identification. And I need to cross as a civilian. An officer travelling outside of Berlin is one thing, but they would have serious questions about my business in the Netherlands. This is easier. Safer."

Audrey still had reservations about this plan, but she had to trust that Friedrich knew the state, knew what to expect from its police services. Their experience at the checkpoint outside Berlin had proven him right so far.

The car slowed to a stop beside the guard and once more, Friedrich rolled down the window. The guard was young, but he had dark circles beneath his eyes; Audrey wondered if he had been on shift all night.

"*Guten Morgen*," Friedrich said, and he slung his elbow over the window ledge again. This time Audrey wondered whether it was a deliberate attempt to appear relaxed, or if Friedrich had developed a habit of exhibiting his rank whenever the need to manipulate others presented itself.

"*Guten Morgen*," the guard replied. He ducked his head briefly to glance at Audrey, Ilse, and Daniel. "Papers."

Friedrich withdrew his civilian one, along with the others, from his jacket pocket. As the guard flipped through the documents, Friedrich drummed his fingers on the outside of the car door, smiling politely, but the guard ignored him. He looked over at Audrey and motioned for her to bring her face closer to the window, which she did. He glanced at the photo on her papers and back again, then repeated the process with Ilse. When he reached Friedrich's papers, his brow knitted.

"Herr Schmidt?" he asked.

"Yes?" Friedrich said.

"Walter Schmidt?"

"Yes."

"Of Schuttorf?"

Friedrich nodded. Aldous had deliberately chosen a town close enough to the Dutch border for the travellers to plausibly be heading over to visit family nearby in the Netherlands, and the name Walter Schmidt was common enough to avoid attention.

In the front seat, Daniel began to squirm, unhappy that the vehicle had stopped moving. Ilse cooed and bounced him more vigorously. Beside her, Friedrich coughed. The guard studied him again.

"Becker!" the guard shouted over his shoulder, and Audrey flinched. A second guard emerged from the small lean-to and strode over to them.

"Walter Schmidt," the first guard said to the other, an older, stockier man with a noticeable scar along his chin.

There was a silent moment when Becker reviewed the papers, then Friedrich. Daniel was now crying in earnest, and the din made Audrey clench her fists in her lap.

"Get out of the vehicle," Becker demanded. "Everyone."

Audrey's heart hammered a tattoo against her tonsils as she locked eyes with Ilse, who was next to tears, and Audrey willed her to suppress her emotion. What was happening? Friedrich had said they'd be fine. But here he was nodding and opening the car door. He moved to help Ilse out of the passenger seat.

"Stop!" The guards both shouted, cocking their pistols. "Turn around!"

Friedrich's eyes met Audrey's for half a moment, and she feared the apology she glimpsed in their depths. He turned around, hands in the air. Audrey slowly climbed out of the car. Ilse was already out, standing beside her door, futilely shushing Daniel. He was red in the face, drool shining around his mouth as his screams split the morning air and echoed across the nearby fields. But the officers' attention—and their pistols—were solely on Friedrich.

"Is there a problem, Officers?" Friedrich asked them.

"Walter Schmidt?" The first officer repeated.

"*Yes*," said Friedrich, his tone irritable. "I have told you so. As have my papers."

Despite her fear, Audrey was impressed with his performance. He must have been sweating beneath his jacket, but if the character of Walter Schmidt had nothing to hide, he would indeed be aggravated by this scrutiny and delay. Still, defiance under the circumstances took courage, and perhaps for the first time, she fully appreciated the extent of Friedrich Müller's bravery in taking on the Reich. Until now, it had existed in concept, and in action only within the safety of the Kaplans' comfortable sitting room as they discussed what they *might do* in resistance to Hitler. But in this moment, she observed a different version of the man. More warrior than idealist intellectual.

"Please either explain your concern or allow my family and me to be on our way," Friedrich went on.

"Wait here," Becker said, and disappeared back into the booth, leaving the first guard on watch. Daniel continued to wail.

"Quiet that child!" he barked.

"He needs a new nappy," Ilse said, her voice wavering. "They're in my bag in the front seat."

"Let her get the baby changed," Friedrich said. "It will stop the wailing."

The guard assented, and Audrey sidestepped over to Ilse and retrieved the bag from the car. She laid a cloth down on the gravel at their feet and Ilse changed Daniel, soothing him with her soft voice. Once he quieted, the sound of the morning sparrows twittering in the hedges along the fence line came into focus. Audrey stood and surveyed the Dutch landscape just across the border. They were *so* close. The landscape looked identical to the lush greenery where they currently stood, yet it glowed somehow. It was a beacon of safety, unlike the dangerous terrain of Germany. She watched as Ilse scooped up Daniel and pulled another bottle from her bag. Her hands were trembling. Audrey and Friedrich had to get them to safety. They had to.

The second guard, Becker, returned with a sheet of paper, which he thrust at his comrade. They muttered to one another, too low for Audrey to hear, and both squinted at Friedrich, who still held his hands in the air.

"I will need to search the vehicle," Becker said, flicking his hand at Audrey and Ilse as though waving away some irritant. The previous bite in his voice was gone.

They stepped back from the car, then the guard began his search, tossing items out onto the road as he went. As he opened their travelling cases, pawed through clothing and sundries, Audrey was thankful that Friedrich had abandoned his uniform behind the oak tree earlier. Seemingly satisfied, he slammed a door shut and beckoned to his comrade to lower his weapon. Audrey's heart leapt.

The guards approached Friedrich and spoke in low tones. After a brief exchange, Friedrich nodded, then gestured to Ilse and Audrey that they were leaving. As he helped Ilse into the front with Daniel, Audrey quickly collected the items the guard had scattered and climbed into the back.

"What happened?" she demanded.

"It would seem Aldous chose a name that was a little *too* common," Friedrich said, taking shaky breaths. "There is a Walter Schmidt wanted for robbery and battery two towns over."

Audrey gasped.

"Fortunately," Friedrich continued, "I do not match his physical description even remotely. Good God, my heart is racing." He cursed under his breath.

"So are they letting us through?" Ilse asked, eyes wide.

"Yes, they're letting us through. You're going to be safe now. You and Daniel." He held her gaze, touched her hand.

Audrey cleared her throat. "All right. Let's get the hell out of here. How much longer?"

Friedrich looked back at her. "We're nearly there. Less than an hour, I'd wager."

When they crossed the border, the mood inside the car lightened as the elation of success and freedom set in. They had done it. They had gotten Ilse and Daniel out. They continued through the countryside toward the Von Albrecht home in the Dutch woods, just outside Enschede. The sun was shining in earnest now.

In better spirits with a clean nappy and a full belly, Daniel babbled in Ilse's lap as Friedrich talked about his childhood in the south, near Munich.

"These woods remind me of the ones I used to run to when I didn't want to go to bed," he said, and his lip twitched as his eyes slid into the middle distance of his memory. "My mother hated the forest. Wouldn't come after me. She'd send my sister Gisela in to drag me out instead. I drove her mad, I think."

Ilse watched him. "You miss your family, don't you?"

"Well, that was my stepmother," he said. "I do wish I'd had more of a relationship with my real mother. But she's safe in Oxford. And that gives me comfort."

Ilse swayed as the car rolled over a bump in the road. "Do you think you'll see her again?"

Friedrich shifted his hands on the steering wheel. "I hope so. Though none of us knows what all of this will bring to our doorstep. I would hope a great many people will be reunited with their loved ones in the end."

Ilse held Daniel closer to her and stared out the windscreen.

Not long after, Friedrich handed Audrey the directions he'd been given to the Von Albrechts', and she navigated them the final few minutes. They pulled off the main road onto what could hardly be called a side road—it was more of a beaten path through the forest—and Friedrich had to slow the car to a crawl to avoid bottoming out on the large tree roots and holes of the forest floor. The house was well concealed, and Audrey was reassured. After a kilometre or so, the path widened at the edge of a clearing and a large stone house came into view.

"What's that?" Ilse said suddenly. "There, on the grass. Just there."

Audrey craned her neck.

"Oh fuck," Friedrich swore, braking to a stop.

"What is it?" Audrey demanded. "What do you see?"

"There's a body," Ilse said shakily. "There's a body on the lawn. A man, I think."

Friedrich shifted gears and backed the car into the woods again, a good twenty feet away from the clearing.

"Stay here," he said sharply, opening his door.

"What are you doing?" Audrey hissed. "You don't have your gun!"

"Yes, I do," Friedrich said, and he disappeared beneath the car for several seconds before emerging, pistol in his hand.

He strode toward the house, gun raised.

"I'm going, too," Audrey said, scrambling out of the back and hurrying after him.

"Audrey, no!" Ilse called. "Wait!"

"Audrey, for God's sake," Friedrich muttered. "Stay behind me then. *Right* behind me. And keep an eye on the trees."

She crept along in his wake as he entered the clearing. A crow took flight from a nearby tree, cawing and flapping its wings. Audrey scanned the tree line but saw no other sign of movement.

They reached the prone man on the ground. The grass around him was smeared with dark brown, dried blood. Audrey looked away as her stomach turned, but Friedrich knelt beside him.

"Who is he?" she asked.

"I'm guessing Henrik Von Albrecht, Wendelein's husband. He matches the description I was given, and this is their house. He's been shot in the chest. Dead a while. At least a day or two." Friedrich was still for a moment, then slid the man's eyelids shut.

As he rose, Audrey took a deep breath. "Friedrich—" she began, but he cut across her.

"Do you smell that?"

She sniffed the air, then looked up at the house. "Smoke."

"Not from the chimney though," he said, pointing. "The house is smouldering."

It was. Dark grey curls drifted skyward from the roof and what remained of the broken and burned-out windows. The grass around the foundation of the building was scorched and littered with debris. This place was meant to keep Ilse safe from harm, but all that remained was the blistered detritus of a defeated possibility.

"This was targeted," Audrey said. "It has to have been."

"Yes."

They stood together on the lawn as the reality of their circumstances hit. Everything they had done, the risks they had taken to get Ilse and Daniel here, were all for naught. They would have to turn around and go back to Berlin. Audrey's mind began to spiral. To escape to the Netherlands had been their best answer to the cell's ultimatum, and the futility of the whole venture settled itself inside her chest like some crouching spider.

She glanced back at the woods, the car. How would she break the news to Ilse? What would happen to them now?

The sun shone overhead, glowing against the robin's-egg-blue sky, the hint of early spring, and a breeze blew through the clearing. The man's body and the smoking house clashed impossibly with the idyllic scenery.

A thought occurred to Audrey. "What about his wife? Wendelein?"

"She could be anywhere. Abducted? She could have made it farther than him and been shot in the woods."

They both scanned the edge of the forest around them.

"It's too big to search," Audrey said dully, turning her attention back to the house. "She could be inside. Let's go look."

The front door was open, scorched from flame.

"I don't know whether it's safe to go in," Friedrich said. "Likely not. It could collapse at any moment given the state it's in."

"Nothing we're doing is safe, Friedrich. We have to at least look," Audrey said.

He sighed in resignation. "Come on, then."

They entered the house, squinting as their eyes adjusted to the dim light. Sun shone through the windows, but it was much darker than the clearing. The air was heavy with the scent of smoke, and the burned floorboards beneath their feet creaked and cracked with every footfall.

"Hello?" Audrey called out, but there was no reply.

They didn't make it farther than the sitting room before Friedrich stopped her. "There's no one here," he said. "Not alive, anyway. They must have been found out."

"By whom?"

"I do not know. But there is no other explanation for this. We need to leave now. The local authorities might show up, and we have no reason to be here that they would accept. Or the people who targeted the Von

Albrechts could return. We have no real idea what we just walked into. We need to leave, Audrey. I'm serious."

When Audrey didn't move, Friedrich faced her square-on. "None of us wants this to be true. But it is. We will think of something else."

"There is nothing else, Friedrich. There's no other option," Audrey pressed, panic rising in her chest. "We've been over—"

He held her shoulders. "We cannot rail against what is true, Audrey," he said. "No matter how much we wish it were not. There is nothing these people can do for us now, God help them. I promise you we will find another answer."

"How? How will we keep her safe now?"

"Because we *must*!" he snapped.

He turned from her, but Audrey remained still. "You love her, don't you?" she blurted.

Friedrich halted, looked back. She knew by the expression of angst on his face that she was right, and dismay settled on her like the ash floating around this burned-out house. Her eyes stung with it.

Friedrich shifted his feet.

"I do," he said, and though she'd expected it, the admission cut her. "And I know you do too."

They stared at one another in the remains of the Von Albrecht sitting room as silence stretched between them. Tears threatened, but Audrey beat them back. He could never know how much she loved Ilse, could never love her like Audrey did, anchored with the compounding weight of a lifetime of friendship.

Audrey swept past him without a word and into the harsh light of the clearing. The crow was pecking at the dead man's body now, and took flight in alarm as Audrey strode past, its shrill cry echoing the turmoil in her heart.

Chapter 23

Audrey

BERLIN, GERMANY | MARCH 1939

Audrey stomped her boots on the porch, trying to knock some warmth into her toes. She cupped her coffee in her hands, breathed in the aromatic steam that was always a comfort to her. Her thighs were cold from sitting on the stone stoop, but she didn't care. She needed to be outside the confines of the house, revive herself in the fresh air.

It was still dark, the streetlights on. She'd woken well before dawn, her mind restlessly trying to work out what to do next. They'd arrived back in Berlin the previous afternoon in a state of disbelief, stiff from the lengthy round-trip journey. None of them said much to one another. Friedrich had told them to eat, sleep, and they would regroup in the morning.

Audrey stared across the street at the Richters' house without really seeing it. What she wouldn't give to go back, just for a while, to how things used to be. To live there again with her father and Sophie. To go back to that beautiful time when she had no idea that any of this lurked in their future.

She shook back her coat sleeve to glance at her watch.

5:49 a.m.

She thought of Ludwig's threat, his ultimatum for Ilse and Daniel to be gone in forty-eight hours. Not even a day remained. And what would happen once the cell discovered Friedrich and Audrey hadn't abided by their demands? Her sleepless night had presented an idea, though she was doubtful of Ilse's reaction to it.

She exhaled a cloud of fog and went inside. Ilse was awake now, seated in the lounge off her father's study, a fire flickering in the grate.

"Hi," she said as Audrey entered. "Daniel's still asleep. Yesterday exhausted him, poor thing." She was curled up on the sofa in her robe and slippers, feet tucked under her, as usual. "What were you doing outside? It's freezing."

"I know," Audrey said. "I needed some air."

"I know how that is," Ilse said with a mild bite. "I was looking forward to more fresh air."

Audrey sighed and took a seat next to her. "You were willing to go to the Netherlands for Daniel."

Ilse watched her, nodded.

"I know it's farther away, but would you be willing to go to my aunt's, in Alnwick? In England? And maybe I would go with you this time?"

"But it's so much farther away, Audrey, *so* much more risk to get there, especially with Daniel. I told you I wouldn't go to England with you those first days after"—her voice shook on the rough terrain of the memory—"after all this started, because I need to be here. I never wanted to leave this house in the first place, and that remains true. If there is a war coming, like Friedrich says, how could I possibly get back to Berlin from England when Ephraim and Mama return? Even with an English passport? I—"

"But it's *dire* now, Ilse, with Ludwig's threats, you can't . . ." Understanding hit her in the face.

"What?" Ilse asked.

"You don't want to leave him, do you?"

Ilse swallowed, fixed her eyes on her own knees. "Daniel? Of course I won't."

"Friedrich," Audrey said. "I mean Friedrich, Ilse."

Ilse was silent, and Audrey felt something release inside herself, a pressure that had been building for months. Despite her feelings for Ilse, the future she yearned for with her and could not have, their shared past still remained. That friendship, that sisterhood, still existed beneath the layers of complication.

"You've been my best friend my whole life," Audrey said. "And you still are. I know we've grown apart a little under these circumstances. But if you won't be honest with me, I don't know what's become of us."

Tears came to Ilse's eyes. "I'm sorry. You're right about everything you just said. The truth is, I feel safe with him. I feel protected. And he's kind, we have a connection."

Audrey wrestled down the knot in her throat, the realization that she alone wasn't enough to make Ilse feel safe.

"Hello." Friedrich appeared in the doorway, dressed in civilian wear, and Audrey and Ilse leaned back, wiping their eyes. He took a seat in the large red armchair across from them, looking about as exhausted as Audrey felt. "I will get straight to the point," he said, his eyes on Ilse. "I have given the matter a great deal of thought since we left Enschede, and I think we need to get married."

Audrey's stomach swooped. Ilse's mouth hung open.

"*What?*" Ilse said.

Friedrich opened his hands, imploring. "At this juncture, with no other safe house available—at least in the short term—it is the *only* course of action I see remaining."

"Why?" Audrey demanded.

Friedrich kept his gaze on Ilse. "Seeing what happened to the Von Albrecht cell has been sobering. It is entirely likely that, at some point,

I will get killed during our resistance efforts. If I do, us being married will ensure that my wealth is transferred to you. It will be more than enough to support you and Daniel for some time to come. As it stands, your familial wealth has been absorbed by the Reich, and I do not have the power to recover it."

Audrey knew this, but the reality still bowled her over. "But how does that protect her, all of us, from Ludwig's threats?" she asked. "He wants her *gone*, as does Claus. You heard what he—"

"That is the second point I would like to make," Friedrich said. "None of them are aware that the safe house was destroyed, though I must tell Aldous, as he was the connection and he will find out through some other channel. But in the immediate term, I suggest we tell them all that Ilse and Daniel are in the Netherlands, and if we have another incident like the other night, where your presence is revealed," he continued, eyes on Ilse again, "we would then have ammunition against Thurman's accusations in the form of your and Daniel's false identification *and* our registered marriage. I cannot imagine it would be worth the risk for him to pursue the matter, knowing he could be embarrassed if he cannot prove Ilse's true identity. He isn't about to personally search the house for you. We may yet be able to buy ourselves some time, and this scheme safeguards us. Aldous is sympathetic, as you know, and I believe I can convince Claus to drop the issue. He's reasonable. I think he was simply caught off guard."

Audrey and Ilse sat side by side in the prickly silence, contemplating the proposal.

Friedrich clasped his hands together in front of him. "I know it would not be a love match for you," he told Ilse. "But it would allow you to remain here, in your home. Still hiding on Friday evenings, but . . . here, nevertheless."

Audrey watched for Ilse's reaction, but her face was inscrutable. After a long moment, she spoke.

"Could we have a Jewish ceremony?" she asked. She did not deny it being a love match.

Friedrich shook his head. "I don't think there would be a ceremony at all. Too much risk. It would be on paper. It wouldn't need to mean anything, though, if you do not want it to." He cleared his throat. "It would be playacting. A show. Audrey can attest," he added. He turned to her for validation, but Audrey couldn't answer.

Ilse rose, and the atmosphere in the room shifted. "The two of you may have muddied your identities to the point where you do not even know yourselves anymore—"

"Ilse!" Audrey protested, stung.

"But my faith is not just a part of who I am. It *is* who I am. You told me I needed to give up my name, my home, my way of life, and I did that. But I cannot surrender my faith to this cause. I cannot betray it, or dilute it, because if I do, what is any of this for? Am I staying alive to become someone else entirely? Someone I no longer understand, or trust? Am I to look in the mirror and see a Nazi's Christian wife?"

Audrey understood her objection. They were living now in some alternative world, a nightmarish shadow of everything they had known. Ilse was just trying to hold tight to the things that mattered in the hope that there would still be something to recognize when the world finally righted itself.

Friedrich's face was pinched with emotion.

Ilse stood in front of him, expectant. "How can you ask that of me, Friedrich?"

He exhaled sharply. "Do you think it easy for me, Ilse? It is my faith, too, in case you have forgotten. Do you think I don't struggle *every single day* as I don my uniform? That I don't look in the mirror and think of my mother and loathe myself for all of it?"

"Then why do you do it?"

"Because this is bigger than me," Friedrich said simply. "I am inconsequential. All that matters is the good I am able to do from this position of power. I believe God can see past the insignia on my uniform, and know my soul. Know that the clothes I wear and the character I play are not who I truly am inside. I thought you knew that too."

She clenched her jaw.

"And you would not be surrendering your faith to our cause. You would *exchange* it, temporarily, for your and Daniel's survival, Ilse. All I—all Audrey and I want is to ensure your safety. We care for you. Very deeply."

Audrey looked away from them. She didn't want to see his feelings reflected in Ilse's eyes, golden in the firelight.

The silence stretched out until Ilse took a steadying breath. "Can you give us a moment, please?" Her voice was hoarse with fatigue.

Friedrich rose from his chair and stomped toward the kitchen. Ilse threw herself back down beside Audrey.

"It's the only answer, isn't it?"

Audrey couldn't decide whether her world would fall apart or be held together if Ilse married Friedrich. It still made more sense to Audrey that they try to get her to England, where she would have the physical freedoms the Von Albrecht home had offered her. But Audrey steeled herself to reply with what she knew Ilse wanted to hear.

"Yes. I think it is."

On a Thursday night in late March, Audrey was squeezed next to Rolf Weber at The Adlon. The upholstered half-moon booth was spacious enough for them, Gerta Roth and her friend Marianne, and Otto Basner and his secretary, but Weber purposefully pressed up against Audrey, his breath steamy against her neck. The air was thick with jazz, noisy conversation, and a bluish haze of cigarette smoke. Audrey preferred the more spirited, edgier swing jazz she'd listened to when she was back in England—the sort the Americans and the rest of Europe enjoyed now—if it was ever played. But the instrumentals at German clubs, including the premier Adlon lounge, were limited to the jazz prescribed by Goebbels and the Ministry of Propaganda and Public Enlightenment: written and performed by Third Reich–approved artists and considered acceptable for the ears of good Germans.

"I love this song," Gerta Roth said, standing and pulling Marianne to her feet. "Let's dance."

Her husband, Ernst, hadn't come with her tonight. Hitler was on a speaking tour, which had taken Ernst out of town for nearly two weeks, but Gerta didn't let that stop her from having fun, and plenty of it. She was a plain-looking woman with a fiery disposition at odds with her mouse-brown hair and short stature.

Gerta flashed Audrey a broad grin. "Ada? You *never* dance! Come on!"

Audrey had come to suspect that valuable information was not going to come directly from Weber, who never danced, but preferred to sit close to Audrey and play with her hair. Despite her attempts to flirt information out of him, he always rebuffed any talk of work. With each overpriced glass of spirits, his comments became more risqué, his hands more curious. She hadn't yet learned a damn thing of value, but Weber still served a purpose: he was the vehicle for Audrey to access the Roths and any details they might possess about Hitler's schedule.

Audrey smiled and made to stand up, but Weber seized her arm and shook his head.

"Uh, Rolf, you're such a fossil!" Gerta rolled her eyes at Weber, but he waved her away.

Another half hour passed whilst Audrey sat in quiet, suggestive conversation with Weber, her insides burning with frustration and disgust. When Otto and his secretary left, he leaned in to kiss her neck and she willed herself not to bristle, casting her eyes over to the dance floor. Gerta was now hanging off Marianne, who appeared to be supporting her.

She gestured away from the floor and Gerta nodded, putting a hand to her mouth. They were heading for the ladies' toilets, and Audrey spied an opportunity. The brass continued to blare as Weber turned Audrey's face to him, pressed his lips onto hers, leaving behind the taste of gin and dominance. A sort of growl slipped through his mouth, a sound of impatient longing, and she pulled away, smiled demurely.

"I'm just going to freshen up," she shouted over the din. He nodded, and released his grip on her.

"Five minutes," he said.

She slid from the booth with a feeling of having slipped a trap, and hurried toward the toilets.

"Ada!" Gerta exclaimed. She was standing at the sinks. Marianne was clearly in a stall. Gerta slid a little on the tile floor as she reached for Audrey, who was glad, for her sake, that Ernst wasn't here tonight. Women in the Reich weren't meant to drink to excess, and he wouldn't have liked her behaviour. Audrey hoped Weber wouldn't mention it to him.

"Are you okay?" Audrey asked.

"Ugh, yes. It's those gin and tonics."

In the stall, Marianne urinated with a little sigh.

"I think when you're done here, we should get you a taxi," Audrey suggested. She thought for a beat. "I'll ride with you." She would figure out some way to dodge Weber. She hadn't yet had a chance like this, alone with Gerta, and wasn't about to squander it.

Gerta gave a childlike frown. "There's no one waiting for me, what does it matter? Ernst won't even be home until Saturday. They're in Frankfurt until tomorrow."

Excitement flared. This was what Audrey had hoped for. "You said they've been all over for this speaking tour?" she asked.

"Yes, he hasn't even telegrammed from the hotels," Gerta complained. "In eight days!"

"But then he'll be back for a while, right?"

Gerta turned to the mirror and patted her hair, tried to fix a rogue strand. She grasped it between her fingers on the second attempt. "Yes. A week. No." She shook her head. "What day is it? Two weeks. Two weeks. Then we're going to Hanover."

The stall door slammed and Marianne came out, washed her hands with the hotel's expensive soap. The pungent scent of lily-of-the-valley filled the room as Gerta continued to struggle with her hair.

"Let me," Audrey said, moving behind her. Repinning Gerta's errant curls, she casually asked, "What are you doing in Hanover? A little get-away?"

"Sort of," Gerta said. "Ernst is driving the Führer, but we're going to stay over, visit a couple of friends. Get a smart hotel."

A little shiver danced across Audrey's shoulders.

"Come on," Marianne said, ignoring Audrey. "I'm hungry. Let's go for dinner." She seized Gerta's arm, but Audrey caught the other and held fast. Marianne shrugged and exited the bathroom, muttering about her hunger. A cacophony of loud brass swelled for a moment before the polished wooden door swung shut.

"What's the Führer doing there?" Audrey pressed, blood pulsing through her temples.

Gerta stepped back, thoughtful, and swayed. "I think it's some Hitler Youth thing," she said. "At the Opera House."

Audrey's heart raced. She needed to know when, but she didn't want to risk Gerta's suspicions by asking more. Or was Gerta too drunk to remember that she'd revealed anything at all? It was a gamble. Not one she was willing to take. Hopefully knowing the day would be enough.

"Well, I'm so glad the two of you will get a chance to spend some time together," she said brightly.

Gerta smiled, though her expression was pained. "I know I should feel fortunate that we're so close to the Führer," she said, leaning into Audrey, her eyes unfocused. "But sometimes it feels like he might ruin us."

Chapter 24

Audrey

BERLIN, GERMANY | MARCH 1939

Friedrich!" Audrey called the moment she crossed the threshold of the house. Then she realized it was nearly eleven o'clock. Daniel and Ilse would have been asleep for hours now, maybe Friedrich, too, but this news could not wait. She felt a surge of exhilaration that—finally—she could deliver something of value. She kicked off her shoes. "Friedrich," she said again, quieter this time as she rushed down the hall. "Are you down here?"

Footsteps sounded and then he appeared, concern on his face. "What is it?" he demanded, taking in her windswept hair and bright eyes. "You're so late, is everything all—"

"Yes," she said, breathless. "I have news. Come. Sit."

He followed her into the sitting room, though neither sat down. She still wore her coat.

"Weber took me for drinks, but it was Gerta Roth who did all the talking."

"What?"

"She was drunk, and told me all about how she and Ernst hardly have time together, but that they're going to be in Hanover weekend after next, starting Friday." She grinned. "Hitler will be speaking at the Staatsoper Opera House on the Saturday. I couldn't get the time without drawing suspicion, but I think—"

"It is enough," Friedrich said, his expression clearing. "They will release more in the news the day before. But with date and location, we can plan. This is brilliant, Audrey. Brilliant!" He moved to embrace her, then rather awkwardly clapped her on the shoulder instead. "Well done. *Well done.*"

Audrey basked in the praise for a moment before the elation fell away. "There's more. The opportunity is not without complications." She pinched her lips. "He's speaking to an assembly of the Hitler Youth."

Friedrich's shoulders slumped. "Goddamnit. Are you serious?"

"Yes. I think we need to talk to the others."

Friedrich looked to the ceiling, then back down at her. "Yes. Yes, we do."

"It's late though."

He glanced at the mantel clock. "I know. But we need to discuss this immediately. I'll go telephone them."

Audrey and Friedrich spent the better part of an hour working through the possibilities until Ludwig, Claus, and Aldous arrived.

Audrey peered out the window, checking that their late visit hadn't drawn attention, but the street was deserted. She twitched the curtains closed, then nodded at Friedrich.

"We'll get straight to the point," he said. "Hitler will be giving a speech Saturday after next, in Hanover. At the Opera House."

All three of them froze for a fleeting moment, then Ludwig let out a low "Yes!" Claus looked excited, Aldous impassive.

"How did you learn this?" Claus asked.

Friedrich smiled at Audrey. "Audrey can explain."

Ludwig crossed his arms over his chest as Audrey recounted what had happened that evening, hesitating when she relayed the news about the event being a gathering of the Hitler Youth. The charge of excitement hanging over the room dissipated like smoke in a cold wind.

"Children?" Claus asked. His eyes pierced Friedrich's, and Audrey knew they were in for a fight. "We can't attack him with children in the line of fire, Fred. Come on now."

"Why not?" Ludwig challenged him.

"Do we seriously need to have that conversation?" Claus rolled his stalky shoulders back, and Audrey remembered he had a family. "We're not doing this."

"Why not?"

"Because they're *children*, Thurman," Claus said.

"We could try to make sure we aim for him when he's not near them," Friedrich said. "Audrey—"

"We may not get another chance like this," Ludwig interrupted. "We've had a valuable leak, and we need to use it. There've been a slew of attempts, and the bastard keeps evading death. We have a responsibility to act!"

"We have a responsibility to not kill kids, Lud." Claus shook his head in disbelief. "Listen to yourself."

Friedrich raised his voice. "Gentlemen!"

"What do you care?" Ludwig fired at Claus.

"I'm not in the business of killing children, you prick."

"Do you know how many children the Reich has already sent to their deaths?" Audrey challenged him.

Claus's nostrils flared.

"She has a point," Aldous piped up. "But I do think we need to consider—"

"Consider what? This is madness," Claus snapped. "We're not doing it. I can't build a bomb that won't have collateral damage. It just cannot be done."

"Other people are going to die, Claus," Ludwig shouted, and Audrey winced, hoped to God he wouldn't wake Daniel. "Unless you want to try to snipe him. But I'll remind you that we've been over that option before. None of us is a precise enough shot to guarantee it, and the shooter is certainly going to be killed by Hitler's security team. Pointing a gun at the Führer's fucking head is pretty obvious. Planting a timed bomb in advance and walking away—less so."

"What do you propose we do, Fred?" Aldous asked, turning from Ludwig. "Did you have a plan in mind?"

Claus scoffed. "You all just want—"

"Yes, we do." Audrey cut across Claus, but shot him a conciliatory look. "I think there might be a way to do this that would drastically decrease the likelihood of collateral injury to the children."

The room was silent, skeptical. Then Aldous spoke.

"Let's hear it."

"I know the Staatsoper Opera House in Hanover," she said. "I saw performances there when I was younger. I remember the layout and the area around it reasonably well. It's in an old quarter of the city, so I doubt much has changed in a decade." The men looked at her, listening, and she ploughed on. "As Ludwig says, shooting him isn't a viable option. What we need is some distance on the kill, to keep ourselves and any potential bystanders safe. I propose we avoid trying to reach him at the pulpit or anywhere else on the actual premises where the children are likely to be," she said, gaining confidence with her plan as she spoke. "I say we target his motorcar. It'll be parked on the street outside, either in front or behind the building. From what I remember of the Opera House, they'll probably park the car behind the theatre, as opposed to the front, which would be too exposed. The car will still be surrounded by security, of course, but if we can place a bomb underneath the vehicle at some point during the speech, it will go off *after* he's left in the car."

Aldous was nodding. "This could work," he said.

Ludwig muttered something affirmative and poured himself a

drink. Claus met eyes with Audrey, uncertain, but no longer angry.

"That means the likely casualties would only extend to his driver and body men," Friedrich added. "Perhaps a few people on the street, or in a neighbouring vehicle, if they happen to have the misfortune of being in the wrong place at the wrong time, but that's negligible. The number of lives we would be saving after the fact are incalculable. This is worth the risk, worth the sacrifice." He glared around the room. "And you all know it."

Audrey felt a stirring of guilt at using Gerta Roth's information to plan an assassination involving her husband. But this was bigger than any one man. As Friedrich had said, this was bigger than all of them.

"I agree," Ludwig said. "We should proceed."

The fact that he'd only agreed once Friedrich had given her proposal his support set Audrey's teeth on edge, but she let the slight go with an exhale.

"How precise can you make your timer on the explosive device?" Friedrich asked Claus.

He thought for a moment. "Pretty damn precise. I'm good. How long would we need, do you think?"

Friedrich considered it. "We have no way of knowing where Hitler is headed once in the motorcar. But the timer would need to be at least, what, two or three minutes perhaps, from when he enters the vehicle to when it's clear of the theatre. Add in the time in between planting it, to Hitler actually entering the vehicle . . ." He cocked his head. "I'd wager maybe twenty minutes?"

"How do we plant the explosive, Claus?" Aldous asked.

"I'd have to do it myself," Claus said. "The rest of you needn't put yourselves in any real danger, don't fret. But we would need some kind of diversion so I could attach it to the underside of his car."

Audrey didn't skip a beat. "I can do that. Of course."

"We would need fake identification to pass for security personnel or some such."

Aldous nodded. "I just need a sample. You all know I can't be of any help on-site, with this," he said, tapping the handle of his cane. "I'm not exactly quick on my feet, nor inconspicuous."

"If Audrey can draw security away from the motorcar, Claus and I could offer to stay with the vehicle whilst they go investigate," Friedrich offered.

"That works," Claus agreed. "Can't see why anyone would object if we're in uniform. We can give false names if we need to."

"Then you can plant the device?" Friedrich asked him.

"Yes."

"How long would you need to actually plant it?" Audrey asked.

"Maybe five minutes."

"And then what?" Aldous said.

Claus sighed. "We plant it and, well . . . get the living hell out of there. Lud, can you be ready and waiting with our car?"

Ludwig nodded curtly.

"But would they notice if Hitler's car is unattended when they finally get back to it?" Aldous asked. "Would that send up a red flag?"

Ludwig shrugged gruffly. "If Audrey can create enough of a diversion, it's possible his security might be too distracted to notice. Difficult to say. But there's usually more security on arrival than on departure, once they've already determined the location is clear."

"But I think we would have to risk that anyway," Claus said. "We don't want to be anywhere near that fucking car when the device goes off."

"We can discuss risk and likelihood until the hair on my ass turns grey," Ludwig boomed. "Every man is here because he knows this must be done. We accepted the risk at our first meeting. The fact remains this is a *real* chance to eliminate him."

"With any luck, it's the only chance we will need," Friedrich said.

A heavy silence befell the group as the prospect of murdering Hitler, and the subsequent fallout, descended on them. After several long moments, Aldous leaned on his cane and pushed himself up.

"Well," he said, "let's get to it, then. We've got work to do if we're going to bring down the damn Reich two weeks from now. The pawns need to be in place before we try to take the king."

The following evening after Daniel was asleep, Audrey, Ilse, and Friedrich gathered in the sitting room. The fire crackled in the grate, warming them for what was sure to be a chilling conversation.

As Friedrich and Audrey filled Ilse in on the plan, she sat silently.

"I know none of us wants to think about the worst possible outcome with this venture," Friedrich said, his hands clasped between his knees, dark eyes on Ilse. "But we need to discuss it."

Ilse's nostrils flared. "You mean what happens to me and Daniel if you both get killed? Or arrested?"

Audrey reached for Ilse's hand, pressing through that invisible barrier to the woman she had loved, in one way or another, for so long.

"Neither Friedrich nor I will be near the bomb," she said. "The plan is for us to be long gone before the detonation takes place. We will do everything we can to return safely, Ilse. I promise."

"It sounds terribly unsafe," Ilse said. "Mad, even."

Friedrich nodded. "I know. But Audrey is right. We've planned this so that we will be as far away from the risk of harm as we possibly can. And Ilse . . . no matter what happens here, if we succeed, the risk will always have been worth it. Surely you must see that. You and I, together, must accept this risk. For the sake of our people. For Daniel's future, and the future of every Jewish child. It is for them that we do this."

Ilse's eyes welled with tears as Audrey's heart ached from the outskirts.

You and I, together.

Friedrich ran his fingers through his hair. "There are four possible outcomes here," he said, all business. "The first possibility is that we fail but survive. In that case, Audrey and I return home and continue as we are. The second and third possibilities are that we fail and die, or succeed and die." His voice was rougher now, as though he'd wrapped it in jute cloth. "If we succeed, the death of Adolf Hitler won't necessarily mean immediate freedom for Jews. We cannot know the precise impact his demise will have, though obviously we hope it will be substantial, enough to trigger, or at least hasten, the fall of the Reich. But you would need to lie low, risk nothing unnecessarily. There would be no small amount of shame or suspicion attached to the widow of a dead traitor. If we fail," Friedrich continued, "I think you need to seriously reconsider Audrey's suggestion to flee to her aunt in England. I will speak to Aldous in advance of this operation, but I know he would help you."

Audrey stared at a spot on the sage green paisley-patterned rug at her feet. Hearing Friedrich so frankly describe the aftermath of their deaths was arresting.

"And the fourth outcome?" Ilse asked quietly.

Friedrich forced a small smile. "We succeed and survive. We move forward here, together, in what will hopefully be a peaceful new Germany."

"*Im yirtsé hashém*," Ilse said. God willing.

Friedrich shifted in his chair. "Our marriage certificate has been filed with the registrar's office, so if I die, all my wealth passes to you. If the worst does happen, I would appreciate it if you could send a certain sum to my mother. I will leave her details with you. Please keep them protected. I would prefer you memorize them, then destroy them."

Ilse brushed away a tear. "Of course. Of course, I will."

A cloak of despondency settled on Audrey. How little would it matter if she, not Friedrich, perished in the attempt? If she died and Friedrich lived, he would return home to Ilse. They might even have a real future together, if her feelings for him continued to grow from the seedling clearly taking hold in her heart. Audrey bore jealousy for Friedrich, certainly, but she could not deny that with his machinations in place, regardless of what happened to Audrey now, Ilse's future might be secured, and she simultaneously appreciated and resented him for it.

They all stared into the flames. There wasn't much more to say.

"I'm going up," Ilse said. "Get a decent sleep before Daniel wakes up. Three in the morning, like clockwork, it seems. Good night."

Ilse's footsteps retreated upstairs, and Friedrich and Audrey sat a while longer, each lost in their own thoughts.

Friedrich broke the silence. "Do you want a drink, Audrey?"

"God, yes."

He returned with a pair of overfilled glasses, though in light of the conversation, Audrey welcomed the generous pour. He sat down again and took a sip, then held the glass up to the firelight, examining it.

"Do you know the history of this drink, Schwartzhog? The legend behind it?" he asked.

Audrey shook her head and drank deeply of the familiar, spicy liqueur.

"Back in the sixteenth century, a German noble family was attacked one night by envious rivals. But a black boar on the property started to squeal, and the family woke, fought off the attackers, and survived. They put the black boar on their crest to honour it for saving them from a terrible fate, and named their liquor after it."

Audrey gazed into the syrupy depths of her glass, mulling over Friedrich's tale. "Is that really true?"

"So they say."

She ran her finger around the edge of the glass. "And did the boar survive?"

Friedrich looked puzzled. "What?"

"Did the boar survive?" she repeated. "It squealed enough to wake the family, so I assume it was heard by the attackers too."

Friedrich's mouth twisted into a contemplative pucker. "I've never thought about that, to be honest. It's just a legend. You think it died, then?"

Audrey took another sip. "Yes," she said quietly. "I think it died. It might have died a hero, but it died a hero with a slit throat."

Friedrich watched her for a moment, then set his glass down on the table between them. "As much as I hate to say it, that reminds me . . . I have something for you." He pulled a small brown paper bag from inside his jacket and opened it to reveal two black coat buttons. He handed her one. "This is a cyanide capsule. Made to look like a coat button. It is a last resort, a safety catch."

"Friedrich," Audrey said, feeling sick. "I don't want this." She made to hand it back to him, but he pulled away.

"You may not think you do right now, but if you are arrested, it is almost a certainty that you will be subjected to torture so they can find out what you know of the Red Orchestra and our resistance efforts. I assure you, a quick death by poisoning is a far better fate than anything the SS can dream up for you. I need you to trust me on that."

Audrey studied his face, more serious than she had ever seen it. What had he witnessed, or heard of, in his professional life? "I can't—"

"Sew it into the inside of your pocket, or hide it in the sole of your shoe," he said. "When you are searched, it looks like an extra button. But when you decide you want it, rip it out and crush it between your teeth. Do not think twice, or you'll hesitate, and those seconds could mean the difference between a quick or a drawn-out death."

Staring down at the pill-button, Audrey felt more out of her depth than ever. This all felt like a dream sometimes, a story from someone else's life. She was just a pianist. Not much more than a girl. When had she become a spy, an assassin?

Her eyes welled with emotion and she took another large gulp of the liquor. "Friedrich," she said, and she was grateful to the Schwartzhog for depressing her nerves. "If I don't make it out of this alive, I need you to promise me you'll take care of her."

They looked at each other, perhaps seeing one another fully for the first time.

"I will," he said.

"She cares for you too. She feels safe with you." It was an effort to say it, but she did anyway. "That's something I haven't been able to give her. Being a woman . . ." She trailed off, angry at all of it. That women needed men for protection. That they lived in a world that was designed and run and ruined by men. That Ilse wanted a man instead of her. She was lightheaded now, but it made it easier to say what she must. "Love her like she's the best thing to ever happen to you. Because she will be. That is a certainty."

"I will," he said.

Audrey felt the smooth button clenched in her hand. "Promise me."

"I promise. I will take care of her, and love her. For the both of us."

She downed the rest of her drink and bade Friedrich good night, then retrieved her grey coat from the hall closet. Upstairs, she built a small fire in the grate and fetched her sewing kit from the dresser, selecting an ash-coloured thread. She held it up in the firelight to measure before snipping it off and feeding it, with a shaky hand, through the needle head. She tied a knot and began to work, thinking of Ilse and Friedrich and murdering Adolf Hitler, all the while wondering why she bothered to find a matching thread to sew her death into the pocket of her coat.

Chapter 25

Audrey

BERLIN, GERMANY | APRIL 1939

I guess this is it, then." Friedrich exhaled a long stream of nerves, his breath visible in the cold air.

The morning of the assassination attempt had dawned with a plunge in temperature and a dusting of snow, and Audrey and Friedrich sat together in the automobile he had hired under a false name, going over their mental checklist. It was early, barely light out, but their journey would take about four hours. They would pick up Claus on their way out of town near an abandoned warehouse that would render no witnesses. Ludwig was driving alone to avoid the others being seen in his car prior to the attack, and would wait in his vehicle near the Opera House to reconvene with them once the mission was complete. Aldous had taken the train to Hanover alone the week before, for reconnaissance and to map out the area, and Audrey was pleased when he confirmed her recollections of the Opera House and its neighbourhood.

Friedrich looked at Audrey from under the rim of his cap. She had never seen him so unsettled, though she could hardly blame him. This was the riskiest, most intense day of any of their lives. But she felt composed. She was ready for this. So much had been building toward it, they'd all put so much on the line. She'd tolerated Weber's revolting advances and gropes for the scrap of critical information that had led to this day, and a balloon of hope buoyed her. This might be the end of it. They might make it out alive. Germany might wake to a new and brighter future the next day where Ruth, Ephraim, and Ilse were free.

Audrey had said her goodbye to Ilse upstairs before they came down for breakfast. They held each other, and Ilse had cried, but Audrey kept her emotions in check. She'd already said everything she needed to say. Being Ilse's best and longest friend would be enough, because it had to be. She would love what they were and had been, and let go of what she wanted them to be. And, Audrey thought, an optimistic mindset tilting toward success was essential for what they were about to do. Tears would not help.

As they pulled away from the curb, she looked back at the Kaplans' house. The past few months, the house had been a small haven, a private island in the middle of the red and black sea. This might be the last time she would see it, the place that had been her home in practice for three years, and in spirit far longer than that.

The first day she crossed the street to meet Ilse flashed before her, Sophie's admonishments echoing in her mind. With a surge of determination, she pushed it all down and forced herself to look away.

The car was freezing, and she stuck her gloved hands into her coat pockets. "When are they going to put some kind of heating system in these damn things?" she mused.

"I hear they have them in America," Friedrich said.

Audrey smirked. "If we end up as fugitives, I say we hop a boat to Boston, then."

Friedrich laughed, and she glanced sideways at him. She'd never seen him really laugh before. She knew he was nervous, but there was a glow about him that warmed her.

They drove to the city's edge in relative silence, each contemplating the day before them. Claus was waiting with his back against a brown brick warehouse, a briefcase-sized canvas bag beside him. The car jostled as he climbed into the back seat. Audrey and Friedrich turned to him, and all three sets of eyes fell on the bag.

"That's it?" Friedrich asked.

Claus nodded. "Yeah. Enough TNT to change the world."

"And blow up our car?"

Claus chuckled. "No, fortunately. It's far less sensitive than the alternatives. It's pretty much safe until I connect it to the detonators."

Friedrich faced the wheel. "If you say so."

"I do. Relax, Fred."

The ride to Hanover was uneventful and beautiful. The sun rose and shone as they drove along a quiet motorway, passing few other vehicles. It was the same route they had taken on their way to Enschede. The fields were frosted and shimmering, but Audrey could tell in the summer months they would be green and lush with crops. It still seemed too idyllic for a country that was on its way to becoming the epicentre of a war. She wondered how long it could remain untouched. Perhaps forever, if they succeeded today.

They reached Hanover with an hour to spare before Hitler was due to deliver his speech. As they passed the imposing Staatsoper Opera House with its soaring three storeys of stone arches, they spotted several groups of children already gathering in the courtyard out front, the brown bloomers of the Hitler Youth uniform visible beneath the hems of their wool coats. Audrey would have guessed they ranged from around seven years old to midteens, judging by their height. Friedrich kept his eyes on the road, but she saw Claus scan the assembled crowd.

"So many damn kids," he muttered.

They turned a corner and Friedrich nodded at his window. "There's

Ludwig's car. Beside the bank. Remember where it is." Audrey took note of the green sign above the bank door, committing it to memory.

Friedrich parked several blocks away, near the train station amid a string of other similar-looking vehicles that could serve as a convenient camouflage. Audrey watched the bustle of pedestrians, office girls hurrying past in heels and long coats, families with battered travelling cases, and some military men in crisp uniforms.

"No point sitting here," Claus said. "Let's fucking do this. Audrey: wait five minutes and then follow me. Fred, another five after her."

Audrey and Friedrich nodded, and Claus exited the car, threading his way into the throng. They sat in silence for a moment, and Audrey went through the plan in her mind for the tenth time. She would blend into the crowd of parents and Hitler Youth leaders whilst Claus and Friedrich located Hitler's motorcar, which she was sure would be parked somewhere behind the Opera House. The armour-plated black Mercedes-Benz was always easily identifiable by its parade flags; the Führer's sense of grandeur trumped the idea that discretion might be safer.

After Hitler had finished speaking to the children, Audrey would engage some feminine hysterics to draw the SS officers away from the vehicle. Claus would then plant the bomb and set the timer for the agreed-upon twenty minutes. The three of them would make their way to Ludwig's car, and be on the motorway back to Berlin before the blast. They wouldn't know whether they had succeeded until that evening's news hit the wires. Audrey imagined sitting with Friedrich and Ilse, nursing a glass and listening to Hitler's death announced on the wireless.

She tried to put that wondrous thought out of her mind now as she fussed with the collar of her coat.

"You next, Fräulein," Friedrich said.

She opened the car door and stepped into the snow-frosted street.

"Audrey," she heard behind her. She leaned down to the window. "Please be careful." Fear flickered in Friedrich's eyes.

She attempted a wry smile. "I'll see you soon. I promise."

She set her feet in the direction of the Opera House. When she entered the building five minutes later, sweat trickled down her back from nerves despite the cold weather. She nipped into the ladies' to mop her forehead, but when she glanced at the ornate, gold-framed mirror above the marble sink, she was startled to see Ada's severe face staring back at her, eyes somehow even colder than their usual grey. She was glad, really. It was better that she couldn't see herself underneath Ada's harsh exterior. She took a deep breath, bracing herself for the task at hand, and exited, head held high.

Groups of children swarmed the theatre lobby, a sea of brown caps, buckled boots, and bloomers, pea coats and scarves slung over little arms whose sleeves bore the swastika. Seeing the symbol so proudly showcased on eight-year-old children was unnerving. They chased one another, faces glowing with excitement at being in such an opulent place, ready to hear the Führer himself tell them how the Party was purifying their great country and the lands beyond, how the Third Reich would establish a glorious, virtuous Germany, how they and their brothers and sisters would be the curators of the new world Hitler was creating for them. Audrey picked her way through the crowd and wondered what these children thought of their new activities. She supposed not much, at least not the younger ones. The older ones were being trained in what was essentially military combat. She watched a group of older boys, about Ephraim's age, and fought a surge of heat, thinking of the thugs who'd attacked him.

She composed herself and slid into a row at the very back of the auditorium, which looked the same as it had years ago when she'd been here under much different and happier circumstances.

Her eyes scanned the crowd for Claus or Friedrich, but she didn't see either of them. *They should have located Hitler's car by now*, she thought, heart fluttering. Was everything going to plan? What if the car wasn't where they expected it to be? What if they had already been found out? She hated that she couldn't contact them, confirm whether she should be going ahead with her task. She felt blind. She turned her attention to the three tiers of balcony seats towering above her. The audience was settled now; the chatter of hundreds of children echoed up into the high ceiling.

A minute later, a hush fell. Audrey glanced at her watch: it was already eleven o'clock and Adolf Hitler himself was striding out onto the stage.

This kinglike icon of a man had seduced and captivated the German people. His photograph was in newspapers and on the walls of every office in the Third Reich, but it was entirely different to see him in the flesh, to watch how his small body moved, how he waved to a crowd, how his eyes surveyed the faces before him, calculating. Audrey felt sure, in that moment, that if the Führer's eyes fell on her, he would see her immediately for the imposter she was. His were eyes that pierced and undressed a person. They were inescapable.

The knowledge that the cell was about to try to assassinate this man, that he might be dead at their hands before the hour was out, triggered an odd combination of thrill, terror, and an overwhelming sense of power that Audrey had never felt before.

He began his speech, its contents predictably propagandistic.

The Jewish people were a dangerous blight on the face of a pure Aryan society. This "alien race" had to be removed. They must all unite to defend the "National Community." The children were encouraged to spy on their friends and families.

Looking out over the hundreds of children sitting rapt in the auditorium, Audrey weighed the concept of innocence. Hitler had created a veritable network of eyes that could see into each Aryan home, sit at the dinner tables of resisters and Jewish sympathizers, reporting back to their leaders any thought or sentiment their parents or friends might have that wasn't in keeping with the Reich's policies and philosophies. It was a masterstroke, this army of little soldier-spies.

She tried her best to tune out his words by ruminating on the timing of her next move. The children couldn't be expected to pay attention to a speech for longer than twenty minutes or so, she was sure. The plan had been for Audrey to create a diversion with a report of a man with a gun at the front of the Opera House. She was certain the Führer wouldn't tolerate someone leaving in the middle of his speech, so she bided her time.

When he finished, he saluted the crowd and Audrey felt a chill skip down her spine at the sound of hundreds of children's voices chanting "Heil Hitler!" She saluted along with them, as she must, then darted back to the lobby, exiting the theatre the way she had come. Blinking against the sudden brightness, she hurried around the side of the building toward the back doors, taking care on the thin layer of snow. Sure enough, she spotted a cluster of guards milling around. Hitler's car was parked in the centre of a black motorcade, red flags fluttering on the bonnets in the cold breeze.

She took a moment to gather herself, then set her features into an expression of panicked anguish and raced over to the guards. They all looked up at her approach, shading their eyes with their hands. She waved her arm, hailing them.

"Excuse me!" she shouted in a high voice. "Sir! Anyone! Help! Please!"

Two of the four guards stepped toward her. They all looked eerily alike, aside from their difference in height. Light brown hair and clean-shaven faces over the collars of their identical uniforms.

"Fräulein?" one of them asked.

"Oh, thank God," Audrey said. "I didn't know what to do. There was a man out front, on the lawn, with a gun, I saw him enter the theatre just now. He—"

"Out front?" another guard snapped at her, alert.

"Yes! In the building now, I should think. Oh God!" she wailed in false hysterics, flapping her gloved hands, forcing tears to her eyes. "Please hurry! You must get the Führer out! The Führer!"

All four guards sprinted toward the front of the large building, drawing their weapons, but one shouted to his comrade to remain with the car. The man seemed young, hardly older than the teenagers inside. He fell back in obedience. Audrey swore, wondering what else she could possibly do. But her card was played now. There was no way she could lure this guard away without raising suspicion, especially once the others discovered there was no assassin.

There was nothing for it. Audrey turned from the scene, hoping Claus and Friedrich could figure out the next step, that she hadn't ruined everything by failing to draw all the guards. Ducking behind a barren hedge a few yards away, she peered back at the car. Several agonizing minutes passed where nothing happened. And then, with a leap in her stomach, she spotted Friedrich, Claus just behind him. Friedrich strode up to the remaining guard with an air of confident authority and said something to him, indicating Claus, who nodded. The large duffel bag was slung over his shoulder.

Audrey watched the exchange, breathless. The young guard shook his head, but when Friedrich responded, the guard reluctantly stepped away from the vehicle. At that moment, Claus dropped to the ground with the bag and disappeared underneath the car whilst Friedrich made conversation with the guard, his eyes flitting to the back doors of the Opera House every few seconds.

The bomb was being set.

Audrey tore her gaze away. It was time to get to the getaway car. She walked as fast as she could without running. The whole mission suddenly seemed far more real, more dangerous. *This is mad*, she thought, dodging the other pedestrians. Finally, she turned a corner and the bright green sign above the bank came into view; Ludwig's car was still parked beneath it. Her heels clicked on the pavement in time with the bomb that was now ticking underneath the Führer's seat. She slid into the back and shut the door.

Ludwig twisted to see her. "Well?"

"I don't know," Audrey answered, panting. "They started to set the device, but they're still there. They need to get out before the other guards come back, or someone raises an alarm."

He faced the front. "We'll know soon enough."

They waited another torturous few minutes before Audrey spotted Friedrich walking toward them.

"There's Friedrich!"

He wasn't running, which she took as a good sign. He met her eyes as he approached, and she saw her own relief reflected in them. She slid across the seat to make room.

"It's done," he said, chest heaving. "Claus is right behind me."

"Yes!" Ludwig hammered his hands on the steering wheel. "Yes!"

Friedrich covered Audrey's hand on top of her knee. "Your diversion was brilliant. Well done."

"I couldn't get them all away though," she said.

"It's all right. The guard who stayed behind was still wet behind the ears. I told him Claus was there to fix the vehicle. He didn't put up much of a fight. We were in uniform. There's Claus now."

Their comrade threw himself into the front seat beside Ludwig. "Fucking hell," he swore. "We did it, gents. And lady," he added. "Let's get out of here. I need a goddamn drink."

"How much time do we have before it goes off?" Ludwig asked.

"About five minutes, I'd say. I didn't get a chance to note the time before we hightailed it out of there. Good job, Audrey," he said, turning in his seat. "Whatever you did, it worked."

"Thank you. Told you I'd be useful."

He grinned. "Let's go," he said to Ludwig, who hesitated.

"Should we wait and see whether it's worked?" he asked.

Claus looked incredulous. "We don't want to be anywhere near that thing, Ludwig."

"But we're blocks away," he argued. "We'd see the smoke, hear it from here, surely? But not—"

"We're not risking that!" Friedrich snapped. "You don't think after that thing goes off, they won't be cordoning off the whole damn city? Blocking the motorways? Drive, man! We need to be back in our homes before this even hits the wires! Go!"

Ludwig's jaw twitched, but he put the car into gear. They had to pass the Opera House on their way to the motorway. As they approached, all four sets of eyes snapped to the laneway behind the theatre. Several uniformed men were there now, along with a photographer, whose tall tripod was set up a few feet away from the car. They drove a little farther along the road—Ludwig slowed down as much as he could—until the other side of Hitler's car came into view.

Audrey gasped in horror.

"No! No no no no no!" Claus shouted.

The subject of the photographer's attention was a lineup of children positioned along one side of the vehicle, one row standing, another kneeling, the smallest of them seated on the pavement in front. Hitler Youth leaders bracketed them on either side, chivvying them into place. There were over a dozen of them, smiles gleaming as they laughed for the camera, thrilled at the honour of being chosen for a photo opportunity with the Führer's car.

"Is he there too?" Ludwig demanded. "Do you see him? Does anyone see him?!" He jerked the car over to the side of the street.

"No," Claus said. "He's not there. He's not there."

"What do we do?" Audrey breathed.

"Claus!" Friedrich shouted.

But it was too late. Claus had already opened the car door and was sprinting across the snow-covered lawn.

Chapter 26

Audrey

HANOVER, GERMANY | APRIL 1939

Claus!" Friedrich shouted, opening his door.

"Get him back here!" Ludwig bellowed. "Get him back! Let it go off!"

Friedrich tore after Claus.

"Friedrich!" Audrey screamed, then, without thinking, followed.

How much time was left on the bomb? She glanced at her watch. Two minutes, if that? She jogged toward the parked motorcade, slipping a little on the snow. She stopped twenty feet away. She could see the faces of the children clearly now, some still smiling, others watching the commotion playing out behind them as Claus argued with one of the security team. Friedrich approached at a forced walk, hailed the original guard, drawing his attention away from Claus, who hit the ground and disappeared under the vehicle. Audrey inched closer, her own pulse thudding in her ears. A woman walked in front of her, hand in hand with two young children.

"Get out of here!" Audrey yelled at her. "Get your children out of here, go! Run!"

The woman's face crumpled in alarm and confusion. "Excuse me?"

Audrey shoved her shoulder and she lurched forward. One of the children nearly tripped. "Go!" Audrey cried, grey eyes wide as they bored into the woman's.

She hurried off as shouting started near the motorcade. Friedrich was arguing with the guards. The children were staring at him, turned away from the camera and the photographer, who looked on, puzzled.

Less than one minute.

"There's a bomb under the car!" Friedrich said, his hands in the air in surrender. "Let him get it!" He indicated Claus's exposed boots.

But they didn't. Claus was dragged out, swearing and kicking. His face was red and wild-eyed as he grappled with the officers. His hat was knocked to the ground and his sandy hair fell sweaty over his forehead. Their hands were all over him. A gun was being drawn.

"Run!" he screamed at Friedrich. "Run!"

Friedrich hesitated only a moment, then turned. He flew toward Audrey, coattails lifting on the wind, boots pounding the frosty ground. Then he had her hand, and they were sprinting to the car.

Some of the children were crying, upset by the disturbance. Audrey would remember the sound for the rest of her life. She would hear it in the middle of the night, wake in bed drenched in sweat, knowing those voices would be frozen in delicate youth forever.

A shot cracked through the air, and Friedrich cried out and tripped. Another shot. People in the surrounding streets were shrieking now. A few more stumbled steps. Blood streaking the snow beneath their feet. And then they were back in the car and it started to move. Audrey registered Ludwig's voice throwing questions at them, but all she could focus on was holding her scarf against the wound in Friedrich's thigh as he gripped her shoulder.

And then she felt it. The car shook with a force stronger than anything she'd ever experienced. The explosion was inside her stomach, her chest, her throat. She thought her eardrums might blow out, and ducked her head instinctively, still pressing her scarf into Friedrich's leg. He was breathing heavily, eyes closed. Audrey began to sob as Ludwig sped onto the motorway and out of Hanover, away from the scene of the crime. Away from Claus's untimely death and the unnecessary, unintended deaths of all those children.

Away from the best chance they would ever have to kill Adolf Hitler.

They arrived back in Berlin in the early afternoon. The drive felt agonizingly long as Audrey fretted over Friedrich, who drifted in and out of consciousness. Finally, Ludwig pulled up outside the Kaplans' house. Praying none of the neighbours were watching, Audrey helped Friedrich out of the car, steadying him against her on the pavement. Ludwig came round to help so Audrey could unlock the front door.

Ludwig staggered up the steps, bearing Friedrich's weight, and they tripped over the threshold and into the kitchen, where they dumped Friedrich into a chair.

"Christ!" he hissed as they extended his leg and propped it on the table. "Fuck!"

His pant leg was soaked and shining red. Blood was smeared across the floor. Audrey spun round and bolted back to the foyer. It wouldn't do for anyone passing the house to see a trail of blood leading up to the front door. She spotted three footprints in the slush of the street. With her foot, she shuffled snow over the red prints. It was good enough for now, anyway. She darted inside.

Friedrich had stopped grumbling and was slumped in the chair, pale and breathing heavily. Ludwig was rolling up his pant leg to get a better look at the wound. Audrey felt her insides jerk at the sight of the mangled skin and blood.

"There's so much blood, Ludwig. We have to take him to a hospital. We must."

Ludwig shook his head. "We can't. A member of the SS with a serious bullet wound? They will make inquiries that we cannot answer. And by now, news will be spreading. Witnesses will know the guards fired shots at a retreating man and woman moments before the bomb went off. They will be looking for people with bullet wounds. Hospitals don't get those every day."

"Then what do we do?" Audrey tried to master her own panic.

Ludwig stepped back. "Friedrich knew what he was getting into."

"What do you mean?"

"I mean we all knew the risk we were assuming with this mission," he said. "We knew what could happen, what would likely happen. We were all prepared to pay the price. Claus knew that. Fred did too." He moved farther from the table, as though Friedrich had something catching that he was keen to avoid.

"Don't talk about him like he's dead already!" Audrey snapped.

Friedrich's skin was ashen, his eyes closed. Audrey knew that what Ludwig said was true; they couldn't take him to the hospital, or they would all be found out and executed. But he needed medical care, a doctor who could be paid off, or—

Ilse.

Her mind darted its way through a silent maze of strategy.

"You're right," she told Ludwig. "Go. Just go. It's better that we not be found together right now, anyway. I'll tend to him the best I can and if he dies, we'll figure it out then. Telephone Aldous, and I'll call you later with an update. Go, Thurman. Don't be seen leaving."

His moustache quivered at being told what to do by a woman, and Audrey in particular, but she was long past caring.

He swept from the room without so much as a backward glance. She barely waited until the door slammed shut before thundering up the stairs to Ilse, nearly hitting her when she flung open the bedroom door. Ilse was standing there in a state of agitation.

She pulled Audrey into a crushing hug. "What's happened? Did you kill him?"

Behind her, Audrey spied Daniel asleep in the crib. "No," she replied, dragging Ilse out into the hallway.

Ilse's lip began to tremble. "Well is everyone all right? I heard Ludwig, and—"

"Friedrich has been shot."

Ilse blanched. "Where?"

"In the thigh."

"Is the bullet still inside?"

"I don't know."

Ilse darted back into her room and emerged with her sewing basket and scissors. "Grab some towels and a basin from the bathroom."

Audrey did as she was told, then followed Ilse downstairs. She was sweating all over.

When they entered the kitchen, Ilse let out a gasp at the sight of Friedrich's leg and the blood pooling on the floor. She snatched one of the towels out of Audrey's hands, kneeling down to inspect him.

"He was shot from the back?"

"Yes."

"There's no exit wound here," Ilse said. "And it's a small enough hole. I think the bullet is still inside." She straightened. "How long has it been?"

The day already felt like a week. "Four hours, maybe?"

"Okay." Ilse was nodding as though convincing herself of something. "I think . . . I think if the shot alone were going to kill him, he would be dead already."

"What do you mean, the shot alone?" Audrey asked.

"I mean if the bullet had hit an artery, he'd already be dead. Friedrich?" she said loudly, tapping his face. "Friedrich?" His eyes fluttered half-open. "We need to get the bullet out. But if I try, I could make you bleed more. It could get infected either way. But I'll do—I'll do my best."

Infected. Audrey remembered all the soldiers she'd seen as a child, the ones who lost entire limbs in the Great War; her father had told her he'd witnessed men's legs being sawed off due to gangrene.

But Friedrich was murmuring his consent.

"I need a knife," Ilse said. She rummaged in a kitchen drawer and extracted two small paring knives. "This might work. Audrey, get some vodka from the sideboard. He's going to need it."

Ilse washed the knives and her sewing needles and scissors whilst Audrey retrieved the bottle from the sitting room. Once again, it was Ilse coming to their aid. Ilse had always called Audrey the brave one, but as one crisis led into the next on this mad mission, it became clear that Ilse had no understanding of the depth of her own courage.

After setting out the knives, her sewing kit, and the towels on the table, Ilse sliced Friedrich's pant leg with the scissors, then gently wiped away the blood to get a clearer view of the wound, grimacing as she did so. Audrey couldn't be sure, but the blood flow appeared to be slowing. Though she didn't know whether that was reassuring or not.

"Have you ever done this before?" she asked Ilse, who shook her head.

"Give him the vodka," she said. "And you might want to feed his belt between his teeth."

Audrey awkwardly fiddled with Friedrich's belt buckle. Once loosened, she had him bite down on the leather.

Removing the bullet was a gruesome process. Audrey did her best to steel her nerves as Ilse crouched down awkwardly behind Friedrich's thigh and began to push aside shreds of flesh, digging into the wound as fresh blood filled the hole and dripped onto the towel Audrey had placed on the floor. Friedrich groaned and cried out several times, and Audrey had to hold his leg down. She felt sick, both at the sight of the wound and the fact that they were causing him such agony, but in a few horrible minutes, it was done. Ilse dropped the bullet onto the floor with a small clunk and let out a sigh. She rolled her shoulders, then, with steady hands, began stitching up the wound.

"You're quite good at that," Audrey said, and the memory of Ephraim's attack crashed over her in a painful wave. Ilse had stitched up her own brother at this same table, and Audrey wondered how many wounds the world would inflict on her before she lost the will to try to repair them.

"Sutures are one of the first things you learn," Ilse replied. "I might have learnt how to do this kind of surgery if I'd been able to continue studying, but . . ." She snipped the end of the thread, stood, and set the needle down on the table. "That's it."

Friedrich was unconscious again; the physical toll coupled with the medicinal alcohol had knocked him out thoroughly.

"All we can do is pray there's no infection," Ilse said, as she fashioned a makeshift bandage out of the towels and Friedrich's belt. "We'll have to keep him hydrated and fed, and keep the area clean and dry."

She moved to the sink and began scrubbing the blood from her hands and arms.

Audrey studied Friedrich's pale face. "Does he have a decent chance, you think?"

Ilse's eyes welled with tears. "I honestly don't know. I wish I did. He needs rest. The couch in the lounge will have to do. There's no way we can get him upstairs."

With some effort, they settled Friedrich into a comfortable position, leg raised on a pile of cushions. Then Audrey went to the front door and slid all the locks shut, sealing them inside their fragile sanctuary. Leaning against the door, she breathed in the smell of the house, grateful beyond belief that she had come home in one piece.

After a minute, she went to the lounge, pausing in the doorway at the scene before her. Ilse had draped a blanket over Friedrich and was caressing his brow. It was an intimate moment. Audrey cleared her throat, and Ilse withdrew her hand.

Avoiding Ilse's gaze, Audrey set about building a fire, then poured herself a Schwartzhog and flicked on the wireless atop the spindly cherrywood table in the corner of the room. She needed to check for news of the bombing, to hear what the authorities suspected, to know whether wolves paced outside the door. Voices murmured in crackly tones. Some novel being read aloud. No news yet.

"What happened?" Ilse asked after a beat. "You didn't get him?"

Audrey took a long drink. "No. We got close though. We really did."

"Did anyone else get hurt?"

Angry tears threatened. "Claus is dead."

Ilse gasped. "Oh God. I'm sorry. You liked him well enough, didn't you?"

"Yeah. Well enough. But he had a wife, children."

"He died a hero," Ilse said. "I hope that brings some comfort to his family."

Audrey had no idea whether Claus's wife knew of his involvement in the resistance, or what the authorities would tell her had transpired. Would there be anything left of him to identify? Audrey wondered with a surge of nausea. His family might not even know of his death for some time.

"Are you okay?" Ilse leaned forward. The golden flames illuminated her face, casting shadows around her brow and nose, the curve of her upper lip.

"No," Audrey said, her chin trembling. "Ilse, we . . ."

"What?"

The tears slipped from the corners of Audrey's eyes now. She wiped them away with a cold hand.

"We killed a group of children. By mistake."

Slowly, she relayed the painful truth as Ilse listened in stunned silence. She was desperate to explain their actions, for Ilse to understand, because she already felt the seeds of this disaster sowing into her veins where their roots would burrow and spread, a great forest of guilt and doubt that would forever cast shade on her conviction.

"What would you have done if Hitler *had* been there with the children?" Ilse asked.

Audrey felt wretched. She couldn't answer. She couldn't meet Ilse's eyes. All she could do was bury her face in her hands and sob.

Ilse pulled her close then and Audrey rested her head on her shoulder as she cried out her grief and shame.

"So what happens next?" Ilse asked when Audrey's breathing had steadied.

"I've no idea," Audrey said. "I don't know what Claus's death or Friedrich's injury means for our resistance efforts. Perhaps our cell has just run its course. We tried. We failed."

She thought of how many lives had been lost in the attempt.

How much more death would there be until someone finally stopped him?

Upstairs, Daniel let out a little cry.

"He'll be hungry," Ilse said, rising. She looked at Friedrich, still asleep, her eyes clouded with concern. "I just hope—" Her voice broke. "I hope he makes it. I'm so grateful you both came home."

Audrey couldn't tell Ilse how imperative it was that Friedrich survive. They'd already been forced to dispose of one body from this house; their deniability would evaporate if another Nazi official was found dead on the premises. Audrey would certainly be investigated, and then where would they be?

Dead. All of them. Dead.

Audrey nodded. "Me too."

Evening fell and the wind howled outside the window. Audrey knew she should try to sleep, but she was too restless, her body still humming with adrenaline and sorrow. She drank her way through a third of a bottle of Schwartzhog, trying to drown out the faces of the children. Wandering into the sitting room, she flicked on the lamps and slid onto the piano bench. She placed her glass directly over the water ring Vogt had left, as though she could cover up the stain, convince herself it wasn't there.

She didn't want to wake Friedrich or Daniel, so she set her fingers on the keys and began to play silently, moving them across the keyboard with a whisper-gentle touch. She could hear the piece in her mind, anyway, and the music blended with images of Ilse's face. Her finger lifted off the ivory on the last note, and she slouched, staring into the middle distance. Drink in hand, she meandered back into the lounge. She listened for a while, but there was still nothing about it on the wireless. Her mind drifted, guided by alcohol, to a sweet fantasy that maybe it hadn't happened at all. Maybe this was a dreadful dream. She watched Friedrich's chest rise and fall, willing him to live, and finally fell asleep just as dusk crept its way into the shadowy room.

Chapter 27

Kate

ALNWICK, ENGLAND | DECEMBER 2010

Is that what gives you the nightmares?" Kate asks Audrey, her words struggling up and over the lump of emotion in her throat. "The children?"

Audrey stares at the snowfall outside, her face paler than usual in the late morning light. Her knotty hands are clenched together in her lap, coffee long forgotten and cold in the blue ceramic mug beside her. "Mostly, yes," she says. "I see their faces. Or at least, what my mind has created for their faces."

Kate sets the pen down on her notebook, wondering what to say. When they sat down this morning, Sophie and Ozzie snoozing at their feet, Audrey had told Kate this would be one of the most difficult things for her to recount, and that Kate was the only person, aside from Ilse, that she had ever spoken to about it. Kate hadn't known what exactly to expect. She'd wondered if perhaps she was about to hear how Audrey sustained the injuries to her fingers, or that Ruth and Ephraim were dead. But she wasn't prepared for this.

She takes a deep breath and a bracing drink of cold water from the glass beside her. People use the term "collateral damage" in reference to war. So sanitized and unspecified. But the damage, the loss, are the real people who happened to be in the wrong place when others chose to kill each other. Human beings with names and families and dreams.

Children.

"It's a very strange grief, you see," Audrey says. "An incomparable guilt, really. There is no one in the world who could quite understand it. There's no support, and certainly no sympathy. And why would there be? We killed children in the pursuit of something that might have been impossible from the start. There were two dozen attempts on Hitler's life over the years—that we know about—and no one ever managed it. It's incomprehensible that no one ever succeeded. Our cell got closer than many, but . . ." She clears her throat in one quick bark. "I haven't ever forgiven myself for it, and it has been singularly lonesome to carry that burden. To be frank," she says, "it will be a relief to be rid of it when my time comes."

"You meant to kill Hitler," Kate says quietly. "Who ended up murdering tens of millions, directly and indirectly, over the course of the war. Surely that intention counts for something."

"I doubt the parents of those children would agree." A log pops in the fireplace. "*It will always have been worth it*, Friedrich had said. But we didn't make one modicum of difference. Hitler continued to live and breathe and kill whilst a dozen Aryan families mourned the deaths of their children, and, as we now know, millions of Jewish parents mourned the deaths of theirs, or were murdered right alongside them. Held their little hands as they were shoved in front of the same firing squads, or into gas . . ."

Her breath comes in heaving waves, her eyes wide and watering.

"Audrey—" Kate reaches for her hand, grasps the age-speckled skin in hers, fighting her own tears now.

"Me telling you all of this, and you recording it . . . it's a reckoning. Finally." Audrey takes another deep breath, as though trying to draw forgiveness from the air itself. "Those children formed the basis of my nightmares my whole life, but I would always wake, wait for my heart rate to still, and push it from my mind, like a fool." She releases Kate's hand and sits up a little straighter. "They were in training to be Nazis. So who knows what they would have grown up to be. But at the time, they were still only children. Just children. And no one ever took responsibility for their deaths." She blinks rapidly. "It's time someone did. That *I* did."

Responsibility for their deaths . . .

"So . . . thank you for being willing to listen. And for, well . . ." Audrey's lips pucker into a tight screw. "For not judging me too harshly, I hope."

Suddenly, Kate is sobbing. She buries her face in her hands as she dips into her memories of the accident, that chasm in her mind where self-loathing and denial lurk at the bottom.

"Kate?" Audrey's voice filters in. "I know this was upsetting. I'm so sorry. Let's take a break, get some fresh coffee."

Kate raises her head, takes in Audrey's thinning white hair, her remarkable yet aged grey eyes. They're full of genuine concern for Kate, who didn't mean to drag this up now. But it's time she took responsibility, too, just like Audrey is. For her parents' deaths, her role in them. And it's time she was more honest with Audrey, time she returned her trust.

She sits forward on the edge of the navy armchair as Ozzie approaches, rests his head between her knees, offering his oversized, glossy ears as treatment for Kate's trembling hands.

"I was driving the car when my parents were killed," she says. "I let you believe I was a passenger. But it was my fault."

Audrey tuts. "I'm so sorry, dear. That must be a terrible burden to bear."

Kate shakes her head, finally looking up at Audrey. Their chairs used to feel much farther apart.

"But terrible accidents happen every day, Kate. You—"

"Except it wasn't an accident. Not really." A chill runs through Kate despite the heat emanating from the fireplace. "It's far, far worse than that."

Chapter 28

Kate

LUTTERWORTH, ENGLAND | FEBRUARY 2010

"Give me the keys, Dad," Kate said, holding out her gloved hand as they made their way down the path from her aunt's house to the street. The surprise birthday party for her mother's sister had been a success, but the champagne flowed like a new faucet and her dad had been half in the bag an hour before the cake had even been brought out. Kate hated it when he got like this. She spent most of the party sitting in a corner, sipping a ginger ale to ease the nausea and refusing the seafood canapes her uncle thrust at her on a metal tray.

"Ah, yeah. Here," her dad said, rummaging around in his trouser pocket.

"You sure you don't mind, dear?" Kate's mum asked vaguely. She wasn't generally much of a drinker, but the festive air of her sister's sixty-fifth birthday seemed to have gotten the better of her too.

"It's fine," Kate said, trying to keep the irritation from her voice. When she agreed to ride with them to Lutterworth, she suspected this might happen. And now it would be past midnight when they got back to London. "But what would have happened if I hadn't been here?"

she asked, unlocking the car with a chirp that cut through the cold winter air.

Her mother didn't answer, just climbed in the back, leaving the front passenger seat for Kate's dad.

Kate stopped outside the driver's side of the small red Toyota and checked her mobile. Sure enough, there was another text from Adam, even more petulant than the last three volleys had been. She didn't know whether to laugh or scream.

You've known what my job is like since before we got married. You knew what you were getting into. I'm doing this for all of us. Why can't you see that?

He was supposed to join them tonight, but this afternoon Kate had told him not to bother. Adam had a demanding advertising job in the City, but he'd been telling Kate he would start dialing it back, refusing extra work and events that weren't strictly necessary. But he hadn't, and Kate couldn't tell whether he was addicted to it or just didn't want to spend time with her. They'd been arguing for the past two days, and the last thing she wanted was to be confined in a car with him, both of them seething, for a four-hour round-trip plus a family function where everyone would be fawning over how happy they must be. The truth was that they were happy—most of the time. But when they weren't—like now—the lows were low.

Kate threw herself into the car and replied.

Except there won't be an "us" if you're never home.

She tossed the mobile back into her purse and set it down on the console beside her.

"You know the car will talk to you now, eh?" her dad said, eyes sparkling with champagne as he buckled himself in on the second try. "You just hook it up and—"

"Yeah, thanks, Dad," Kate said, angrily adjusting the seat and mirrors. The last thing she needed was for her parents' car to read out angry texts from her husband.

Both of Kate's parents had fallen asleep by the time she merged onto the M1. Traffic was light this time of night, but the earlier snow had turned to freezing rain, and the motorway was slick. A wind gusted from the west and Kate fought the wheel as her mind replayed the ongoing fight with Adam.

Twenty minutes later, she heard her phone vibrate inside her purse. She reached over and felt around for it, pulled it out, then glanced down.

Is that some threat to leave me if I don't cave to you? WTF

Kate bit her lip hard to stop herself from shouting. Anger and resentment churned in her chest as she stared at the screen. She managed to type out three words with her thumb before something the size of a train collided with them. They spun, and Kate knew a brief, terror-stricken sensation of weightlessness as the car flipped over and everything went dark.

She wasn't sure when she woke up in the hospital, only that she did. It was a while before the sounds she heard—women's voices calling to one another, the tinny tones of an intercom, the rattling of wheels on a tile floor—nudged her to open her eyes.

The blue and green pattern of the curtain beside her came into view, but it was out of focus. Adam was standing at the end of her bed with a tall man in what she took for a police uniform, and a shorter blond woman wearing bottle-green scrubs. Kate couldn't make out the details of any of their faces. She needed her glasses. The blur in her eyes was as thick as the fog in her mind that dulled her senses. As she watched the group converse in low tones for several long moments, she struggled to piece together what had happened, why she was in a hospital bed with an IV in her arm. Her cheek and arm stung like hell, and her hips ached. Looking down, she saw that her forearm was wrapped in gauze, and panic began to sift its way through the cracks in her confusion.

Adam was saying something. Asking something. The woman in green responded, nodding a lot as she did.

Adam paused, then swore, reached an arm out and leaned his weight against the beige plastic bed rail.

"But is the baby okay?"

A grave silence followed, punctured by the incessant beeping of the heart monitor beside Kate, confirming that she was still alive when she might not want to be.

Chapter 29

Kate

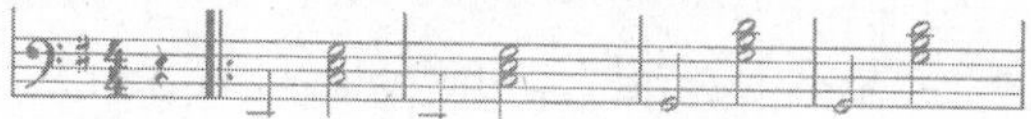

ALNWICK, ENGLAND | DECEMBER 2010

When Audrey told Kate about the bombing of Hitler's car, Kate's body had run cold, her systems paused, as though everything inside her needed a moment of respite. She feels similarly as she finishes her own story, finally surrendering it into Audrey's keeping.

"The other driver was fine. He was in a lorry. The only witness was the driver of a car far behind us. She said we both tried to change lanes at the same time. But I didn't. I drifted because I wasn't paying attention." More tears fall, coursing down the length of the scar on her cheek, a river of regret. "We'd just started to tell people I was pregnant. And every time we looked at each other in the weeks and months afterward, we just saw the child we were supposed to have. Blamed each other for everything." She blows her swollen nose. "We stuck it out for a while, into the summer, but when the, er, when the due date came round, that was really the end of it, I think. All that loss, just . . ." Her mind casts out for the right words, comes back to what Audrey had said: *an incomparable guilt.* "We couldn't bridge the gap it made. We weren't enough for each other anymore. And I think there just wasn't enough will left in either of us to try."

Audrey watches her as she wrestles against the pain. "Countless relationships have broken down under far less strain than that, dear," she says. "Do not be too harsh with yourself. You've said your marriage was never perfect. A cracked foundation doesn't stand a chance against an earthquake like that."

"It just . . ." Kate shifts in her chair. "I'm such a careful person. I plan ahead, I calculate. I don't take risks. I pride myself on not making a lot of mistakes. I spent a lifetime like that, careful and meticulous, and I slip just once, *once*, Audrey, and . . ." She splays her hands out, palms up, beseeching. "I killed all of them. It's all on me—"

She dissolves entirely now, sinking into the darkness. This time it's Audrey who reaches for Kate's hand and holds it until Kate is ready to come back to the surface.

Eventually her sobs slow, and Audrey passes her a tissue.

"You made a mistake," Audrey says. "And it won't be your last, no matter how hard you try. But so much was out of your control: your parents' inebriation. The lorry being in the next lane at that very moment. The rain." Kate looks into her eyes, bright green into faded grey. Audrey shakes her head. "There isn't any plan, Kate," she says gently. "For you or me or anyone else. There never was. Life is a game of inches. Nothing more or less than that. I survived the war. Others didn't. You survived the crash. They didn't. There is no rhyme or reason to chance. It just *is*."

Kate lets the thought settle. "It's so hard to think of it that way," she says. "It's so—"

"Frightening."

"Yeah. It just . . . Sometimes it's all I can think about—that I'm here, and they're not. And why. Why?"

She hears Ian's voice in her head. *There's no cheating it, no making sense of it.*

"I know, dear," Audrey says. "That's the price of survival."

Kate swallows hard. "Ian said something similar. About him and Doug."

"And he's quite right."

Ozzie and Sophie have gone back to sleep, curled together on the dog bed. Kate glances at the clock by the doorway to the foyer.

"Shit," she says. "I'm meant to be having lunch with him. He's picking me up in fifteen. I'll just ring him and tell him—"

"You will do no such thing," Audrey says, blinking Kate back into focus.

"But this isn't the time," Kate says, brow furrowed. "We can easily go tomorrow. After everything we just—"

"There's never a right time, dear. For anything. Besides, we're here to record my past, but not at the expense of your enjoyable present," Audrey says with half a smile. "And your future, for that matter. He's falling in love with you, you know."

Kate's stomach flips.

Audrey eyes her pointedly. "You haven't told him all this, have you?"

"Not all of it."

"You're going to have to."

"I know. I don't know if I can today. But I will soon. I promise."

They sit together in the tall chairs by the fire for another few minutes. The exhaustion that follows emotional release has begun to set in on both of them. Audrey is staring off out the window, her eyelids heavy. But Kate feels closer to her than ever, as though some clouded veil that hung between them has lifted.

"Go be with that boy, Kate," Audrey says with a sigh. "You still have so much ahead of you. Make the most of it, I beg you."

"Okay, if you're sure." She scrutinizes Audrey's face. "But you're a bit pale."

"I'm fine," Audrey says. "Just tired. And don't Old Lady me. I've made it through more than one snowy afternoon alone. I assure you, I'll manage."

“There,” Ian says, replacing the shovel. Kate steps forward to kiss him. The butterflies in her stomach are swirling in a cyclone of emotion and hormones, and a minute later she pulls away from him, though it’s clear he could have gone on like that for at least another hour.

“Was that about the shovelling?” he asks. “Because if it was, I’ll happily go back and do the whole car park twice.” He turns to leave.

Kate smiles, pulls his arm. “Come on. I need to make dinner for Audrey. She looked a bit peaky when I left her earlier.”

She’d gone out as Audrey insisted, and was, in the end, glad she did. It was a welcome reprieve from the gravity of their conversation. She needed to air out her thoughts in the crisp December afternoon as she and Ian ate their lunch in the cozy warmth of the Barter’s cafe, then wandered down the high street for a long while nursing takeaway coffees. She hadn’t told him how weighty her morning had been. There was time for that later. What she needed was to hold his hand and talk about inconsequential things, topics that weren’t life or death or loss, and remember that she could, in fact, have a future. And maybe a future with him.

They step over the threshold into the comfort of the Oakwood entryway, and Kate startles at Ozzie’s bark from the floor above. He’s not usually a barker.

“Oz?” Kate calls. “What’s up?” Another three barks.

“What’s he doing?” Ian asks.

“I’m not sure,” she mutters, making for the stairs. A sense of unease hits her as she sprints up the staircase. Ozzie is whining outside Audrey’s room.

“Ozzie, what’s wrong?” She darts down the hall, aware of Ian’s presence close on her heels. Audrey’s door is open and she looks in. “Oh my God! Oh my God! Audrey?”

Audrey is flat on her back on the woven tan rug beside the bed. Her chest is rising and falling in ragged breaths as tears slip from the corners of her eyes back into her white temples.

"Call an ambulance," Kate says, but Ian is already dialing.

A moment later he's giving the address to a dispatcher. Audrey clutches at Kate's hands.

"You're okay," Kate says. "You're going to be fine. We're here, Audrey. We're right here with you. We've got you."

But she's lying, of course. In moments like this, there is nothing but fear. Cold and searing and all-consuming. When we don't know what's coming next, or if there will even be a next. There is only this moment, this rotten grip of terror, as the people we love lie to our faces because they are just as afraid of the truth as we are.

"You're going to be fine," Kate says again.

Glass exploding like a bomb full of diamonds.

Blood on the leather car seats. Her mother's face, white and red and grey.

"You're going to be fine."

Kate and Ian sit side by side in the waiting room at the hospital emergency department, fingers entwined on Ian's knee. They've been here for an hour and a half. Audrey was taken into triage within minutes of her arrival, but they haven't heard from a nurse or doctor since.

"She's going to be okay," Ian says, squeezing her hand in reassurance.

Kate manages a small smile of gratitude, but her stomach churns. She spent most of the ride with her eyes shut against the lights of the ambulance in front of them, wondering whether Audrey would even make it to the hospital alive. She hasn't been inside a hospital since the accident, and it's taking everything she's got to stay calm.

"Did you get a hold of Sue?" she asks.

"Couldn't reach her, but I left a message."

Another half hour passes before a doctor emerges from behind the swinging doors of the ER.

"Kate Mercer?" he asks. He's balding extensively, and the harsh lighting reflects off his forehead.

Ms. Mercer? We're going to need to ask you a few questions . . .

"Yes," Kate says, swatting away the memories that keep pecking at her brain. She releases Ian's hand and stands up. "How is she?"

The doctor's expression is serious behind his round glasses. "She's stable. It's a bit of an odd thing," he says. "She presented as a heart attack, but the ECG showed no indication of a cardiac event."

Kate feels the clench in her own chest loosen slightly at his words. "Oh. Well that's good, right?"

"Generally, yes," he says. A doctor is paged over the intercom. "We examined her medical history, and based on that, and what she's told us, we ran some tests to determine whether the chest pain and the fall might have been related to the cancer. But we can't see any indication of a connection."

A wave of cold ripples down Kate's body from her head to her legs. Beside her, Ian nods at the doctor, slides one arm around her waist.

"I'm sorry, the what?"

"The cancer. She's named you both as her next of kin, Ms. Mercer. You are aware that she has a terminal case?"

Kate's mouth has gone dry. "I, er . . ."

"She declined any chemotherapy or radiation months ago. She's on medication now to keep her comfortable. But we still don't think this is related. Ruling out other possibilities, I'm wondering whether this might have been psychosomatic. A panic attack, of sorts. Do you know if she's prone to them, or has been under any particular sort of stress lately?"

Kate stares at him. "Other than a terminal diagnosis, you mean?"

The doctor nods. "Something more acute that might have triggered this episode. Something out of the ordinary."

This is all Kate's fault. "We've had some difficult conversations lately."

"Can a panic attack do something like this though?" Ian asks. "Seems a bit extreme."

The doctor nods again. "Often panic attacks are mistaken for, and mimic, heart attacks. Chest pain, sweating, rapid heart rate, et cetera. It can be frightening for the patient, and the stress and fear can exacerbate the symptoms in a cyclical way," he says. "But when we rule out clinical explanations for the symptoms, that's pretty much what we're left with."

"Can we see her?" Kate asks. "Is she awake?"

"Yes. Come on through. We're going to keep her here overnight to monitor her, as a precaution, given her age and health situation. But I suspect we'll discharge her in the morning."

They follow the doctor through the swinging doors into another brightly lit corridor. Kate hurries along behind him with Ian at her side, her mind blank. They turn several corners before the doctor stops outside a patient room and gestures for them to go in. He hurries off, but they remain in the hallway.

"She's terminal?" Kate whispers to Ian.

A nurse passes by, pumps a squirt of hand sanitizer into his palm from the dispenser on the wall, and nods somberly at them. Kate's nostrils fill with the chemical scent of illness.

Ian looks at her, face drawn in the shadow of the overhead lights, and something about the pity in his eyes makes her pause.

"Did you know?" she asks him.

He sighs. "Yeah. I did."

Kate takes a step back, stung. "Why didn't you tell me?"

He shoves his hands into his trouser pockets. "I'm sorry. She told me in confidence, and I thought—"

"You know how close I've gotten to her," Kate hisses. "You know what she means to me, Ian." She's fighting back tears now. "Why would you keep this from me? How long have you known?"

Ian shrugs. "A month or two, I guess. Sometime back in the fall. She pulled me into the office and told me."

Kate bites down on her bottom lip as she recalls that day Ian came out of Audrey's office looking upset.

"I'm sorry," he said. "I am."

"Did she tell you not to tell me?"

Ian shakes his head. "No. But you'd only just arrived."

"And what about after?" Kate fires back, blinking hard. Her mobile buzzes in her purse. She ignores it.

"Kate," Ian says, stepping toward her again. She's inclined to push him away, but doesn't. "I think this is a conversation you need to have with *her*, not me."

She takes a deep breath. "Fine. Yeah."

"Let's just go talk to her."

Kate leads the way into the room. There's no one in the bed nearest the door, but Audrey is lying awake, propped up in the bed on the far side of the room. Her hair is a little disheveled, frizzing around her head, and the blue hospital gown sags on her shoulders. Kate wonders whether it's the effect of the hospital bed that makes her appear so diminished and small, or whether she'd just been blind to it before.

"Hello," Audrey says with a sigh.

"Audrey." Kate reaches for her hand. Ian takes a seat on the other side of the bed.

Audrey takes one of Ian's hands, too, and squeezes them both gently. "I'm sorry I gave you both such a turn," she says, frowning. "This is utterly embarrassing. They say I didn't even have a proper heart attack. Distress, or some such stupid thing."

"I'm so sorry, Audrey," Kate says. "The things we've been talking about, I never should have pushed you to do it."

Audrey fixes Kate with a look that is somehow both tender and condescending. "Kate. I would expect that you would understand me well enough now to know that I never would have relayed my story to you if I didn't truly want to."

Kate swallows hard, grips Audrey's hand tighter.

"So," Audrey continues, "before you go getting any silly ideas, I will tell you straightaway that this is *not your fault*."

Out of the corner of her eye, Kate sees Ian glance over at her. "Okay. If you say so."

"I do."

"Why didn't you tell me about the cancer?" Kate asks.

Audrey looks at Ian, then back at Kate. "I'm sorry, dear."

"How long have you known?"

"About a year. They told me it was a done deal a few months ago."

Ian is staring at a spot on Audrey's hospital blanket, eyes unfocused.

"How much time do you have, then?" Kate asks.

Audrey shrugs. "They're not sure. But I think long enough to finish our chats, anyway. And I would like to, now we've come so far." She pinches her lips.

The tears slip from the corners of Kate's eyes now. "Okay."

"Ian," Audrey says, looking up at him. "Would you be a dear and go fetch me some ice chips? It's drier than rye toast in here."

"Sure," he says, blinking. "Back in a few."

Audrey watches him leave, but Kate keeps her eyes on her friend.

"I'm sorry I didn't tell you," Audrey says.

"Ian didn't either."

"He and I have such a history. He's as good as a grandson to me, as you know. And when I told him, you and I didn't have, well . . . what we have now."

"Yeah. That's what he said."

"And he's right. But I suppose, over the past while . . ." She reaches for Kate's other hand. "You've had so much loss, Kate. I suppose I felt badly adding to your burden."

A single tear slides down Audrey's cheek, faltering a little on the deep crevices in her mottled skin.

"Now then," she says. "The pair of you should go. Get a good night's sleep. You look exhausted."

"I don't want to leave you." Kate's voice cracks on a swollen throat. "And I don't want you to leave me."

Audrey smiles tightly. "I'd said you could stay on until Christmas. I think I can extend your contract now, if you'd like. It seems to have worked out."

A watery, reluctant laugh escapes Kate. She nods.

Audrey cups her wet cheek. "I'm not dying tonight. I'll still be here tomorrow. We'll talk then."

"And then what?" Kate asks.

"Well, you shall have me until you don't, and we'll just have to make the most of the time we have left, won't we?"

The next morning, Kate wakes to a scratchy sensation on her hand. She blinks several times in the dim light, her brain sluggish to rouse itself. A brown blob comes into view before Kate reaches for her glasses on the bedside table.

"Oh, Oz," she mutters. "I know. We're late for breakfast, aren't we?"

Beside her, Ian turns over onto his side, stretches his bare arms up over his head. "Morning."

Kate smiles at him. "Morning."

After he'd driven her back to the Oakwood from the hospital, Kate had led him inside and up the stairs, and for the first time in a long while, she felt like she was on the right path. It wasn't fully illuminated yet, she couldn't see very far ahead, but she knew she should hold true and see where it led. Live her life.

It was strange, though, to see anyone other than her husband in bed next to her, like a remake of a film with new actors. But sleeping with Ian was the first excitement she'd felt in months. Under his soft and meticulous touch, she felt as though she was thawing, that it was finally spring after a year of winters. It gave her hope, and made her wonder what kind of heat the summer could bring.

"Should I make us some breakfast?" she asks Ian now.

He runs a hand through her hair and shifts his hips a little closer. She knows he wants her again, and the knowledge sends warmth through her whole body.

"Trying to get rid of me so fast?" he teases.

"No. But Audrey's going to be discharged this morning and I'll need to be ready to go get her."

"Not alone, I'll come, too," Ian says.

The realization that he doesn't want to leave her, that he cares for both her and Audrey, hits her so hard that her heart starts to race.

Ian holds her gaze for a moment. "How are you feeling?"

"I'm all right, I guess. Processing."

"Do you think . . ." Ian starts. "Do you think you'll have enough time to finish? For her to tell you the rest of the story?"

Kate's nose starts to tickle. "I hope so. I still don't know how it all ends." She's desperate to know what happened to Ilse, and to Audrey's hands. How she ended up here in the first place.

"The good news is you get to be there for that bit."

"What bit?"

"The end."

Ian reaches a hand up, runs his thumb gently along the scar on her cheek, then kisses her temple. She wraps her arms around him and holds on to his body like a life raft.

A while later, they dress and head downstairs to feed themselves and the dogs. It's chilly on the main floor, and just as Kate goes to ask Ian to build a fire, there's a loud knock at the front door.

"Who could that be?" Ian asks.

"No idea."

She opens the door to see a man standing on the snow-covered porch. He huffs his breath out into the cold air, like a puff of smoke from a fire that's about to rage, and her stomach drops.

"Hey, Kate," Adam says.

Ian is at her elbow now, face quizzical. "Can we help you?" he asks.

"Adam," Kate begins, "what—?"

"Can I come in?" Adam says, stomping his feet in the leather boots Kate gave him last Christmas. "It's freezing."

She lets him pass in a state of disbelief, her mind skipping ahead to how she's going to explain this to Ian, who has stepped back into the hall.

"I'm sorry," he says, "but who are you?"

Ozzie bounds around the corner from the sitting room, drawn by Adam's voice. He runs over to him in a blur of brown, the tags on his collar jingling. Adam looks from Ian to Kate and back again.

"I'm her husband. Who are you?"

Chapter 30

Kate

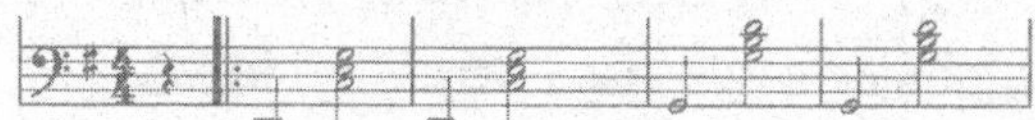

ALNWICK, ENGLAND | DECEMBER 2010

Your husband?" Ian asks, facing her. "*What?*"

Kate's face and hands are starting to tingle. She hasn't had a full-blown anxiety attack in months, and she can tell this one is going to make up for lost time.

"Kate?" The hurt and confusion glazing his features breaks her heart. She knows the look on her own face is all the confirmation he needs. "You're married?"

"Yes, but Ian—"

"I can't believe this. I can't believe this, Kate."

"Ian—"

"You said you had an *ex.* I thought . . . never mind. I have to go pick up Audrey." He brushes past Adam to the coatrack, then breezes out the open door in a frigid gust.

"Ian!" Kate calls again, but he peels out down the laneway. "God-damnit," she mutters.

"What did I just walk into?" Adam asks behind her.

She shuts the door and turns, crossing her arms. Adam is here. At the Oakwood. Kate takes in his sandy, styled hair, the grey wool coat atop his slim shoulders. He looks exactly the same, yet is somehow unfamiliar to her now. "What are you *doing* here?"

"I called three times last night, Kate. You didn't answer, didn't call me back."

"You know I don't look at my phone much now. And we had an emergency."

Concern ripples across his face. "Are you okay?"

"I'm fine. It was Audrey. The owner. My boss. My—" She exhales. *My friend. My saving grace. The woman who pulled me back from the brink.* "Never mind."

"And the guy?"

She looks him square-on. "Why are you here?" she repeats.

"I have the divorce papers." He taps his messenger bag.

She lets her breath out. "Right. Okay." But the anger surges. "I thought you'd courier them or something. Jesus, Adam."

"I was in Glasgow this week at a conference. I'm on my way back to London. That's why I tried to call you last night, to tell you I was coming round."

She shakes her head. "You could have couriered them."

Adam shifts his feet, and a little snow falls off, melting into the entryway carpet. "I wanted to talk to you."

"Okay, let's talk," she says, bringing him into the sitting room even though all she wants to do is go find Ian, explain and apologize.

Adam settles in a chair by the fire, Ozzie pressed excitedly against his knees, tail wagging. She sinks into the opposite chair, looking at him expectantly.

"How have you been?" he asks.

She opens her mouth on a curt reply, but catches herself. His expression is genuine. He came all the way here to talk to her, check up on her. She should lower her guard a little.

"Actually, I'm okay," she says. "This place has been good for me."

"I'm glad to hear it. Really," he says. "But you do know you're in the middle of nowhere, right? I had to take a train and then a taxi to get here." He lets out a small chuckle.

"It might seem that way to you," she says, without heat. "But it's home for a lot of people. Me included."

He strokes Ozzie's head. "Home, eh?"

"Yeah. Believe it or not. My parents stayed here on their honeymoon. That's why I picked it."

He watches her. "I didn't know they came up here."

"Yeah."

His brow contorts in the way it does when he's considering something. "I think about ours a lot," he says. "Hawaii." They'd spent ten days in bed and diving into the blue pools, drank late into the night in front of bonfires after watching the sun set from Wailea Beach. It was paradise, but it feels like a memory from someone else's life now. Adam looks down at the dog, clears his throat. "I miss this guy. He like it here too?"

Kate smiles a little. "Yeah. He's got a girlfriend. Sophie." She points to the small black lump on the dog bed.

"Didn't even see her there. Well . . . that's nice, buddy," he says, and Ozzie retreats, curls up with Sophie.

"I sometimes feel like the mistress now," Kate says. "The girl he cuddles with on the side. I've been completely usurped."

After a moment, Adam reaches down and withdraws a manila envelope from his bag on the rug. "So, here are the papers."

"Right. Yeah," Kate says, heart fluttering a little.

"I sold the flat," he says. "It fetched a good price. That's all here in the divorce settlement. We split it."

Kate nods. "Thanks for handling that."

"Yeah."

"Do you have a pen?"

She reads through, feeling the burn of his eyes on her. She signs the pages indicated with little red flags, one at a time. It feels at once mundane and profound, to sign off on her marriage like this, to put her signature to all her failures. Claiming, yet releasing them. She signs the final page, hands it back to Adam. They stare at one another.

Adam speaks first. "We had a good run for a while, didn't we? There were better times. Especially in those first few years. I know it was never perfect, but . . ." His shoulders droop a little. Kate nods, her eyes prickling uncomfortably.

He clears his throat, tears forming in the green eyes that did her in all those years ago. She remembers the last time she saw him cry, that day at the hospital when the bottom fell out of their lives.

"Do you still blame me?" she asks.

He takes a deep breath. "No. And I think you've blamed yourself enough for the both of us."

He meets her eyes squarely. There's a sadness in his that she hadn't been able to see through the haze of her own grief and guilt, and she fully understands, for the first time, that their dreams share the same ghost.

"But a lot of it's on me, Kate. I'm sorry about the fighting. About work. About . . . about texting you that night. I was tired, and angry. I shouldn't have—"

"I shouldn't have answered."

There's silence, and in it Kate hears that last message, the one that changed everything, and for a moment she can't breathe. Sometimes a tragedy brings people together, and sometimes it's too big to overcome. A great millstone too heavy to shift, and impossible to carry.

"I still care about you, you know," Adam says. "I always will. And I'm sorry I didn't care enough when it really mattered."

"I care about you, too," she says. She involuntarily rubs the base of her ring finger with her thumb, surprised to see that the groove has mostly disappeared. "Do you want your rings back?" she asks.

He shakes his head. "No. I mean . . . they're worth something, right?"

Kate frowns. "I don't want to sell them."

"No, no. I just mean they're a reminder, I guess. That at one point, things were good. Great, even. I'd like us to remember we had that. I think it's hopeful for the future, right? Maybe we can both find that again somewhere." He pauses. "The guy that left, are you . . . ?"

Kate nods. "Yeah. Ian."

There's a flicker of sadness, but nothing malicious. No jealousy. "I hope I didn't mess anything up for you."

Kate shrugs, straightens. That'll be her next reconciliation. "No, it'll be okay. I'll sort it out."

They sit for a while in the cold sitting room as the finality of it all comes to rest on them. Kate wonders if this will be the last time they ever see each other, and the ache of their shared loss stirs inside her. No matter where they go, or who they're with, they'll always be connected to one another by that thread. The one woven from the battered fibers of their unraveled life.

"Well," Kate says finally. "You're never going to get a taxi to come back out here. Let me drive you to the station."

Half an hour later, Kate is standing up at the kitchen counter, picking at a small bowl of cereal after she dropped Adam off at the train. With his arrival, she and Ian hadn't eaten breakfast, and though she felt she should eat something, her appetite is lacking. She feels genuine relief after the conversation with Adam, a true sense that some of the weight she's been carrying for the past year has lifted, and she's grateful for that. But she's on edge for Ian to bring Audrey back so she can explain everything that just happened. Tell him how she really feels. They hadn't even had a chance to enjoy the afterglow of their first night together before it was interrupted.

When she hears the front door open, she sets the bowl down with a clatter and hurries to the hall, but Audrey is alone. "Where's Ian?"

Audrey gives her an exasperated look. "He's left," she says. "He needs space. I told him to walk me to the door and I'd be fine."

Kate wants to rush past Audrey and find him, but instead she steps forward to take Audrey's coat. "How are you?"

"What I am is desperate for a cup of coffee that doesn't taste like wood chips," she says. "No wonder everyone feels utterly wretched in hospital. Go put on a pot, and we shall discuss the whole thing." Her voice is quieter, weaker than usual.

Audrey is already settled with Sophie on her lap when Kate brings the coffee into the sitting room. Wordlessly, Kate sets the mugs down on the side table, then builds a fire to warm the room.

Audrey takes her mug and inhales deeply. "Dear God, I thought they were trying to hasten my already imminent demise with that pig-slop instant brew."

Kate bites her lip at the dark humour. "Audrey—"

"I know, I know. I shouldn't jest." She takes a careful sip, though Kate doesn't fill Audrey's mug as full as she used to. "But still . . . as I said last night, we should, er, hurry things along. I've more to say. As do you," she adds, white brow furrowed over her cup. "I understand your ex-husband made an appearance, and that this was a great surprise to Ian. Why didn't you tell him?"

Kate sighs as her insides squirm. "I wanted to see where things were headed. I didn't think I needed to yet, and I didn't want to talk about it. It had no bearing on us, really. I had no idea Adam was going to drop in like that. But Ian took off before I could explain; he wouldn't even listen."

"He was reacting to the fact that you had lied to him, Kate. You know why he—"

"Yes, I know," Kate says. "I know about his fiancée."

She bounds up out of her chair and goes to the frosted window, looks out over the white lawns surrounding the inn. The snow is entirely undisturbed. Not even a rabbit track runs through it. It covers up everything beneath in a smooth layer of powder.

"Oh, Kate," Audrey says. "Have I not taught you by now what *not* to do? The only way avoidance will serve you is to exhaust you completely. You can get some distance on it, think you've won, but when you finally stop to rest, you've got no energy left to face it once it catches up to you. If you have any hope of moving forward, of a future with Ian, you must deal with your past, just as I have been," she adds. "It has been painful and complex and I don't like it. But it's necessary."

Kate fiddles with the gold rope on the curtain. If she isn't careful, it's going to fray between her fingers.

She can still repair things with Ian. She's sure he'll hear her out if she's as transparent as he is with her. She knows now how rare it is to find someone so open, but the openness does make them more vulnerable, more easily hurt. She should have seen that.

She sits back down in the chair, kitty-corner to Audrey. "I'll give him some space for today, if you think he needs it," she says. "I'll talk to him tomorrow."

Audrey nods. "Never, ever lose anyone you don't have to," she says. "Life will take your loved ones without warning or permission, as we both very well know. And we must endure those losses as part of life. But never let petty circumstance and disagreement separate you; life is too short to let pride get in the way of love."

Kate opens and shuts her mouth. *Love.*

"It may be," Audrey says, "that when all is said and done, you aren't right for each other for the rest of your lives. But we never know how much time we have left, Kate. Seize even temporary happiness and peace. Please. I wish I had."

She pats Kate's forearm. Her hand lingers there, and she gives a little squeeze, her knotted knuckles protruding. Kate takes a deep breath, and finally a sip of her own coffee, her mind turning to Audrey's loves: Ian's grandfather, and Ilse. She looks up at her aged friend and sadness clutches at her heart. However much time Kate herself has left, it's certainly more than Audrey.

"How did your fingers get like that?" she asks quietly. "You still haven't told me."

Audrey lifts her hand and rests it on Sophie's back. "Ah. Well," she says, caressing the knuckles. "Someone thought I was playing the wrong sort of piano."

Chapter 31

Audrey

BERLIN, GERMANY | MAY 1939

She was dreaming of the children. They were running about, ten feet beneath her whilst she sat on the edge of a massive grave, smiling as she watched them play among a sea of dead bodies. But somehow it was not a gruesome scene; they played with the spirits of the others, who knew now that they were not alone. Audrey felt a pull, or perhaps a push, her own longing nudging her in the back. She should join them. It's what she deserved. Her shoe fell off, tumbling down and down into the endless grave.

A small boy with eyes like a robin's egg looked up at her perched on the edge of the pit, her bare foot dangling a little below the other as she prepared to jump in.

"It's nearly time," he called, his little voice echoing in the grey sky above her.

A girl appeared beside him. She looked just like Ilse had when she was that age. "Audrey," she said.

Audrey tried to answer, but couldn't.

"Audrey. Audrey!"

She was teetering over the edge now. Then something pulled her back and her eyes fluttered open. There was no grey sky above her, just the white ceiling of her bedroom and Ilse's worried face.

"Audrey."

Her heart was beating in time to a woodpecker. She blinked quickly to clear the images of the children. They always lingered for a while after she woke. She pushed herself upright. "Is it morning?"

"Not quite," Ilse said. "You were moaning again, and it woke me."

"I'm sorry." Audrey ran a hand over her clammy forehead. "I'm sorry."

It had been a month since the disaster in Hanover, and the faces of the children had haunted her ever since. It was her punishment, she figured, since no one had yet come after their cell. The papers had called it a terrible tragedy, reporting that the gas tank of Hitler's car somehow malfunctioned, causing the explosion. Automobile and combustion experts attested to the car's volatility.

"The Ministry of Public Enlightenment is populated with highly skilled storytellers," Friedrich had told her. "Anything becomes true to the masses if they want it to be. Resistance is bad for optics and morale. It is far better for everyone to assume he has unanimous support, is universally adored." But behind closed doors, Friedrich said, Hitler was demanding that a head roll.

Friedrich had recovered well from his wound, and without infection, thanks to Ilse's skilled ministrations and aftercare. He had taken some time off work—allegedly to visit his sister Gisela in Vienna—to let his leg heal without questions from anyone in his office. There was a quiet internal investigation happening, he said, and was trying his best to redirect their efforts toward a ghost cell in Moscow.

The resistance group had disbanded. Claus, who had not been seen nor heard from by his supervisor or wife, was now wanted under suspicion of desertion. Aldous visited from time to time to share a drink with Friedrich, but Ludwig had disappeared from their lives entirely.

He hadn't even checked in on Friedrich in the days following his injury, which Audrey found cruel, but privately she didn't mind if she never saw his face again.

"All you all right?" Ilse asked, knowing she wasn't.

Audrey shook her head. "Friedrich keeps saying it's over."

"I know."

"It'll never be over."

"I know."

The house was quiet. Daniel was still asleep.

Audrey sat up in bed and seized the bedcovers pooled around her. "I just don't know what happens now," she said. "I don't know what to do."

Ilse's brow furrowed in concern. "I think you should talk to Friedrich."

"About what?"

"About what's next. It's clear you can't go on like this."

Audrey hung her head, swallowed. "I don't really know why I'm still going in to work. I feel like we've reached the end of this. With Claus and Ludwig gone, and what we did . . ."

Sabotaging the Third Reich provided profound meaning, but the role of Ada Jakob exhausted her. She was ready to hang up the costume. She didn't have the thirst for action that she'd had when she asked to join the Red Orchestra. They had the blood of children and their own comrade on their hands now. The cards were dealt, the hand was bad, and it was a wise person who recognized when it was time to fold.

She supposed she could look into taking up her studies again, finishing her program at the *konservatorium*. It had been a dream for so long, and she still played when she could, but the aspirations she'd had seemed adolescent now. Frivolous. She'd changed as everything else had, hardened and matured.

Ilse squeezed her shoulder. "Daniel will be up soon. Go talk to Friedrich."

Audrey bathed, dressed, and twisted her messy hair up into a bun in an attempt to tame it, then found Friedrich in the lounge off Ira's study, newspaper in hand. Audrey averted her eyes from the paper, allowing them to land instead on the crease in Friedrich's high forehead. Despite the SS's instructions and the Ministry of Public Enlightenment's efforts to cover up the truth of the explosion, the death of the children and several SS personnel meant it was still headline news. Audrey had been avoiding the papers at home and the office as much as she could, but spotted a headline the previous week about the planned funerals for the children. She'd had to dart into the toilets at work to vomit, dodging Frau Schulze's scrutinizing glare.

Audrey sat down on the couch. "With Claus and Ludwig gone," she began, "I'm not sure what our cell can accomplish. Where do we go from here?"

Friedrich nodded. "Ilse came down a while ago, told me you needed to talk." He sighed. "I've thought of little else lately, to be honest. Besides the pain in my bloody leg." He shifted it with a wince. "It took years to establish my relationships with Ludwig, Claus, and Vogt. I've been giving some consideration to poking around at a couple of other men I know in government and the Wehrmacht, see whether I might find new like-minded comrades for us, but I am walking a fine line here. I've been trying to throw off the investigation as best I can, but I can only do so much without rousing suspicion or being fired for not doing my job properly. And not doing your job properly in this administration is dangerous. They believe everyone has a slavish devotion to Hitler and the regime. How well you do your job is equated to your love for the Führer. Subpar performance is suspect."

They were quiet for a while as the mantel clock ticked, their thoughts drifting outside the walls of the Kaplan home to the grey marble offices of the SS headquarters and the Department of Property Reclamation, the decrees that would continue to come, restricting and ending life for Germany's Jews. As always, Audrey's thoughts came back to the Opera

House. The car. The bomb and the blood. Her heart ached for all of it. It was all too big, too merciless.

"Do you think maybe we're looking at this wrong, at this point?" she asked quietly.

Friedrich seemed to rouse from his own reverie. "How do you mean?"

Audrey cast her eyes down at her fingers. "Instead of trying to create change on a grand scale, should we focus on what's right in front of us?" She looked up at him. "Maybe staying safe now, not taking risks, can ensure three Jews remain safe, including the person we both love." Her eyes were shining with a hopeful sorrow. "If we can't save the rest of them . . ."

Friedrich glanced toward the staircase, toward Ilse and Daniel, whose voices floated down to them, soft petals on the wind.

"I would not say you're wrong," he said, eyes still on the stairs. "But it also feels like a betrayal to stop trying. To myself, and my people. To Ilse. And Daniel." He turned his gaze to Audrey. "When I first decided to do this, I knew I would likely die. And I accepted that. Though I didn't . . . My life was much more straightforward. I did not have anything in particular to live for when all this began."

Audrey tried to ignore the pressure in her chest. "And now you do."

"Yes."

Friedrich and Ilse had grown even closer over the past few weeks, drawn together as Ilse cared for Friedrich's injury with tenderness, and by Daniel, who interacted with Friedrich now as though he were indeed his father. They were in love, and Audrey did her best to feel glad for Ilse's happiness, that something of what she wanted out of her life—to have a family of her own—had been salvaged from the wreckage.

But Audrey wasn't sure where that left her. Nothing felt like home anymore. Not this version of Berlin, certainly. Not her father's house in Kensington, which now sat empty and deserted. Her aunt in Alnwick was her only family, but that didn't feel like home either. All that felt like home was Ilse, wherever she was.

"Your purpose is the same as mine, except . . ." She pressed her lips together. "Your purpose actually needs you."

"Ilse still needs you," he said immediately. It was generous of him.

"I can't offer her anything she can't get from you," she said.

"Well . . . there are mutterings about another invasion. Poland, this time." He shook his head. "If that happens, I cannot see how we can continue to avoid another war. It is only a matter of time. And then, my work may take me away from Berlin. It depends how far Germany's reach continues to expand, whether they set up SS offices in the occupied countries. But she would need you here. If I'm away, she would need you."

"I'll always do anything to protect her." Audrey straightened in her chair. "The truth is, I don't know how much longer I can fully resist Weber." She flushed. "Even before all this happened, I wasn't sure. He's clearly impatient, and if I don't give in willingly, I'm afraid he might just take what he wants, regardless. And it's not . . ." She trailed off.

The click of his belt buckle.

Her hair dampened with blood.

"I don't think me sacrificing that will yield anything more valuable than the information we already got about Hanover. If we were to continue any kind of broad-scale resistance, I would need a new mission anyway."

"I agree," Friedrich said. "But I don't know how we're going to extract you from Weber's office. No one ever leaves their job, for all the reasons I just outlined."

She chewed her lip, considering. "Well . . . the women do. I know how I can quit."

Friedrich raised his eyebrows. Audrey filled him in on Johanna's predicament, the suspicions about what had happened to Ursula.

"It will be entirely believable," she said, thinking of her recent vomiting episode with a wave of relief. "Without question." Frau Schulze would ensure everyone in the entire ministry, well beyond Weber's office, would suspect pregnancy as the impetus of her departure.

"But what will you tell Weber?" he asked.

They both stared at the coffee table between them, the morning light reflecting on its polished surface.

"A beau," Friedrich said finally. "He would be spurned if you left for your own reasons, but he will accept it if another man has claim to you."

"Claim to me?" Audrey exhaled through a growl.

Friedrich shrugged. "I'm sorry. But tell him your beau has insisted you leave your job so you can get married. Men like Weber don't tolerate working wives."

Audrey scoffed, but knew he was right. "Okay," she said. "I'll do it. I'll do it tomorrow."

Audrey turned off the lamps in the lounge. It was nearing nine o'clock, and Ilse had retreated upstairs a while ago to bathe Daniel and get him into bed. They'd had a lovely afternoon together, just the two of them whilst Daniel napped, and Friedrich went out to visit Aldous for a couple of hours, returning before dinner. After deciding to quit her job, Audrey had felt lighter than she had in a long time, and she and Ilse had drunk cold glasses of ginger ale and played two-person bridge like they used to when they were girls. Audrey still wasn't very good, which they'd both had a good laugh about. A sense of relief came over her, that perhaps they could just stay like this, hide out in relative contentment until the end of the coming war—which surely couldn't last as long or be as bad as the Great War. Maybe she didn't need to think into the future just yet. Maybe being here with Ilse in the present could be enough for now.

Audrey had just checked for the evening post when she heard a male voice outside, and a loud knock sounded on the front door. It was late for door-to-door salesmen. She debated answering, but with a tired air, unlatched the lock. Her stomach fell through the floor.

Three SS officers stood on the porch, their severe faces partially illuminated by yellow light from the streetlamps. Behind them was a woman, her face in shadow.

Audrey recovered herself and adopted a welcoming yet puzzled expression appropriate to the face of a loyal German who opened her door to three officers late in the evening. Perhaps they were here to speak to Friedrich. Perhaps there was no cause for alarm.

"*Guten Abend*," she said. "How can I help you, gentlemen?"

Two of them exchanged a glance. Another spoke. "Ada Jakob?" He was tall and heavily decorated.

"Y-yes," she said.

"We need to come in."

"Of course." Audrey waved them through.

"Who's there?" she heard Friedrich call from down the hall. She felt a modicum of relief as he strode toward them. "What is this?" he asked, dark brow furrowed.

"Obersturmbannführer Müller?" the same man said. He was evidently the spokesman. He saluted.

Audrey took in the men, then her eyes moved to the woman. She was shorter than Audrey, a little plain-looking, but somehow familiar, with an angry look in her eye.

"Heil Hitler. I am Obersturmbannführer Ziegler. We are here for Ada Jakob."

Audrey's breath hitched. She looked from him to the woman again, and a cold wave came over her, as though she'd been doused with a bucket of frigid water.

She knew where she'd seen her before . . .

Ziegler faced the woman now. "Frau Braun? You confirm this is the same woman?"

She nodded fervently. "Yes, sir. I never forgot her eyes. She yelled at me and my children to flee on the pavement outside the Opera House in Hanover. Shoved me. She was in a panic. And then . . ." She trailed off with a look of mingled fear and disgust.

"Very well. Ada Jakob, you are under arrest on suspicion of crimes against the state," Ziegler said.

"No." Audrey blinked at Friedrich. "No. No . . ." Her body felt disconnected from her brain.

Another of the men stepped forward and seized her arms. She watched, stunned, as the cold metal cuffs clicked into place. Adrenaline coursed through her like hot oil.

Friedrich's voice filtered through, loud and outraged. "What is this?! I demand—"

"Frau Braun has placed Ada Jakob at the scene of the explosion on the fifteenth of April in Hanover."

Audrey could see Friedrich calculating. Everyone in the higher ranks knew it wasn't the gas tank that had exploded. But not Ada Jakob. She was too junior.

"That was an accident, wasn't it?" she said, her voice wavering.

Friedrich bristled, began to argue with Ziegler.

One of the men opened the door onto the cool evening, preparing to leave, to take her God only knew where. But there was another woman on the porch. She stepped forward into the light and Audrey gaped.

Gerta Roth's face was red, eyes glistening with tears. "I knew it!" she shouted. "I knew it was you! You killed my husband." And she slapped Audrey across the face with a powerful vengeance that shocked her out of her disbelief.

"Frau Roth!" Ziegler barked. "I told you to wait on the pavement!"

Gerta retreated down the front steps. Frau Braun had joined her, arm around her shoulders.

Audrey's eyes were watering.

Friedrich was still arguing with Ziegler, and for a second, she wondered if there was still a way out of this. But then it hit her: Friedrich's defense of her now would only stoke the flames of suspicion that so easily jumped from one person to the next. She thought of Ilse upstairs, keeping Daniel quiet in bed as fear swelled at the sounds of commotion below. And she knew, in that moment, that Friedrich had to turn on her. He had to let her draw the attention away.

Audrey caught his eyes, gave a slight shake of her head, imploring him to stop, to not put himself at risk. In the depths of his dark pupils she saw his understanding, and the pain. Saw what it cost him to do it.

He hesitated for a heartbeat, then renounced her. "Fine, take her," he spat, flicking a hand in disgust. "Get this traitor out of my house."

PART IV

Love brought us to one death.

—Dante Alighieri, *Inferno*

Chapter 32

Audrey

BERLIN, GERMANY | MAY 1939

The cell in the basement of the Reich Security Main Office was a small, poorly lit room that smelled of damp and distress. It made Audrey wonder who had occupied this place before her, and what their fate had been, whether they were dead or alive. Was the stench in the toilet beside her all that remained of some poor soul who had come before? What a dreadfully arresting thought, that one could depart this earth and leave behind nothing but the sour smell of urine in some dank basement cell.

She was guarded by two Nazis who looked so much alike that she wondered if they might be twins. But a lot of them looked alike to her now, especially the young ones. The same haircuts, colouring, and pale lashes encircling steely eyes that seemed to have lost any glimmer of life.

Her transfer to the SS headquarters on the Prinz-Albrecht-Strasse was a blur of grey suits and bright lights. They had shoved her into this cell where she'd been waiting for at least an hour whilst her brain whirred with questions and possibilities, each more terrifying than the last. Horrific fantasies chased each other around her spiralling mind, and she was nearly sick with worry about Friedrich and Ilse, hoping with every fibre of her being that Friedrich's ostensive loyalties remained uncontested.

But beyond Frau Braun's testimony, what—and how much—did the SS know? And why in the hell had Gerta Roth been there? There was a rattling sound on the other side of the door and a man entered, tall and thin with a narrow chin that would have been strengthened by a beard.

"Ada Jakob, my name is Graf," he said. There was a clipboard in his hands. He remained standing, so Audrey was forced to look up at him. "I am here to ask you some questions about your whereabouts on the fifteenth of April."

She had to at least try to get herself out of this. "There isn't much to say," she said, moistening her dry lips. "There's been some mistake, sir. I was here, in Berlin. At home."

Graf stared at her. "Can anyone corroborate that? You live with Obersturmbannführer Friedrich Müller, correct?"

Audrey thought fast.

"Yes, I live with him," she said. "But he doesn't know much about me. He's very busy, you see. He's at the office much of the time."

Graf watched her. "He was not at home with you on the day in question?"

She couldn't give a firm yes or no in case Friedrich was asked and offered a different answer. "I don't know whether he was at home. I was in my bedroom. I didn't see him." She wanted desperately to ask whether they'd spoken to him yet.

"Mm," Graf grunted. "And no one else can confirm your whereabouts?"

Fear flared, but she shook her head. "No. But I—"

"You were positively identified near the scene of the explosion at the Staatsoper Opera House that killed nineteen children, five officers, and two staff," Graf continued, then summarized Frau Braun's testimony. "You clearly had knowledge of what was about to transpire."

Audrey stared at him for several seconds, then let out a long, silent exhale. How astounding, that a single, instinctive moment of benevolence could completely destroy a person.

"I don't know what you're talking about, as I wasn't there," Audrey said, with an effort at dispassion.

Graf smirked. "I'm not sure you fully understand the gravity of the situation, Fräulein Jakob. You would do well to appreciate what is at stake. We know the Führer's car did not malfunction."

Audrey tried a different tack, feigned shock. "But sir, it was all over the news. The engine—"

"We write the news. Someone attempted to murder the Führer. We know that the person in question was you. We have a witness attesting to that fact. And . . ." He unclipped a stack of crumpled-looking papers from the clipboard and laid them out on the cement floor, facing her, as though she were playing solitaire. "These were found in your desk in the Department of Property Reclamation. Schematics for detonators matching the traces of devices recovered at the scene. A map of the city of Hanover, notes encircling the Opera House."

Shivers of fear gripped her now. Her eyes darted over the documents. Where had they come from? She wondered briefly whether they had been recovered from Claus's house, or Aldous's, but knew they never would have been so sloppy as to retain them. These had to be a fabrication.

"Those aren't mine," she said emphatically. "I've never seen them before in my life. There's been some sort of mistake. I don't even understand what these are!"

Graf studied her, expectant. She squinted in the glare of the overhead light.

She stood to meet his gaze. "Only a fool would bring something this incriminating into an office crawling with Party and military officials. Did you plant them?"

A vein in his forehead pulsed. "Who were you working with?" he demanded. "Was it Friedrich Müller?"

They could not suspect Friedrich. She needed to put an ocean of space between them. He needed to believe her. She summoned all her strength.

"No one," she snapped. "I wasn't working with anyone *because I didn't do anything.* And besides, Müller isn't clever enough, anyway."

His eyes narrowed. "You are a pianist, are you not, Ada Jakob?"

Her breath suspended as Ilse's words filled her mind. *Somehow, they know everything about everyone . . .*

If they knew she was a pianist, what else did they know? Her heart pounded. Did they have Friedrich in custody? Had he already told them everything about her, to secure his own innocence? She clenched her fists as though preparing to fight, and grasped for a neutral response.

"I hardly see how that's relevant."

"You don't?"

"No."

"Are you a pianist?" he asked again.

Where the hell is he going with this? "Yes. Why?"

His eyebrows nearly disappeared into his hairline. "You are?"

She watched him.

"And what sorts of messages have you been sending to your conductor on your piano?" he asked quietly.

Audrey leaned her neck forward slightly, as though getting a closer look at him might help clarify this bizarre line of questioning. "I have no—"

Graf lunged at her so fast she barely saw him move. In an instant, he shoved her to the floor. She shot out her hands, cuffed in a grotesque mockery of prayer, to cushion her fall, but her knees and forearms hit the ground. A shadow fell across her as Graf stepped in front of the light.

"We know you had something to do with this, you clever little bitch," he spat. "And evidence has a way of finding us when we need it. Good luck with the firing squad, Fräulein Jakob. Heil Hitler."

He raised his leg, then brought it down hard. She cried out as blinding pain coursed through her fingers. The crunch of her fragile bones filled her ears.

"That's from Gerta. Ought to stop you from playing your little piano," he snarled.

His footsteps retreated to the door, and he left her there, sobbing, cradling her broken fingers.

Hours passed. Perhaps a day. And the pain didn't lessen. Her fingers were swollen and throbbing. She was exhausted, she wanted to sleep, but the fierce ache in her hands and the sickening apprehension of what awaited her had prevented any chance of rest. A part of her wondered what the point of sleep would be, anyway. To be well-rested for her impending execution?

At the sound of keys in the cell door, she scrambled awkwardly to her feet. Friedrich walked in, coat slung over his arm.

"Ada Jakob," he said, pointedly crisp for the benefit of the guard behind him.

She fought her elated relief at the sight of him and bowed her head. "Herr Müller."

The guard closed the door, then retreated. For a moment they said nothing. Then Friedrich craned his neck to see through the small rectangular window.

"He's gone down the hall," he muttered, then strode toward her and pulled her into a hug. "Audrey, good God."

She closed her eyes against the comfort and wondered if this would be her last ever embrace. She breathed in the smell of him, the starch from his shirt, the hint of rosemary from the airing cupboard, and wished he were Ilse.

"What's happened?" she demanded as they pulled apart. "Is Ilse okay?"

"Yes, she's safe." He took a deep breath. "Devastated though. They asked to search your room this morning. But they were apologetic, and left quickly. They asked me whether I knew anything of your plans, and of course I played it off, offended, said you kept to yourself and all of it. I think they believe you acted alone. The . . . machinations of a madwoman."

Audrey's insides burned. "But how did that woman, Braun—?"

"She's a friend of Gerta Roth's. From what I've been able to glean, she never swallowed the gas tank story because of your warning. She finally brought it up with Gerta, who recognized her description of you." His brown eyes raked her grey ones, her hair. "Gerta told her brother. He's SS too. And . . ." His shoulders slumped. "Now she gets her revenge for her husband's death, and her brother gets to deliver Hitler the head he's been screaming for."

Audrey stared at him, stunned.

"I am so sorry," Friedrich pled. "I—" He reached for her hands, but on instinct, she recoiled. He stared at them. "Audrey!" he gasped, looking up at her in agony.

"The interrogator, Graf, kept asking me if I played the piano," she said, tears stinging her eyes. "I said yes, and then he asked me what I'd sent back to my conductor, I—"

Friedrich swore.

"What?"

He seemed reluctant to answer.

"What?"

"He didn't mean it directly. Counterintelligence refers to radio transmitters as pianists. Their radios are pianos, their leaders are conductors. It's code."

She was hollow inside.

"He crushed my fingers," she said, her voice breaking.

Friedrich had no response. Some echoes sounded down the hall, and Audrey realized they hadn't much time left. The knowledge seeped like acid into her bloodstream. She felt it course from her chest down to her toes. She began to pace.

"They've told me I'll be tried by a judge," she said. "He'll find me guilty, won't he?"

Friedrich's eyes lowered. "Yes. I suspect it will be a farce."

She stopped. "And a death sentence will follow?"

"Most likely."

She knew it, Graf had said it. It made sense. But somehow hearing the words fall from Friedrich's mouth crystallized the reality in her mind. She struggled to absorb it. This had all happened so fast.

"I brought you your coat," Friedrich said, and only as he handed it to her did she notice that it was hers slung over his arm, not his own. She took it from him, slowly, with dawning realization. She ran her hand over the front pocket, felt the shallow lump of the cyanide button.

"It's going to get cold later," he said quietly. "You may find you want it."

She cleared her burning throat. "I need you to promise me again—"

"I will," he said immediately. "You have my word, Audrey. I will take care of Ilse as long as and in every way that she will allow." His eyes were wet. "But I cannot help but feel it should be me in this cell. I got you into this. I was prepared to pay the price."

Audrey looked down at the broken hands that had once created something beautiful out of nothing, filling rooms with soaring music. "I've known for a while that if it came to it, I would be the black boar. Because you're the one she needs, the one she wants." She forced a weak smile. "And because I would do anything for her." A tear slid down her cheek, so salty it stung. Her mind ran ahead of her into the shining years beyond, the ones she would never see, where Ilse would grow older and more beautiful and maybe, perhaps, reunite with Ruth and Ephraim. "Please tell her, again, that I love her," Audrey said. Her heart was beating for both of them.

Friedrich embraced her once more then, and she whispered in his ear. "The last thing I shall do for her is die."

Chapter 33

Audrey

BERLIN, GERMANY | MAY 1939

"Ada Jakob."

The morning after Friedrich's visit, Audrey heard the name called from inside the courtroom. She had grown so accustomed to it, taken on the mantle of the character she'd created to fool Weber. And now Ada was going to die right alongside her after sharing some half-life existence that, in the end, caused nothing but death.

Two guards guided her into the courtroom, hands gripping her arms. They needn't have bothered; her legs and hands were bound, her fingers hot and throbbing. She couldn't have opened a door to flee if she'd even had the chance.

The courtroom wasn't grand; the few rows of benches on either side of the aisle were empty but for two clerks whose necks were bowed, scribbling notes, and a young, besuited man with a briefcase near the front of the room.

They shuffled down the short aisle to where the judge sat at his desk on a platform. The guards released their hold on her, and she stood, facing the judge, preparing for the blade to fall.

"Where is counsel for the accused?" the judge asked, glancing up from his notes through small spectacles.

"Here, your honour." The young man with the briefcase raised a vague hand.

Audrey had never seen him before. No one told her she had a barrister to represent her. Hope flared for a fraction of a second, then she realized he was merely a prop for the stage, and a harsh laugh escaped her. The judge fixed her in his gaze. His eyes were bright blue, sharp, and she could tell this was a man who could see right through people. Good. She was exhausted by pretending to be someone else, anyway.

"*Guten Morgen, mein Herr*," she said, meeting his eye.

"*Guten Morgen*, Fräulein Jakob," he replied. There was a long moment where he continued to observe her, grey brows furrowed above a straight nose. He took in her dirty dress, her overall disheveled appearance, and the amused expression on her face. Then he glanced at the pages in his hands. "You are charged with crimes against the state, Ada Jakob. How do you answer these charges?"

The whole time she'd sat in that jail cell, all through the night, of all the things that went through her mind, her answer to the charges hadn't been one of them. She had figured this entire process would be a sham, just as Friedrich had warned her—and it clearly was. There was only one outcome. All she could preserve now was her integrity.

She loosened her shoulders. "Not guilty, *mein Herr*. Not guilty."

The guard to her right shifted his feet.

"Do you understand why you are here?" the judge asked.

He must have seen the flicker of mirth pass across her face, because he frowned in confusion.

"Truth be told, not entirely, sir," she said.

"You have not been duly informed of the crime of which you are accused?"

Audrey scoffed. "I have been informed, yes."

He rested his hands on the desk. "I must say, I find it difficult to believe that a woman of your intellectual comportment would be capable of the machinations presented in the evidence before me." He addressed the two guards. "What has this woman's behaviour been like during her time in custody?"

They exchanged a glance. "Much like this, your honour," one answered.

He nodded. "Fräulein Jakob, the sentence for such a crime against the Reich is death by firing squad."

Audrey's heart skipped. She was exhausted, heartbroken. But one thing she did know was that there was no point in allowing them to see her fear. Not now. She twitched her chin a fraction higher. "Yes, sir. I understand. Thank you, *mein Herr.*"

The judge tilted his head. "Did you hear what I said, Fräulein?"

"Yes, sir. Thank you."

"Do you understand the fate that awaits you? You have twice thanked me for telling you that you are about to be executed."

"Yes, sir." She imagined they wasted no time in dispatching traitors. She might only have hours remaining in her life. But after so much uncertainty, perhaps it was a welcome sense of finality. The fight was done. She had lost. And Ilse would live. "When will the execution take place?" she asked.

He shifted in his large, high-backed chair. "They are conducted just after sundown."

She pressed her bound wrist into the outer pocket of her coat, felt the cyanide button. She wouldn't die with her body riddled with Nazi bullets, and that knowledge satisfied her.

She bowed to the judge. "Thank you, sir."

He set her file aside. "That is not the . . . typical reaction to such news, I must say. Are you deranged, Ada Jakob? Are you meant to be in an institution?" He looked to the guards again, as though seeking confirmation of his suspicion.

Audrey considered the question, wondering whether he might be right. She probably was mad to have stayed in Berlin whilst her father urged her to return to England. She could not contemplate her life without Ilse, and because of that, she would now face death without her. Love, after all, made people do mad things. She blinked hard, determined not to allow weakness to own her final hours.

The judge tapped the tip of his middle finger on the desk. "I am going to be plain with you, Fräulein Jakob: you are a most peculiar case. I have never seen such blatant disregard for the prospect of impending execution, nor such courage from a woman, in any capacity, and that—along with your general demeanour—leads me to seriously call into question your sanity."

Audrey waited.

"In addition, I have never been forced to hand down a death sentence to a woman, in all my years on this bench. I am, frankly, disinclined to besmirch that record." He sat up a little straighter. "Ada Jakob, I hereby sentence you to life imprisonment. You will be transported to the prison at Vechta forthwith." He slammed his gavel in a resigned sort of way. "Next case."

Audrey and the other prisoners shuffled along in a single file, heads bent against the wind, for ten minutes toward a compound she could just make out against the sky. She looked up, eyes watering in the chilly air, to see a large, looming building surrounded by a wrought-iron fence. Lights in the dozen or so windows punctured the dark stone.

The journey to Vechta had taken hours. Hours in which Audrey alternated between studying her fellow prisoners and staring down at her own shoes, doing her best to tune out the aching throb of her fingers. She was still wearing her coat, which was fortunate, as the train was draftier than a country barn and chilled by damp. But she had moved the cyanide pill to the sole of her shoe.

After her sentencing, she'd been returned to her cell for the night with nothing to do but think—and plan, still in disbelief that she was not dead in some unmarked traitor's grave on the outskirts of Berlin. She'd assumed her coat would be taken from her when she was forced into some sort of institutional garb, so in her cell, she pulled off one of her shoes, peeled up the sole with her unbroken left index finger, and slid the cyanide pill beneath. Escaping a death sentence had given her some small shred of hope to cling to, that she might yet have a life somewhere ahead of her. But keeping the pill allowed her to maintain some shadow of control. She could still choose to end her life if and when she wanted to.

The guards led them now into an inner courtyard, a reprieve from the bitter wind, and Audrey took in her surroundings. The main building was set up in a square formation, with the courtyard in the centre. Iron bars secured all the windows. The group stopped outside an open door with a plaque overhead that read HEADMISTRESS'S OFFICE. Audrey raised an eyebrow. They must have converted a girls' school into a prison. The tentacles of the Reich had crept and stretched and wrapped their sinewy limbs around all of Germany's institutions. They took what they wanted, and few had the power or ability to resist. Those who did were sent here.

The women shivered in the cold, waiting.

After another few minutes, they were brought into the building to their left, which housed what Audrey presumed were classrooms in a previous life. They stood in line in the silent hallway as each woman was shunted forward into one of the rooms, emerging minutes later dressed in the same stiff grey dress and sweater, carrying a folded blanket. Many had tears in their eyes, whilst those who had already accepted their fate wore dead expressions.

When Audrey reached the front of the line, the guard beside her uncuffed her wrists, and she exhaled gratefully as a bruise bloomed in the dim light.

"Next," a voice called from inside the room. A middle-aged woman was standing beside a table piled with clothes and folded blankets, a clipboard in hand. "Name."

"Ada Jakob," she answered.

The woman referred to her list. "Jakob, Jakob . . . here you are." Sizing Audrey up, she selected a long dress and sweater from one of the piles. "Take off your clothes and put these on."

Audrey hesitated, then chose her words carefully. "Do you give me shoes too?"

"Why, what's wrong with the ones you've got?" the woman barked.

"Nothing. They're fine." Audrey slid them off, then stripped off her old clothes, tugging on the new dress and sweater. They were bulky but fit. She slipped her shoes back on quickly. "What do I—"

"Give me your old clothes," the woman said, hands extended. Audrey scooped them up and passed them to her. "Here's your blanket. Guard!" she called. "Cellblock D. Cell four. Bunk one," the woman told him. "Next!"

The guard gave Audrey a shove in the shoulder. "Walk."

They moved down the dimly lit hallway into the next wing of the prison toward Cellblock D. The polished wood floors that would have felt homey when the building was a dormitory seemed incongruous now with the prison. Audrey tried to note any exits on her way by, but saw none. The guard stopped in front of a cell. As he unlocked it, the jangling of the keys echoing down the corridor, Audrey saw a shadow move through the tiny window in the door.

The guard pushed her inside. "It's already lights-out, so no talking." Then he left, locking the door again behind him.

Audrey stood in front of her new cellmate: a curious, haughty woman with a pale face.

"I'm Ada," she said, then wondered why. It had become so automatic.

The woman tapped her long fingernail on the wall as she stared at Audrey. "What are you in for?" she finally asked.

Her voice was deeper than Audrey expected. A stage voice, she thought. A voice accustomed to people listening to it, obeying it. Audrey considered her answer for a moment. There was little point in lying.

"My name is actually Audrey James. I was arrested for my activity in a resistance cell in Berlin. We tried to kill Hitler."

The woman waited a moment, then threw her head back and laughed heartily, as though they were at a picture show together and the leading man just cracked a good joke. Audrey glanced back at the cell door, afraid a guard would come tell them off, or worse.

"What's your name?" Audrey asked.

The woman stepped toward her. She wore her confidence with poise, draped around her shoulders like a glossy fox fur.

"I am Wendelein Von Albrecht," she said, extending her hand. "From Enschede. I believe you were meant to be my houseguest."

Chapter 34

Kate

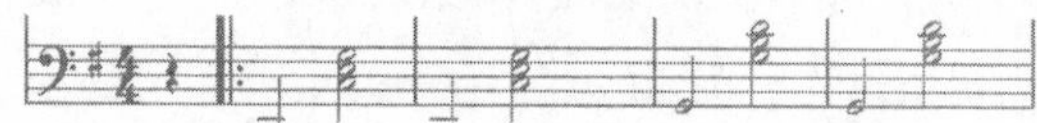

ALNWICK, ENGLAND | DECEMBER 2010

Kate is taking Audrey to an office just off the high street, on the second floor above a small charity shop. The brass plaque on the brick wall next to the door reads JOHN MACGREGOR, ESTATE SOLICITOR. Audrey has her cane, but Kate still helps her up the narrow stairs and down a stuffy carpeted hallway that seems to absorb all sound.

Audrey's moving particularly slowly today. It took a toll on her to recount the moment the Gestapo finally arrived on the Kaplans' doorstep, and her fatigue has lingered. That was, Kate sadly assumed, also the last time she ever saw Ilse. The interrogation that destroyed her fingers had clearly left its mark on her soul as well as her hands.

"Did it prevent you from playing again?" Kate had asked gently.

Audrey looked down at her fingers, eyes glinting with anger. "Oh yes. It certainly did."

"I'm so sorry."

"Thank you. But others fared far worse. This was a small price to pay."

"Are you sure this isn't too much to talk about, so soon after your . . . episode?" Kate had asked.

"There's no such thing as too soon at this point, dear. We don't know how much more time we have for me to get it all out." Audrey had been quiet for a moment then. "It's funny," she said, with an expression that suggested it was anything but. "I've been living on borrowed time for so long, yet right now, I feel a surprising need to borrow just a little bit more."

Kate did her best not to flinch at the mention of Audrey's impending death, tried to follow her lead and focus on the time still remaining, how best to spend it. She hasn't wanted to ask what happens next, after Audrey dies. She assumes the Oakwood will be sold off, which may well be the topic of Audrey's appointment with her solicitor today.

As they enter the office, memories of the aftermath of Kate's parents' deaths come flooding back: meeting with their lawyer, signing piles of documents she didn't even read or understand whilst Adam sat in the chair beside her, asking questions she can't recall now. She tries to ignore the palpitations.

After she gets Audrey settled in the tiny waiting area, Audrey pats her arm affectionately. "Good luck, dear. If you can't knock some sense into that boy, then I shall."

Kate's plan is to try to find Ian whilst she waits for Audrey to finish her appointment. If this were Adam, her previous life, she would have gotten herself all dolled up for such a gesture, to look as appealing and polished as possible. But this is Ian, and she's hardly worn makeup since she arrived here. She's not hiding anything anymore, so she goes fresh-faced.

She thought of calling to set up a time, but she wasn't sure he would pick up. She tries his flat first. No one answers. She chews her cheek, then goes to the bookshop.

The fireplaces are all lit, as usual, and Kate shivers with comfort at the blast of warm air as she enters, the heavy door swinging shut behind her. Ian's not at the cash desk, so she looks through the aisles of books, but doesn't find him lurking anywhere or helping a patron either. She heads to the café, orders a hazelnut latte, and settles herself at the table she and Ian usually share, when it's available, in a corner by the fireplace. As she sips her drink, her mind wanders back to happier days.

She finishes her coffee and is rising to leave when she hears Ian's voice, laughing with Charlene, today's barista. A sense of kismet settles on her, and she wonders for a moment whether they were meant to meet here today, to work things out. But the thought is instantly interrupted by Audrey's voice, telling her that everything in life is nothing more or less than random chance. He works here. He happened to be working today.

It's just good luck for a change.

She wrestles the butterflies as she waits for him to come around the corner, which he does a moment later, heading for their usual table, just like Kate did. He stops in his tracks, jacket in one hand, coffee in the other, and they stare at one another. She steps toward him.

"Ian," she begins.

He shakes his head, but he doesn't walk away.

"Have you been waiting for me to get off work?"

"No. I couldn't find you, actually. And I wanted a coffee."

"At our table?"

"Yes." She pauses, licks her lips. "I'm sorry, Ian. I'm so sorry. There's a lot I need to tell you."

He takes a seat, and she sits as well, feeling a measure of hope.

He meets her eyes square-on. "Why now? You seemed fine lying about it for long enough."

"I know."

"Do you?"

"Of course I do."

"Then why did you do it, Kate?" He glances over his shoulder, but the nearest patrons are several tables away. "You know, I thought we had something special. Unless you want to explain why you lied, there's no chance for this. For us. I told you about my ex, what she did—"

"I know. But you could have waited for me to explain yesterday. I called after you."

He shifts in his seat, heaves a sigh.

"Give me something real, Kate. Something that isn't a lie."

Looking into his dark eyes, it hits her that there's more on the line than she thought. People always talk about falling in love like it's a standardized state of being, that the experience is the same for everyone, every time. But it isn't. She didn't recognize it because it was so different than it was with Adam. She works to find the right words, but she knows that all he really wants is the plain, unedited truth. Bare and open, just like him.

"I know I was wrong to lie. But I did it because I'm falling in love with you," she says, heart hammering. He doesn't move, just continues to stare. "My marriage really is over; I just wasn't divorced on paper yet, and I wanted to start fresh with you, without all the goddamn baggage." She'd tried to avoid it, but she knows now that you can't. You just have to learn to carry it. The muscles of your trauma strengthen, and eventually it weighs less than it did at the start. "And because I lost a pregnancy in the accident along with my parents, and I've felt nothing but fucking lonely and broken ever since, and I think you might actually be able to make me feel like a whole person again, and it all kind of terrifies me." She gallops to the end of the emotional sprint and exhales shakily.

Ian's eyes are on her, one hand still holding his forgotten coffee. The colour is rising in his neck. He's still invested. And he wouldn't have sat down to talk in the first place if he didn't want to try to fix this.

He blinks fast. "I'm so sorry, Kate. I was being a prat. Come here."

They push their chairs back with a choral scrape and embrace each other. She presses her eyes shut, relief flooding her body as she sinks into the comfort of his chest, a bed of cable cotton and peace, the scent of coffee and warm wood.

Kate spends a good portion of the afternoon upstairs in her room. After her conversation with Ian, she'd picked up Audrey, and the pair of them stopped at the supermarket before making their way back to the Oakwood. Both were quiet, each absorbed in her own thoughts of the past.

She takes a hot bath, closes her eyes and inhales the steam. Lets the soapy rose-scented water rinse the soot from the memories as her thoughts flow over one another, of Adam and the pregnancy. Her parents. Audrey. The future she's glimpsed with Ian.

It's dusk by the time she dries off and changes into pyjamas. She turns on the lamps, then pulls out the box of photos from the floor of the wardrobe where she stashed them the day she moved in. She finds the ones that prompted her to google the Oakwood in the first place, and shuffles through them again. They look different to her now that she knows the place so well. Outside, the steely grey sky grows darker by the minute. She looks forward to the spring, when the lawns will be lush and green, casting shadow over the winding, narrow road, the gardens full of wildflowers and thistle, just like in the photo.

Kate sets aside the picture of her parents beside the sign, makes a mental note to ask Audrey if it would be all right to hang it in the lobby or the library. But then she realizes the Oakwood might not be home for her much longer and she'll want to take the picture with her wherever she ends up next. She thinks of Ian, wonders what sort of life they might have together, and where.

She goes to her dresser, removes the little jewellery box with the locket inside. She holds the small oval in her hands and runs a thumb over the surface, thinking of her parents staying in this room. She had to come all the way up here just to find them—and herself—again. She can bring them with her into the new life she's forging, but only if she has the courage to listen to Audrey. To forgive herself. After a pause, Kate heads back into the bathroom, where she dampens a Q-tip and cleans the dried blood off the clasp. Condensation still encircles the edges of the mirror, but she sees her reflection clearly. Her red hair is damp and a little frizzy, slung over one shoulder. She puts the necklace on and caresses the silver, cool against her hot skin as she reunites with a lost piece of herself.

Chapter 35

Audrey

VECHTA, GERMANY | SPRING - AUTUMN 1939

The morning after their arrival at the prison, a loud voice called for Audrey outside her cell. Her heart skipped as keys rattled in the lock, and a guard entered.

For a moment, hope flared—that they were going to tell her there'd been a mistake, that Friedrich had found some way to secure her release.

"You're next for Dr. Adler," the guard said, beckoning.

Audrey looked to Wendelein, who was lounging on the top bunk. "They just want to check for VD and lice," she said, flipping over onto her stomach and peering down at Audrey. "All the prisons do it."

The night before, they had curled up in their bunks under insufficient blankets, listening to the motors and screams of planes flying overhead from the Luftwaffe airfield nearby as they laid out all that had happened to them in the preceding months, and how each had ended up at Vechta. Wen told Audrey about her time with the Red Orchestra, aiding both the Dutch and German resistance efforts. She still didn't know how their cell had been discovered, but could only assume one of their contacts had turned, or been interrogated beyond toleration and given them up in exchange for some leniency. Wen had evaded capture for three weeks before she was arrested and sent to her first prison, from whence she'd escaped—twice.

The first time, she'd bribed a guard who fancied her to leave the outer gate unlocked at the end of his watch. But he reneged on the deal, alerted his superior, and she had been on the run for only thirty minutes before she was recaptured and sent back. The second time, she managed to goad two of her fellow inmates into a fistfight to distract the guards, allowing her to slip out through a gap under the fence that she had slowly tunnelled during their exercise hours.

"For some reason they didn't just shoot me, the idiots," Wen had said with a scoff. "They sent me here instead."

Audrey found Wen almost mythological in existence: a baroness of high pedigree; a rebellious, educated woman with a hatred of authority and a thirst for adrenaline. She seemed to fear nothing but captivity.

Audrey followed behind the guard now, cradling her aching hands. She didn't want to undergo the physical examination, but perhaps the doctor might be able to set her broken fingers.

Dr. Adler was an older gentleman, heavyset with grey hair and glasses, and was surprisingly gentle, a welcome reprieve from the harsh shoves and barks of the guards. He *tsked* as he assessed her bruised fingers over the top of his spectacles. "What happened to them?"

Audrey told him baldly of the assault, and he winced.

"And when was that?" he asked.

Audrey shrugged. Time had slipped by during her arrest and detainment, too fast for her to grasp it, yet somehow torturously slow.

"I don't know exactly," she said. "A week, maybe?"

Dr. Adler frowned. "I shall do my best. You'll need to be able to work," he added quietly, glancing at the closed door beyond which stood the guard. "Things will be worse for you if you can't work."

There were five broken fingers between her two hands, and each had to be set individually. Audrey bit down and tried not to cry out as

Dr. Adler worked, apologizing after every crunching thrust. By the time he was finished, they were both sweating, and Audrey panted in pain. But it was duller now, less pronounced. Her fingers felt hot.

"Try to move them a little. Just a little," Dr. Adler said.

She hesitated but did. "It's better than before," she said, as tears slipped down her cheeks. "A bit."

"Let's hope it takes," he said. "Enough to get by, anyway."

Vechta Prison, Audrey soon learned, was effectively a workhouse for homegrown German and Allied irritants, women like her and Wendelein who acted as resisters to the Reich, either within Germany or in the surrounding countries. It became evident that Germany was in full-on preparation mode for a war, and the women of Vechta were being utilized as free factory labour. They knitted socks for faceless German soldiers, men whose names they didn't know, whom they would never meet, and who, at the rate things were going with Hitler's rumoured new agreement with the Soviets, might very well be lying dead on a battlefield with three bullets in their chest by the time the socks reached their regiment. Other one-off projects were sometimes set up in the mess hall—assembling radio transmitters or sewing parachutes by hand.

Once her fingers healed well enough, Audrey took her spot on a bench in the mess hall. Her nanny, Sophie, had taught her needlepoint, but not knitting, as her father had believed it to be an activity more fit for the likes of servants and middle-class grandmothers. So it was in prison that Audrey learned how to manage the needles, modifying the proper form and accepting help from Wen to accommodate the limitations of her damaged hands. She had grieved the loss of them, and put to rest any feeble dream of ever playing the piano again. That skill, that joy, along with so much else, was now part of a past life to which she could never return. But she played music in her head. She was still composing Ilse's theme in her mind, trying to polish that always-unfinished piece of herself as she toiled away at her workstation.

During the countless hours spent in the factory, the laundry, or tending the prison garden, Audrey's thoughts swirled around nothing but Ilse. Daniel and Friedrich too. What they were doing, whether they remained safe and undetected. Her nights were filled with vivid nightmares of what might have happened to them, and, as always, the explosion in Hanover, the confused faces of the children in their fleeting, final moments.

She and Wen were desperate for information from the outside, and they strained their ears for snippets of news whenever the guards gossiped to each other in low tones. From what they overheard, it sounded as though Europe was on the precipice of war. Just as Ira, her father, and Friedrich had predicted.

When they weren't knitting or repairing radios, they peeled mountains of potatoes for the thin, revolting soup that allegedly constituted a meal. Potatoes made up the bulk of it—there never seemed to be any shortage of them—but the rest came from the slop from the adjoining men's prison, the bones and carrot peelings left over from their heartier stews. As always seemed to be the case, women were meant to subsist on the dregs that remained once men had had their fill.

She and Wen were always starving—intellectually as well as physically.

A month after her arrival, a loud knock at their cell door jarred them both.

"Books!" a woman's voice called from outside.

"Yes, please!" Audrey had said, rolling off her bunk. Newspapers weren't allowed, and she worried her mind had begun to dull, disconnect. There was no intellectual stimulation beyond her conversations with Wen, and the thought of a book thrilled her. The guard had opened the door and a tiny young woman named Hannah entered with a rusty metal cart. She was one of the youngest prisoners, and allegedly a member of the White Rose student protest group in Munich—the distributors of the resistance leaflets. Their leaders had been murdered and the rest imprisoned, but Hannah was so mild that Audrey wondered sometimes whether her arrest had been a mistake.

She and Wen pawed through the two dozen titles, several of which Audrey had already read, then she stopped, smiled, and pulled out a battered copy of Dante's *Divine Comedy*. After everything that had come after, she never actually finished it at the Kaplans'. She ran her hand over the cover, warmed by its familiarity. Reading it in the Kaplans' sitting room, she never would have imagined she would finish it in a prison cell. But there was little about her life now that she *had* imagined. They were all at the centre of a great tempest that tossed them around at will, landing them in places that hardly resembled their previous lives.

"A comedy?" Wen said with a grin. "Not a bad idea."

Audrey laughed aloud, which felt both wonderful and foreign. "It's not a comedy," she said. "I assure you."

On one scorching afternoon in early September when Audrey and a few others were digging up the last of the season's potatoes, the guard's whistle sounded, announcing the end of their shift. Audrey slowly rose from her knees, wiping her dripping brow with the back of her soiled hand. The fingers had healed now, but imperfectly. They no longer hurt, but several were crooked, the knuckles enlarged and bumpy.

The prisoners hadn't been given enough water or food for this sort of exertion in this heat, and she felt faint. She squinted into the sun, noticed the three guards on duty in the yard were huddled together. One of them gesticulated in anger, and Audrey wondered what the fuss was about, but she knew better than to stare. She took advantage of the moment to slip two potatoes into the pocket of her apron, something she always did when she got the chance.

After loading the last of her potato harvest into the rusted wheelbarrow, she fell in line with the other inmates. The muscles in her arms flexed as she wheeled the load to the kitchen doors at the back of the prison. They bulged beneath her thin flesh, giving the appearance of a ball stuffed into a transparent stocking. She had never had such muscle mass in all her life, yet had never been so weak.

She returned the empty wheelbarrow to the garden shed, then traipsed back to her cell, dirty and exhausted. They were only allowed one bath per week, so she would have to wash as best she could in the shallow basin on the floor. She always thought of Ilse when she washed in the basin, of those first weeks before Müller revealed himself, the indignity she suffered without complaint. She hoped Ilse was still in a position of being able to have a proper hot bath. She hoped to God everything had stayed stable for her and Friedrich. She thought of little else, especially late at night with no work to distract her racing thoughts.

The hall guard unlocked her cell and Audrey entered to find Wen there, on her feet, pacing back and forth.

"You're back already?" Audrey asked. "I thought—"

"Did you hear?" Wen said, eyes bright.

"Hear what?"

Wen ceased her pacing, glanced at the door as it shut with a clang.

"What?" Audrey pressed.

"The guards are all talking about it," she said. "We're finally at war. Britain and France have declared war on Germany."

It was all anyone could talk about for the next several weeks. As the autumn wore on and the cooler weather moved in, so too did a new sense of excitement among the guards, though it was laced with a tense thread of trepidation. They were now openly discussing the war and there was plenty to overhear, if you knew enough to keep your head down and your ears open. Germany had invaded Poland, and was joined by the Soviets a few weeks later. No one knew what would happen next, only that it seemed clear Hitler had no intention of withdrawing.

Audrey wondered whether the war was the beginning of the end of her tribulation, or would spell the end of everything for everyone. She couldn't know, of course. No one could. But she thought a little too often about what things might have looked like had they succeeded in killing Hitler in Hanover. She might still have been arrested and sent to prison, but they wouldn't have been at war. Perhaps Ephraim and Ruth and the other detained Jews would have been released by now. Perhaps, as Ira had hoped, reason would have prevailed.

Perhaps. Though Audrey had come to understand that there were many questions in a person's life that might just remain unresolved. In some cases, the lack of answers was agonizing. In others, it could be a mercy.

"Where are you?" Wen asked her from the top bunk as they relaxed in their cell after dinner one night in mid-December.

It was a question they often posed one another. They each knew the telltale expression when one disappeared into the past—somewhere they both travelled to often, visiting their lost loved ones and haunting themselves with the ghosts they couldn't manage to exorcise. For Wen, it was her dead husband, Henrik, and the lost pregnancy before he was killed. And for Audrey, always Berlin. Always Ilse.

"Mail!" A voice boomed from the hall before Audrey could respond to Wen. The tiny window near the top of the cell door slid open and an ivory envelope dropped onto the floor with a flutter like birds' wings. Footsteps retreated.

"Mail?" Audrey's brow furrowed. "What?"

She stood in her sock feet, staring at the letter. Ada Jakob's name and the prison were on the front in handwriting she would know anywhere, but there was no return address. The gold wax seal had been broken.

"What is it?" Wen asked.

With a jolt of electricity Audrey opened the envelope and unfolded the paper, a thick, deluxe gauge. Audrey scanned it, hardly hearing Wen's continued inquiries. Her hand came to her mouth, and she burst into tears as some great levee in her chest gave way.

"It's from Ilse," she choked, looking up at Wen, who had come to her, face full of concern. Wen reached out, and Audrey grasped her cold hand in her own mangled one. "She's fine. She's alive. They're all alive."

Chapter 36

Audrey

VECHTA, GERMANY | WINTER - SPRING 1945

Audrey took her time walking down the long hall toward the cell she and Wen had shared for the past six years, clutching Ilse's newest correspondence. She had learned never to rush anywhere if she wasn't required to by a guard. She had no energy to waste, and nothing of consequence to hurry to.

"Here," she said to Wen, withdrawing from her apron one of the two raw potatoes she had saved during her kitchen shift. "Dessert."

She was so sick of potatoes she could have spat, and the prepping and peeling was torture for her hands. But the fact was, without the tubers, the Vechta women might well have just starved to death. As it was, Audrey and Wen were emaciated versions of themselves. Three years into her sentence, Audrey had swapped her original uniform for a set that looked as though it belonged on a child. Her hair had thinned and was starting to fall out. Sometimes she wondered why the Reich didn't just let them starve and save a whole lot of bother and money. But, she supposed, the prisoners' deaths would also mean the end of the supply of free labour. They were provided just enough to stay alive.

"Did you get another letter?" Wen asked, biting down gingerly on her potato. The prison diet was causing her teeth to decay, and she'd already lost a few.

Audrey nodded. When she'd received Ilse's first letter, she'd been shocked that post was allowed in the prison—and that she was permitted to write back. But of course, everything was vetted. Ilse's letters always arrived open, and sometimes redacted with thick black pen. Ilse was careful anyway: there was never any return name or address, and she deliberately left out any identifying detail, using only initials for Friedrich and Daniel. But Audrey loved the sight of her meticulous, swooping penmanship. The loops of the letters encircled her like a velvet tether, pulling her back toward Ilse.

Audrey wrote back via Aldous's address, where Friedrich would pick them up. But she edited her own letters too. She couldn't stand the thought of Ilse knowing how terrible things were for her, and she assumed any negative reports on the living conditions would be tossed into the bin before they even left the prison. She'd stopped asking questions about the war because Ilse's responses to those never arrived. So she wrote a lot about the many excitements and frivolities of their shared past, the birds she spotted along the tree line near the exercise yard, and peppered Ilse with questions about what was happening at home. She wrote more slowly now, holding the pencil awkwardly to keep her penmanship tidy. She could have dictated to Wen, but wanted Ilse to read words from her own hand as she reached out to her across the divide.

Ilse couldn't say some things explicitly, but in coded language, she explained that it was Friedrich who had finally tracked down where Audrey was. It had taken him six months. He'd had to be covert, avoid raising suspicion in the aftermath of Audrey's arrest. He had also withdrawn from direct involvement in organized resistance, though he still looked for opportunities to protect other resisters and cells by misdirecting investigations in counterintelligence. Audrey was grateful that Ilse and Daniel were safer as a result, and it was also a sign of Friedrich's deepening love for Ilse that he was no longer willing to risk his own imprisonment.

Friedrich and Ilse were living as husband and wife now, and Audrey found her joy for Ilse was only marginally tinted with envy. Ilse was safe and happy, and that's what mattered. That was what Audrey had traded her own liberty for.

"What does Ilse say?" Wen asked now, patting the spot beside her. Her fingers were thin as twigs. With her parents and husband dead, Wen never received letters, and she looked forward to hearing about Ilse's life almost as much as Audrey did.

Audrey read the most recent missive aloud to Wen as she nibbled on her potato. It was full of stories of domestic life and a cryptic reference to the recent bombings in Berlin that Audrey had heard the guards talking about.

"Daniel is doing mathematics!" Wen exclaimed when Audrey finished. "It feels like just yesterday he was learning to feed himself, doesn't it?"

"Yes," she said, folding up Ilse's letter. "And no."

She considered the weight of the intervening years.

Most days, she felt as though she had always lived in this prison, so eternal was the sense of captivity. In the first year, Wen had tried to plan their escape, but couldn't find a crack to wedge open. She thought the prison director, a Reich government employee but a reasonable enough woman, might be bribed. There were rumours that her son was killed on the Eastern front when the USSR turned its coat; others whispered that she was Jewish, which was a possibility, Audrey thought, remembering Friedrich's own duplicity. Though there were no Jewish prisoners here, as far as she could tell. From the stories that trickled in, Audrey had pieced together the truth about the deportations, the purpose of the camps in Germany and Poland. She'd never had much hope for Ruth and Ephraim's safe return, but the flicker of optimism she'd tried to shield from the storm had long since been snuffed out.

It felt sometimes like they had been at Vechta for a century, but Ilse's updates about Daniel's rapid growth had a way of revealing how quickly time actually moved.

The women sat on the edge of the bed, staring at the cement wall across from them for a long while.

"You still love her, don't you?" Wen asked.

Audrey nodded. "Oh, yes. Do you still love Henrik?"

Wen sighed. "Yes. I believe I will forever. Isn't that absurd? I have nothing to live for on the outside. I keep on going here for . . . what? The memory of a dead man."

"How is it absurd to live for Henrik's memory?" Audrey asked gently. "Keeping yourself alive means keeping him alive, too, Wen. He would only be truly gone if you weren't here to remember him."

Wen was quiet. Some women shouted down the hall; a metal door slammed.

"We knew what we were getting into," Wen said. "We did. I think we just always thought we'd survive it. Isn't that foolish?"

Audrey gave Wen a squeeze. "No. I think it was hopeful."

Wen scoffed through a stuffed nose. "Hope makes fools of us all, doesn't it?"

Audrey thought of Ilse's continued insistence to remain in the house in case her mother and brother returned. Of the men firing bullets and bombs at one another on land, at sea, and in the air. Of the women, the nurses, secretaries, and factory workers. They were all fighting, right at this very moment, to ensure there was something left of the world for those who came after. The entire war was about hope that the future could bring something better. The beat of their pounding, fearful, courageous hearts would echo down through the generations.

Hope would be the world's inheritance at the end of all the bloodshed.

"Perhaps," Audrey said. "But what would we be without it?"

In March, Audrey and Wen—along with twenty or so other prisoners—were tasked with splicing wires for bomb igniters. It was painfully tedious, and Audrey's fingers made it difficult. She had to set the wires at a strange angle for the small, blunt knife that was her stripping tool. It wasn't sharp enough to do much damage to a person, but the guards had nevertheless chosen the work group carefully. Looking around, Audrey realized the group was mostly full of inmates who never caused trouble, and those like Wen whose spirits had been broken long ago.

They were lined up at the long tables in the mess hall, backs hunched over their work, which was lit poorly by a few barred windows and a handful of bare lightbulbs. Talking was permitted so long as they were reasonably quiet, but many of the women had said all there was to say to one another years ago. There were a few newer prisoners though; Audrey could identify them immediately as they still had fat on their bones, and they were the chattiest.

Audrey had no idea how much time had passed as they worked. There were no clocks anywhere; the inmates were simply told where to go in the moment it was demanded of them. As Audrey worked, she allowed her mind to drift to Ilse's theme. She'd finished it during the thousands of hours of labour over the past few years. She missed all music, but at least was able to keep this piece with her wherever she went. Though she knew she could never play it again herself, she had some hope that someday she could write it down and hire someone to play it for Ilse. Some unshattered pianist who could finish what she'd started.

The voice of a new inmate broke through the music in her mind. The woman was telling the group about her sister, who lived near the Polish border, where there were a number of ghettos. Audrey tried to tune her out, but when she described the Nazi purge of the encampments, Audrey turned to Wen.

"Why would they be purging the ghettos?" she whispered, setting aside a blue wire and picking up a red one.

"I was just thinking the same," Wen muttered. "Must mean something's changed, anyway. Berlin is being bombed. Maybe Germany's retreating from Poland?"

Audrey reached now for the yellow wire, the longest of the three.

"Made the children dig their own graves," the woman was saying in a distraught tone that carried down the table. "Little ones, not ten years old, mind. Just buried them straight alive, poor souls. Klara said the earth atop the pit moved for three days before it finally stopped."

Audrey's hands froze. She was grateful, in that moment, that her stomach was always empty, because otherwise she would have vomited.

Beside her, Wen shuddered. "Good God."

Audrey's ears were ringing, eyes itching with the threat of tears. She stared down at the multicoloured wires in front of her. She was still holding the yellow one, the one that needed to be twisted together with the end of the red one and then folded over, securing the pieces together.

Words from the White Rose leaflet came rushing back in a gale of awareness.

Crimes that infinitely outdistance every human measure . . .

She held the wire and knife as her body buzzed with a sensation she'd nearly forgotten: the compulsion to act. She'd been in prison for six years—physically, emotionally, and psychologically reduced to a faded version of herself. But beneath the crust of exhaustion and despair, she recalled the version who'd thrown herself in Weber's licentious path, who brought Daniel home, who didn't break, as her fingers had, during interrogation in the basement of the Gestapo headquarters. That version of Audrey still had something left to give, some ounce of resistance remaining.

So she began to splice the wires wrong. Maybe she could ensure some German bombs didn't detonate. Maybe she could still save someone from this seat on the long wooden bench in the middle of the Vechta prison mess hall.

Wen glanced over at her hands. "Do you need help?" she muttered.

"No."

"But you're doing it wrong. You need to secure the—"

"I *know*."

Chapter 37

Audrey

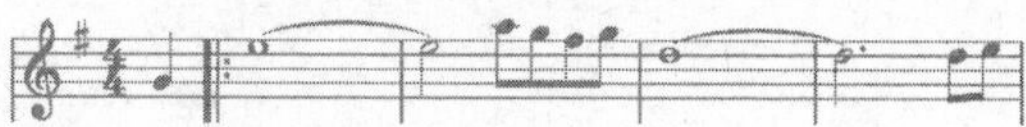

VECHTA, GERMANY | APRIL 1945

Audrey and Wen shuffled side by side in the small inner courtyard. It was their daily exercise hour, and the women all walked in the same direction like some sluggish human cyclone, heads bent against the relentlessly bitter wind.

Audrey was just thinking how she would rather have walked laps around her own cell when, out of nowhere, the air itself broke apart. Some unseen force shook the ground, and the women screamed. They instinctively ducked down with their hands covering their heads, as though that might help in the slightest. The guards shouted, and four more bombs fell nearby. Audrey remained on the frosted ground, thinking this might be the end, but Wen rose on unsteady legs, staring at the sky as a plane crossed over the prison compound.

"What are they doing?!" one of the inmates cried. "What is it?"

Audrey lifted a hand to shield her eyes from the glare as she looked up at Wen. A grin cracked across her friend's cheeks the way it had that very first night in their cell, and she laughed aloud, a cloud of hot breath bursting in front of her mouth.

"It's the Allies," she said. Her amber eyes danced, watering with cold and relief. "They're here."

Audrey kept her eyes on the sky as Wen's words sank in. She hardly dared believe that perhaps, after so long, this nightmare might be coming to an end.

Another week passed before the area surrounding the prison was shelled again. It was clear now that the airfield to the east of the prison was the Allies' target. She and Wen lay in their bunks in the middle of the night, feeling the reverberation of the bombs falling as the air raid siren wailed in the distance.

"They're so close, sometimes," Wen said from the bunk above. "Does it frighten you?"

Audrey shook her head, though Wen couldn't see her. "No. Surprisingly. Are you afraid?"

Wen snorted. "No. This kitty has already used her nine lives. You know I'm living on borrowed time now anyway."

"I think we all are," Audrey said.

Wen dangled one arm over the edge of the bunk, and Audrey took hold of it. They lay like that for a long while until Audrey felt her friend's fingers start to grow heavy with sleep. Audrey gently released them, and she heard Wen turn over on the mattress, adjust the blanket.

"Hey, Audrey," she said. "What—"

A roar unlike anything they had yet heard shattered the relative quiet of the prison. A second later, they felt the vibration of a blast so close that for a fleeting moment Audrey fully expected to die. A chunk of the wall above the cell door crashed to the floor. A chorus of screams issued from down the hall.

Audrey threw off the covers, springing from the bunk. "I think they've hit the prison!" she yelled, her mouth dry.

Another bomb ripped through the air and shook the earth as Wen leapt down from her bed. Chaos sounded outside the door. A shell whistled overhead and they both hit the floor.

When the walls stopped shuddering, they rose to their feet.

"Let us out!" Wen cried, hammering on the door. "For God's sake, let us out!"

The other women were banging on their own doors, and guards continued to shout to one another beneath the constant air raid siren shrieking its warning call into the night.

Wen turned to Audrey. "This is it, isn't? This might be it!"

Audrey swallowed. How many were already dead? She didn't want to die in this prison, not like this. "They're still after the airfield, but there's a chance the bombs will miss us here."

Wen looked confused. "I don't mean to die. I mean to escape!"

"Escape?" Audrey said, breathing fast.

"Get your coat," Wen said, grabbing her own.

Audrey pulled hers on and they both slid into their shoes.

There was a jangle of keys down the hall.

"Someone's coming." Wen pressed her cheek against the window, straining to see. "They're unlocking the doors! Get ready."

A guard was outside their door now. "Inmates, stand back!" he called.

They did, though Audrey could tell Wen was summoning all her available strength, readying for a fight.

The door opened and the ashen-faced guard beckoned them forward. "Move, move, single file, to the rear doors, go!"

They complied, scurrying down the hall. Audrey yelped as another bomb shook the building, but Wen practically ran ahead of her now, following the other women rushing out of the cellblock. They burst out into the cold air of the courtyard at the back of the prison. Most of the inmates were already assembled, watching the sky with frightened faces. Then Audrey smelled smoke. The sky was alight. The men's wing of the prison, just to the east, was engulfed in flames.

Audrey spotted the prison director. She ordered everyone toward the gate and the guards began poking them into a herd. Audrey seized Wen's arm, heart in her throat when she saw the rifle in the nearest guard's hands.

They're just going to shoot us, she thought, *and abandon the prison.*

The male prisoners were already burning to death just yards away . . .

The prison director shouted over the tumult. "Ladies!"

Another shell rent the air, and everyone crouched, screaming. When the shock subsided, they all rose on unsteady legs.

"Ladies!" she shouted again. "I'm opening the gates. You can stay here and take your chances with the bombs, or leave. But the surrounding fields are full of mines. The choice is yours."

Audrey's jaw dropped. Wen gasped beside her. The other women were yelling questions, crying. Two guards stepped forward and unlocked the iron gates, swung them open with an almighty creak, but no one moved.

Incredulous, Audrey glanced at the director. She shouted at one of the guards, something about assembling the *Kubelwagens* for the staff—the prison's utility vehicles. She wasn't even watching what the inmates were doing. Was this a trick? If they left, would the guards just pick them off from the watchtower and claim they tried to escape? Or was the end of the war really so close? If the Allies were here, then Nazi Germany's days were over—and the director knew it. If they released all the prisoners, the staff could leave, too, and have a chance to flee home to their families.

A haze of smoke hovered over them. The flames from the men's prison were shooting into the sky, an eerie midnight sunset, and the sound of desperate wails carried across the wind, mingling with the shriek of the siren. Audrey couldn't stay here. Clutching Wen's hand, she stepped forward, distancing herself from those dreadful sounds. Wen followed without hesitation.

They reached the front of the crowd and walked through the gate, into the night. Audrey's body tensed, but no shot rang through the air, no bullet ripped a hole in her chest. Other women were trailing them now, some sticking together in pairs whilst others set out on their own. None of them looked back. A sense of terror mixed with elation at their sudden, unexpected freedom descended on Audrey.

"Go, Audrey, go!" Wen urged.

"Which way?" she shouted over the siren, struggling to catch her bearings in the chaos. The men's prison and the airfield—the target of the Allied bombs—were to the east. To the west, the woods.

"Left, to the woods," Wen said. "West. The Dutch border is close. We need to get out of Germany."

Others had the same idea, and a group of them broke into a jog around the side of the prison fence. They pulled up short when they saw the guards from the men's prison milling around at the back. The Nazis fingered their rifles, some looking serious and some laughing, imitating the screams of the inmates as they burned to death inside.

They spotted the women, and several were suddenly alert, pointing their guns at them.

I was right, Audrey thought, with a sickening swoop of fear. *This is for sport. A spring hunt.*

One shot cracked and they all screamed. A woman fell not far from Wen and Audrey, shot through the neck. Her head was nearly severed from her body, blood shining in the light from the burning prison and its searchlights. Audrey looked away, waiting for her own death to come.

"What are you doing?" one of the guards said to the sniper. "Don't waste your bullets."

More laughter.

"Have at it, ladies!" another called, gesturing to the empty field to the west: the only way into the protection of the woods, the only way toward the Allies.

The minefield. The fail-safe for the prison.

"Wagers on how long it takes to get 'em all?" a guard shouted to his comrades.

"We have to go," Wen said, panting beside her. "We have to."

Audrey saw herself reflected in Wen's eyes along with the orange glow of the sky. What were the chances they would make it? How thoroughly was the field booby-trapped? Another Allied plane screamed overhead, a shell quaking the ground once more as the airfield took another hit. Audrey closed her eyes at the sound, breath heaving. She opened them again as a woman to her right shouted.

One of the inmates had either lost her mind or found her courage, and sprinted forward. They all watched for a full minute as she fled across the field toward the woods. She made it halfway before she hit a mine. The blast shocked Audrey to her core. She was already so weak, running only on blistering adrenaline. And the sight of the woman's body blown sideways, no longer in one piece, made her knees falter.

Another shot went off behind them. One of the Nazi guards fired at the ground near one pair of inmates, deliberately missing them by two feet.

"Get a move on, you cunts!" he called. His fellows guffawed cruelly.

"Audrey, we have to go," Wen said again, breathing hard.

They could either take their chances or stay here until the guards got bored and used them for target practice anyway. They had no choice.

"Stay behind me," Audrey told her.

She broke into a sprint, barely feeling her feet touch the ground as she ran, and she imagined for a moment that perhaps she was flying, impervious to the web of mines lurking in the dark soil beneath the grass. She kept her eyes on the tree line ahead of her. Her goal. Her refuge.

She would not look down at her grave.

The siren from the airfield faded. Audrey barely registered the sound of Wen's heaving breath and the blasts behind her as their unfortunate fellows met their ends. Lost limbs. All Audrey heard was the rush of her own blood in her ears as she flew across the field faster than she had ever run in her life, never diverting from her straight path.

The trees were growing closer.

A flood of instinctive willpower pushed her on.

Then she was surrounded by trees and darkness, the canopy of evergreens shutting out the unnatural orange night sky. She fell to her hands and knees, gasping for air, sweat dripping from her forehead, eyes burning from the cold wind. She caught her breath, then spun round and faced the edge of the wood again. The density of the trees only barely dampened the screams from the women who didn't die cleanly.

Audrey pushed herself up and stumbled back to the edge of the forest. The field was littered with bodies, and pieces of bodies. She could see them all in the light from the fire and, for a fleeting moment, was sure she must be dead too. One girl had stopped in the centre of the field. It was Hannah, the tiny White Rose resister. She shivered with terror, afraid to move any farther. Another woman was moaning for Jesus somewhere on Audrey's left, too far into the field for her to try to haul the unfortunate woman to safety. But from the looks of it, her death was imminent.

And there was Wen. At the very edge of the field. She must have hit the mine right at the end, because her body was blasted forward to settle beneath one of the first trees.

Audrey rushed to her and fell to her knees. Tears sprang to her eyes as she saw the catastrophic damage to Wen's leg. Blood was pouring from somewhere in her abdomen too.

"Oh, Wen," she gasped, cradling her friend in her lap. Wen's body was shaking from shock and blood loss. She was so far gone, she wasn't even screaming from the pain. "I'm so sorry, Wen," Audrey cried, brushing

Wen's hair back from her forehead. A tear coursed down Wen's pale face. "We tried. We tried."

Wen managed the ghost of a smile. "I—told—you," she said, her words stuttering with the force of her chills. "This kitty used up—all her lives. Got lucky. Right the—end." She lifted a trembling arm and pointed at the edge of the minefield.

She was so close to making it. Inches.

The other dying woman stopped moaning. The air raid siren went silent. The assault must be over. A cold wind brushed the tips of its fingers over Audrey and Wen, entwined together on the frigid ground.

"You were so brave, Wen," Audrey said through her tears. "So brave."

Wen locked eyes with her, amber into grey. "So—you."

Her shakes were getting worse, her breathing shallow, and Audrey couldn't bear to see her suffer any longer. She braced Wen's weight with one arm and slid her own shoe off with the other hand. She wiggled her fingers beneath the sole and found the cyanide pill.

"Here," she said. "Take this. It'll help the pain."

Wen opened her mouth without question, like a child to a trusted parent, and Audrey placed the pill between her remaining back teeth.

"Bite down."

The effect was as instant as Friedrich had told her it would be. Wen shuddered for a moment, harder than before, and Audrey embraced her tightly until she felt her breathing stop. Her body grew heavy.

Audrey choked on a sob, lowering Wen to the ground again. The night sky was luminous in her eyes, staring, unseeing. Audrey gently slid the lids shut.

"So brave," she whispered.

A sudden gunshot split the quiet air from far off in the distance, and out of the corner of her eye Audrey saw Hannah, the lone young girl in the centre of the field, drop to the frozen ground.

Chapter 38

Kate

ALNWICK, ENGLAND | DECEMBER 2010

Kate wipes away a tear, still in a state of shock over all that Audrey has just recounted. She sets her pen down on her notebook but keeps the voice recorder rolling. Audrey is staring out the large front windows of the Oakwood at the trees lining the drive. They're all bare now, a white morning frost coating their branches, and Kate wonders if she sees the forest outside Vechta.

Kate sits for a minute, absorbing it all like ice water into a sponge. How it all makes sense now. Why Audrey is the way she is. The nightmares and guilt. She shifts uncomfortably as a shiver grips her.

The fire is fading. She rises to tend it. Her necklace swings out of her cowl-neck sweater as she kneels to add another log and bits of newspaper. It's become an odd point of pride that she can keep the flames going on these cold winter days. She knows Audrey needs the warmth. Since returning from the hospital, she's lost more weight, more strength, more independence. Kate had to help her down the stairs and to her chair this morning and Audrey never gave a word of complaint. She's aware of her decline; it's ratcheted up her sense of urgency, but it's clear she also doesn't want to omit or trim any detail. The experiences became a part of her, lined the cells in her body, and she doesn't want them to die with her. She needs to drain them, set them carefully aside for preservation, before her body fails. She's just covered six years in the last few days.

Once the fire is roaring, Kate returns to her chair. Both dogs are at Audrey's feet now. They always know. Audrey faces her now, blinking away the images of the prison escape and Wen's tragic death that still project behind her eyes.

"So," Kate begins tentatively. "What happened after that? Where did you go?"

Audrey clears her throat, winces, and takes a large sip of water, her hand shaking, but her voice is a little stronger than when she spoke of Wen's fate a few minutes ago. "The Allies had clearly made it to Germany. We only knew that their planes were there, but not much else. Wen had said to run for the Dutch border, so I did. It seemed the only thing to do, really. Even though the Nazis were everywhere, staying in the country that had imprisoned me felt foolish. And I wasn't really thinking. I was in shock, I'm sure. So shocked that I failed to notice I hadn't put my shoe back on until I was miles away, on the other side of that wooded area." She pauses. "I don't remember much from that first night, to be honest with you."

She stares into the middle distance.

"Have you ever read Dante's *Divine Comedy*, Kate?"

Kate shakes her head.

"In the *Inferno* volume, the ninth circle of hell is a frozen lake, reserved for traitors. That's what my journey felt like. Most of what I remember was that it was freezing. Bloody goddamn freezing. And there was a part of me that felt as though I must have deserved it somehow. That it was my penance for all of it, that the land itself was punishing me for my betrayal of Germany." Sophie paws at her leg, and she lifts her into her lap with a groan. "I was following the small towns on the way, because they did provide some refuge. I broke into a barn one night, at a farm outside of Lindern, I think. I slept in the hay under a horse blanket. A young woman found me in the early hours, pail in hand to milk the cows. She didn't say much, didn't even ask who I was, which made me think it wasn't the first time they'd sheltered someone. She gave me milk, and I drank as much as I could. She let me take the horse blanket too. At any rate, I eventually made it to the border. Somehow. I'm sure I veered off course because I ended up farther north. I didn't even realize I was in the Netherlands until I saw a group of soldiers that weren't German. Turned out to be Canadians. I wept with relief when I heard them speaking English. I learned soon enough that they'd just liberated the Netherlands, that the dominoes were beginning to fall. I could hardly believe it. The war was nearly over. And I had survived."

A pause stretches between them, and Kate suspects Audrey is thinking of Wen, how close she'd come to surviving too.

"Others died, lost entire limbs. Me?" She holds up her gnarled hands. "This was my damage. This—and frostbite on my baby toe. They had to remove it at the field hospital."

"I'm sorry," Kate says, unsure how many times she's said that since Audrey began telling her story. "How long were you at the hospital?"

"About a month, I think. Through the end of April and into May. They took good care of me. They had mostly men's clothes there, but my nurse, Eloise, was about my size. She gave me some clothes, and they hung off my frame. I felt a little more like a real person, but at the same time had this sense that I was donning a costume for a play. Like I was sort of this … pleasant imposter in my own life. It took some time to learn how to walk properly again. It's strange how one toe can impact your balance so much. I did better in my younger years, but that's why I need the bloody cane now." She begins to cough, pauses for a sip of water.

"And when did you learn that Hitler was dead?" Kate asks.

"Well, news trickled into the hospital over a few weeks, and we eventually started to get newspapers there. They said he'd shot himself in his bunker in Berlin, and that his woman killed herself, too, with cyanide, and all that did was remind me of Wen's face, of her gasping her last breaths in my arms." She shrugs. "I think by that point I was just glad he was dead. It meant the war would be over soon. People at the hospital celebrated, toasted. Cried. Others sat on their beds, just in a state of disbelief, I think. I couldn't help but think how the war might have ended years earlier if we'd been successful that day in Hanover. How different life would have been. How different I might have been." Audrey clears her throat again. "I remember taking a bath at the hospital and scrubbing my skin with this scrap of soap until it was pink and raw, trying to wash away the grime of the war. But the residue was indelible, I think. I wasn't the person I was before. I was a survivor, and forever marked with the stain."

She looks up at Kate, who nods, thumbing her necklace and thinking of her parents. "That burden must have felt even heavier when you learned about the extent of the camps. The Holocaust," she says.

"Yes, but that came later," Audrey says. "There'd been rumours and stories at the prison about the deportation of Jews to work camps, that people were dying there. But the full truth about the extermination camps didn't reach us until the Allied soldiers started to liberate them. Once they began to sort through the evidence, the debris of all that had happened over those six years. Back then news took days or even weeks to reach people. But when I was in the hospital, all I could think about was Ilse. About getting back to her. Berlin had been bombed all to hell, and I was worried sick. I could hardly wait to see her again, hold her."

Kate smiles through stinging eyes. Reuniting with Ilse was the dream Audrey had allowed to consume her during the hundreds of dark nights at Vechta. It had fed her as her body weakened, sustained the flame of her soul when the cold gusts threatened to snuff it out.

"Returning to her was all that mattered at that point," Audrey says.

Kate tries to imagine the uncertainty, especially after everything Audrey had been through. Curiosity burns inside her. "And did you?" she asks. "Did you make it back to her? Was she still alive?"

Audrey takes a deep breath, but her throat catches, and she wheezes.

"Let me get you more water," Kate says, swiping her glass.

Audrey nods, covering her mouth as the coughs rack her body.

Kate returns a moment later with a full glass of water, and as she leans down to hand it to Audrey, the older woman pales.

"Audrey, are you all right?" Kate asks, concerned.

"Kate . . ." she rasps. Her eyes are locked on Kate's neck.

"What's the matter? What is it?"

"Who are you?" Audrey looks up at her, an expression of utter disbelief on her face. Something well beyond confusion.

"Er," Kate breathes. Is this some sign of cognitive degeneration? Kate's own grandparents died before their memories did. She doesn't know exactly how to handle this. She offers a small smile, wishing Ian were here. "I'm Kate, Audrey. I'm—"

"No," Audrey says, her voice deathly low. "I mean *who are you*, and what are you doing with Ilse's locket?"

Chapter 39

Audrey

BERLIN, GERMANY | MAY 1945

Audrey's stomach began to flutter as her train neared Berlin, and she feared she might be sick when it pulled into the station. But as she disembarked and made her way through the crowd toward the busy street, she noted the absence of the Nazi insignia, the scores of imposing flags that used to drape throughout the city. It felt like the morning after a storm, when light filters through the grim, grey dawn. But the city had been badly bombed in the Battle of Berlin just weeks ago.

At the field hospital in the Netherlands, Audrey had been glued to the newspapers covering the Allied Soviet invasion of the city, at once elated by the liberation and terrified for Ilse. Her last letter had come in February and she'd still been safe then. Audrey had wanted to write from the hospital, to make sure she was still all right, but her nurse said there was no point. No post would reach Berlin. Not when Germany was falling back, the end of the war finally in sight.

Now, though, Audrey saw just how extensive the Soviet assaults had been, and her anxiety about Ilse's welfare crested. There were piles of rubble everywhere from countless destroyed buildings. Others were missing their windows and blackened with soot. The streets were filthy, the dust only just beginning to settle. Her feet carried her, with a slight limp, over the old Moltkebrucke bridge, which was still standing, then through the streets that were at once familiar and unrecognizable. She took them in with a reserved, painful nostalgia.

When she rounded the end of the Kaplans' street, she gasped at the line of row houses. Several doors down, two houses had been nearly destroyed, their roofs all but gone. A few wooden beams and patches of shingles remained, hanging at strange angles. The windows were no longer there; Audrey could see inside the front rooms where most of the walls had been entirely blown away.

She ran now as best she could toward the Kaplans' and let out a cry of relief to see the front door and windows intact. There was even a light on in the sitting room. She summited the steps, paused for a deep breath, then knocked.

A long moment passed before the door opened. Audrey's throat tightened at the sight of an unfamiliar woman standing in front of her.

What had happened to Ilse? Her thoughts swirled, each more horrific than the last. She saw the Gestapo shouting, dragging Ilse out into the snow as she screamed her protest. Daniel crying in her arms. An officer threatening them with a gun to the head, shoving them into the back of a van headed for the same place all the Jews had gone. This woman and her Nazi husband moving their furniture in the next day.

"Hello," the woman said. She was a bit older than Audrey, with light brown hair. "Can I help you?"

Audrey didn't know what to say. Did she dare ask for Ilse?

"Ma'am, are you quite all right?" The woman was concerned now. Perhaps she thought Audrey a madwoman. A vagrant or a beggar. She was sure she must look the part.

"Er—" Audrey stuttered, swallowing her fear. "Perhaps I have the wrong house."

There was the sound of small feet running and a boy appeared at the woman's elbow. Audrey took in his clipped dark hair and pleated trousers, the eyes she'd known she would remember for the rest of her life.

"Daniel?" she breathed.

"Yes?" he said.

"Is Ilse here?" Audrey asked the woman now, heart pounding in desperation. "Friedrich?"

"Oh!" she replied. "Are you a friend?"

Audrey nodded warily. "Yes. My name is Audrey. Audrey James."

Recognition flooded the woman's face. "Hello, Audrey. I am Gisela Müller, Friedrich's sister. He said you would come. I prayed you would. And soon."

The fog lifted. Gisela. The sister who had dragged Friedrich out of the forest when he was a child . . . But her being here—what did that mean?

Before she could ask, Gisela ushered her in.

Daniel shut the door behind Audrey, and they stared at one another. She recalled the distinct memory of feeling his body lifeless against hers. He was a miracle.

"You're so big now," she said, then to Gisela, "I knew Daniel when he was just a baby. I used to live here."

"I know," Gisela said. "You'd better sit down. I'll make some tea. I believe we have a great deal to discuss, Fräulein James."

"I'd like to see Ilse first. Where is she?" Audrey asked, heading toward the stairs.

"She's sleeping right now."

"I'm sure she won't mind me waking her, I—"

"I don't think Ilse ought to be disturbed at the moment."

"Where is Friedrich, then?" Audrey asked, struggling to keep the frustration from her voice.

But Gisela ignored her, turning to Daniel. "Go play quietly in your room please, Daniel. I must speak to this lady."

Daniel obliged. When he was gone, Gisela led Audrey into the sitting room.

"What's going on?" Audrey pressed, heat rising in her face. "Where is Friedrich?"

"He was arrested two weeks ago," Gisela said. "After Germany surrendered, the Allies came for the officials. I assume he is in prison. I do not know where."

Audrey lowered herself to the couch. She shouldn't be surprised. Technically, Friedrich was SS. Of course he'd be arrested, but she'd hoped . . . She looked at Gisela. "I'm sorry. Did he tell you . . . Do you know what he was doing before the war? What he was really doing?"

Gisela nodded. Audrey saw the light from the window reflecting on the tears in her eyes, like a glimmer on glass. "I do. I am proud of him."

"You are?"

"Yes. And he told me about you. You resisted with him. He said you went to prison for it, but you never gave him away."

Audrey looked down at her fingers. "It was the right thing to do. Ilse and Daniel needed Friedrich more than they needed me."

Gisela touched Audrey's hand. "I'm thankful you did. Friedrich may be my half brother, but we grew up as siblings. I never knew of my father's affair until later. I understood why Friedrich left to go fight Hitler. It was for his mother. For himself."

Audrey studied Gisela's face, afraid to ask the question that burned in her mind. Afraid of the answer. "Why are you here, Gisela?"

"About a year ago," Gisela said, "Friedrich wrote to me and asked me to come. Ilse was unwell and he couldn't manage caring for her and Daniel whilst also maintaining his cover at work."

"Unwell?" Audrey repeated, as fear surged in her chest. "What's wrong?"

Gisela sighed. "She had been short of breath, even just going up the stairs. She fainted on several occasions, once whilst at the stove, and sustained a bad shoulder injury. She was weak, and getting weaker. Friedrich managed to find a sympathetic doctor, who thinks it's some sort of heart condition."

Audrey shook her head. "This doesn't make any sense. She's so young."

"The doctor says the problem has likely been there for years. Possibly her whole life. But it has worsened in the past year."

"Why?"

Gisela shook her head.

"What's the treatment?" Audrey asked.

Gisela glanced away.

"Gisela."

"There is none," she said quietly. "The doctor has been here several times in the past few weeks. She hasn't long left, I'm afraid." Gisela paused. "Ilse is dying, Audrey."

Her words echoed in Audrey's ears.

"I am terribly sorry," Gisela went on. "But it is in God's hands now."

Audrey didn't want to believe it. She tried not to. This simply couldn't be.

"She never said anything," she said, stricken. "Why wouldn't she tell me?"

Gisela's eyes were full of sympathy. "She did not want to worry you, she said. You had enough—"

Audrey rose. "I need to see her."

On the stairs, the familiarity of the house hit Audrey like a sharp blow to the chest. She had hoped to come back, but it had always felt like a distant dream that might never come true. And now this homecoming burned, sour and acidic.

Outside Ilse's room, she hesitated, afraid to startle her, but there was no way her arrival would not come as a shock.

She knocked.

Ilse's voice came through. "Come in."

Audrey's gut clenched at the sound, and the sudden realization that she might not have much longer to hear it, if what Gisela said was true. She swallowed the lump in her throat and turned the handle with a creak.

And there was her best friend in all the world, her dearest love, sitting up in bed in her nightgown, a light blue crocheted blanket slung round her shoulders.

"Audrey!" Ilse gasped, and her chin started to tremble. "Oh my God. Oh my God." She held out her arms and Audrey rushed into them, wrapping her own around Ilse's small body. Before Audrey's arrest, Ilse had gained back some of the weight she'd lost in hiding, but she'd lost it all again, plus some. Her fragility was a shock, and Audrey tried not to squeeze too tightly.

Audrey pulled back. There was no weakness in Ilse's dark eyes, though. "Ilse—"

Her friend shook her head, at a loss for words. They were finally here. Together. Both alive, after all that had happened, after so many wretched years of separation. Warm spring sunlight crept in through the window, which was opened a crack; the chirp of birds and the scent of lilac wafted in on the breeze. The bedside table lamp was on, a notebook and pencil set beside it.

Ilse was smiling through heaving sobs, and Audrey leaned in and held her again, inhaling her. Her hair tickled the side of Audrey's cheek.

"Is it true?" Audrey managed.

Ilse exhaled, trying to steady her breath. "I'm sorry I didn't tell you," she whispered. "I couldn't bear it. I had hoped it would all turn out to be nothing of concern. It got better sometimes, then worse, then . . ." She cleared her gummy throat, and pulled away gently. "You were in *prison*. I only wanted to bring you good news, speak of happy things. Happier times." Her voice wavered. "But you haven't been honest with me either," she said, taking in Audrey's jutting shoulders and collarbone. "You're skin and bones, and your hands . . ." She took them in her own. "Friedrich told me about the interrogation. I'm so sorry, Audrey. But tell me everything now, please. We must lay it all out."

Audrey sighed. She knew Ilse thought she wanted to know, but she didn't. Not really. Audrey didn't even think she could bear to relay it all, anyway. Not yet. So she settled for some half-truths, telling Ilse her tale but stopping short of the full story where the reality became too unbearable. She didn't tell her about how Wen had died. She couldn't bear to speak of death with Ilse, who followed Audrey's story for the better part of an hour, all the way up to her own front door that afternoon. When she finished, they both sat for a minute in silence.

"You're still here because some judge thought you unusually brave," Ilse said.

"Or mad," Audrey said.

Ilse smiled weakly. "Why does that not surprise me?"

Audrey squeezed her hand. "And Friedrich? Gisela told me."

Ilse averted her gaze. "He's been so good to me. I know I told you some of it in my letters, but I want you to know that. I really did come to love him. Truly. And he loves me. We're a good match. And now he won't be here when—" She looked at Audrey, eyes red. "We talked about fleeing, before Berlin fell, to try to avoid his arrest. But I was too ill to travel, and he wouldn't leave me. He said he hoped to be able to prove himself, but . . ." Audrey watched her with sympathy. "He was wonderful with Daniel too. He was as good as a father. It was a joy to watch. God, poor Daniel. He was so distraught when Friedrich was arrested. He still asks for him. All I can tell him is that he's gone. How can I ever explain this to him?"

"We would have been lost without Friedrich," Audrey admitted.

"I'm so grateful he called for Gisela when he did, once it was clear that things would be getting more difficult," Ilse said. "I resisted it at first, but thank God, given what happened. She's been so kind to me too. I've been very fortunate."

How had things gone so wrong with the world that after all that had happened to Ilse, she still considered herself one of the lucky ones?

Audrey swallowed. "And the doctor, he's quite sure there's no treatment?"

"Yes. He's sure. But you know"—she lifted her eyes to the ceiling, blinking hard—"I'm finding I don't mind so much. Not really. It's . . ."

Audrey waited whilst she searched the heavens for the words.

"I'm happy, in a way. Relieved, perhaps? I believe I'll be with my family. Somewhere. Somehow. I've missed them so much."

"I know. But we don't know yet, about—"

"We do," Ilse said, renewed tears shining in her brown eyes. "Friedrich found out last year. He was finally able to track them down. They were moved to the Dachau camp, then separated at one point, which made it more difficult. Mama . . ." She took a shaky breath. "Mama died in forty-two at Dachau. January ninth. All the record said was that she was ill." Her shoulders fell. "And Ephraim was transferred to a camp at Mauthausen, for labour. He was murdered." Her tone rose as she forced the words from her throat. "In a gas chamber. Last March. The sixteenth."

Tears poured down Audrey's cheeks, and nausea surged, tinged with as much rage as she could spare the energy for. "Oh Ilse. Why didn't you tell me?"

Ilse reached for her face, brushed away the tears with her thumbs. "This is why. I couldn't bear to deliver you more heartache, make things any more difficult for you than they already were."

They held each other again for a long while, entwining their grief like a pair of thorn-covered vines. A ray of spring sunlight shone in a bar across Ilse's bedspread. Audrey looked down at the pattern of forget-me-nots. The flower that represented true love.

"I've thought about those dates," Ilse said, sitting back against the headboard now. "Tried to recall what I was doing. Busy with Daniel, no doubt. But I must have risen and eaten and played with him and gone to bed and never felt a thing. Don't you think that's odd? I thought I would have known, would have felt it somehow in my heart. I think that's part of the reason I never believed they were dead. Why I wanted to wait. But at least I'm not waiting for them anymore." She tried to smile. "They're all waiting for me now."

"Don't say that, Ilse," Audrey murmured, her heart breaking all over again. She leaned forward and laid her head in Ilse's warm lap.

"I've come to terms with it, Audrey, and you must, too," Ilse said, stroking her thin hair. "Do you ever think about what would have happened if you'd found the dress you wanted at Hertie's? If we hadn't gone over the street to that little gown shop? We would have still been with my parents, and then . . . It just makes no sense. That I survived, and they didn't. Because of a happenstance like that. And now? Maybe I was just never meant to live through this. Maybe nothing we did mattered."

Audrey took a deep breath and surfaced, mopping her face with her sleeve. "I've thought about it. Of course I have. But our efforts weren't all for nothing. We got you six more years that you wouldn't have had if you'd been there with your family that day. You got to be a *mother*, Ilse. You fulfilled a dream. That has to have been worth it. It is for me. That you got to live a little longer. That you get to be here, at home, at—at the end." It took strenuous effort to maintain her composure. She would need to be strong for Ilse one last time.

"You went to such trouble for me," Ilse said. "To help me. You saved my life. You endured so much, Audrey."

"Not as much as many," Audrey muttered.

"I can't ever thank you enough for it. And I don't think I did at the time, really. Not like I should have."

"I would do it all again. All of it." And she meant it.

"All of our partings have felt impossible to endure," Ilse said. "But we'll only have to say goodbye once more." Audrey's heart was barbed with grief. "I love you, Audrey," Ilse said.

"I love you too."

Audrey shifted, resting her head on Ilse's shoulder. At long last, she felt as though she had come home. She closed her eyes, soaking in the comfort.

They stayed like that for a long time. Birds twittered in the tree outside the window. Spring was here, and summer would arrive just as surely afterward, no matter who died or lived or what wonderful or horrible things happened in the world. Summer would still come.

"My great regret is leaving Daniel so young," Ilse said, breaking the silence. "Here," she said, leaning forward and reaching around behind her neck. She unclasped her mother's necklace and held it out for Audrey. "Will you give this to him for me? When he's older? I want him to have something of mine. Of the family's."

The chain pooled in the palm of Audrey's hand. What she had always taken for a pendant was actually a small locket, the family monogram *K* ornately engraved in the centre.

"Of course," Audrey said, closing her fingers around the silver.

A long time passed, each of the women lost in her own thoughts. It was peaceful, and soon Audrey began to think Ilse had fallen asleep again, but then she spoke, murmuring into Audrey's shoulder.

"Before I go, there's something else I need to ask you."

Audrey lingered in the doorway of the Kaplan house as she watched the solicitor leave. The boulevard trees were in full leaf now, but the summer colours and scents were diminished this year, as though painted over with a sheen of grey. The warm July breeze touched her skin and her mind traveled back. Time moved fast and expired quickly at the best of times; even more so under the incubating heat of a war.

How many times had she crossed this street to go play with Ilse? If she listened, she could still hear their little girls' voices on the wind, chanting out skipping rhymes. She could see the withered shadows of their bouncing ringlets, their buckled shoes on the road. Their childhood selves were suspended in time on this street, and always would be, even though Ilse was now gone.

She had died quietly in her sleep a week ago. Audrey was at the piano with Daniel, teaching him how to play Ilse's theme when Gisela came downstairs with a full breakfast tray. Audrey knew what had happened by the look on her face. Gisela set the tray down on the coffee table and pulled Audrey into a hug. She was much shorter, but held her tightly as Audrey wept. Daniel looked up at the two of them with wide brown eyes that were keen for answers. Answers, Audrey feared, she might never be able to give him.

Only one family from Ilse's synagogue had come back from the camps. A woman named Anna who was once pretty but returned from Auschwitz with thin, short hair, dull eyes, and a limp. She came home with her teenage son, just one of the five children who were taken with her and her husband in the winter of '42. Ilse had left her name and address, and a few hours after Ilse's death, Audrey knocked on Anna's door. Anna didn't say much, just followed her back to the house and directed Audrey on how to prepare Ilse's body. She wished she could honour her friend more thoroughly, but this was the best they could do under the circumstances.

Ilse was buried in the Kaplan family plot on the Grosse Hamburgerstrasse alongside her paternal grandparents. Audrey stood beside the grave, holding Daniel's little hand as he cried for his mama. She was at a loss for what to say that might soothe him. They didn't sit shiva in any formal way, but Audrey stayed at the house for a week after Ilse's death, delaying the inevitable.

Now she glanced at the stack of documents from the solicitor in her hand and turned to go back inside. She stopped for a moment, leaned against the doorway between the hall and sitting room, remembering how it was Ludwig Thurman's usual spot. She wondered on occasion what had become of him. Was he arrested along with Friedrich? Or had he managed to turn his coat effectively enough to avoid capture? She shook the questions from her head. After all he'd done—or rather not done—she found she didn't really care what had become of him.

Daniel was sitting at Ruth's piano in his blue collared shirt and suspenders, feet grazing the pedals as he picked at the high notes, the summer sun illuminating his hair from the sitting room window.

When Ilse asked Audrey that day up in her bedroom if she would take Daniel, she had agreed, of course. Audrey couldn't bear to deny anything Ilse wanted or needed, particularly in those final weeks. She would have fought a bear or cut off another one of her own toes if Ilse had asked her to.

"Thank you, Audrey," Ilse had said through more tears. "I didn't know what I was going to do. Gisela made some enquiries with an orphanage right after Friedrich's arrest. But you turning up here has answered my prayers."

Ilse knew Audrey never wanted to be a mother, knew the prospect terrified her. Ilse always thought that her resistance was based on a fear of childbirth, given how her own mother had died. She'd presumed Audrey was actually all right with the concept itself. But she was wrong.

Gisela came out of the kitchen, wiping her hands on a dish towel. "Lunch is nearly ready. Everything settled with the solicitor?"

"Yes," Audrey said.

In April, when it became clear that Germany was on the brink of surrender, Friedrich had withdrawn most of his money and put it in a trust for Daniel. Audrey would now manage the account until he came of age to inherit.

"Good," Gisela said. "I think, then, it is time I return to Austria."

Audrey nodded. "Thank you for staying so long, and for everything you've done for Ilse, and for Daniel. For me. You've been a good friend to us all when most would have abandoned the responsibility quite some time ago. I'm very grateful to you."

Gisela inclined her head. "It is what Friedrich would have wanted. He thought very highly of you, I hope you know. And besides, I have—had—grown fond of Ilse. She was very special to Friedrich."

His name hung in the empty space between them.

"Are you going to try to learn what's happened to him?" Audrey asked.

"Yes, of course. I have already made some enquiries, but it is difficult to get accurate information. I think the administration of justice is going to be challenging. It may be years before it is all sorted out."

"I hope they'll be fair to him," Audrey said. "He wasn't like the others."

"But he wore the insignia. He lived in a commandeered Jewish home. The version of himself that he put forward to mask his true intentions and sentiments was thorough. It will be difficult for him to prove otherwise, I fear. On paper, he is as guilty as the rest."

Audrey knew she was right, but it was hard to hear it all the same. She pitied him, knew how it would have felt for him to be arrested and taken from Ilse, unsure of what would happen to her.

"My thoughts go with you," she said to Gisela. "When you do find him, please tell him thank you. For everything. I'm indebted to you both."

Gisela managed a smile. "I shall. What is next for you?"

Audrey sighed. "There's nothing for me here, now. It doesn't feel like home anymore. I don't really have one." She looked over at Daniel. "But I'm going to need help. I can't do this alone. I have an aunt in England, the only family I have left. I figure that's as good a place as any. For now, anyway."

Gisela nodded. "We will all have to forge new paths for ourselves in this overturned world. Find our way. May the stars light your journey, Audrey James."

Chapter 40

Kate

ALNWICK, ENGLAND | DECEMBER 2010

Audrey, what do you mean?" Kate asks, touching the silver locket in the folds of her cowl neck.

"That is Ilse's locket," Audrey says. "*My Ilse*. How do you have it?"

Kate's brow furrows. "My parents gave it to me on my twentieth birthday. It has my initial on it, see?"

Audrey's eyes are wide. "I would know that locket anywhere. Let me see it."

"What?"

"I need to see it," she snaps.

"Okay, fine," Kate mutters, unclasping the necklace and wondering what the hell is going on. She passes it to Audrey, who picks up her glasses from the table beside her chair, perches them on the end of her nose.

Kate watches her examine it, the small oval piece with a scrolled *K* on the front. "It was a gift," she says again. "I haven't worn it since the accident, and—"

"I need to open it," Audrey says, cutting her off. "What's inside?"

"Photos," Kate says. "Of my grandparents."

"My fingers can't manage it. I need you to open it."

"O—okay," Kate says.

"Don't give me that face. I'm not senile."

"Okay," she says again, and presses on the tiny clasp to expose the inside of the locket. "Look."

Audrey lets out a deep breath and slouches back down a little in her chair, eyes still on the photos. She runs a hand over her forehead. "I'm sorry, Kate," she says. "We've been digging up so much from the past, I think I'm seeing things that just aren't there."

Kate purses her lips, wondering if she should ring Ian. Something is clearly not right. "Should I call someone, Audrey?" she asks. "I think—"

"Wait. Have you ever—" Audrey's voice cracks, and she sits up a bit straighter in her chair again. "Have you ever taken those photos out? Did you put them inside?"

"No. They were in there when my parents gave it to me."

Audrey frowns, eyes on the locket, and then she pins them on Kate. "What is—was—your father's name, Kate?"

"Joseph Barber."

Audrey stares at her, disbelief and fear and a dozen other emotions flickering across her face, one after the other.

"Audrey, *what is going on*?" Kate demands. "Tell me! I'm worried about you."

Audrey holds up a hand, the misshapen fingers trembling. "Are you lying to me, Kate? You said you had stopped lying."

"What do you mean, lying?"

"Have you been lying all along? You didn't just stumble across that job advert, did you? You knew what this place was."

"I don't know what you're talking about," Kate says, palms out in frustration. "I told you, my parents—"

"Came here for their honeymoon, you said?"

"Yes!" Kate is scrambling to catch up. "They met you then. I have a photo. I was retracing their steps, like I told you, and—"

"Bring me the photo," Audrey says shakily. "*Now*."

Kate backs away, exasperated, and leaves the room, heading upstairs, still utterly perplexed. She seizes the photo from her dresser, then thunders back down to the sitting room.

"Here," she says, striding toward Audrey with the picture held aloft. "Look."

Audrey brings one hand to her cheek, staring at the photo. Her eyes are wet.

"Audrey, for the love of God, tell me what's going on," Kate pleads. "What does this locket you say is Ilse's have to do with my dad?"

Audrey exhales fully, and a tear slides down her wrinkled cheek. "Kate, your father was Ilse's son. Your father was Daniel Abrams."

Kate freezes. How can that be? Then an eerie sense of understanding trickles down from the crown of her head as she considers what she knows about her dad. He was adopted, but he'd never spoken about where he came from. Not even the one time Kate had asked, when she was ten years old and doing a family tree project at school. Her mother had told her he didn't know anything about his heritage other than that he was Jewish.

"How can this be true?" she asks, her ears ringing.

Audrey pinches her eyes shut as though she can't bear to witness the conversation anymore.

"Audrey?" Kate presses.

"Because it *is* true," she says, looking at Kate. "That photo wasn't taken during your parents' honeymoon. It was taken when your father came to meet me after tracking me down. *I* took it."

"But the photos . . ." Kate trails off, then remembers: the photos from this trip were stuffed between the pages of the honeymoon album. Kate had made an assumption, but they weren't from the same trip. Her eyes start to prick as the bizarre acceptance sets in. "But you said you were going to bring Daniel to Alnwick. Wasn't that your plan?"

"Christ." Audrey shifts in her seat with Sophie firmly entrenched in the valley of her lap. "I did. I brought him here after Berlin. I tried to make a go of it. I really did." Her eyes are shining. "For Ilse's sake, because I said I would."

"Well, what happened?"

Audrey looks to the ceiling as though appealing for help from above. "Sit down, Kate," she says. "Please."

Kate obliges, eyes locked on Audrey as her mind trips over itself in an effort to piece this all together.

Audrey takes a long drink of water, sets it back down with a tap on the wooden coaster. "When we left Berlin, we came straight to London so that I could manage my father's estate. Get everything sorted, sell the Kensington house, et cetera. It had all just been sitting there on ice since his death in '38. I visited the solicitor in Lombard Street, but he'd been killed during the invasion of Sicily, so I dealt instead with *his* father. He was one of the most hollowed-out men I've ever encountered, just shattered by the loss of his only son. In any event," Audrey continues in a hard tone, "there was no home to sell. The house on Argyll Road had been destroyed during the Blitz."

Kate gasped.

"I went to see it with Daniel. Ours and the one to the north of it had been hit. Fortunately, ours had been empty." She takes a deep breath. "But my father's neighbours, the Andersons, were home. Both were killed, but their twin boys had already been evacuated to the country. Lucky devils or poor little bastards, I've never decided." She shakes her head.

"So," Kate ventures, "if you had gone home when your father wanted you to . . ."

"There's a good chance I would have been killed in the Blitz, yes. I can't ever know, but risking my life to stay in Berlin might have actually saved it." Her lips twist into a wretched grimace. "We stayed in a hotel whilst I sorted out my father's estate, then Daniel and I left London for the Oakwood. My aunt Minna was a help, and I did my best, but Daniel wasn't adjusting well. He was heartbroken at the loss of his mother, as was I. I descended into a deep depression that I couldn't seem to pull myself out of. All I could think about was the dead. Ilse, Wen, the other women who died on that minefield. The children we killed whilst trying to save the lives of countless others. Claus, the Kaplans, Daniel's family. All the boys who wouldn't be coming home to their mothers, the unnamed dead who hadn't even yet been tallied. And my mother, who died trying to give me a life that made no sense to me now. Somehow I was the only one left standing."

She strokes Sophie and steadies her breathing.

"I felt rather useless to Daniel then. He was a seven-year-old boy, active and inquisitive. And here we were, out in the middle of nowhere, really." She gestures at the window and the frozen, sweeping property beyond.

Kate imagines her father at seven years old, kicking a ball around the grounds of the Oakwood. How could he have kept all this from her?

"He couldn't make friends, and I don't know if there were any Jewish children round here back then. None that I knew of, anyway. And that was a big part of it."

"A big part of what?" Kate sniffs.

"I couldn't raise him in his own faith, and I had none of my own left to pass on to him. I didn't want to be a mother, and to be honest with you . . ." Her voice is thick with emotion. "After all he had been through, I thought he deserved more than a reluctant mother." Audrey meets Kate's eyes, whose tears mirror her own. "Promises are difficult to keep. Even for well-meaning people. But the way I see it, well . . . the promise I made to Ilse was that I would take care of him. And in the end, finding him a home with his own people, where he could live a good life with parents who wanted and loved him, felt like the best thing I could do to care for him. To honour her, and what she would have wanted for him, had she lived."

The question forms in Kate's mind, but Audrey beats her to it. "I tried to find some Abrams or Kaplan relatives in England, or even on the continent. But everything was such a disaster in the aftermath of the war and the genocide. I doubt there would have even been relatives to find, but the search was practically impossible. Europe was a shambles, still piecing itself back into something vaguely resembling its former self. So I took him to a Jewish orphanage in London. Most of the children who came over on the *kindertransports* in the thirties were now orphaned. There were plenty of them in need of homes. He was placed with your grandparents, the Barbers. And that's, well . . ."

A long silence follows. Kate glances at the black voice recorder on the table between them. It's still running, recording the threads of Audrey's history that have just intertwined with hers.

Kate doesn't know where to begin. She's grappling with the sense of understanding this brings about her dad's addiction. He was a high-functioning alcoholic, and she always knew he was trying to drown something. But it was too far below the surface for her to see what it was.

"So, that's why my dad came here," she says. "He was looking for you."

Audrey nods. "Yes. He tracked me down through the adoption agency records in London, around the time he was, what, twenty-eight? I'd left my information there, with this address, when I dropped him off. I still had Friedrich's trust fund to bequeath him, and I reckoned he would have questions. One day. And of course, he did."

"Did you tell him everything you told me?"

"Most of it. He remembered me, remembered this place. And Ilse, and Friedrich. He asked me why I didn't keep him, but I think—I hope—in the end, he understood. He had a lovely childhood, he said. Loving parents."

"He did," Kate whispers. "My Bubbe and Zayde. They were older. He was their only child, and they doted on him." She smiles sadly. "And me."

"But I think . . ." Audrey shakes her head. "He had so many upheavals, so young. And his memories of Ilse were complicated."

"How do you mean?"

"Well, the earliest memories he had were of her, but also of Friedrich, a man who left the house every day in a Nazi uniform. A man whom he called Papa, who played with him, hugged him, just as a father would. I explained it all. Who Friedrich was, who Ilse was. What we had all tried to do, and how we failed. Friedrich's double life, and mine. Ilse's, too, in a sense. And I gave him Ruth's necklace, as Ilse had asked me to. But to tell the truth, I've never been convinced he believed me. Not entirely."

Kate nods. He would have assumed Ilse and Friedrich were Nazis. She can only imagine what those memories of Friedrich must have done to her dad once he learned of the Holocaust more broadly.

"I hoped the photos in Ilse's necklace would help, over time," Audrey says. "I would be surprised if he ever spoke of that bit to anyone. Possibly not even your mother. And the Barbers only ever told him that he was adopted from Berlin at the end of the war, when he had no family left."

"Did they know more than that?" Kate asks.

Something akin to shame colours Audrey's face. "They only knew what I had told the orphanage in London. For obvious reasons, I kept it simple." She takes a deep breath. "He did ask for the address of the Abramses, said he needed to go learn more. I never forgot that house. I saw it in my dreams, for God's sake. I assumed they had all died, but he said he needed to know for certain. Though I'm not sure he was ready for what he found."

A chill runs down Kate's spine. This is her family history. "What did he find?"

Audrey hesitates. "The Abramses were all murdered at Mauthausen. He wrote to me, just once, to tell me what he had learned. It was mostly . . . informative in tone." She sighs. "I think his feelings about me were very complicated. I don't know how much closure I was ever able to bring, or whether it would have been better for him if he'd never sought me out. It is so difficult to know what knowledge will do to us. I think a part of him wished I hadn't found him in the house that day."

Kate's nose begins to swell, and she rolls her shoulders inward against the pain in her chest. She fingers the necklace in her hands and starts to sob. The Abramses, and the Kaplans, too, in a way—these were her ancestors. And if not for Audrey, Kate wouldn't be alive at all.

Her father was a sole survivor, as she is now. A twisted connection she now shares with him, a paradox that folds in on itself. But she'll never be able to tell him that she understands him now, finally. Never have a chance to ask him how to live with it. Her stomach feels as though it's rotting. It was horrendous enough to be responsible for her parents' deaths, but now, knowing that her dad had escaped such odds, that he was lucky to have even made it to childhood to begin with, just makes it all feel that much more senseless. But all she can do now is honour her family. See it all as a gift, like Ian does.

Just live.

"Why did he never tell me any of this?"

"Oh, Kate," Audrey says. "Come here."

Kate kneels at Audrey's chair as the old woman's arms enclose her. Sophie licks her arm, and Ozzie scoots closer too. They all hold one another for a long time. The animals stare up at their mistresses with wide eyes, knowing something has happened but unsure of what it means. Kate isn't entirely sure what it means yet either. But a dam of some sort has broken, she knows that much.

When she pulls away, she snatches a tissue from the coffee table and notices the lamplight reflecting off the glossy tan surface of the baby grand piano. "Why did you bring the piano back?" she asks. "Isn't it just a constant reminder of all the loss? Of Ilse, and the Kaplans? Your gift?"

"Yes," Audrey says. "That's why I wanted it. And why I never had the water ring removed. Forgive me for asking, but if you could erase those scars, would you?"

Kate pauses. There was a time, months ago, when she would have said yes unequivocally. But she knows better now. The scars and the memories they hold are a part of her. Even if she'd tried, they wouldn't ever actually be erased. She would still see them beneath the surface. She's about to respond when a thought occurs to her. "Did my dad play your piano when he was here? He was a player. Not professionally or anything, but he was good. I think . . . I think it was therapy for him, in a way. He'd play a lot more when his depression was winning."

Audrey smiles sadly. "Yes, he did. I even showed him 'Ilse's Theme,' taught him how to play it. Again. He . . ." Her voice cracks. "He remembered it from when she was dying."

A realization hits Kate with a hard jolt to the chest. "Does Ian know it?"

Audrey nods. "The composition is in the piano bench. I wrote it out and asked him to learn it so I could hear it again, somewhere other than my own dusty mind."

"He played it the first day I met him, when you were at the doctor. There was something about it, like I knew it . . ." A warmth spreads in Kate's chest, despite the heartache the day has brought.

"Well," Audrey says quietly. "I'm glad your father played it. It helps keep Ilse's memory alive."

"Could I . . ." Kate hesitates. "Would it be okay if I had a look at the letter my dad sent?"

"I'll swap you. Your dad's letter for a few minutes with that necklace."

Kate helps her up from her chair.

"Just give me a moment," Audrey says.

Kate sits back in her chair again and watches the gold and orange flames dance and crackle in the fireplace. Somehow everything has changed, and all too late for her to do much about it besides mourn. It's an odd conflict when happiness and sadness coexist in your heart. It's tight yet expansive, warm but painful.

"Took me a minute," Audrey says, returning from the office. "Here."

Kate takes the letter, a leap in her chest, and passes the locket back to Audrey. The two women sit in silence, examining their shared treasures as though they were indeed rare gems. Reading through her dad's letter, fresh tears drip down Kate's face. It's strange, she thinks, when we reach adulthood and realize that our parents are just flawed humans like we are; when the veneer wears away, and we find a person who's just doing the best they can with what they have to work with, the trauma they're lugging with them each day.

She glances over at Audrey, who looks up from the locket with glassy eyes. "What is it?" Kate asks, then sees that Audrey has removed the tiny photos of Kate's grandparents. "Hey, what are you doing?"

"Look," Audrey says, handing her the necklace.

There are two portraits inside, sepia-toned and aged, and Kate's breath catches.

"That's her, then. Ilse."

"And her brother Ephraim."

Kate takes in the dark-haired young woman with large eyes, arched brows, and a small mouth beneath a straight nose and high cheekbones. She's friendly looking, despite the neutral expression she's adopted for the photo. She looks pretty much how Kate had pictured her, but it's striking and emotional to finally see the face of the woman who captured Audrey's heart, altering the course of her life, and who nursed Kate's father back to life and loved him as though he were her own.

"These were in my necklace the whole time," she whispers. Her father's family secret had lain against her own skin for years, and she hadn't any idea.

"Just behind your own photos."

"How did you know to look?"

Audrey gives a little shrug. "I wondered what else your father would have done with them."

"Do you think he ever planned to tell me?"

"We can't know, of course," Audrey says. "Although he did give you the necklace without removing them first. He must have known you'd discover them at some point. Maybe on some level he wanted you to."

"It seems strange to cover these up again with my own photos. Do you want them? Do you have another photo of Ilse?"

"No," Audrey says. "But I think it's lovely, actually. You'll keep your own family close for your sake, and you'll keep Ilse close for your dad's."

"And yours," Kate says, a tear slipping into her lap.

"Thank you, dear. That means a great deal to me."

Kate can feel her exhaustion finally taking over.

"Where are they buried?" Audrey asks. "Your parents?"

"In London. The Liberal Jewish Cemetery. It's interfaith, so he and my mum could be buried together. Why?"

Audrey sits up. "I think I would like to go visit his grave."

Kate looks down at her lap. "I haven't been since the funeral."

"Then I think we should go. Together. I want to visit my father's grave too. To say goodbye before I say hello again."

"Where is he?"

"Brompton Cemetery, in Chelsea. Not too far from yours."

Kate fingers the locket, avoiding Audrey's gaze. "I'm just not sure I'm ready to go back again."

"I think you need to go back whether you're ready or not," Audrey says. "In my experience, a person will never do anything if they always wait until they're ready. We have to make ourselves uncomfortable, Kate, in order to move. Otherwise we get stuck, stagnating, until we lose the ability to move anywhere at all."

"I know," Kate says, tapping the tip of her finger at a spot on her glass. She keeps her eyes downcast. "But I'm afraid."

"I know, dear," Audrey says gently. "We all are."

Chapter 41

Kate

LONDON, ENGLAND | JANUARY 2011

Kate pulls up to the curb outside their bed-and-breakfast in Kensington and turns off the ignition. Her nerves, which were already on edge from her impending visit to the cemetery, are all pins and needles. She'd happily forgotten how anxiety-inducing it is to drive in the city in rush hour traffic. Audrey's right, though—this trip is necessary. Kate fled her life too quickly to tie up any loose ends, which have a way of unravelling at the most inconvenient of times.

But the shadow of finality hovering over them is undeniable. For both Kate and Audrey, this journey is at once a homecoming and a goodbye. That's part of what Audrey has been trying to tell her: she has to turn and face her past, her mistakes. She lets out a breath and glances at Audrey, whose lips are pursed in a thin line. She coughs a little.

After they check in, Audrey lies down to take a quick nap before dinner and Kate heads to the room next door. She sends Ian a text that they've arrived safe and sound. She had filled him in about all the developments, and he'd been as supportive as she possibly could have wanted. She and Audrey invited him to come with them, but he'd declined, offering instead to stay home with the dogs.

"Audrey and I have our own history already sorted," he'd said, brushing a strand of hair back off Kate's face in the warmth of the Rose Room's bed. "Now it's your turn. I think this is something the two of you should do together."

The following day dawns cloudy and cold. Audrey and Kate sit down to breakfast and a large pot of coffee in the dining room of the hotel before setting out for Brompton Cemetery, then on to the Liberal Jewish Cemetery.

"When was the last time you visited?" Kate asks her in the back of a taxi.

They didn't drive Kate's car, so they wouldn't have to worry about parking and walking. Audrey tried to wave Kate down, claiming the taxi was too expensive and they should take the bus, but Kate held firm.

"Not for decades," Audrey says. She stares pensively out the window at the hustle and bustle of the street as the taxi winds its way down Old Brompton Road to the grand cemetery entrance. "Everything is so much faster now," she muses. "Everyone's so hurried. I wonder why. All they're really rushing toward is death."

They exit the car and Audrey loops her arm with Kate's, leading her down a long winding path bordered by tall bare trees that will be lush come springtime, providing plenty of shade for those visiting the graves below, their branches extending outward like comforting arms, soothing the bereaved.

"I've always liked cemeteries, you know," Audrey says beside her. "They give a lot of people the creeps, or they're superstitious about them. But I find them to be very peaceful. Quiet, still. Treed and cool. And there's a sort of relief in them. The lives of the people buried inside might have been cut short by accident or disease, whilst others ended later, at the proper time. But there's this sense of rest that you don't encounter many other places."

They walk another minute or so until Audrey points to a set of three gravestones a little way off the path. "Right there."

They step around the other stones, some so ancient the names and dates can't be made out, the identities erased by rain and wind and the calloused hands of time. And what a tragedy that seems to Kate, that no one visits those graves anymore; the deceased's loved ones are long gone themselves. And so moss grows over the stone and it sinks into the earth as the person below is forgotten. She wonders how many unremembered souls there are in this one cemetery alone, and it hits her in that moment, perhaps harder than it ever has, how fleeting a single life is. How enormous, yet insignificant. It's astonishing how readily people waste time with no consideration that eventually—and maybe without warning—they're going to run out of it.

Audrey comes to a halt in front of the stones. She's quiet for a while, and Kate waits, supporting Audrey's arm. A wind whips up and lifts the fringe off Kate's forehead.

"I do wish I'd been here for my father's burial," Audrey finally says. "Would you help me?"

With Kate's assistance, Audrey kneels on the snow-dusted grass in front of the plot and sets one of the bouquets of flowers they bought near the hotel—white lilies—in front. She places a gloved hand on her father's stone, lingering for a moment, eyes closed. Kate wonders what she's telling him.

"Thank you," Audrey says, as Kate helps her back up.

Another couple passes by on the path behind them, talking in low tones.

"That's my plot beside him," Audrey says, pointing. They both stare at the empty space. A bird calls from a nearby tree. "I thought it would feel more frightening to see my final resting place now that I'm nearing the end. But . . ."

"I don't want you to go," Kate says, her arm around Audrey's shoulders. "I'm so sick of goodbyes."

In such a short time, Audrey has become irreplaceable in her life. Kate understands how Audrey felt, having finally returned to Ilse only to have her die not long after.

Audrey squeezes Kate a little with her small arm. "But now you'll know where to find me. I'll be right here, if you need me. Only next time you'll talk, and I'll just listen." Audrey pauses. "Do what I never could, Kate," she says, "and forgive yourself for what you did. Please."

Kate nods, on the verge of tears now in this melancholy spot. "I'm trying."

Chapter 42

Kate

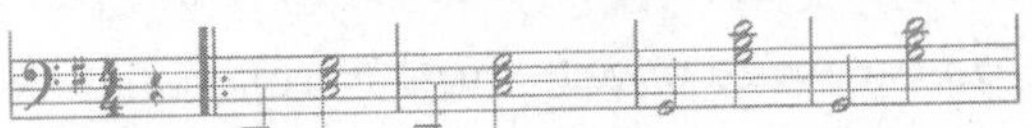

ALNWICK, ENGLAND | APRIL 2011

Kate looks up from her laptop and takes a sip of coffee. She's been working furiously on polishing Audrey's story and, at Audrey's request, searching for more details on what happened to Friedrich Müller.

The buds are just beginning to burst on the trees surrounding the Oakwood. The daffodils and hyacinths are already in bloom at the stone gateway by the road, and in a few weeks, the spectacular cherry blossoms in the Alnwick Garden will make their seasonal appearance, drawing tourists from around the world. But Kate has kept the bookings closed. All the botanically titled rooms at the guesthouse remain vacant except for Rose and Elder, where Audrey is resting in palliative care.

As she keeps telling Kate, she's lived for months after they told her there was nothing more to be done. "From birth, we're all on borrowed time, anyway, Kate. Or maybe it's stolen. Or gifted. I never really worked that bit out. Perhaps you will. But whatever it is, it is fleeting."

Kate stands and walks to her bedroom window, looking down at the garden behind the hotel where Ian is building a set of new raised beds for herbs. The sleeves on his beige sweater are pushed up, and his hair falls a little across his forehead as he stoops to measure a piece of timber. Last weekend he relaid the patio stones and power-washed the outdoor furniture. His love language, Kate now understands, is to quietly assist behind the scenes. He's been spending a lot of time at the Oakwood to be with Kate, but particularly since Audrey was declared palliative, alternating between talking to her in the hours she is awake and lucid, and keeping himself occupied with maintenance whilst she sleeps.

The sound of a bell tinkles from the floor below and Kate smiles. Audrey had resolutely refused either a mobile phone or the employment of a baby monitor to call Kate for whatever she might need. But she did allow a small brass bell, borrowed from the dormant reception desk in the foyer. "Far more dignified," she'd said.

Good timing, Kate thinks. She gathers the pad with her notes about Friedrich and heads to Audrey's room. Audrey is sitting up in bed, braided white hair falling over one bony shoulder.

"Heya," Kate says, smiling even though every time she sees Audrey so wasted and tired, she just wants to cry. "What do you need?"

"Good afternoon, dear," Audrey says before a coughing fit overtakes her. Kate refills her glass in the bathroom sink and Audrey sips it gratefully. "I would commit a moderate crime for some Marmite and egg on toast," she says, a little raspy. "Heavy on the butter, too, hell, why not. And some coffee. I appear to have slept through breakfast."

Kate returns fifteen minutes later with a tray, then settles herself at the end of the bed as Audrey starts to eat.

"So, you had asked me to learn whatever I could about what became of Friedrich," Kate says.

Audrey's chewing slows. She takes a deep breath and another sip of coffee. "What did you find out?"

Kate glances down at her notes. "After his arrest in '45, there's a gap in information, but we can assume he was sent to prison for a few years, because he was tried at Nuremberg along with the other general staff and high command of the German armed forces in March of 1948, after they did the initial round of trials for the primary leaders of the Reich. He was found guilty of conspiracy to commit war crimes and crimes against humanity. Generally aiding and abetting the Nazi regime."

Audrey nods. "That's unsurprising. Did he plead guilty or not?"

"He pled not guilty," Kate says gently.

Audrey sighs. "Good. That's good."

"He received a life sentence and was sent to Spandau Prison in Berlin, along with a load of other convicted Nazi officials." Kate pauses, her heart heavy. "He died there, in 1963. There's one report that he was stabbed to death by another inmate, some kind of altercation. There isn't much detail. I'm sorry, Audrey."

Audrey sets aside her toast and egg. "Thank you for doing that, Kate." Her eyes slide out of focus for a minute, and Kate waits for her to come back from where she's drifted off to. "And what of the others?" she asks.

"There isn't much," Kate says, frowning. "I couldn't find anything about Aldous Stoltz or Claus Von Holten. But Ludwig Thurman was also tried, in the same batch of trials at Nuremberg as Friedrich. He was found guilty, but there's no other mention of him. I guess we can assume he was either pardoned at some point, or died in prison too." Kate voices a train of thought that's been dogging her. "If you don't mind, Audrey, when I was trying to find all this, I found the website of a facility—sort of a museum—called the German Resistance Memorial Center. Have you heard of it?"

"No."

Kate takes a deep breath. "They've compiled all the available information on the German people who tried to resist Hitler. Students, like that White Rose group you mentioned. Academics, activists. And some people in the Nazi ranks too."

Audrey watches her silently.

"This place has memorialized these resisters for what they tried to accomplish, and I wondered . . . Do you have any interest in sending them your story? They don't have anything about your cell in their archives."

Audrey shrugs. "No, I wouldn't imagine they do. There was no information to find on us, was there?"

Kate waits.

"I told you I thought it was time someone took responsibility for the deaths of those children in Hanover. Perhaps this is how I can do that." Audrey licks her lips. "Do what you can, I suppose. Send my account to this museum. See what they say."

"All right. I will."

As Audrey finishes her breakfast, Kate can tell her mind is far from the Elder Room.

"Is Ian here today?" Audrey asks, dabbing her mouth with a napkin.

"Yeah. He's doing the garden beds out back."

"I'm so very glad the two of you found one another."

Kate blushes a little, worried her grin is too much for the somber circumstances. "We only did because of you. We wouldn't have, otherwise."

Audrey squints at her, considering. "You found each other because of your parents, actually. In chasing them, you found him. Think of it that way."

They exchange an emotional glance.

"And you're in love?" Audrey asks.

Kate nods. "It's . . ."

"On a cellular level?" Audrey's broken fingers come up to rest on Ruth's necklace, the photo of Ilse. Kate lent it to her back in January, so she could keep Ilse close.

"Yes," Kate says, filled with warmth. "Do you need anything else right now?"

"Yes, could you pass me the telephone, please?" Audrey indicates the landline on her bedside table, an old gold-plated relic of a thing that looks like it was pulled straight from a 1940s film set.

Kate moves the dozen orange plastic prescription bottles, sets the glass of water aside, and places the phone in Audrey's lap. Then she lifts the breakfast tray, heads downstairs and allows herself to cry as she does the washing up, her salty tears sinking into the sudsy water.

A while later, the sound of the piano drifts into her ears. Ian must be back inside now. She dries her hands, wiping her face on the tea cloth, too, and pushes through the swinging kitchen door, the music growing louder with each step. Leaning in the doorway of the library, she watches Ian's brow pinch in concentration, his neck stooped just a little over the keys. Ozzie is splayed out on the floor beside the piano. He's so attached to Ian.

When Kate walks over, Ian looks up, smiles a little crookedly as he continues to play. She runs her hand over his back, then lifts his chin to her, kissing him.

"Thanks," he says. "How's she doing?"

"Okay. You know."

When he finishes the piece, Ian goes to stoke the sitting room fire, and Kate's about to get them each a coffee when there's a knock at the door.

They both pause, glance at one another.

"Sue maybe?" Ian says, turning back to the fire.

Kate opens the door onto the cool spring air. There's an official-looking man standing on the porch in an expensive suit.

"Hi," she says. "Can I help you?"

"Ms. Mercer?" he asks.

"Yes."

"My name is John MacGregor. I am Audrey James's estate solicitor." She recalls his name from the office plaque when she took Audrey to see him back in December. "I need to have a word with you, if I may. Mr. Smythe, too," he says.

"Er, sure." She leads him into the sitting room, curious. "Is everything all right?"

"Yes. But I do need to have a word with you both." He glances suggestively at the chairs and couch.

"Okay," Kate says, looking at Ian.

Mr. MacGregor sits down in what is usually Audrey's chair, and Kate and Ian take seats on the long couch.

"I appreciate that this is a little unorthodox, though having known Audrey for years, I find that hardly surprising." A grin plays around his mouth, and he continues. "Audrey just rang and asked me to come speak to you both now, as opposed to after her passing. Her estate settlement is fairly straightforward. As I'm sure you know, Audrey will pass without issue—without children"—he clarifies for their blank stares—"and she has left her considerable estate of inherited family fortune and the Oakwood Inn to the pair of you, jointly."

His words filter through the buzzing in Kate's ears. "Excuse me?" She glances sideways at Ian, who looks as confused as she feels.

The lawyer cocks his head to the side and a small grin twitches at the corner of his mouth. "She has bequeathed her estate to both of you. It would appear that this comes as a surprise."

"I think there's been some kind of mistake," Ian says.

"There is no mistake, Mr. Smythe. You are to inherit jointly. Audrey has been very clear on this matter."

Both Kate and Ian continue to stare at him, dumbfounded.

"There will be a significant amount of paperwork for you to fill out, but the thrust is, you both stand to inherit substantially. I am here to assist you with the process, when the time comes."

"What do you mean by estate?" Ian asks. "That's the hotel?"

"No, no, Mr. Smythe. The Oakwood is a separate bequest. Audrey's estate is her family fortune. Approximately two million pounds."

"E—excuse me?" Kate asks.

Mr. MacGregor smiles at them as though they're in on some kind of joke. Surely they must be. "Audrey inherited a considerable sum when her father passed prematurely. I believe it was around thirty thousand pounds at the time. But that was 1938, and Audrey has invested much of that inheritance since the midforties, with a robust return."

Kate opens and closes her mouth. Ian's face has turned beet red. The flecks of grey in his temples stand out sharper against the blush.

"Well, I believe that's all for now," Mr. MacGregor says. "I will be in touch about the paperwork upon Audrey's passing."

Several long moments after the door shuts behind the solicitor, Ian finally speaks. "What the bloody hell just happened?"

Kate's mind is reeling. "I don't know. We need to go talk to her."

They stop outside her room. Kate leans her head in and knocks on the door frame, but she can see Audrey is still sitting up in bed, glass of water in hand, as though she expected the visit.

"Audrey?"

"Come in," she says with an amused sort of air.

Kate moves into the room, Ian right behind her. "Mr. MacGregor just left."

"Yes. Come here," Audrey says, gesturing to them both.

They join her on either side of her bed. Sophie is curled up at the foot of it, fast asleep. She hasn't left Audrey's side for two days now, leaving poor Ozzie in a state of dejection.

Audrey grips each of their hands with her own. "As Kate well knows by now, the Oakwood turned out to be my most unexpected place of refuge and peace at a terrible juncture in my life," she says. "And I leave it in your safekeeping, the pair of you, because you have come to love it nearly as much as I did."

"But Audrey—" Ian begins.

"You cannot deny a dying woman what she wants," Audrey says, her tone heavy.

Kate knows she's thinking of Ilse and Daniel, and she squeezes Audrey's hand. The set of her jaw reflects the fierce determination that lies beneath the aging pale skin.

"Please take care of it, and each other," Audrey says, glancing at them each in turn.

Kate's heart swells with the knowledge that she won't have to leave this place that's become her home, where her parents walked the halls and her dad lived for a while as a boy, where Audrey's spirit will always linger in the smell of coffee and Marmite.

"Audrey, you still can't give us all that money." Ian says.

"I can do absolutely whatever I want with my fortune." Audrey scowls, making it clear any further argument would be futile. "And this is what I want."

Ian swipes at his eyes with his free hand, then leans over to hug her. She whispers something in his ear that Kate doesn't catch. When they break apart, Audrey cups his cheek in her hand, brushes away a tear with her thumb. Ian nods.

"I will," he says.

"Thank you."

Ian leaves the room, touching Kate's shoulder on the way by, his head down.

Audrey's shoulders slump. "I'm very tired."

Kate helps her lie down, tucks the blanket in like a mother would, then Audrey pats the edge of the bed, and Kate sits.

"Thank you for being such a willing steward of my pain," Audrey says. "I know it wasn't easy to hear everything I had to say. But look at what it brought us both in the end. I think that alone has made it worthwhile." Audrey runs her hand over Sophie, whose little body rises and falls on soft exhalations. "Take care of her, will you?"

"Of course," Kate says. "Oz will too."

"Thank you."

"Is there anything else you need me to do?"

Audrey is quiet a moment, staring into Kate's eyes. "Just talk about me," she says. "And Ilse. About Friedrich, and your mum and dad. Tell people about them. Tell these stories. When we are the only ones left to remember someone, we have a responsibility to let them live on through our memories, our stories. I do love you, Kate. I wish I had known you sooner. But time always makes fools of us all."

"I love you, too," Kate chokes out.

Grief holds her lungs in its sharp talons. She catches a few snippets of notes from the piano downstairs, notes she knows well now.

"Can I see her again, please?" Audrey asks.

"Of course," Kate manages, her throat thick. She reaches behind Audrey's neck and unclasps Ruth's necklace, opens it, and passes it into Audrey's hands. She holds it with the fingers that shattered and eventually healed enough to be functional, but never quite the same as they were before.

Audrey smiles a little, and the tears slip back into her white temples as her head rests against the cool pillowcase.

"Ilse taught me a great many things, whether she realized it or not," she says, fingering the tiny photo. "How to love so deeply, and on so many levels. How to survive after losing all the people you love." She smiles through misty eyes as she travels back in time to Ilse's bedroom, that day in the spring of 1945, filled with brown eyes and sorrow and the scent of lilacs. "And she also taught me how to die."

Kate has tried so hard to keep herself composed for Audrey's sake, but the tears are in full flow now, her nose red and swollen.

"Do you hear that?" Audrey asks. She folds the locket into the palm of her hand and crosses her arms over her chest. She closes her eyes. "He's playing her song."

Epilogue

BERLIN, GERMANY | SEPTEMBER 2013

Kate glances once more at the map on her mobile, the little pin showing the location of the address she inputted before they left the hotel. It's a bright, cool Tuesday afternoon in the middle of September, and the sun shines down on them as a soft breeze blows. Kate has never been to Berlin before, and was surprised to travel somewhere foreign with the sense that she was going home.

Audrey had left her the Kaplans' and Abramses' addresses so that Kate could do her own research after she was gone. She'd let herself sink into the work after Audrey died, using her spare time in the evenings after they finally opened the Oakwood up to guests in the midsummer. After polishing the memoir, she'd sent it to the German Resistance Memorial Center. They were thrilled to hear about this cell of the Red Orchestra, but warned her that with only one woman's testimony to go on, they would need to cross-reference Audrey's account with any other information they could find on the other members of the cell before they could make any sort of official addition to the memorial. Kate kept her expectations low. She wasn't sure whether Audrey and her comrades' complex contributions would ever be recognized there, but she was doing right by Audrey to try, and that was enough for her.

"How much farther?" Ian asks her.

"Just around the next corner, I think," Kate says, with a tingle of anticipation.

There are two row houses sitting right at the curve of the road, tall and proud.

"This is it," she says quietly.

Ian looks over at her, watching for her reaction, and she's touched that he wants to know if she's okay.

She stares up at the house, a large grey-brick structure, and thinks of her father's birth family, the grandparents and aunts and uncles she would never meet. Kate and Ian will be going to the Memorial to the Murdered Jews of Europe later in the week, before they head back home. She wants to see if she can find the Abramses' and Kaplans' names. It would soothe her to pay her respects and honour her lost family. She carries their legacy in her veins, and so does the baby girl growing inside her.

She runs her hand over her gently swelling belly now, thinking of her father, left alone somewhere upstairs in this very house, soiled and screaming and orphaned at not even a year old. Her face crumples.

"Come here," Ian says, pulling her into a tight hug. Kate takes a minute to let it out, but as she buries her head in Ian's chest, something catches her eye on the pavement below.

"Ian, look."

She blinks through wet lashes. Inlaid in the cement are six small square brass markers with inscriptions. The names of Ezra, Zelda, Sarah, Samuel, Reuben, and Rebecca Abrams are engraved in capital letters on each of the stones. Beneath the names are birth dates, deportation dates, and death dates.

A tear drips onto Sarah's name, and Ian rubs soft circles on her back.

"Do you know if your dad ever came here?" he asks.

Kate shakes her head. "Audrey didn't say, but I think he would have told her if he had. In his letter he just said he'd finally learned they all died, and where. Maybe it was just too much for him to come."

As Kate stands, Ian snaps a photo of the plaques. The front door of the house opens, and a middle-aged woman walks out onto the step in slippers and a red apron.

"Can I help you?" she asks.

Kate opens her mouth to apologize, then doesn't. "Hi," she says instead. "My dad's family lived here. Before the war. The Abramses," she says, indicating the plaques near her feet.

"Oh, my," the woman says, coming down the stairs. "I'm so sorry. Welcome. They're called stumbling stones," she explains. "They're all over the city. Markers for the victims." Her face is pained. "I knew they were Abramses. Knew they were here, but . . . which one was your dad?" she asks.

"He's not here, actually," Kate says. "His name was Daniel. He was rescued from the house. He was just a baby."

She leaves it at that. The woman nods, doesn't press the matter.

"Mazel," she says, indicating Kate's belly.

"Thank you."

"Please stay as long as you like."

Ian thanks her, and she disappears back into the house.

It takes Kate a while before she's ready to move on, then they walk a few streets over, to the Kaplans' large row house.

"There it is," Kate says.

It looks just like its fellows, lined up like spines on a bookshelf all along the street, but to Kate, it seems to shine with some inexplicable, radiant light.

Birds sing in the trees along the boulevard. A breeze flutters the leaves, and Kate can almost hear the music from Ruth's piano floating on it, the notes from "Ilse's Theme" that led Audrey home to her loved ones.

Kate rests her hand on the curved stone railing of the porch, cool beneath her fingers, thinking of all that happened here. It fills her up now, with grief and love and something warm that stings. She runs a hand over her belly again, knowing she'll want to bring her daughter back here someday, when she's old enough to learn.

To understand, and remember.

Piano

Ilse's Theme

For *The Secret History of Audrey James*

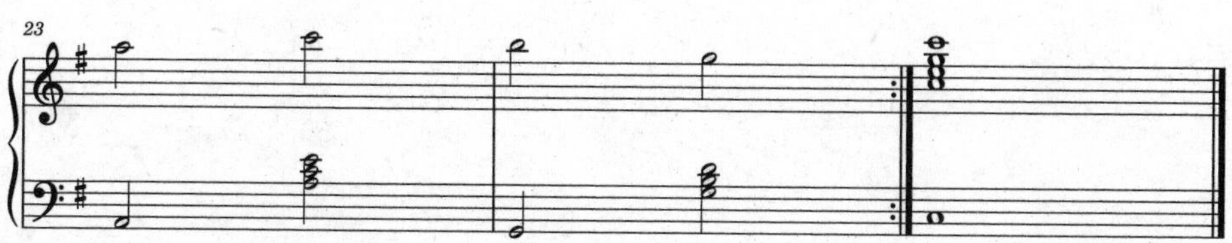

Author's Note

Dear Reader,

So, funny story . . . I didn't actually set out to write a World War II novel. It just sort of happened.

AUDREY AND MONA

I'm always on the lookout for untold—or undertold—stories, and while meandering down one of my frequent Historical Facts Rabbit Holes, I came across a woman named Mona Parsons. To the best of anyone's knowledge, she was the only Canadian civilian woman to be sentenced to death and imprisoned by the Nazis during World War II. After learning about her, I found I couldn't *not* use her story for inspiration. She lived an incredible life, a story you almost wouldn't believe if someone told you (or wrote a novel inspired by it), and I was honoured to borrow from her experiences to construct Audrey's character and story line. Mona's biography is extensive, but to summarize: She was born in Nova Scotia, Canada, and became an actress and then a nurse before marrying a millionaire in New York and moving to the Netherlands.

She and her husband joined the Dutch resistance and sheltered downed Allied airmen, smuggling them to safety.

While Audrey's story certainly doesn't follow Mona's at every turn, I did fold several elements of Mona's life history into Audrey's character, including her theatrical and musical skills, her involvement in a resistance movement against the Nazis, her arrest for anti-Nazi/traitorous actions and subsequent imprisonment, her remarkable escape from prison during an Allied air raid, and her discovery—half-starved and bleeding—on a dirt road near Vlagtwedde by the North Nova Scotia Highlanders who had just assisted with the liberation of the Netherlands.

If you had difficulty believing that a judge would commute a convicted traitor's death sentence, you would be wrong. This indeed happened to Mona; she apparently responded to the death sentence with such stone-cold courage that the judge told her to appeal, and it was later commuted to life with hard labour. For the sake of brevity, I depicted Audrey imprisoned only at Vechta, but in reality, Mona Parsons was moved around to several different prisons over the course of a few years before she was finally transferred to Vechta, where her weight reduced to about ninety pounds but she continued to try to effect some change via resistance. She incorrectly spliced wires while manufacturing German bomb igniters, just like Audrey did, hoping she might be able to save some lives from a distance. Mona escaped during an Allied air raid, making her way across Germany to the Dutch border. The prison director at Vechta did in fact open the gates when the men's wing of the prison caught fire, telling the women that they could stay and be killed by the bombs, or take their chances on foot.

However, to the best of my knowledge, Mona never sprinted across a German minefield. That scene comes from my own family history. My grandfather was a bombardier in World War II. His Lancaster was shot down over German-occupied France, and of the seven men on the plane, only he and one other man survived. They became separated in the immediate aftermath of the crash, and my grandpa got up and ran through a field, watching in terror as armed German soldiers laughed at him. They weren't shooting because they didn't want to waste their bullets. They were waiting for him to hit a mine, but he never did. By some miracle or outrageous stroke of luck, he got safely to the other side, where he was then captured, given a cigarette in acknowledgement of his recent feat, and taken as a prisoner of war. He spent nearly a year eating rotten Brussels sprouts in a POW camp (the inspiration behind Audrey's hatred of potatoes) before he was traded for medical supplies. Like so many people who served, my grandpa rarely talked about his experience in the war, and only opened up about these shocking stories as he was nearing the end of his life.

I wouldn't be here, and you wouldn't be holding this book, if my grandpa had hit one of those mines. So when I found myself writing a World War II novel, I decided I wanted to include that piece of my family history in the narrative, and it dovetailed so naturally onto Mona's real-life escape from Vechta prison. I also thought it particularly fitting for a story that explores the nature of luck, chance, and accidents, and the often cruel—but occasionally wonderful—randomness of life.

Among other smaller details, the water ring on the piano that holds some significance in the novel was also borrowed from Mona's history. When she and her husband were arrested, a group of Nazis occupied their house, and at some point left water rings on top of Mona's prized, rare honey oak piano. When she returned to Canada from the Netherlands after the war, she brought the piano back with her and never had the water rings removed, as a reminder of the wounds the war had inflicted. This is one of the reasons I chose to make Audrey a pianist and pull the thread of the piano through the story, all the way to its connection with Kate, her father, and "Ilse's Theme." So much of the story touches on the scars we bear after trauma, and how we learn to live in new skin that will never be quite the same as it was before the injury.

After the war, Mona Parsons received citations from both the Royal Air Force, on behalf of the British, and President Dwight Eisenhower, on behalf of the Americans, for her outstanding courage in aiding the Allied effort and saving the lives of those soldiers. To date, she has never been officially recognized by the Canadian government, though in 2017, a statue in her honour was unveiled in her hometown of Wolfville, Nova Scotia, and in 2023 she was recognized on a Canada Post Remembrance Day stamp. Her tombstone names her as "wife of Major General H. W. Foster," with no reference to her extraordinary life and heroism.

You can learn lots more about Mona Parsons online, or pick up the biography by Andria Hill-Lehr.

THE WOMAN IN THE ATTIC

There are so many stories to tell about World War II, partly because the collateral damage and reach of the war was so extensive. But it means, as a writer and an historical researcher, that there is such a rich pool of inspiration to draw from, and I'm always keen to braid as many stories together as my editors will allow.

Audrey's efforts to try to protect Ilse were inspired by the true story of Elsa Koditschek, a Jewish woman who managed to hide from the Nazis in her own attic in Vienna, even after a high-ranking Nazi officer—Herbert Gerbing—moved in downstairs when the SS confiscated her home. Elsa fled upon receiving a deportation order, and spent years hiding with non-Jewish friends before desperate circumstances pushed her to leave. Out of options, she returned to the last place anyone would look for her: her own attic. She was kept hidden by a sympathetic tenant who lived on the second floor of the house while Gerbing occupied the main floor. He entertained other officers in Elsa's back garden and organized the deportation of Jewish people across Europe from the comfort of her sitting room below. There's also a fascinating piece of this story that involves an Egon Schiele painting Elsa had to sell to help herself survive, the long road to discovering the provenance of the artwork decades later, and the sale of the multimillion-dollar piece. I wasn't able to squeeze it into this narrative (believe me, I tried), but I highly recommend you look it up for further reading.

KRISTALLNACHT

The research authors undertake as part of the writing process can be distressing, but it's necessary in order to craft stories that animate the history books and move readers on a very personal, human level. I knew, when I set out for greater detail about Kristallnacht than I had learned during my own education about Nazi Germany and the Holocaust, that it was going to be emotional. But as I got into the weeds on this research, I was more deeply disturbed than I had anticipated by the witness and survivor accounts of home invasion and destruction. It was beyond what I had imagined, because a great deal of the coverage of Kristallnacht focuses on the destruction of Jewish synagogues, businesses, and schools on November 9–10, 1938. But with lists provided by Nazi Party officers and city officials, thousands (if not tens of thousands) of Jewish homes and apartments were also destroyed, looted, and vandalized beyond repair, in many cases making them uninhabitable and rendering the families homeless. Survivor accounts detail the beatings, sexual assaults, and murders that occurred during these home invasions on this night of systematic terror.

What happened to the Kaplan family home was not uncommon during the pogrom, and carried devastating consequences for the families.

THE GERMAN RESISTANCE

When I began my research for this book, digging into the types of resistance groups that existed during the war, I found a reference to a group of rebel cells in Germany and German-occupied Europe that were collectively called *Rote Kapelle* (Red Orchestra) by the Nazis, who believed they had ties to the Soviets and were far more closely connected than they actually were. I was so intrigued by this piece of history that I decided to place my character inspired by Mona Parsons within a resistance organization in Germany instead of the Netherlands.

Some of these resisters were Nazi officers themselves, who, like the characters in the book, had diverse reasons for fighting back against the Third Reich and Hitler. Many believed that he would end up destroying Germany itself. Others had more altruistic and humanitarian motivations, and I'm sure others dreamed of usurping Hitler and seizing power for themselves. Among the general public, several different types of resistance groups existed outside the Rote Kapelle, mostly made up of Jewish people, Sinti, Roma, scientists, artists, humanists, youth, communists, workers' unions, students, and those who resisted the regime based on their Christian faith and passivism.

The White Rose resistance group that makes a cameo is pulled right from the history books. They were a small association of students at the University of Munich who distributed leaflets, openly decried the Nazi regime and its genocidal actions, and urged students and other members of the German public to defy and sabotage the government in any way possible. The text Audrey finds pasted to the column of the Brandenburg Gate is a direct quote from the first leaflet of the White Rose. Two of their founding members, siblings Hans and Sophie Scholl, were executed alongside a third resister, Christoph Probst, in February 1943. The rest of the members—along with the philosophy professor who supported their actions—were also eventually arrested and murdered. Hans Scholl's final words before his execution by guillotine were "Let freedom live!"

Many individuals made attempts on Hitler's life throughout the war. There are dozens of documented assassination attempts from 1932 onward. Some readers may be familiar with the culmination of these, what came to be known as the July 20 Plot, in 1944. It was an intricate attempted coup carried out by a group of Nazi officers who aimed to end the war by murdering Hitler at his East Prussian headquarters at Rastenburg. They tried to kill him with a bomb in a suitcase, but he escaped the blast with minor injuries. More than six hundred people who were in some way involved in the coup attempt were arrested in the aftermath. More than a hundred were sentenced to death and immediately murdered, and far more died later by suicide or in prison.

The German Resistance Memorial Center in Berlin has permanent exhibits to commemorate all of these courageous resisters, and their online resources were invaluable in my research process for this book. I would strongly encourage you to learn more by accessing their online exhibit at gdw-berlin.de.

TAKING LIBERTY

One of the biggest challenges for historical fiction authors is choosing when to stick close to the historical record, and when to bend or ignore the facts and dates for the sake of fiction. The Reich Security Office (within the SS) did actually refer to radio operators as pianists, their radios as pianos, and their leaders as conductors, but I've taken liberty with the timeline, as those code terms were only used once Germany finally decrypted radio transmissions in 1942. I also took creative license to use the White Rose group in 1939, though they operated over the course of 1942–43, and *The Great British Bake Off* premiered in August of 2010, not November. But those poor delicious lemon cupcakes did get eliminated.

ON A PERSONAL NOTE

In grade eight, we were learning all about Canadian Confederation, and the men who made it happen. During that class, I stuck my hand in the air and quite innocently asked my female teacher, "What were the women doing?" You see, I was wondering what their wives and daughters were up to while these Very Important Men met and drank scotch in Very Important Rooms to discuss politics and make decisions for everyone else. In answer to my question, I was sent to the principal's office for insubordination. For posing questions unrelated to the course content. *For daring to ask what the women were doing.*

Needless to say, I wasn't in trouble with my parents, who congratulated me and took me out to Pizza Hut. But ever since that day, I have not stopped asking what the women were doing. It's the question that drives my research and my novels, and I will keep asking it over and over again to try to help fill in the blanks of our history books where no one bothered to talk about what the women were doing.

I can't wait to share my next novel with you, which brings us back to Toronto in the 1960s and covers the historic treatment of women's mental health and incarceration (spoiler alert: it's been awful).

I hope you will continue to join me.

Heather

P.S. Enjoy the Easter eggs.

Acknowledgements

First thanks go to my invaluable champion of an agent, Hayley Steed. There aren't enough Reese's peanut butter cups in the world for me to adequately express my gratitude, but I am the luckiest of authors to be able to call you my friend and teammate. Thank you, always, for everything you do (I know I'm probably only aware of about 70 percent of what you *actually* do behind the scenes for me and my career), and for so graciously putting up with me pitching you a new book idea approximately every 3.7 weeks.

Thanks to Sarah St. Pierre, Adrienne Kerr, Rita Silva, Cali Platek, and the team at Simon & Schuster Canada for your work on this project. To Olivia Barber and Olivia Robertshaw at Hodder UK for their valuable feedback on the first and second drafts, respectively, and to Kate Norman for guiding it to production. Thank you to my former UK editor and author friend Sara Nisha Adams for your support for the original story, its reimagination, and for taking the time to so eloquently describe what Islington smells like in the autumn (I've only ever visited London in the spring!).

One of the most wonderful surprises of my new career is the

opportunity it's afforded for me to really get to know some incredible women I otherwise would have only been able to admire from a distance. It's an honour and a joy to be part of this community.

Thank you to my talented author pals Genevieve Graham, Charlene Carr, Natalie Jenner, Marissa Stapley, Amita Parikh, and Ellen Keith for your generosity of spirit and willingness to lend an ear, and to my additional early readers Kristin Harmel, Patti Callaghan Henry, Janet Skeslien Charles, Louise Fein, Karma Brown, Rachel McMillan, Caroline Bishop, Andie Newton, Roberta Rich, and Margaret DeRosia for taking time away from your own busy lives and projects to provide such generous endorsements for *Audrey*. And thank you to Kate Quinn for gently preparing me for the fact that the whole process of releasing a novel into the world will never become any less nerve-racking than it was the first time. Swallowing moths, indeed!

Special thanks to Jim for composing "Ilse's Theme," and somehow knowing precisely the sound I was going for. It was so special to be able to listen to it play in real life (and in my head) while I finished off this story.

I began writing the draft of this book when I was on maternity leave with my first child. As a rookie mum, I had no idea how difficult it would truly be to write a good novel with a newborn in tow, hormonal, and more bone-crushingly exhausted than I'd ever felt in my life. I'd written novels before, so I knew what was required to make that happen, but I'd never raised a baby before, and I still had a lot to learn on the job about being a mum. I also wildly underestimated the impact chronic, severe sleep deprivation and distraction would have on my mental energy and creative juices. I'm a firm believer that success rarely—if ever—happens in a vacuum, and I simply could *not* have accomplished this feat without the support of my family: the countless hours of quality childcare provided by my parents, Auntie K, and my mother-in-law, and my husband's love, reassurance, and well-timed snack deliveries. I cannot thank you all enough for what you did to enable me to continue on with my writing career after having a baby.

If not for the pandemic and having a newborn, I would have been thrilled to visit the German Resistance Memorial Center in person when I first began writing the book. But when my brother announced that he was going to be visiting Berlin, I all but demanded he visit the GRMC for me to collect photos and hard copies of resistance documents. He also returned with several heartrending photos of the "stumbling stone" plaques around the city that commemorate the victims of the Holocaust, and which inspired the inclusion of the epilogue. So special thanks are due to my bro for being such a *great* bro to this housebound new mama.

And finally, thank *you*, readers.

I will be forever stunned by your response to my debut *Looking for Jane.* Many writers need to write, in the same way we need a myriad of other sustenance in our lives, from water, to love, and meaning. My heart needed to write *Jane* because I thought it was about time we started actually *talking* about the things we had only before whispered about. I hoped it might get published. I hoped a few people might read it. And then you took a story that, in my astonished mind, is still just scribbled sentences in my dogeared notebook, and you started talking.

You helped *Jane* reach tens of thousands of readers across Canada and around the world, you gifted it to each other, recommended it, waited months to check it out from your local libraries, and chose it for your book clubs because the themes in it resonated on a profoundly personal level. Since *Jane*'s publication, I've received hundreds of messages from readers sharing stories of heartbreak, horror, relief, connection, understanding, and hope—all the emotions I felt while writing it, and that is such a beautiful thing: that what I felt in my heart came out on the page and found its way into yours. For writers, having readers connect to our stories is the greatest professional joy and triumph, and we would be nothing without you.